NICK & GREG

Other published works by John Roman Baker

Novels
No Fixed Ground
The Dark Antagonist
The Paris Syndrome
The Sea and the City
The Vicious Age

Short Stories
Brighton Darkness

Plays
The Crying Celibate Tears Trilogy
The Prostitution Plays

Poetry
Cast Down
The Deserted Shore
Gethsemane
Poèmes à Tristan

NICK & GREG

John Roman Baker

WILKINSON HOUSE

Nick & Greg
Copyright © John Roman Baker 2016
The moral right of the author has been asserted.

Published by Wilkinson House Ltd, September 2016

FIRST EDITION
978-1-899713-51-6
Trade Paperback

Wilkinson House Ltd.,
20-22 Wenlock Road,
London, N1 7GU
United Kingdom

www.wilkinsonhouse.com
info@wilkinsonhouse.com

Cover design: Rod Evan

British Library Cataloguing-in-Publication Data
A catalogue record for this book is available
from the British Library.

Dedicated to the towns of
Brighton and Hove

This, he thought with perfect certainty, this after all is to be young. It is for this. Now we have the strength to make our memories, out of hard stuff, out of steel and crystal.

Mary Renault, *The Charioteer*

Often I have been acquainted with the worst of living:
It was the suffocated rivulet gasping,
It was the dried out leaf curling tight,
It was the horse in its fall into dying.

No good in the knowledge of divine Indifference:
It was the statue in the near sleep of noon,
The cloud, and above, a falcon soaring.

Eugenio Montale, *Spesso il male di vivere ho incontrato*
(freely translated by John Roman Baker, April 2016)

CHAPTERS

ONE

He was kicking a ball in St Ann's Well Gardens. Nick was watching him, sitting with his back to the pond. The boy had noticed him and between kicks would look over; it was a smiling, cheeky look that seemed to ask for attention. Nick saw how strong his legs were, and that the shorts he was wearing were dirty with mud. The ground was wet from a downpour the night before and the late autumn grass looked thin and worn after too much use and abuse. The gardens had been crowded all through the summer months, and well into October there had been picnics.

"Come and join me."

The cry was cheerful and Nick, feeling self-conscious in his coat and long trousers, shook his head in silence. But he smiled at the boy and raised his hand in a half wave half gesture of recognition.

"Scared of getting your clothes dirty?"

The boy kicked the ball in Nick's direction and it landed under the long seat he was on. He realised, looking down, that his legs had been wide open like a goalpost. In the next moment the boy was on his knees in front of him and without looking up at Nick retrieved the ball.

"Sorry," he said, looking up. His face was smeared with dirt, but he had bright blue eyes and Nick found them very attractive.

"What's your name?" the boy asked.

"Nick."

"I'm Greg."

Nick said hello and Greg sat down next to him.

"I hope it doesn't fucking rain," Greg said, looking up at the sky. "Always happens at the weekend, doesn't it?"

"I don't come here often at the weekends. I thought there would be more people."

"What do you expect in November?"

"It's warm. The sun's out."

"Not for long. Look at those clouds coming in from Worthing."

Nick laughed. Greg's voice was much deeper than his, and he was impressed by the forbidden swear word he had used— *fucking*. The last time he had used the word *bloody* his mother had hit him.

"Do you swear much?" he asked, turning to stare at Greg.

"Course I do. Shit. Fuck. Cunt. Didn't anyone talk like that to you before? Must be a fucking polite school you go to."

"No, they use words like bloody and even shit sometimes."

Greg replied with a sneer in his voice, "Should hope so. Everyone shits. It's the most natural word in the English language. As for bloody, even my seven year old sister says that. It's nothing."

Nick remained silent. He turned away from Greg and looked at the trees beyond the open space of grass. The trees still had a lot of leaves, but they were turning browner than the earth beneath them. Then suddenly he felt a sharp nudge in his side.

"Dressed up like that and sitting like that, you look like an old man. I bet you're younger than me, but you look years older."

"I was fourteen a few weeks ago."

"Stand up."

"Why?"

"I want to see how tall you are. Your legs seem quite long, but the rest of you looks shorter."

Feeling embarrassed, but obeying Greg, Nick stood up.

"Thought so."

"What?"

"You are shorter than me."

"Prove it."

Greg stood and faced Nick. He was about a head taller. Nick wasn't very good at assessing height, and he thought he may have been as tall as Greg. After all, he didn't look in mirrors much and his mother never measured his height against a wall like some other children's parents did.

"Does it matter?" he asked defiantly.

Greg shrugged, then ran out onto the grass and began kicking the ball again. It was around three in the afternoon and a few people began to appear, most of them walking their dogs. One Alsatian was especially interested in the ball and ran after it when Greg gave it a second kick. Greg looked back at Nick who was still standing on the gravel by the seat and called out, "Look, even *he* is more eager than you are."

"He's a dog," Nick shouted back, stating the obvious. "I'm not as stupid as a dog."

"And he doesn't sound posh like you when he opens his mouth. Thank God all fucking dogs bark more or less the same."

The Alsatian, shocked by their shouting voices, bounded away, and running to the ball, Greg picked it up and returned to where Nick was standing.

"Don't you like sport?" he asked.

"It's alright. I don't do much of it."

"What school d'you go to?"

"A small one. You wouldn't know it. Clifton College."

"Posh is it?" Greg shrugged again. "Oh, fuck it. It doesn't matter. I don't care what sort of school you go to. I never passed my Eleven-Plus. I go to the Knoll cos I live in Portslade."

Nick rarely went to Portslade and had no idea where the Knoll was. He wondered what kind of school it was, especially if they all swore like Greg. Clearly it must have a big playground, so that in all the noise the words could not be identified. At his private school, they had only a small playing area and it was supervised. He looked down at the ground and mumbled that he had better start out for home.

"Where's that?" Greg asked.

"Montpelier Road. I live in the big red house, next to the tennis court."

"A flat is it?"

"Yes."

"I live in a house. Dad will own it soon. He makes good money in his electrical shop."

His voice sounded defiant and boasting. There was also an edge of anger in it, as if he had to assert something over Nick.

"Why don't we do something?" he said.

"Do you really want to?" Nick asked with a dull sound in his voice, although inside he felt excited and eager to stay with this bold and adventurous boy he had just met.

"Don't talk to me like a sodding wimp. Would I ask you if I didn't want to? I know a boy called Charlie. He lives around here. We could go and see if he's in. He's got a TV. We could see what's on."

Nick, who lived alone with his mother, did not have a TV. She liked the radio and often in the evenings he would listen to concerts and plays with her. She was separated from his father and lived a solitary life except for Nick who kept her company most of the time. He certainly couldn't offer to take Greg back to *his* flat. None of the kids he knew at school had ever gone back to his place, and as his mother was in ill-health, they would not have been welcome.

"I thought television didn't start until the evening," he said.

"Haven't you got a set?"

"We're thinking about it."

"Your mum and dad?"

"My mother. My father is dead," he lied.

"What did he die of?"

Nick paused. He went through a mental list of illnesses that could possibly lead to death. He knew about pneumonia and cancer and tuberculosis. Then he thought of the obvious: the one he didn't have to describe any symptoms of.

"Heart attack," he said.

"Quiet or noisy? I had an uncle who died of a heart attack. Bloody cried out as he went, or that's what my dad said. It's supposed to be fucking awful painful."

14

"I don't know. He died in the street."

The lie was becoming more and more elaborate. But Nick was ashamed of admitting there had been a separation between his parents. It was almost as shameful as admitting you were illegitimate, or that you had been adopted because neither of your real parents wanted you.

"Couldn't the ambulance men have saved him if they'd come in time?"

"Yes, I suppose so," Nick replied, running out of more ideas for this lie. He had been brought up as a Catholic and had been to a Catholic primary school. Lying was a venial sin, not a mortal one, but all the same he didn't like to tell them. He might go to Purgatory if he told too many and didn't go to confession after. He hated confession and usually avoided it. He hated the darkness of the place and the mumbling of the priests. Then he reminded himself that deep down he didn't really believe God existed. He had realised that in St Mary Magdalen's church one day while gazing around at all the gaudy statues, especially the one of the Virgin Mary, or had it been St Mary Magdalen herself? It had all seemed so improbable suddenly—a God up there, way beyond the clouds, paying attention to him. He had been about eight or nine at the time and he was so thin and small he thought it would be impossible for a God to notice him, even if He did exist. Then he felt guilty and crossed himself just the same. He was almost tempted to say a few Hail Marys, but then gave up the thought and looked vacantly at the altar. The priest was raising the monstrance, which was an inappropriate time to look up, and he lowered his eyes quickly. He knew the word *atheist,* as he had been told by a particularly nasty master at school, who had given him a rabbit punch for inattention, that atheists were doomed to damnation. He decided there must be a Hell and a Purgatory and that place Limbo for dead unbaptised babies and for people who had been dead before Christ, and that not believing in God would take him to one of them. He sighed at the comforting thought that he had at least escaped the possibility of Limbo as he had been baptised there in the font of St Mary Magdalen's itself. He tried to think of Heaven without the existence of God, then gave up.

"What you so quiet for?"

Greg's deep voice roused him out of his thoughts. He looked at the boy, coming as it were from a place of deep meditation and quite suddenly Greg appeared to him as some sort of earthly but radiant angel. He looked at Greg and stared down at his sturdy legs. He saw hair growing on them and felt an impulse to reach out and touch them. He liked hair on men's legs. It was then he realised he hadn't asked Greg how old he was. This vision was no angel, but pure human boy! And he looked old enough to be as much as sixteen.

"Can you get into X-films?" Nick asked suddenly.

Greg laughed.

"What you asking that for?"

"Don't know. Just wondered."

"I saw my first X-film months ago. They let me in no problem. S'pose I look old enough."

"How old are you?"

"Year older than you. Born in December. I'll be fifteen next month."

"So you're really fourteen like me."

"I'm not like you at all. Bet you haven't even got pubic hair yet?"

Nick had pubic hair, but he blushed at the nakedness of the word. It sounded exciting coming out of Greg's mouth though and he felt his penis grow hard. Frightened that it showed, he put his hand down in front of him. Then he remembered he was wearing a coat, and his erection couldn't show through trousers and a coat. He began walking and Greg moved quickly after him.

"I was just asking," Greg said. "I knew a boy who had pubic hair at the age of ten."

Nick laughed, not believing.

16

"How do you know?" he asked. He knew this was a daring question to ask, but he had to. His mind was full of images of the hair around Greg's penis and by asking he was prolonging what was a forbidden conversation. He imagined himself being caned for this at school.

"In know cos he dropped his trousers and showed me," Greg said. "His cock was bigger than I thought it would be as well. Bloody abnormal, I told him."

They reached the park entrance on Furze Hill and it was here that Greg steered the conversation into another area.

"D'you like science fiction comics?" he asked.

Nick liked them very much and told him so.

"I know this shop near the Theatre Royal. In Gardner Street. Want to come with me and look at some?"

"What time does it close?"

"Half four. We've still got time if we hurry. He doesn't have any horror comics like my older brother has though. Fuck knows where he got them from. I saw one and it had a woman's head being cut off by this monster. It was in colour and there was blood everywhere."

Nick didn't much like the thought of that, but he looked up at Greg's eager face and noticed again the sparkling blue eyes. He wouldn't like it at all if there were real monsters and he saw this possibly new friend having his head cut off.

"Let's run," he said, all too ready to show he was fast at running. He had to begin to impress Greg.

Brighton and Hove was their playground—from St Ann's Well Gardens to Black Rock. They ran a lot, laughed a lot, and Nick, while he was with Greg, began to swear as much as he did. Only he wouldn't use the word *cunt*. A deep reservation made him refuse to use this most forbidden of words. He had heard a drunk in the street say it when he was with his mother. She had turned on the man, a living burning flame of reproval, standing there in her red dress, and had said to him, loudly and clearly, "You disgusting man. Aren't you ashamed of yourself?" The drunk had looked at her and laughed through his broken teeth, "What, ain't you got one, Missus?" His mother had drawn Nick quickly away, and they went onto the West Pier where, as she said, "The wind will blow the nastiness and the cobwebs away." Now when Greg used that word, which he did less frequently than the others, Nick looked disapprovingly at him. "Don't be such a kid," Greg would say, then pinch him on the arm cheekily and run on ahead.

Every now and then, they would steal comics from the shops in the warren of squalid houses that led down from the station. It was easy to do, especially in the one on Trafalgar Street where the man who ran it was too blind to see what they were up to. Greg would always pick out the more lurid ones—the ones that resembled the films Nick was too young to see.

One day they sneaked into the back of the shop, unseen by the nearly blind man. In the back room, they discovered an adult section full of hardback and paperback books and also a pile of older comics, dating from a few years before, which were hard-core horror. Some had scantily dressed women being carried by a monster or a creature or a thing. Nick got very confused about why these objects of horror had such different names.

"Why is he called an *It*?" he whispered, as Greg singled out a comic called *It Came from the Gruesome Lands*. Greg was looking at a picture of a woman being dismembered by a man with only half a recognisable face, the other half being skeletal, when Nick asked him.

"It's just to make it more exciting," Greg replied, still very much immersed in the images he was following with his eyes.

"So what is the difference between a creature and a monster?" Nick insisted.

Greg looked up then, torn away from the excitement for a moment's reflection.

"Monsters do more," he said simply at last, closing the

comic, then stealing it away into his inside jacket pocket.

Nick felt slightly ashamed at asking such a childish question then nodded his head in agreement. Since he had met Greg, being an avid reader, he had quickly read both Mary Shelley's *Frankenstein*, which he had found very heavily written, followed by Bram Stoker's *Dracula*, which was equally heavily written but much more to his taste. But he was not sure he agreed with Greg. Frankenstein's creature was called a monster, so it was perfectly clear that you could be both at the same time.

"Can we go and see one of those films?" he asked. "If we're together I'm sure I can get in with you. There are so many X horror films on at the moment. I know you're taller and bigger than me, but you've often said my face looks older."

"After Christmas and my birthday," Greg replied then neatly slipped a few more of the comics inside his jacket. "Now let's make a fucking run for it," he said.

The shopkeeper did not see them as they left, Greg carrying his forbidden cargo.

Often they would go and see Charlie. Charlie lived in St Michael's Place, which was considered a rough street to live on and had police cars going up and down it all the time. It was taller than the other streets in the Montpelier area and appeared narrower. This was accentuated by the impression that the sun rarely shone down into it. Nick's mother had told him, with inevitable severity, that only drug addicts and prostitutes lived there. She called them low-life and told him he must never loiter near or go along that street as only bad things happened there.

Greg laughed when Nick told him that.

"I bet she got that out of the local papers," he said.

"She doesn't read the local papers."

"Then she don't know nothing," Greg added, accentuating the bad grammar he had learned from detective series on TV.

"She's not stupid," Nick said defensively.

"Well, don't tell Charlie it's a bad street," Greg said on the first day they visited it. "His parents had a lot of trouble getting their flat. At first the landlord said he wouldn't take in teenagers. Too much noise for the house, he said, which just shows how quiet the place is."

Charlie lived on the top floor of one of the tall houses on the west side of St Michael's Place, near the corner of Victoria Road, across which was the much more expensive and desirable Montpelier Villas. Greg said some famous people lived there, even someone on television, but he wasn't sure of the man's name.

"It's Gilbert something," he said. "It's a quiz thing. We don't watch it in our house. It clashes with something Dad likes on the other side."

"I don't watch it either," Charlie added, proud of the television set his parents rented.

Charlie was an overweight boy who loved sweets, which he ate copiously while he was alone and his parents were at work. He was too greedy to share them with anyone who went to see him, including Nick and Greg. Greg who was constantly hungry resented him for this. Whenever Charlie was out of the room he would steal a few and put them in his pockets. Later he would share them with Nick. As for Charlie, he would often skip school to watch TV, even for the most boring of programmes. He said that he liked to watch anything that moved and Nick although he liked Charlie, thought he was lazy and that part of him being fat was due to the fact he rarely went out of doors.

One afternoon when Charlie was sitting engrossed on the sofa watching something abysmal, Greg asked if he could see *it* in the bedroom. *It* turned out to be a magazine in the bottom drawer of a chest of drawers facing the bed. The magazine had photographs of nearly naked women in it. Charlie said he had stolen it from a special shop, but would not say where the shop was.

"Just for an hour," Greg said.

"Alright," Charlie replied, "but remember to listen out for any noise in here. Mum and dad might come home early."

Greg replied that he would listen out for them, and then asked if he could take Nick in with him. Charlie looked at Greg, nodded his head, then turned back to stare at the television.

"What happens if one of his parents does come back?" Nick asked as Greg closed the bedroom door behind them.

Greg said nothing in reply, and went straight to the bottom drawer for the magazine. He then lay on the bed and opened the magazine to a wide double spread of pages in the middle.

"I like these," Greg said, then beckoned to Nick to join him. Nick sat on the edge of the bed and looked carefully at the picture. It was of a woman lying on a pink bed much bigger than the one they were on. She was dressed in a semi-transparent nightdress, which revealed nothing clearly. One of her hands was poised above her groin. The picture was very gaudily coloured and the woman did not appeal to Nick at all. But all the same he was aroused by a tension in the air that he knew was sexual.

"What is she doing?" he asked, his voice a little hoarse with suppressed excitement at what Greg might say.

"She's about to have a wank," Greg said quickly. He then looked up at Nick from his prone position and asked Nick to lie down next to him.

"I don't know how women do it," Nick replied, complying with Greg's request to lie next to him.

"They finger their cunts," Greg added crudely. "They put their fingers inside themselves."

As he said this, he began rubbing at his own groin. Nick at first turned away. Then, getting an erection himself, began to look down at what Greg was doing.

"I wonder who's got the biggest," Greg whispered as if the words were explosive enough to be heard by Charlie in the living room. "Shall I push my trousers down? This picture's got me turned on. Are you turned on?"

"Yes," Nick said, but it was the prospect of seeing Greg's penis that was really turning him on.

"Then let's do it shall we?"

Greg turned his head to look at Nick. Their heads almost touched. Nick saw the wide smile, the open mouth and the perfect teeth. He noticed some saliva at the corner of Greg's lower lip, and the sight of this white liquid substance made his penis stiffen to its full hardness.

"Okay," he said.

Nick could hardly breathe he was so tense.

"Take yours out first and show me," Greg murmured, still looking at Nick's face with his sweet smile.

"Why me?"

"I want to see if you are bigger than me."

Then Greg turned his head away and resumed looking at the full length spread of the woman in the magazine beside him.

Nick unzipped his trousers and fumbled with unsteady hands to get his trousers down to his knees. He still had his underwear on, but his erection clearly showed and there was a damp patch revealing his pre-cum.

"Yeah, I can see you're big. Almost as big as me."

Greg bent slightly upwards. His eyes had a glazed sort of look as he stared down at Nick's underwear. He then quickly pushed down his own trousers to his ankles, edging himself further up to push his underwear down as well. His penis sprang out, thick and red with blood with a thick bush of black hair around it. It was almost the same colour as the hair on his head, but looked much darker.

"I haven't got as much hair as you," Nick said.

"Then push your fucking underwear down and fucking well show me how much you have got."

Nick did. His penis wasn't as big as Greg's nor was it anywhere near as hairy. Greg looked at it closely.

"I'm longer and thicker than you. You've nothing to

complain about though. By the time you reach my age you'll be as big as me. Anyway, some boys are just not as hairy as other boys, that's all."

The words were said quickly and excitedly. Nick looked at Greg's erection again and then at his own. He was glad Greg approved of what he saw.

"Now let's wank and imagine we are both fucking her."

There was an impatient urgency in Greg's voice, as if the excitement was too much for him and he was tired of the preliminaries.

"But you've got the magazine on your side of the bed," Nick said, trying to convince Greg that this was his real object of desire.

"You've seen her. You can imagine her. Come on, let's do it, and no noise, remember? We don't want Charlie coming in."

"Have you ever wanked with Charlie?" Nick asked.

"Don't be stupid. I don't even know how he can find his cock in that roll of fat. I don't wank with just anyone. Now for fuck's sake let's get on with it. I'm ready to burst."

They both came, almost simultaneously. Greg looked at the picture most of the time, but sometimes turned to look to see how Nick was progressing. Nick concentrated on what Greg was doing with his hand. He stared fixedly at the foreskin as it came up and down, covering, then revealing the deep red tip.

"I'm almost there," Greg panted.

He came a few moments before Nick and couldn't suppress a cry as he did. Nick was too far gone to take notice of the cry, and was quiet when he climaxed.

"Shit, I hope we didn't get any of it on the bedspread," Greg said casually, his voice now back to normal. Then he wiped himself down with a dirty handkerchief retrieved from his trouser pocket.

"You got one?"

"No," Nick lied.

He did have one, but he wanted Greg's. He took it and felt Greg's wet sperm touch his own penis. For Nick, this was the most exciting moment of the afternoon, but of course he could not say so.

"You okay?" Greg asked, pulling up his trousers.

"Yes," Nick said, clenching the handkerchief tightly in his hand.

Charlie didn't look at them when they came out of the bedroom. He was engrossed in an educational programme which made Greg laugh.

"Charlie, how can you watch that crap?" he asked. "Don't you ever want to go out some afternoons to the cinema like the rest of us? For fuck's sake, your size alone would get you into an X-film."

"Shut up about my size," Charlie replied, without turning around. "I'm okay as I am. Anyway, I don't want to see some cruddy creature from outer space or whatever it is you get off on."

Greg went towards the sofa and stood in front of Charlie.

"There's sex films."

"That's what I mean about getting off. Anyway, what do you see? Not much I bet. Just a lot of talk."

"But Charlie, it's fun."

Greg pointed to the screen. Lines of interference were running up and down it.

"This isn't fun and you can barely see it. And don't you get enough of that educational shit at school? Or is it because you hardly ever go to school that you watch this?"

Nick stood by the bedroom door and watched them. He had a feeling this was not the first time they had talked like this, and for some reason he felt like an outsider. He was also not feeling quite so casual about the sex that had just happened between them a short while ago on the bed. He was surprised Greg looked so cool about it—just as cool as before he went into the room. Because Nick felt something of their mutual masturbation showed on him, he expected it to show

24

on Greg. But how could it show? Wasn't he being stupidly young in thinking that it would? He was sure that he himself looked as if something had happened to him. His mind recalled the moment when Greg had shot his sperm over his stomach and, on seeing that, he too had ejaculated. He felt his face grow hot with the thought of it. Could it be possible that Greg had dismissed all such images and that he genuinely thought it was something everyday, like going to the toilet? He clutched at the damp handkerchief which was now in his pocket. It was a reminder of the act done and the pleasure shared. Greg at least couldn't deny to himself that it had been shared. As for Nick, it had been his first time with anyone else, and he felt changed by it. He was also nervous that if he joined Greg in front of the sofa with Charlie, the shock and the still remaining excitement would show. Then he was shaken out of his thoughts by Greg shouting his name.

"Nick, what the hell are you standing there for like some spare part that doesn't know what to do with itself? Come and give me backup. Tell Charlie he should go out more often when he skips classes. That man on the screen for shit's sake is talking about trigonometry." He laughed. "Trigonometry! I can't even fucking spell it. Can you?"

Nick stepped forward and spelled out the word.

"Smart-arse," Greg replied. "I bet you know fuck all about how to do it though."

Nick lied and said he did not know how to do it, which he did. He thought the lie would make Greg feel good, and he wanted to make him feel good. He did not want to let him down. "It's just a word that came up in a game of Scrabble we played at home last Christmas," he added.

"Sure?"

Greg stared at him with his bright blue eyes and Nick wanted so much to return to the bedroom and to lie again on the bed close to Greg with their heads nearly touching. He had looked him in the eyes so closely and intimately.

"I happen to be interested in Trigonometry," Charlie said.

"Then why don't you go to classes more often?"

Greg cast his piercing clear look at Charlie. To Nick it looked like a sudden visual attack. The same look you would see in a predatory bird's eyes as it swooped down to seize a mouse.

"You know why," Charlie mumbled but did not explain further. He then added as if to defend himself, "and anyway, if I wasn't in so often how could you come around as much as you do? I'm doing you a favour aren't I? Now get out of the way. You're blocking my view."

To Nick it appeared that the big mouse had won this battle. With simple questions he had warded off the predator and Greg looked distinctly unhappy about it.

"Tell me about how this trigonometry thing works then," Greg said, re-armed and returning to the fray.

"Why should I?"

"I think you're bluffing."

"Don't care a sod what you think."

Greg turned from Charlie to the television set and with a quick swoop, turned it off. Nick was shocked. Charlie lowered his head. He looked defeated and Nick felt ashamed of Greg.

"Greg, I think we should go," he said, then added, "at least, I must go."

Greg stared at him hard. His face looked rigid with anger.

"No, you wait for me. You wait 'til I'm ready to go."

A moment after he said this, his face relaxed, his mouth widening into one of his brightest smiles. If Nick had known more, he would have realised that this was the attack of the seducer. It was the same smile that had won Nick over in St Ann's Well Gardens. Succumbing to it, he sat down next to Charlie on the sofa.

"I think you should let Charlie have his programme back," he said mildly. "I don't mind watching it."

"I do!"

The smile had gone and the ugly look returned. Nick

watched as Greg started to move restlessly around the room, picking up one object after another. His jerky movements looked openly aggressive, as if he wanted a real fight, fists and all. Charlie seemed to notice this as well and rose to the bait, telling Greg to stop messing with things his parents would notice had been moved.

"You sure as hell have a lot of crap here Charlie," Greg said, picking up a porcelain shepherdess.

"It's not my business what they choose," Charlie replied. "Anyway, is your home in Portslade any better?"

"We have all brand new furniture," Greg sneered. "Clean lines. Modern stuff. And there's not so much fucking dust on it. At least my mum dusts."

"Mind your own business," Charlie said.

Greg didn't reply to this, but began to kick a tennis ball that was lying on the floor. Nick thought of him kicking the football when he had first seen him. But Greg grew tired of the ball, probably because he had accidentally kicked it under the TV set and he didn't fancy humiliating himself by stretching out on the floor to hunt for it among the jungle of stuff that was hidden behind there.

"Let's play some music," he said, jumping around. "You've got a record player, Charlie. You got *Rock Around the Clock*, haven't you?"

"Yeah," Charlie replied sullenly.

"Then let's put it on."

Heaving himself up from the sofa, Charlie ambled over to where the record player was and took out a pile of records from the cabinet beside it. Greg pounced on them at once and hooted with laughter.

"You've got Doris Day! You've got fucking Doris Day. What the hell is she doing in here? Don't tell me you listen to her."

"My mum likes Doris Day. She went to see a film of hers years back," Charlie explained defensively. "And my dad likes her as well."

Nick added politely that his mother liked Doris Day as well, and that every time she sang on the radio, she turned the sound up. He wanted to protect Charlie from more mockery. In reality, his mother hardly ever listened to popular music. Every time it came on, she turned the radio off or switched to another station, saying how soppy and vulgar it was. She associated contemporary popular music with the low-life of the worst parts of Brighton, calling it common and vulgar. When she heard *Rock Around the Clock* for the first time, she said disgustedly that it sounded like the end of civilisation as she knew it and that poor Ivor Novello would turn in his grave if he had the misfortune to hear it in the afterlife. She was very much concerned—if doubtful—about the afterlife.

Still hunting through the jumbled records, Greg eventually found Bill Haley and he immediately put the record on. It jumped at first, caught in several scratched grooves and Greg looked harshly at the machine as if he wanted to kick it. Nick thought he would, but then the record settled down and with the volume turned up full, the music blared out.

"Come on, Charlie, let's rock 'n' roll," he shouted over it.

Charlie looked appalled at the thought, but was not given any time to reply before Greg grabbed him, taking the male role, and forced him to dance. Charlie complied at once, much to Nick's surprise, allowing himself to be thrown back, then forwards. The centre of the living room suddenly became a dance floor.

"Stop making with the elephant waltz," Greg cried out as he attempted to whirl Charlie around. Nick looked on, realising he was deliberately trying to make Charlie look ridiculous and grotesque.

"Let's get more of your roll into this rock," Greg jeered. "You make a fucking awful partner, Charlie. A real fat girl. How am I supposed to throw you up or between my legs? How am I supposed to do that with your weight?"

This was nasty and Nick tried to think how to intervene, but knew that things had gone too far. Why was Greg behaving like this? Why was he taking it out on Charlie? He wondered if it had anything to do with him and what had taken place between him and Greg on the bed, but this thought pattern was too complex to explore, so he let it go. Then, just as he was about to cry out to Greg to stop, Charlie rebelled at the humiliation and broke away.

"I won't let you," he said. His voice was shaking and he looked as if he was near to tears. He shouted at Greg as loud as he could to mask the fact that he was near to crying, "You've played it twice and that's enough."

"Wrong. Three times," Greg added.

"The neighbours will complain to my parents. You know they will. Then you'll never, never be allowed to come here again. Not ever, do you understand?"

He emphasised the word *never* by stomping his heavy foot on the carpet. A Toby Jug fell off the mantelpiece in the racket and smashed into pieces.

"Look what you've done!" he screamed.

"You did it, Charlie. You did it. Gettin' all het up about a bit of Rock 'n' Roll. For fuck's sake, the neighbours have heard it all before."

Nick went over and picked up the pieces of the Toby Jug. It was broken beyond all repair, and he knew just by looking at Charlie's face that the ornament meant a lot to Charlie's family.

"Greg, I want to go," he said, placing the pieces on the living room table. "We've caused enough trouble here and it's getting late."

"Mummy waiting at home, is she?" Greg sneered, looking at Nick. It was the first time he had really looked at Nick since they had left the bedroom. It was a troubled look that had a mixture of like and dislike in it. His eyes seemed to both plead for and reject Nick.

"She got high tea waiting for you with cakes and scones and everything?"

Nick said nothing and sat down again on the sofa. He

didn't want to add to the row that was going on. Now it was Charlie's turn to stare at Greg with something near to hatred on his face.

"You know what you are, Greg?"

"No, tell me."

"You're an Oscar Wilde boy, that's what! And that's worse than being fat."

"You take that back."

"I won't."

Suddenly it was like being in a playground. Nick wondered about Oscar Wilde. He didn't know much about him, except that even mentioning him was almost as forbidden as using the words *fuck* or *cunt*. He had heard the name once at Clifton College in a shouting match that turned into a fight in the classroom that a teacher had to come and break up. All he definitely knew was the name meant a really, really bad man.

"Say you don't mean it," Greg said threateningly.

Charlie was no longer looking for any more trouble and stared down in silence at the floor. Greg's face was white with rage and Nick could see that he was about to physically lay into Charlie. He didn't want that chaos to happen.

"I've never heard the name before," Nick said loudly, trying to put some balm over the turbulent waters.

"I take it back," Charlie murmured.

"And you'll never say it again?" Greg asked, his fists tightly clenched at his sides.

"No."

"Promise?"

"Promise."

"Really promise. On your mum or dad's life promise."

Charlie said nothing at first.

"I want to hear it, Charlie."

After a long pause, Charlie whispered, "On my dad and mum's life."

Greg, still looking pale and angry, turned to Nick and said they could go now.

In silence, they left the physical and emotional wreckage of the flat. The last glimpse Nick had of Charlie was of him standing in the middle of the room with both his hands held up to his face. The sight of him looking so defeated and unhappy made Nick feel sick inside. He had seen a lot of sadness and despair in his young life, but the way Charlie looked was certainly near the top of the list.

Once out on the street, Greg turned to Nick and asked him if he really didn't understand what Charlie had called him.

"Never heard it before," Nick lied.

"He was a murderer, that's what he was. He called me a murderer."

"What did he do?" Nick asked.

"You don't want to know. It would make you sick. Let's just say he would stick disgusting objects into people's bodies until they died."

Nick realised that this was as bad as could be, despite the obscurity of the description, and yet, from far away inside him, he suspected the name meant something else, something even more terrible than a murderer—after all he had read many accounts of hangings for murder in the local papers to know that killing on purpose was common enough. He also suspected Greg was behaving like real grown-ups who lied constantly instead of telling children the truth. As he thought this, a moment of blurred recall flashed itself into his mind. It was of a voice saying the dreadful name in another context. Oscar Wilde. Maybe it had been on the radio, or even in whispers at Clifton College itself.

"It's only a name," he said in a conciliatory way to Greg.

Greg shrugged, then began to run a little. Nick was tired, but ran after him. Reaching Clifton Hill, only a road crossing and a street away from the School where Nick received his distinctly inferior education, Greg surprised him by holding out a hand to grasp his own. His hand was wet with sweat, and Nick, looking at his face, saw that he was dripping with perspiration.

"I'll see you soon," Greg said. Then without another word, he ran down the incline of Clifton Hill towards Montpelier Road, crossed it, and continued to run in the direction of St Ann's Well Gardens. Nick watched him until he disappeared, and he felt empty but also filled with longing to see Greg again. He put his hand in his trouser pocket and Greg's sweat added its magical odour to the rest that was on the handkerchief.

TWO

Christmas 1957 came and went. Nick spent it with his mother and an aunt called Agnes, who was his mother's sister. She lived in a remote town in Northern England and rarely came down to Brighton. The holiday days passed slowly and he wasn't even much interested in his presents. He was given a watch by his mother and a book by his aunt: a *Rupert* annual he was far too old for. He kissed her over powdered face.

"I can never remember how old you are," Agnes said, no doubt suspecting she should have chosen something a bit older for a boy who had reached puberty. She had considered an unabridged edition of *The Three Musketeers*, but thought the prose looked a bit dense and that the book was, in her terms, far too long.

"He'll soon be a man," his mother had said in one of those rare moments of pride. She was always kindest to Nicholas, as she called him, when others were around.

After Christmas Nick saw Greg again. There was no awkwardness at their first meeting though memories of their previous encounter at Charlie's must still have been in both their minds. They were both tactful enough to avoid the issue and Charlie's name was not mentioned once. Greg though never again asked Nick to go to St Michael's Place with him. The meeting came about when Nick looked out of the window onto Montpelier Road and saw Greg pacing up and down in front of the house.

"I'd like to go out," he said to his mother, who was reading a women's magazine in the living room.

"You usually do what you please," she replied without looking up.

In a few minutes he had joined Greg in the street.

"You remembered where I live," he said.

"Thought it best not to come up the steps and ring the bell. Fuck, it's a big creepy old house, isn't it?"

Nick laughed.

"Full of horrors," he said.

"Do you have a ghost?"

"No such luck, but see there over the road," and he pointed with his hand at one of the whitest and cleanest houses facing them. "The house with the green curtains on the ground floor."

"Yes."

"My mother says no dog will go past that house without its hair standing up on end. Some even refuse to go past it at all. It really is haunted."

Greg stared in fascinated amazement.

"You having me on?"

"No, it's true."

"Yeah, but your mum thinks some streets are slums when they're not."

"I passed it one day. It was a hot day, and I went cold all over. I even saw a dog cross the road myself, instead of passing by it."

Greg turned from staring at the house and looked at Nick.

"I'll test it," he said. He looked excited by the thought, and the note of bravado in his voice which had suddenly turned deeper, made Nick want to reach out and touch him, but his nerve failed him and he didn't.

"Want to come with me?" Greg asked, before stepping off the curb.

"No, you do it," Nick replied, wanting to watch him.

On the opposite side of the street, Greg paused for a while, straightening his back and looking for a moment like a gunman in a film approaching his enemy. This was thrill enough for Nick.

"Please prove me right," Nick said aloud to himself and crossed his fingers behind his back.

Slowly Greg moved forward, and on reaching the house, slowed his steps down to a snail's pace. He did not look at the house, but raised his head as if he was looking at the sea, far away at the bottom of the long steep road. After a while he turned round and then made the same journey back again. Once more, he passed the house without looking at it.

"It's a cold day," Nick whispered to himself, "how will he know if there is something."

Greg crossed over the street in front of him. As he came up close, Nick saw that his face was very white.

"I sensed it," he said.

"You did?"

"It was like a cold hand brushing against my face."

"I told you," Nick couldn't refrain from saying.

"And there was a heavy feeling in my head, like it was going to explode."

For a moment there was silence between them. Then Greg broke the severe look on his face with a big broad grin. He nudged Nick with his arm and the grin turned into a merry laugh.

"That was great," he said at last. "I mean it. It was fucking great. And I did feel the cold. Much colder than the weather. The dogs are right."

"You really mean that?" Nick asked, a noticeable doubt creeping into his voice.

"Wouldn't lie to you."

Greg then pulled Nick by the arm down the street, so he had to run to keep up with him. At the corner of Western Road, by the Curzon cinema, they decided to explore the town. They ended up in the Old Steine, by the fountain, and sitting down on a bench facing it, Nick asked how Greg's Christmas had been.

"They all came down to us," he answered flatly.

"How many?"

"Too many. I had to sleep on the floor. I didn't get much sleep. Noise all over the sodding house, and a lot of drinking. I had a few beers, but you should have seen how much the rest of them knocked back."

Nick shook his head in mock dismay, thinking he wouldn't

have liked a house full of drunks. After the incident in the street with his mother and the drunk, he was suspicious of alcohol. He had also secretly tasted some vermouth his aunt had brought down for Christmas and had disliked the taste.

"I drank as well," he said, both exaggerating and boasting.

"What?"

"Vermouth."

"Never heard of it."

Greg stood up.

"Come on," he said, "let's go up into fucking boring old Kemp Town and see how the rich bastards are doing. Might find something good thrown out onto the street after Christmas. I know that's what they do cos I found a brand new suit, in its box, on the doorstep of a Sussex Square house last year. One of the old poofs living there must have chucked it out, not liking the style. Took it home and it fitted me dad."

Walking up Marine Parade, Nick looked with pride at Greg beside him. He felt a sudden pang of joy knowing that he wouldn't want to be walking with anybody else.

When January came, Greg proposed they should try to get into an X-film together.

"What's on?" Nick asked.

They stole an *Evening Argus* from an unsuspecting newsagent while Nick bought a packet of Fruit Gums, and then hunted through the paper until they reached the cinema page. Almost immediately they found an inviting title at the Astoria cinema: *Invasion of the Hell Creatures*.

"Let's go and see that," Nick said, pointing to an image of a bulbous headed creature, carrying a helpless female (as usual) with the smoking ruins of a city and desolation all around. The X certificate was very bold and big and the size of it alone promised a lot. Nick felt almost as excited as he had been with Greg on the bed, but of course in a different way.

"Yeah," Greg said, and then nudged Nick with his arm.

"Just look at that creature's paw, or whatever it is, all over her fucking big tits."

Nick looked, but he was more interested in the creature than the physical contours of the woman in its arms.

At the Astoria, it was easier getting in than Nick had expected. Greg bought the tickets, and although there were a few people in the foyer who might have come up, no one came to question his age. He was an adult at last. Inside the auditorium, Greg led him to the back row of the stalls. They had to sit through a routine film first which was of very little interest, and not a horror film. Then they had an ice cream each and waited for the curtains to reveal the forbidden X certificate and the warning that no one under the age of sixteen should be present.

"Here we go," Greg said.

To their disappointment the film was half horror and half comedy. There were a lot of couples kissing in cars in a wood, but no cities crumbling with devastation. Instead they saw little creatures (was Hell really that small?) scuttling across the screen and a confusing scene with a cow being injected by syringe-like creature fingers. At one point a creature's eye was poked out, but the film was in black and white, so the blood was pitifully unrealistic. It was not what they had hoped for and Greg turned his head to look at Nick.

"Not as good as the one I saw last May," he said. "It was at the Savoy. I thought it would be difficult to get in, because they're careful there, but I'm tall and they didn't even look at me. The cinema was packed, cos the film was really special."

"What was it?"

"*The Curse of Frankenstein.*"

"Was it in colour?"

"Fucking was. Real soaked-in colour. Like you could feel it, and the monster! Unbelievable! His face was all criss-crossed and sewn together by Frankenstein. Saw all the body parts too. Some silly woman fainted in front of me. She screamed and everything. She had to be carried out. And it was a double X programme. Not like this one. The other film was all about a prostitute in Rome. I'd never seen a film about the goings on of a prostitute before. Makes me hard just thinking about it. Not that you saw her cunt or anything. Pity you couldn't have seen that programme with me. Would've made you hard as well."

There was no one in the row of seats other than themselves, and no one to shush them for talking.

"It sounds exciting," Nick said as he imagined them sitting in the cinema together and both of them getting erections. His penis started to stiffen and as if reading his mind, Greg reached out, took Nick's hand and placed it on his groin. Although totally unexpected, the action was totally desired. Nick felt Greg pushing his hand up and down against the bulge of his erection.

"Unzip me," he whispered as one of the little creatures appeared in close-up. It looked as if it was watching them, and Nick realised they were about to do a punishable act in public.

"Take it out and wank me," Greg said. His voice almost pleaded, but as much as he wanted to, Nick couldn't do it.

"I can't," he said and tried to draw his hand away.

"Why the fuck not?"

"The usherette may come. She has a torch."

"Don't be so fucking stupid. She's a lazy bitch. I know this cinema. I've seen her before. She never comes in during a film. Never shows anyone to their place."

I want him, Nick thought. We are in the back row. Lovers usually use the back row to kiss. That's common knowledge, but am I a lover? I can't use the word with Greg. It's forbidden. No one would ever let us be lovers, and certainly not in the back rows of cinemas.

Greg was getting impatient with him now and after a minute or two of waiting for Nick to do what he had asked, he pushed Nick's hand away.

"It doesn't matter," he said. "I thought you'd want it. But

what the fuck, if you're going to make it complicated. I can do it myself when this bloody awful film is over, and I've gone home."

When he heard these words, Nick made a decision. Gulping hard with both dread and joy at what he was about to do, he put his arm around the back of Greg's seat and then with a sudden movement, grabbed Greg's shoulder, forcing him to turn in astonishment towards him. Then he moved his own head close to Greg's and in an instant was kissing him on the mouth. The action was clumsy and awkward. His own mouth was open, but Greg's was clenched shut. There was no response from him and Nick moved away knowing in that instant he had probably destroyed everything. He stared vacantly up at the screen as the creatures were encircled by a group of lovers' cars and were caught in the glare of their headlamps. There was a lot of creature shrieking as the tiny little things were destroyed. Suddenly they were all gone in a puff of smoke and the wood they were in, not to mention the world, was saved from their pathetic savagery. Greg sat in stony silence beside him, as if he too was pinned by the car headlamps. The end of the film was approaching and also the end of Nick's futile attempt at being a lover. Then Greg spoke.

"I'm not like that," he murmured. "I can't be like that. I'm not."

"I'm sorry," Nick said.

The lights in the cinema would soon come on, and Nick did not want to face Greg in the light. He got up from his seat and feeling frustrated and angry with himself, made his way out into the foyer. He looked at the come-on images for the film and thought how much the expectation of a really adult experience had turned out to be a lie. Was this how it was going to be? Always, for him, if he continued to desire boys like Greg? He knew that he was something Greg was not, and the realisation of that difference brought tears to his eyes. He saw a possibly long life before him, and although he still believed God had nothing to do with it, he felt with a shudder that he would be consigned to Hell's eternal flames. Atheists go to Hell, and so do people like me, he thought. The ugly, protruding eyes of the creatures didn't seem to deny this as they stared apathetically in his direction. I have done the one thing, he thought—the kiss—that proves what I am. He was not even conscious that Greg had joined him in the foyer.

"Come on," he heard Greg say, "let's get out of here. Don't be so bloody pitiful for fuck's sake. I still like you. It's no fucking tragedy. I still want you to wank me. It doesn't mean the end for us."

He sounded awkward. His words were edgy and nervous and when Nick looked at him, he saw that his face was pale.

"I shouldn't have acted like that," Nick said.

"Don't blame yourself."

"It was an impulse."

"We all have them. Look at me. I steal. But I guess the adults are right, there have to be sodding limits. And anyway, the back seat of a cinema always does it. I should have chosen the front row, but honestly, I'd prefer you licking me than those creatures. Think how they must look from the front row! Almost in your lap! You've got a better mug than them. Anyway, you're better than a girlfriend. At least you pay for yourself."

"I haven't paid for the ticket yet."

"Give me the money in the street."

Greg's expression was blank and he looked tired after the string of words he had just uttered: spoken with the stuttering speed of a machine gun in a war film.

Out in the darkness of the street, Nick paid for his ticket, and while he did it, he looked at the line of people waiting to go in for the evening performance. Most were couples. A few were openly kissing each other in the queue. The cinema will be full this evening, Nick thought.

"Do you want to go home now like you said?" Nick asked tentatively.

There was a moment's silence. They both looked at the ground. Then Greg looked at Nick with his devastating smile and said, "Let's go for a run and stretch our legs. I'll race you to the Palace Pier."

"Maybe we could go on it?"

"Got any more money?"

Nick reached into his pockets and brought out a handful of coins. Among the brown money were some sixpences and a couple of half-crowns.

"Shit, you're rich."

"Just got my week's pocket money."

"Then let's go on the pier, push pennies, and see if we can get more of them."

Nick put his money back in his pocket and stared at Greg.

"I hope all X-films are not going to be like the one we've just seen," he said to fuel the conversation and the returning ease between them.

"Wait 'til *The Curse of Frankenstein* does the rounds and comes to the Rothbury in Portslade. Then I'll see it again with you."

Nick was not really sure about Portslade. It was not part of his territory, but if he was to keep in contact with Greg he would go there to please him.

"You said it's got lots of blood, and in colour?"

"Buckets of it."

They both laughed, and Nick broke ahead, starting the race to the Palace Pier. He felt exhilarated as the cold air hit him in the face, and he was the first to reach the pier. At that moment he felt like a champion.

As he walked up Montpelier Road, later than he should have been, he felt a premonition that there was something bad waiting for him at home. He looked at the darkened façade of the supposedly haunted house, and the fact that there were no lights on in the windows only added strangely to his fears. It's a house of the dead, he thought, and the thought made him hurry towards the red house where he lived and to the front door. Once inside he made his way to the kitchen, forcing the door open, which had been stuffed at the bottom with material, and found his mother lying out on the lino floor with her head in the gas oven. She had her head half in, half out, and was still conscious and gasping for breath. He thought brutally, with an acute sense of pain, that this was what it was like to be an adult, and without saying a word, rushed forward and gently pulled her out. He laid her out on the floor, and then thought of the gas and turned it off. The room stank of it and it was filling his own lungs. He opened the kitchen windows wide and was glad that a cold wind had spring up and was soon blowing into the kitchen. He looked down at the prone figure of his mother and watched as a shudder passed visibly through her body. For a moment, for one terrible moment, he hoped that she would die and that it would all come to an end for her. Then he rallied himself and, bending down, put his hands under her shoulders and began to drag her out of the room. As he dragged her towards her bedroom, a multitude of confused emotions and thoughts filled him. He thought of his ridiculous need to see an X-film, of the kiss that had been rejected and of all the previous similar events in his young life which had made him want to force his way forward into adulthood. He was confused too about his own passing childhood and the emerging signs and needs of his adolescence. Question after question flooded into his brain, but not once did he think of the figure he was dragging so clumsily towards a bed.

"I must snap out of this," he said aloud to himself, and then, with a great deal of effort, hauled his mother's body upright, then plunged it down onto the bed. The smell of gas still lingered all over the ground floor of the house, so he ran from room to room opening all of the windows.

"I should call for help," he said again aloud, but decided to go it alone. He guessed she had turned on the gas just before he had arrived and that she would live. He was unhappily wise enough to know that she had attempted suicide and that to call a doctor or the police would expose her as a criminal.

He re-entered her bedroom and stood by her bed. The room was now cold with fresh air and her body was shivering. He had no idea what to do next and stood staring as she gasped and opened her mouth, drawing in great gulps of air. He could see too that she had an instinct to live.

"Mother," he said weakly, and she opened her eyes.

"Water. I want water."

He ran back to the kitchen and turned on the tap. The water gushed out and he held a glass under it. He knew the human body was made up of a lot of water and that at that moment he needed it too. He drank first from the glass, draining it in one go, and then returned it for a refill.

"This cannot go on," he said aloud to himself, and stared out of the open window into the darkness. He wanted to go into his own room, with his view of the tennis court. It was on that tennis court years ago that he had seen snow for the first time. What a magic moment that had been. A great pang of sorrow and loss suddenly filled him.

"I must hurry."

He took the full glass to his mother and raising her head with his free hand, helped her drink it down. She spluttered as she drank and some of the water dripped down onto her brightly coloured dress.

"I'm cold."

The words came out as a hoarse croak. He put the empty glass on the table by her bed, then went to a cupboard and took out a spare blanket. The thought crossed his mind that he should undress her and put her into bed, but somehow he could not face seeing her flesh. Instead he placed the blanket on top of her clothed body and then adjusted the pillows so that her head was slightly raised. She murmured inaudible words as he did this, but he paid no attention and concentrated on the details that were left. She had her shoes on and he took them off. He noticed a hole in her stockings and saw that her red painted big toe was jutting out. The sight of it made him feel temporarily sick. He moved the blanket downwards to cover the sight. I don't know what else to do, he thought.

He stood at the head of the bed and stared down at her. The room was very cold now and he was shivering.

"I think the gas has gone," he said automatically. "I think the windows can be closed now."

She made no response to his words, and he was about to lean over to pull the window closed, but decided at the last moment not to do so. She might die yet, he thought, and felt with a sudden surge of emotion that he did not want her to die. He knew, for so many reasons, that she had been a bad mother to him, but still he did not want her to die. Back there in the kitchen he had and he knew that until the day he died he would always remember that for a while he had wanted her dead. Then the thought scuttled out of his brain like a retreating demon and was replaced by the idea that she needed an eiderdown as well as the blanket. He fetched one and placed it over her. Then he looked down at her face. He turned on the lamp on her night table, and the full force of the light fell on her powdered and rouged face. She always wears too much make up, he thought, then smiled down at her.

"Hot," she whispered. "Hot."

"It's necessary," he said.

"Burning inside," she whispered.

He pitied her suffering and his pity was the closest he could feel to real affection and love.

"Now you must sleep," he said.

"Afraid."

The word made him tremble. He was hungry and he felt sick. He knew that if he was not careful, he would fall ill himself. He also knew there was nothing more he could do for her in that room.

"I will leave you to sleep now."

"No."

He rejected the simple cry, the cry that came from deep

inside her, in a place of darkness that he knew he could never enter with her. Or want to.

"I must eat," he said.

"No," she repeated and he left the room.

He put on a sweater and returned to the kitchen. He cut himself a couple of slices of bread and smeared them with some raspberry jam. He made some hot tea and sat at the kitchen table, clasping it between his hands for warmth. He could not bring himself to close the window. He welcomed the cold air as if it was a lifeline. He glanced at the oven and wondered why she had done it, but the weight of the thought was too much for him and he banished it from his mind. The only way for him to keep sane was to empty his mind of all the images he had just seen of her. She is my mother, he thought simply and finally, then closed the inner door inside himself against her existence.

"I am alone," he said aloud.

He wandered into his bedroom and lay down on the bed. He imagined that Greg was lying beside him and that he was naked. He saw with his mind's eye the red tip of Greg's penis. He saw the slit, wet with pre-cum, and the vivid imagining of it made him want to masturbate. He pushed down his trousers and took out his cock. He said the word *cock* over and over again, rejoicing in his joy of it, in his love of it, and with a few rapid jerks of his hand, sperm spurted out all over his stomach. Then he fell asleep, overcome with mental and physical exhaustion. In his dreams he ran with Greg over a wide green field covered with yellow flowers.

He awoke to the sound of his mother's voice. She was shouting at him, but the words were too distant for him to understand them. Then with a sudden realisation he knew he was half clothed and that he had fallen asleep with his trousers down at his ankles and that most of his body was naked to her.

"Disgusting," she said.

He stood rapidly and shakily, then pulled his clothes into a decent state. He dared not look at her, but he could not escape her words. She called him a filthy masturbator and declared that she had never seen such a terrible sight in all her life. She ordered him to turn round and face her and when he did so she slapped him twice, hard across the face.

"So you think you are a man?" she jeered. "You think you are old enough to do such disgusting things. How dare you show such a sight to your own mother."

He hated her then, with a cool and totally detached hatred. He wished that he had let her die. He saw the bright colour of her face, too red with fresh lipstick. He saw that she was totally recovered or appeared to be totally recovered, as if nothing at all had happened the night before. He wanted to be old enough so that he could leave her.

"I saved you," he said, surprised at how steady his voice was.

"To see that?" she screamed back at him.

"I'm old enough," he replied honestly.

"But not to show it."

"I was too tired to get into bed."

"You are fourteen," she persisted. "You may think you are old enough, but doing that dreadful act is a sin. Do you understand that it is sinful as well as disgusting?"

"So is attempted suicide."

He stared at her bravely and she slapped his face again. His skin began to sting and he only just restrained himself from hitting back at her with his hands.

"I walked into another room once," she continued. "And do you know what I saw? Do you dare to know what I saw?"

He said he didn't care.

"I saw your father on a bed with a woman. It was in one of those slums. Over Street. That's where it was. He was lying naked on a bed, wet like you with some filthy prostitute. I had known for months he was seeing her. A friend of mine had seen him enter the house and told me the address. I went there one day and the door was ajar, just like your door was ajar, and there they were, in a room upstairs both naked and in their disgusting state on a bed. She hadn't even enough shame to lock the door of her sordid little room."

"I am not my father," he said, then brushed past her and went back into the kitchen. He was surprised at her strength and wondered how she had recovered so fast.

"But you'll leave me as he left me. You've got enough of your father in you already to do that, and without a moment's remorse."

He stood by the kitchen sink and thought, why doesn't she just shut up and go back to bed? She wanted to kill herself last night and now she is ready to do me in. He poured some water, making some noise of his own to drown out the noise of her words, but she continued talking.

"It's shocking to see your own son like that. To walk in and see you in that state of shame. It made me sick to look at you."

"Then why didn't you just walk out of the door and leave me alone? It is my room after all."

"Do you pay the rent?"

"Father pays the rent."

"But do *you* pay the rent?"

"No."

"Well, then none of the rooms are yours."

"And the toilet?"

"Don't be smart with me. You know what I mean. Nothing is yours until you finish school and begin earning your own living."

He turned to face her. Her face was drawn with anger, but also deeply tired. For a moment he felt like the confused child that in fact he was. He also felt tired of trying to act like a man.

"I saved you last night, mother. Don't you remember?"

She brushed the air with her hand as if dismissing this admission. She sat down heavily at the table and put her head in her hands. Then her body began to shake, and he realised she was beginning to cry.

"What happened, mother?"

He asked this as gently as he could. It was past nine already and he knew he would have to miss school. He couldn't begin to count the number of times he had missed school on account of his mother and her needs. There was her diabetes, and the double hernia that gave her so much trouble, the sleepless nights with the radio on, tuned in to some obscure programme that went on into the early hours of the morning, all these things that he had to contend with, that controlled his life and often prevented him from getting to school. He had even missed his Eleven-Plus because of her health, but he did not want to think about that. He would get along in life without it. He knew that, or liked to think he did.

"I fell," she said, the sound of her voice muffled between her fingers. She was now a helpless victim, and he felt himself being sucked into the vortex of her pain, dismissing mentally the pain that she had put him through.

"How did you fall?"

"I lit the gas, then I forgot something I needed in the bedroom."

"What mother?"

"My pills. The ones I take for my blood pressure in the evening. Usually I remember, but you were late and I was distracted, waiting for you to come home."

This is not a home. It is not a home at all, he thought.

"Then when I came back into the kitchen, I tripped on that broken bit of lino at the entrance and fell into the room towards the oven."

"But you had your head half in the oven," he said, "and there was material from the inside, stuck into the space under the door so as not to let the air in. How did it get there?"

"How can you interrogate me like this?"

He tried to avoid this victim approach and said quietly, "There must have been a reason why you wanted to do what you did."

She was quiet for a while, then the crying turned into sobbing. Eventually her voice began again, on and on about his father and how he had left her and how Agnes her sister had told her not to marry a man like him. She used the word philanderer, but Nick was not sure what it meant, but sensed that it was something even worse than masturbator. He went over to the table and put his hands awkwardly on her shoulders.

"Maybe you don't remember that you intended to do it," he said.

He felt a shrug beneath his fingers and then she stood up and with groggy steps made her way back to the door. It was clear she was still ill and Nick had absolutely no idea how much gas she had inhaled.

"I'll stay here today," he said, "to make sure you're alright."

"Can you call Agnes for me?" she asked weakly.

They had no phone in the house and his father had said that he hadn't enough money to pay for one to be put in. But Nick sensed his father was afraid she would ring him too much and disturb his work. He asked her what she wanted him to tell Agnes.

"That I will pay for her to come down again for a few days. I will pay for it out of the savings. Tell her I am too ill to be left alone. She'll understand."

"But Agnes has just been and gone," Nick replied.

"She'll understand. Ring her. There's some change in the blue bowl in the kitchen cupboard."

After this, she dragged herself to her room and closed the door. He went out and made the call, telling his aunt that his mother had had a bad attack and that she wanted her sister near her.

"What sort of attack?"

He knew he could not mention the forbidden word suicide and lied by saying that he thought it was her heart.

"Then she should be in hospital."

"Maybe she will understand that if she hears it from you."

"Couldn't you get the doctor?" Agnes asked.

"She won't let me."

"Alright, I'll come down, but I'll have to put the cat and the budgies with the neighbours again. They'll be sick and tired of me."

Nick said he was sorry, then added that his money was running out. His aunt said she would be with them the following day in the evening. As he walked back to the house, up from the Western Road, Nick wondered again why his mother had wanted to kill herself. He realised that he would never know, and that all that business about his father perhaps hid a far deeper sickness within her. Adult and child. He knew that he was both, and that at this point in his life, they were held precariously together within him. He ran the rest of the way up the hill, imagining again that Greg was beside him.

THREE

Four years earlier, when Nick was ten, the situation at his home was already very troubled. His father visited every other weekend, and as the weekend approached Nick would feel dread and grow sick at the prospect of it. He was often to be found vomiting up his lunch in the toilets of St Mary Magdalen's Primary School. This was due not only to the stress he was under at home, but also to his disgust at the food he was given at school and the small warm bottles of milk he was forced to drink in the morning. There was one master (the one who gave him a rabbit punch to his neck—an act of barbarity that provoked even his mother to descend in rage upon the school) who was especially vigilant about the drinking of the warm milk. One day Nick rebelled and was given the strap by the headmaster. He tried not to cry but the pain was severe.

"Behave like that again and you'll get it again," he was told.

At home the atmosphere was even more violent. His mother also was keyed up for the twice monthly visits of his father, and the nearer the time came towards it the more frenzied she became. He had a small collection of *Classics Illustrated* which he bought with his minimal pocket money, (he put pennies aside each week so he could eventually spend one and threepence on a desired title). His mother knew he loved these comics and when he was naughty, according to her terms, she would punish him by first smacking him hard and then tearing up a copy of one his beloved comics. One of his most vivid memories was seeing a copy of *Gulliver's Travels* being ripped apart by her hands and then thrown in the garbage.

"Don't you dare cry about it," she said, but he was so afraid of her he found himself incapable of crying the tears he so desperately needed to.

How he dreaded his father's visits. The worst aspects of his parents' marriage came out during those weekends. His mother had married his father in Chichester when she was forty-four, a year after his birth. His father had been fifty-five. Both had been married before, and both marriages had ended: his father's by his first wife's death, his mother's by incompatibility and divorce. He only learnt the details of this many years later when he was in his late teens. By then his mother was dead and his father wrote and told him the truth about their so-called marriage. He revealed that he had never loved her, but had wanted a child as his previous marriage had been childless. He told Nick he had married her for him. But at the age of ten, there was only mystery and dread every time they came together.

During one of those weekends he witnessed a confrontation that stayed with him for the rest of his life. He was far too young to understand what was going on but instead of putting him to bed they seemed to forget about him while they raged at each other in the living room.

"When did you last see your mistress?" his mother screamed.

"Shut up," came the reply.

"You bastard, tell me the truth."

She spat at his father; spat so hard that her saliva trickled down his face.

"Fucking bitch. Why did I choose a bitch like you when I could have had so many other decent women?"

"Decent? When have you ever known a woman, except me, who was decent? Common tramps are what you like. Even your dead wife was a common tramp—"

"Shut up."

"—a common tramp from a broken-down Sussex farm who probably gave herself to every farm boy she could lay her hands on. And because she was a tramp, she gave you the sex you wanted. I know. I know. Remember that night on our so-called honeymoon? You told me what you liked doing with her? Only a born tramp would have allowed you to do *that*."

"Shut up, I tell you."

His father was taller than his mother and when she wouldn't stop taunting him he grabbed her by the throat and bashed her head against the wall. Nick cowered behind a chair and watched as his father beat her again and again on her breasts and on her head. When he had finished she had blood running down her temple.

"I'd kill you if it wasn't for him," he cried.

When Nick heard this, he screamed and ran to his father, hitting him again and again on his legs.

"You can't kill," he cried. "You can't kill. You will go to Hell. I won't let you kill."

His father turned in horror and amazement at his son. As for his mother, she fell to the floor and crawled, bleeding, out of the room.

"You mustn't. You mustn't," Nick wailed.

Then he felt himself lifted up. He felt kisses on his cheek and on the top of his head. At the same time as he was being kissed, he felt the wet sensation of his father's tears falling on his flesh.

"I love you, I love you," his father said.

"Don't want it. Don't want it."

Nick struggled and his father let him down.

"Is she ever good to you at all?" His father wiped the tears from his face as he said these words.

"We go to the theatre. We see plays. Some days she takes me to the cinema. We go to the Embassy where they show black and white films. I like the cinema and sometimes she buys me ice creams."

"Do you love her?"

Nick at ten did not understand the question. He had no idea what love was. On the big screen, he saw what was called love, and in the cinema people on the screen were often nice to each other and called each other darling. He had never been called darling by anybody, and nobody had said they loved him. Only now, in this evening of fury and pain, had he heard his father speak the words, and instead of embracing them he shrank away.

"I don't—" he began.

"Don't what?"

"I don't know. Please, please let me go to my room."

His father carried him there in his arms, and Nick felt embarrassed. He knew he was short for his age, much shorter than he should have been at ten, but all the same, he felt uncomfortable in his father's arms. But he did not protest and passively allowed himself to be put to bed. He watched in relieved silence as his father left the room and turned off the light.

"No," he screamed out.

His father came back in.

"The night light, I must have the night light."

Only when the lamp was turned on and he was alone did he feel temporarily safe. He knew it was possible, but doubted there would be another row that night.

For a while after that weekend life was calmer. His mother left him more or less to himself, and sometimes he thought she was ashamed of herself for what he had seen.

"Don't believe it is always like that," she had said the day after. There was a plaster on her forehead and he felt sad when he looked at it.

"I don't believe anything, mother," he had replied.

He went to school more regularly and even played more often with the few children who were capable of accepting his changing moods. In class he kept his head down and the teachers didn't pick on him or ask him awkward questions they must have known he could not answer. They even took no notice when he avoided the daily bottle of milk. For a while he was happy in this protected solitude and would often go alone to his favourite place, St Ann's Well Gardens, and tease the tadpoles and the fish in the pond. He allowed himself to be a child.

"Would you like to go to the theatre with me tonight?"

He came home one evening to find his mother dressed in her best clothes. She wore the finest of her red dresses (red was her favourite colour) and her hair had been done that afternoon at the hairdressers. He asked what was on, and she mentioned one of her favourite actresses: Dorothy Tutin.

"Where will we sit?" he asked.

"In the stalls. The front row. A special treat."

"Not in the gallery?"

"Not tonight. It's a funny play. Very good, they say."

She gave the title which seemed strange and not particularly funny to him, but he said he would wash himself extra hard and wear his best long trousers.

"Are we going with anyone else?"

"Only Dora. She wants to see it as well."

Dora was the only friend his mother seemed to have—a woman who dressed even more lavishly than her. She wore high heels and liked to show off the top of her body. His mother said Dora had been in the theatre herself when she was young. She had, it seemed, been in the chorus of *The Maid of the Mountains*.

"I'd better hurry," he said.

At six-thirty Dora came to the house. Her make up was so thick she looked as if she was going on the stage herself. When she saw Nick all dressed up in his best jacket, tie and trousers, she gasped.

"How handsome you look. Do you realise how many hearts you are going to break when you grow up?"

Nick blushed. It was the first time he had been complimented like that.

"I envy the girl who's going to get you," she added. "But I'm sure there will be many more before that one."

She reached out and caressed his face.

"I'll be too old for you by that time. Isn't it a pity?"

"Dora, you mustn't talk like that," his mother scolded, then she laughed and turning to Nick said, "Thank God you don't know anything about all that yet."

Nick thought about the times he went to the beach on summer days. He never went into the water and didn't have a bathing costume, but all the same he would sit close to the near naked bodies and watch them attentively. He hated the sight of the wrinkled flesh of old men, and avoided them, but was especially interested when a young man would get up and put a towel around his waist to lower his swimming trunks. He wished the towel would fall so he could see the whole of the young man's body. But these were shameful thoughts. Sinful thoughts. He would never, ever have the courage to confess to them.

"So are we ready?"

Dora insisted on a taxi. It seemed to be more her treat than his mother's. She mentioned quietly in the taxi how she hoped she had bought the right seats in the stalls.

"It was a toss-up between the stalls and the royal circle, but it's so claustrophobic up there when it's full, and this play is sold out."

The Theatre Royal was a blaze of colour and activity as they arrived. It was a first night, and Dora said it was rumoured Laurence Olivier was going to be there with Vivien Leigh.

"I do hope so," his mother replied, and Nick noticed how young she looked when she said that. He had read in one of his books about a girl waiting to go to her first ball, and now, looking at her, he saw that girl in the flesh. Once inside, he looked at the luxury of it all and as usual the two women were playing their respective pianos. His mother hummed along. He heard her say to Dora how much she loved the tunes of Franz Lehar.

Then the lights went down and the play began. The words were too adult for him and he missed a lot, but he loved the whole experience of sitting there, soaking up the atmosphere of strong perfumes and wealth. All around them, men and women were smartly dressed, and they were all polite enough to laugh, often. They even applauded when the curtain went up, just for the set alone. He sat back in his seat and wished that this was his real life: a life he could rely upon to be constant and not degenerate into rows and recriminations. When he turned to look at his mother and saw her upturned face staring at the magic on the stage, he wondered how she could be the same woman. How could she possibly be the same woman who hit him so often? Then Dora handed him a box of chocolates, asked him to choose one, and the thought passed.

That evening was one of the last of the occasional happy times. His mother received a letter to say that the rent was overdue and she once again became a woman frantic with anxiety. He had to accompany her to the callbox and listen to her scream at his father down the phone. Afterwards, she dragged herself up the hill to the flat and sat silently in her faded armchair all evening listening to the radio. He sat watching her, wary that at any minute her despair might unleash itself into anger and that the anger would be directed at him.

"The swine," she said once, then relapsed into silence.

She said goodnight to him and went to bed. Alone, he made his way to his own room. His mother kept him up every night until well past eleven. He knew that however bad she felt, she dreaded not having him near her. He thought of himself as a teddy bear who could talk: a passive comforter with which she could do what she liked. A few days later when the rent had been paid she recovered and even cooked him some decent meals.

The following week on Thursday afternoon, he came home to find his father there. His mother had gone out with Dora as was her habit every Thursday. They usually took a bus to

Rottingdean for tea, and he didn't expect her back until around seven.

"Hello," his father said.

"But it's not the weekend."

He trembled a little at the sight of the man.

"I suppose I'm a surprise."

"Yes," he said, then ran to his room and put away his schoolbooks.

"I've made you tea. It's in the kitchen."

He followed his father into the kitchen. There was a pot of tea ready and a pile of anchovy sandwiches along with a couple of bought cakes.

"Come on, let's tuck in."

Nick sat at the table but he could hardly eat a thing. He nibbled at a sandwich and drank lots of tea. His father remarked gently that he thought lemonade or some other soft drink would suit him better than tea, but he was used to tea and refused.

"I suppose you want to know why I'm here."

Nick nodded his head in silence.

"Come on. At least eat one of those cakes before we say anything more."

Obeying him, Nick picked up the cake and despite himself found it delicious. His mother rarely bought cakes as they were sweet and bad for her diabetes. When he had finished eating he stared at his father.

"Well, I have come to take you away."

Too shocked to reply, Nick stared down at the empty plate. His father tactfully did not break the silence.

"You mean on holiday?" Nick replied at last. It was all he could say. He could imagine nothing else and even that seemed ridiculous. No, he was lying to himself. Deep down he knew precisely what his father meant.

"Why?"

"I think it would be better for you."

He made an attempt to reply, but his father motioned for

him to be quiet. He asked Nick if he could explain further. Nick nodded his head.

"I know you are going to a lousy school. She's the Catholic, not me. I would not have wanted you to go to that place. I bet it's all penance and sin and cruelty. I hate the Catholics."

Nick looked at him and felt tears pricking at his eyes. He too hated the school.

"Do you learn much there, apart from the mumbo jumbo?"

"The usual things."

"What are you good at?" his father asked and then brushed the question away as if it was an irritating fly. "We don't have time to talk about this in detail. I have packed you a small bag. It's in your room, under your bed. I didn't want it to be a shock when you first got home. I hope you don't mind."

Nick did mind, but said nothing.

"I want you to try to be understanding and intelligent about this. You are old enough to realise that your mother is no longer a good influence on your development."

"I don't see why."

"Of course you see why."

"She's ill."

"That's no excuse to ruin a child's life."

Nick opened his mouth to say more, but his father looked at him sternly like one of the teachers at school.

"I want you to come to the station with me. She will be home soon and then it will be too late. Once you're away from here she will find it bloody hard to get you back. We'll talk it out at the station if we must, but not here. You can also have a real think on the way to the station. There's nothing like fresh air to get some sense into the brain. I was brought up on a farm, so I know something about it."

"I don't want to go," Nick said, and this time he could not stop the tears.

"Just walk with me to the station. Please."

His father's voice was soft and gentle. He felt loved by the man, but at the same time he did not want that love—it suddenly seemed a fearful thing, this concept of love. He hoped his mother would suddenly return, but it wasn't anywhere near the time for that despite what his father thought. There were always delays on the bus from Rottingdean and Dora would keep her talking even when they had arrived back in Brighton.

"I ask you again, please come to the station with me. We'll have plenty of time before the train goes. I have the tickets."

Nick got up mechanically from the table and going to his room drew out the small piece of luggage from under the bed. He hadn't a clue what was inside it and didn't care.

"Don't forget your coat."

His father stood in the doorway with a smile on his face. Nick looked at the smile briefly, then picked up his bag and walked past him to the front door where he put on his coat as he had been told to. Why was it that he was treated like a child and ordered about like a child, when the adults he knew always expected him to look and act like a man? He wore long trousers before any of the other boys in his school. He wore a coat in summer and in winter, just to make sure he didn't catch cold. He was always told by his mother not to play with the 'trash on the street' which was her way of describing most of the boys he knew. He never admitted to her that they almost never wanted to play with him. Just the sound of other children's laughter and talk irritated her.

After his father had quickly cleaned up the kitchen, he joined him by the front door and they both went down the steps to Montpelier Road. At first his father tried to make conversation, but Nick was obstinately quiet. He had nothing to say. He began to think bad thoughts. Was his father's extra niceness to him today a sort of blackmail? He had heard the word used often enough in plays and talks on the radio, but he didn't understand the meaning of it properly. All the same, he thought the word had some relevance to the situation he was now in. Were the cakes and smiles a subtle way of persuading him to leave his mother and his only home? The flat was all he had. The rooms in it were his only true place. Was his father intent on punishing his mother and working through him to get to this goal? He was suspicious of all love, even the love that his father had declared.

They walked up Vernon Terrace and crossed Seven Dials to turn up Buckingham Place. He kept up his silence as they reached the top of the hill, and continued to do so as they dipped down Terminus Road towards the station. He saw clouds of steam and smoke from the arriving and departing trains and for a moment he felt the normal excitement of getting onto a train. Maybe he would go with his father as far as London just for the journey and then walk his way back to Brighton. It would be an adventure, possibly the biggest adventure that life would ever offer him. He would see places he had never seen before, like East Croydon and Haywards Heath. He was told they had a mental asylum Haywards Heath and maybe, just maybe, he would meet up with a mad person who was on the run. That would be an extraordinary experience. In that long moment, hundreds of possibilities rushed through his mind, each racing one after another in a too vivid flash across his brain. Hadn't Dick Whittington walked a long way in that pantomime he had seen at the Grand, or was it the Hippodrome? Then his mind darkened. The dirty cramped houses of Terminus Road with their filthy net curtains and their smell of poverty, well below the level of his own and his mother's, reminded him that this was the stage of *his* world that he wanted to spend his life on. He loved Brighton. It was as simple as that. They reached a café on the opposite side of the street from the station entrance and his father found them a place inside by the window.

"Orange or lemonade?"

"I'd like some tea."

His father ambled clumsily to the café counter. Nick looked out of the window and watched as people went in and out of the station. He considered how much he would like to go on a real holiday to somewhere with an exciting name like *Norge*. He had seen *Norge* in a collection of postcards in a second hand shop. There were also names like *Österreich* and he built up many a fantasy about where they were. Even at this desperate time of life-changing choice, he imagined going on a holiday to one of them—just like he sometimes went on mystery tours with his mother on the buses which left from outside the Palace Pier.

"Lemonade. I chose lemonade for you because you really must cut down on tea, and here are a couple of buns to put in your pocket for the journey."

His father placed the glass and the paper bag of greasy buns in front of him. Nick stared at them, then at the lemonade. His mouth was dry, but he wasn't thirsty.

"The buns have icing on top. They used to be your favourites."

Courage suddenly returned to Nick and he murmured, "That was years ago. You should know I don't like them much anymore. I prefer cream cakes now."

It was a petty reproach, but he meant it. His father's face seemed to crumple in on itself with disappointment, and as he lifted the white cup of tea to his lips, his hands shook. Nick looked at his brown freckled hands and felt disgust at how clumsy a drinker he was. Not at all like his mother who held tea in her hand so delicately when they went to her favourite café in Imperial Arcade. But then again, he reminded himself, she seemed to have stopped taking him there.

"I don't want to go with you," he said suddenly. His voice was decisive. He had made a decision. He would choose for himself for once.

"I am your father, but I cannot force you to come," his father said.

"I would scream if you did."

He looked at his father's distraught face and felt no pity.

"Brighton is my home. You can't take me away from my home. I know mother is often unwell, and she is often unkind to me as well, but this place is my home. No one is ever going to drag me away from it. Not for anything. Not even to go to Norge!"

His father smiled sadly.

"Is that how they call it at your school?" he asked.

"I don't know. Maybe."

"In geography. You must have geography lessons there, even though most of them probably wish the world was still flat. Do you know Norge means Norway?"

Looking down at the table, Nick said had seen the name on a stamp.

"Do you like stamps?"

"I don't know."

"If you like stamps you can have lots of them where we're going."

Nick was suddenly curious.

"And where would that be?"

"I have a sister. Betty. You've never met her because your mother doesn't like any part of my family. But I'm sure Betty could love you like a real mother. She's married to a man who works at Pinewood—you know, the big film studios. I know you like films, so wouldn't that be exciting?"

"Does her husband make films?"

Nick gave in to his curiosity, even though he knew he would remain faithful to Brighton.

"He's works on the production side. But Jack Hawkins came to their house for dinner once. Think how grand that would be for you to meet a great actor like him, and other people like him if you lived there."

"But I'm not going to live there," Nick said firmly.

His father sighed and all hope died in his voice as he said, "It seems I have come too late. I should have come years ago. And it's true, I cannot force you to go with me."

"Will you thank Betty all the same for me?"

If nothing else, Nick's mother had trained him to be polite, even if that training had come with blows across his face to make sure he was polite.

"I will," his father said.

"Tell her I saw a Jack Hawkins film last year. At least, I think it was last year—*The Cruel Sea.*"

"I know the picture," came the flat reply.

"So, may I go now please?"

His father silently handed him his packed bag.

"Are you really sure?"

Nick was already standing and as he heard the question, he realised suddenly that this was a decision that would alter the rest of his life. The adult in the child battled within him. The child thought of it as a great adventure to be able to choose like this, but the impending adult questioned deeply, deeply within the surface of his unformed self. He questioned, what if it's better where my father is going? What if it eases the pain that I know I will have to return to?

"Shall I walk home with you? I can miss the train and catch a later one. I'm not sure you should be by yourself. All this must have come as such a shock."

"No, daddy," he said. The old familiar but lost word escaped from his mouth. "You must catch your train. It's not so far for me to walk back, and mother will worry if she returns to find me not there."

"Yes, that's true."

The words sounded completely defeated. Nick looked down at a man who appeared beaten up and broken. He saw tears in his father's eyes.

"Go home now," his father said. Then as Nick was about to open the café door he called him back. "Here, take this. Just in case you need anything. I know your mother hasn't much money to spare."

His father held out a five pound note to Nick. Nick had never seen as much in his mother's purse.

"I can't take it," he said. "It's too much. I would never live long enough to spend it."

The child spoke, and the child was momentarily happy. He

thought of several books he had seen in the best bookshop in Brighton and knew that he could buy them and still have change.

"Go on," his father insisted. "Give me that much pleasure."

Nick took the money and put it in his trouser pocket. He smiled at his father. A big smile. It went way beyond politeness, almost coming from that dangerous region called love.

"Now, don't say anymore. I've made you happy for a while. That's something," his father said.

Nick left the café and made his way up the steep hill that was Terminus Road. A few grimy curtains twitched as he passed by. Despite the five pound note, he suspected that he had lost something, and that only back there in the café could the loss be re-found. All the same, he carried on up the hill.

When he arrived back at the flat, his mother was sitting in the living room. The radio was on and Nick recognised the theme from *Singin' in the Rain*. He quietly placed his small suitcase back under the bed and by the time he went back into the hall the music had changed to *On Moonlight Bay*. He had seen neither film and disliked the music, but knew both songs because they were played so often.

"Your father came for you, didn't he?"

This was the first thing his mother said when he joined her in the living room. She turned off the radio and there was nothing but cold silence for a while. He did not answer her, but sat in the chair furthest from her. He had not liked the music, but he disliked the silence more.

"Well?" she eventually asked.

"Yes," he said, looking at her once. He dreaded a row.

"He left a betting slip behind," she continued. "It was on the floor. He bets on horses, or didn't you know? That's why we're so poor, but I wonder how much he has got put aside."

"I came back," he replied simply.

"How far did you go? I came home earlier than usual. That

was a good hour ago."

She got up from the chair and came towards him. Her face was red with anger and her hands clenched and unclenched at her sides. He knew he was about to be hit and lowered his head, accustomed but still fearful of her blows. She may have defended him from being hit by teachers at school, but she had different standards when it came to her own home.

"Tell me. I want to know."

"Does it matter?"

He looked briefly up, just in time to receive a hard slap across his face.

"Don't you talk to me like that. I asked you a question and I want an answer. How far did you go with him?"

His face stung and his jaw hurt. He mumbled the words, "As far as the station. He wanted to take me far away."

"What made you come back? I wouldn't have cared if you had gone with him. After all, he couldn't have forced you out of this place and down to the station if you hadn't wanted to go with him in the first place."

"I don't know," he said.

She hit him again, this time harder, and he cried out.

"Don't," he said, getting up from the chair and facing her. She was not tall, but he was shorter than her and he wondered for a moment if she was going to kill him. He had read somewhere, perhaps in the *Evening Argus* about a mother murdering her child.

"I'll do what I like with you," she screamed.

Her face came out in deep purple blotches. She had high blood pressure, and every time she got this angry with him, her face became discoloured and ugly.

"Do you hear me?"

He answered the ridiculous, obvious question, with a quiet "yes" and backed away towards the door. It was too late now to get on that train. Why hadn't he gone? The thought of escape now made him want to run, but seeming to sense this, she moved quicker than he and crossed the room, barring his exit by closing the door and standing in front of it.

"Oh no you don't," she said. "I want to hear what happened. I want to know what he said to you. I want to know what words were said to make you want to leave your mother."

He stared up at her and his fear was so great that a trickle of urine ran down his leg. She was in too much of a rage to notice and soon he felt more liquid escape from his body. His underpants were sodden, and he was sure that it must be showing through his trousers. He looked down and saw to his dismay that a puddle of urine had formed on the lino beneath him. At least it won't stain, he thought, thankful that he had missed the patterned carpet in the middle of the room.

"I am sorry," he said.

"What are you sorry about?"

"This."

He pointed to the urine on the floor.

When she saw what had happened she jumped towards him and slapped him again and again.

"You filthy, disgusting child. You did that deliberately, didn't you? Why didn't you ask for the toilet?"

"You are blocking the door."

He began to cry, filled with pain and shame and fear. At that moment, he loathed both himself and her. The Church spoke of Hell. This was Hell.

"I couldn't control it," he said, his voice choked with sobs.

"Stop it. Stop that stupid sobbing. Do you want the people from upstairs to come down? Do you want them to see this filth?"

"No," he whimpered, his sobs lessening.

"Now go to the kitchen and get a cloth. One that is already dirty from under the sink. Bring it back and wipe this dry."

"But it's in my shoes. I'll make the kitchen wet with my shoes."

"Oh, damn you," she said, unusually for her, using a swear word—a mild one, but one that he would have been severely chastised for if he had said it. She pushed past him and went into the kitchen herself, returning after a few minutes with a mop and a pail, and began to do the cleaning up herself.

When she had finished, she looked at him coldly and told him to go to the bathroom, run a bath, and take his dirty clothes off.

He obeyed her at once, mercifully glad to be away from her. He closed the bathroom door behind him and ran the bath. There was no lock on the door and he was afraid she would follow him in. Hesitantly, he took off his clothes. He put his wet underpants, socks and trousers in a heap with other soiled clothes that were waiting to be cleaned. There was no basket and he hated the sight of his disgrace staring at him. He was conscious too of the smell of urine. Then he got into the bath, and at that moment the door opened. He covered his genitals with his hands.

"Please," he said.

"Please what?"

"Please, I don't want you to see me like this. Can't I be alone?"

"I gave birth to you didn't I? Despite your treachery this afternoon, you are my son."

She handed him a bar of soap and he was forced to reveal himself. His penis was small, shrunken with fear. He soaped his body in front of her, but did not stand up.

"Aren't you ashamed?" she asked, relentless in her pursuit.

"Yes," he said, and after replacing the soap on the side of the bath, again covered his genitals with his hands.

"How could you have gone with him like that?"

There was a now miserable whine in her voice. All anger was gone. She stood there as if she were the victim and he the torturer. Her face looked shocked, as if she had heard terrible news, or was about to hear it. She leant in closer towards him and her dark eyes began to cloud over with tears.

"He wanted to part us, and you let him. How much you must have wanted to go to get as far as the station. This is what I cannot get over. I know you came back, but you went. Don't you see? You went!"

The water was cooling around his body and he began to shiver. He was too afraid to move, and even more afraid of another mood change. He told himself she was a sick woman and that she must have been terribly scared that he would not return. Young as he was, he had learnt to internalise blame.

"I came back because I wanted to," he said.

"And you really wanted to? You had no hesitation in making that decision?"

He shook his head, and longed for her to leave him so he could get out of the bath. She had not seen him naked for a long time, and he cringed at the thought that she might be looking at and judging his body. He knew the male penis grew bigger as a boy grows older and he wondered if his had reached the stage where it was shameful for others, even his own mother, to see it.

"I want to get out of the bath please."

He recognised the child in his voice. The pitiful *please* reminded him of his infant and early years. *Please* was one of the first words he had learnt.

"I'll get you a clean towel. The one here needs to go in the wash with the other things."

She glanced at the pile of clothes and other articles waiting to be taken to the laundry. Could she smell the urine? His body became rigid with shame and he looked to the side at the ugly, peeling paper on the wall.

"I'll be back."

He hurried out of the bath and looked at the wet crumpled clothes. He thought of the urine-soaked five pound note in his trousers. He did not want it anymore. The wealth did not matter. It seemed as lost as everything else and he just stood there, covering his lower body with the towel that she had said was ready for the wash. She came back into the room.

"Take that dirty thing off. Here's the clean one."

Her hands held out a big fluffy white towel—the best they

had—and a change of clothes.

"I'll make you a hot drink," she said, placing the things on a side chair, "and you must be hungry."

Without waiting for an answer, she left him. He stood motionless for a while unable to move. He did not realise it, but he was in shock. Then, mechanically, he pulled the dirty towel away from his body and dried himself with the fresh one. Slowly, as if partially paralysed, he put on the clothes she had brought him.

In the kitchen there was food on the table—hot toast covered with baked beans. A cup of cocoa was beside it. Silently, he sat at the table and ate the meal. He drank down the cocoa, said "Thank you" and hoped he had pleased her. If he had pleased her, at least in some small way, she would leave him alone for the rest of the evening.

"I'd like to go to bed early if I may," he said.

"But it's your favourite serial on the radio," she said smiling. "Don't you want to listen to it?"

"I'm very tired."

"Then I will have to be on my own," she replied.

He looked at her and suddenly he felt pity. He imagined the pain she was in, not only at his going off with his father, but the various pains of her illnesses. Despite the hurt she had inflicted upon him, he recognised that her pain was perhaps greater. He had all his life before him, while she had maybe only a limited number of years left. He knew about death. He knew that death was inside him as well, but that it would come later.

"I am sorry I hurt you, mother," he said.

"I expect he bribed you. He bribed me once, and I gave in. I know how he can be. Promises. Always promises. No doubt he promised you a better life."

Nick knew he must not reply. Any word at all could light the fuse of her anger again, and he did not want that to happen. He told himself he loved her, that she was his mother, and that he had a duty to love her. And sometimes she was kind to him. He knew that as well.

"Well, go off to bed then," she said with a sigh. "It will be a long evening for me."

"I hope they play some of the music you like," he said.

"Yes, there is that," she replied and then quite suddenly she clutched him to her and kissed him over and over again on the cheeks of his face that only a short while before she had struck.

FOUR

Agnes did not leave her house in the north, and failed to turn up. Nick, seeing his mother's distress, went of his own accord to call her again. He took some change out of his mother's savings and hoped she would not notice. The phone rang for a long time and Nick was about to press button B to get his money back when the phone was answered. At first there was total silence at the other end.

"Aunt Agnes, is that you?"

"Oh, it's you Nick," she said as if surprised at hearing him. "I'm a bit out of it at the moment. I had a fall you see. Down the stairs. A stupid slip on a torn bit of carpet. I sprained my ankle. I've written to your mother. She should have the letter tomorrow."

"Then you are not coming?" Nick said.

"Hardly. Do you know what a sprained ankle means?"

At that moment, listening to her, Nick understood only too well that she was very much his mother's sister. The same change of tone from pleasant to sarcastic. He did not know her very well, and deep down he knew that he would never want to get to know her.

"I understand," he replied.

"Well, I hope you do. It's not good at my age to fall. The shock of what's happened has left me in such a daze I barely know what time of day it is. Even the cat is going around half starved because I can't move much. Thank God I've got nice neighbours, not that I intrude on their kindness, of course. But here I am prattling on and it's costing you money. Anyway, everything I have to say to your mother is in the letter."

"I will tell her."

"It should be, like I said, in the post tomorrow."

"Goodbye then, Aunt Agnes."

"Goodbye, Nick. Take care."

He put down the receiver and looked bleakly at the black

telephone with its bold white letters of A and B. He pressed button B, but no coins were returned. Walking home, he decided to say nothing to his mother. The letter would come anyway and he was not going to risk another painful scene with her by telling her that Agnes was not coming. That scene, if it had to be, could wait until tomorrow.

The letter arrived from Agnes, but a day or two later than she said it would. His mother read it in silence, folded it carefully and then put it away in a sideboard drawer. Nick, tempted though he was, never attempted to sneak a look at it.

The distress continued. His mother stopped looking after herself. She bathed infrequently, and began to smell. Meals were sporadic and Nick frequently had to fend for himself, eating what was left in the kitchen and having to almost beg his mother for money to stock up on essentials. This continued for a couple of weeks. He was often late for school, or didn't go at all. He would sit with her for hours with the curtains drawn, listening to the radio. He liked the plays best of all, and for an hour or so he could escape into them, listening to dialogue and imaginary fictitious situations. It was at about that time, that he began to think about becoming a writer.

"I'm going to ring Agnes myself," his mother declared after a particularly bad day of depression when she had hardly spoken at all.

"Do you want me to come with you?" he asked.

"No, I'll manage."

She combed her hair, put on some fresh lipstick and a clean dress. Nick saw with sadness that she was determined to look her best for the telephone box and the walk down Montpelier Road.

"Can I go out as well? I'd like to go to St Ann's Well Gardens."

"Yes, but come back before it gets dark."

It was early March and the days were lengthening. Nick realised he could be out for a good couple of hours if he wanted to, but instead of the park, he had another plan. He waited until his mother had left the flat, and then after tidying himself up, decided to visit Dora. In the same drawer as the letter from Agnes, his mother kept a black notebook of names and addresses. Most of them were from a distant past, but Dora's name was one of the exceptions. Her house was nearby in Victoria Street. He had often walked down it when he went to school at St Mary Magdalen's. The piercing spire rose up majestically at the bottom of the street.

He rang the bell and Dora opened the door. The house was a little run down and its façade was in need of a coat of paint, but once inside the place was welcoming and in its own way elegant. Above the marble mantelpiece, Dora had a portrait of herself which had been painted back in her youth. There were signed photographs of actors and actresses he didn't recognise—the men outnumbered the women—and one face attracted his attention. It was of a handsome, young man, staring wistfully from a silver frame. Dora saw his glance and said slowly, "That's Ivor Novello himself. In his youth. The greatest songwriter and actor, and the most wonderful of men to have emerged from this dreadful century."

"I don't know anything about him," he replied truthfully. He had heard his mother mention his name, but that was all.

To his embarrassment, Dora then began to sing the opening lines of *We'll Gather Lilacs in the Spring*. She had a gravelly voice with no direction, like a needle caught in a record's groove. He just about recognised the tune. He had often heard it on the sort of radio programmes his mother liked. She had only hummed to it whereas Dora was now giving it a deadly vocal treatment.

"Mother likes that song," he said loudly and perhaps a bit rudely, as it prevented Dora from singing more.

"Of course she does," she replied, raising a hand to her throat. "I think she met him too when she was younger.

Wanted his autograph if I remember. As for me? Well, my dear, he rather fancied me, you know."

Nick looked at Dora and wondered what the good looking man in the photograph could have seen in her. He just couldn't believe in her as having ever been young and beautiful despite the flattering portrait on the wall.

"Did he want to marry you or something?"

Dora looked as if she wanted to blush, but couldn't. She shrugged her shoulders and tapped the framed photograph with the tips of her fingers.

"Who knows? He never declared himself. He lived in such a world of celebrity, but our dinners together were so discreet. He was like a shy little boy really, and yet at the same time, such a gentleman."

She paused, then added, "Men are not like that anymore. I remember thinking that when I saw *Genevieve* a while ago. Have you seen it, dear? Part of it is set in Brighton, you know. But the men! So common compared to people like Ivor. I sat watching them with their ridiculous cars, thinking, try as you might, you can't fill a screen with magic like Ivor did."

"What kind of cars were they?" Nick asked with sudden interest.

"Edwardian, I think. Oh, it was a very silly film. The only thing of value in it was Kay Kendall's performance. She made up for all the style the men lacked. Dinah Sheridan was good too, but not in the same class. Too ordinary. But Kay Kendall was superb. I'd love to see her on the stage, but who knows, maybe she's more vivid on the screen. The stage can be so testing."

She sighed, then looked at Nick in a pitiful sort of way as if surprised that she had spoken so fervently about something that he could not possibly understand.

"I remember when mother and I went to the theatre with you," he said.

"Oh yes, but that was such a long time ago. You were a very handsome boy then. I see now you are slowly heading towards manhood. It must be a difficult time for you. Not that I would know. I am far too selfish to have ever been bothered with children."

Nick wondered when she was going to ask him to sit down. They were standing in the middle of the living room, and there were no signs from her that she would.

"I've come about mother," he said. "I have to talk to someone."

"Yes dear, I see."

It was then the sign was made. Dora pointed to a plush pink seat, facing a very large faded mauve sofa set against a wall covered with various brightly coloured paintings.

"She is ill," he said, tentatively sitting down. He was glad he had clean trousers on.

"Again?"

It was both a statement and a question. Dora draped herself elegantly along the sofa, taking out a packet of cigarettes from an equally elegant pocket in her long dress which was more suitable for evening wear than for the afternoon. Nick wondered if she hadn't been preparing herself for an evening out when he called. She lit the cigarette and leaning even further back, closed her eyes and inhaled deeply. Nick waited patiently for her attention to return to him.

"Is it her nerves, or is it something physical?" she murmured, her eyes still closed. She didn't look or sound particularly interested, but Nick hoped that she was.

"It's more serious than that, Mrs Webster."

He had found out her second name from the black book, and felt that he should use it out of politeness.

"Call me Dora, dear. I do so hate Mrs Webster."

She opened her eyes and gave him a rather sharp look.

"In the theatre, I was Dora Vandal. I kept the name Webster only for forms and other bureaucratic things. I always think of myself as Mrs Vandal, and I am to my best of friends. As for you, as you are barely out of childhood, I would prefer it if you called me simply Dora."

"In my mother's address book, you are just Mrs Webster," he replied rather coldly.

"Perhaps it's a very old address book from when she only just got to know me. I never flaunt the name Vandal to people I am not so close to."

Nick watched as Dora roused herself a little, sitting straighter on the sofa and stubbing out her cigarette in an ashtray on the side table. She was still in the mood for reverie.

"Dora Vandal makes me feel young," she said slowly. "Some people are old when they are young and young when they are old, you see. I fall into the latter category. It's a pity that the stage today doesn't respect that. All these vulgar young men—especially the writers—hinting at sex more often than not, and its perversions. Only N.C. Hunter shows promise. His *Waters of the Moon* was a play I would have died to be in. Not that I am old, but let's just say I'm a little further along the road."

Nick had nothing to say to all this. He realised that he had not seen Dora much recently. His mother's days out on Thursdays had been private and he had never been asked along. Then he was jerked out of his thoughts by what Dora said next. It sounded real.

"It must be very hard on you, having to deal with her constant sickness more or less on your own. Does she still have to have those daily injections for her diabetes?"

He nodded his head. A nurse did come every day, very early in the morning, and she dreaded it. This was another thread in her life that led to the anxiety, anger, and all the other ugliness he lived with. It was perhaps another reason why she dreaded going to bed at night. He intuitively understood that she did not want the day to end and that she kept him up late as if to postpone the inevitable harrowing visit of the nurse. She always closed her eyes and went white when the needle went in.

"And your dear father?"

Sarcasm sounded loud and hard in Dora's voice.

"He works hard. At the weekends too sometimes."

"Something to do with horse racing, isn't it? Your mother has never been very precise."

Nick was unsure about this as well. Being young, he took it more or less for granted that his father's work was respectable, and he never asked questions. He was more concerned with his own future and his obvious need to leave school as soon as he could. The money was badly needed, and anyway, he barely learned anything of value at Clifton College.

It was now Dora's turn to be irritated and impatient with his inward looking silence. At least she talked her way through her thoughts.

"Why have you come to me?" she asked directly.

"Because you are her best friend."

"I see. That is very flattering, but honestly we are not that close."

"Mother didn't ask me to come. It was my own decision."

"That was very adult of you, Nick, but frankly I have not seen her in quite a while. She may have told you she still sees me, but I can assure you it is not true. My own health has not been so good, and well, I like to live a more secluded life than I did. There are a few local celebrities who come to visit me, but other than them, I keep myself more or less to myself."

"I heard there's a man on television who lives around the corner."

"Oh yes. Gilbert. He's a constant visitor. A bit of a recluse like me, but he makes the effort. But it's dear Alan Melville I like the best."

"Who?"

"You don't have television, do you?"

He looked down when she asked this. It always seemed like a sort of social reproach when people asked this. Something to be ashamed of, like not being rich enough to own one's house or give parties. He knew a lot of people in the posh parts of Brighton gave parties.

"No," he replied flatly, then glanced around him and saw the desired television set in a corner of the room. It was both discreet and glaringly there.

"Alan writes the most delightful plays as well," she added, then returned to chatter on about the merits of having a television in the house.

"It adds so much more to one's life. The radio is so maddening the way you can never see the people. It'll be out of fashion soon. Really, your mother ought to buy one, or at least rent one. So much good entertainment. One doesn't need to go to the theatre so much with a television to provide the fun. None of my friends take it seriously though, especially my well known friends. They may use it for the benefit of their careers, but it's basically just for fun. It's frivolous, but then what's wrong with that? Brighton was born for frivolity. That's why so many old actors love to live here."

She paused, a little out of breath, then launched in again. Nick wondered if she was writing a play herself, the way she loved monologues.

"Television brings us up to date. At its best it holds to the tradition of glamour, unlike these dreadfully serious plays that London now seems to like. What was it—*Look Back in Anger* or something? What tosh!"

Nick began to fidget in his chair. He was very thirsty, but it was obvious Dora was not concerned about his needs. He was, after all, not on a social call, but a call of need. The needy, he knew with a wisdom way beyond his years, never get particularly good treatment.

"I'm afraid I'm taking up your time," he said.

"A little, but I'm sure this is important for you. I wish I could see how I could help. She does have a doctor, doesn't she? I go to a delightful man in Hove. I'm not sure who your mother sees."

He named his mother's doctor.

"Oh yes, he's a National Health man. They can be so difficult about house visits, compared to a doctor who is private. Not all of course. I have heard of some who are idealistic."

Nick wasn't quite sure what she was talking about. It sounded like snobbish rubbish, but he had no answer to it.

"But you must insist with free doctors," she continued. "You really must. Read them the riot act about their duties etc. Or that's what I would do if I was stuck with one."

"Yes," he said, wanting to get out of the house as soon as possible. He knew now that Dora was the last person he could talk to about how and why his mother had attempted to take her life. She had after all committed a criminal act, and he was afraid Dora would betray her in some way.

"But if she is willing to pay," she went on, "I'll be only too pleased to give her the address of mine. He is like one of those doctors before the war. So eager to please."

"Yes."

"Is that all you have to say?"

He stood up and looked down at her.

"I expect she'll be alright," he said. "All she really needs are the comforts a real friend could give."

He was surprised by his own sharpness and directness. Dora looked up at him, and the lines on her face hardened. She had not heard a boy, but a man speaking. It had clearly not pleased her at all.

"Well, I am that of course, but unless you can be more specific about what is wrong with her, I fail to see how I can be of any aid."

"She had a really bad turn," he lied.

"Oh, that!"

She stood up, attaining authority over him by being a little taller.

"Giddiness, was it?"

"Yes."

"Comes with age, dear. *Anno Domini*. That's what we all call it in the club."

He was not sure about Anno Domini and completely at a

loss about the club, so he coughed instead of replying. The living room felt closed in and very stuffy. He noticed the brand of her cigarettes—*Balkan Sobranie*—expensive and far too strong smelling.

"Give her some warm tea with lots of sugar and make her go to bed."

"She's diabetic."

"Then whatever substitute she uses," Dora said irritably. "It will do wonders. Little remedies are often the best. In fact, I think the last possible thing she needs is another person flapping around her. Giddy attacks can mean a lot of things, but having too many people around can cause panic. I know. I've had them. I'm sure it's nothing serious."

"Yes, *Mrs* Vandal," he said.

Greg would have called her a heartless cunt but Nick had the knack of using more subtle weapons. She bristled, visibly, at the word *Mrs*. Had she ever been Mrs Webster? Had she ever married at all? He could have simply said, Dora Vandal, but even to him, that would have been too obvious a slight.

"I'll show you out, shall I?"

He smiled at the dismissal. He wondered if she would show him to the back entrance, but then he recalled that the houses in Victoria Street didn't have back entrances. He forced a friendly smile back at her.

"No, please go back to your sofa," he said. "This house is small enough for me to find my own way to the door."

He turned his back on her and said goodbye. Once out of the front door, he looked up at the tall spire of St Mary Magdalen's and shuddered. On his way back home, he wondered how people in Portslade treated friends in need.

His mother was silent upon his return. She had a cold meal waiting for him in the kitchen and, with a gesture of her hand, motioned to him to go in and eat it. She remained silent afterwards and it was only around eleven thirty with the radio off and the flat quiet that she said, "Aunt Agnes is too unwell to come down. I knew it already. It's a pity I wasted money on the phone that could have been put to a better purpose."

The silence continued for two days and for two days he missed school, not wanting to leave her. Surprisingly, on the third day, she awoke and got straight into a bath. Afterwards, she chatted with him and scolded him mildly for missing out on his education. It was as if a dark cloud had passed and in the afternoon she suggested they went to the Embassy cinema—her favourite cinema that specialised in re-runs of older films. She mentioned the name of an actress he had never heard of and he said, "Yes, what a good idea." She put on her most vivid red dress and they left the house together. She took his arm, and looking at her in the pale sunlight he saw how frail she was. He felt a surge of tenderness, like a boy should feel for his mother.

Nick had made no arrangement to see Greg, so he trusted to chance that he would. His life with his mother resumed its usual routines, and gradually his mind grew easier. She was less concerned now about his comings and goings which gave him greater freedom. He would wander through the town, spending time on the Palace Pier, and then do a tour of the second hand bookshops. He read a lot at home now, managing to shut out the sound of the radio. He had seen the film of *War and Peace* and had been moved by it. He couldn't remember the story too well, but at the end of the film Audrey Hepburn's character commented upon returning to their ruined Moscow house that despite its wounds, it still stood. The sense of hope in her face and voice after so much destruction filled him too with hope. He felt that he too would have to go through a war, and that he too would find a home and lose it, and yet, like her, he would be able to stand, endure it, and continue with his life. I must read the book, he thought.

This was to be his first real entrance into the world of literature. He no longer read just for the excitement of it, but to learn. He began with a battered Penguin edition. It was in two volumes and, at a stretch on his pocket money, he had been able to buy both. He read the first volume quite quickly, but on entering the second, found that he got too bogged down with the description of war. Most of his reading was done in the calm of St Ann's Well Gardens, on the familiar seat where he had first seen Greg. He was battling with an especially hard page when he saw Greg in the distance, up by the well of St Ann itself. He was talking to a red-headed boy who wore shorts and looked no older than thirteen. Greg stood facing him, dressed in a simple white shirt and jacket and wearing long trousers. They seemed to be arguing. It was the first of April, around five in the afternoon. Then he saw something that astonished him. He saw Greg slap the boy across the face, then turn around and walk away from him. Greg was walking towards Nick and Nick hurriedly stuffed his copy of *War and Peace* into his coat pocket, and waited for Greg to notice him, but Greg was looking down and appeared totally immersed in his thoughts. He even cut across the grass in front of Nick without noticing him, avoiding the path that would have led him to walk directly in front of him.

"Greg!" Nick called out. He couldn't let him go now that he had seen him again.

"Oh, it's you."

The look on his face troubled Nick. It was not particularly welcoming.

"Yes," came Nick's weak reply, and a sinking feeling of disappointment hit him in the pit of his stomach.

"It's April Fool's Day," Greg said as he approached the seat. "I wonder who the fool is. You or me?"

"Both of us," Nick replied, and they both suddenly laughed. The tense, inward look on Greg's face disappeared, and once again, Nick was pulled into the magnetic orbit of his smile.

"No football?" Nick asked jokingly.

Greg's trousers and white shirt made him look very grown up.

"I had other things to do," came the casual reply. He scuffed the gravel with his black shoes. The act was more that of a bored child than an adult. Nick noticed that his hair was longer than before, and that it fell forward covering his forehead and almost hiding his eyes.

"You look so much older with your long trousers and your hair the way it is."

"It's just as it always was," Greg replied, brushing his hair back, and staring at Nick. "You can talk, what with your old face and that same old coat. You look about a hundred. And what is that I see there, poking out of your pocket? What you hiding? Is it a dirty book? Is it about sex?"

"No, it's *War and Peace*. Tolstoy."

"What's fucking Tolstoy?"

"He's a Russian writer. It's about the Napoleonic wars."

"Bit before my time. What in shit's name you reading that for? If you like war books, try *From Here to Eternity*. Me dad read that and I found all the juicy bits. Bit more interesting than Napoleon."

"But this is a serious book."

Greg mimicked the way Nick said the word *serious*, then added, "So's fucking *From Here to Eternity*. And it was one of the first A-films I got someone to take me into."

"Who's that boy I saw you with?" Nick asked suddenly.

There was an awkward silence and Greg looked away into the distance towards a group of old men playing bowls on the green.

"Oh, just someone," he said at last.

"A friend?"

Nick was aware that his voice sounded suspicious and had the ring of marking out territory that he thought was his own.

"He clings," Greg said, turning again to Nick and then sitting down beside him.

"What do you mean?"

"What I said. He clings. Like one of those fucking creepers you see climbing up old walls. It's suffocating."

84

Nick wondered if he was a clinger himself and said nothing.

"He just wants too much," Greg said.

"I don't understand."

"Well I bloody do, and today I'd had enough of it. He goes to the Knoll as well and he follows me around like some puppy. He's not even in the same class as me."

"How did you meet?"

"I told you, at fucking school."

Greg's language was as rich as ever, and to his surprise, Nick found it a relief to hear those words again.

"So you fucking hit him across the face?"

Greg turned to look at Nick and laughed.

"Don't put the ripe words in for me," he said. "In your mouth they sound all wrong. Does anybody ever swear in your ancient Russian novel?"

"No."

"Well, they do in the books I like. Not fuck and cunt of course, but all the others—like bastard. When I read the dialogue in those books, I put in ruder words. Bet the bloody authors would have done it if they'd been allowed to. Anyway, books are boring. They never talk like we talk."

"They do so," Nick said, springing up in defence. "Only yesterday in a bookshop in the Lanes—"

"In the sodding Lanes?" Greg interrupted. "What the fuck were you doing there? Gone queer for antiques and tack like that, have you?"

"No, it's just where I get books."

"Steal 'em I hope."

"No, I buy them."

"More fool you."

They both laughed again and Greg punched Nick on the arm.

"Come on old man, what are we going to do today?"

"But it's getting on for six."

"So?"

"Nothing, but it's late."

"You mean mummy's waiting for you?"

"Sod off."

"That's better. So what can I do to corrupt you today?"

Nick thought of Charlie's place and the bed, and blushed. His penis grew hard, and he knew that more than anything he wanted to masturbate, preferably with Greg. He opened his coat, and edged his way forwards on the seat, hoping that his erection showed. His trousers were light coloured and made of a very thin material. He felt his penis straining in his underwear and was proud of the fact that he was capable of making the first move.

"I'm older than I was when we last met," he said. His mouth felt heavy with the words, and his tongue was dry.

"What's on your mind, Nick?" Greg said, glancing obviously at the displacement of Nick's clothes.

"I don't know."

"I think you do."

"We could run."

"That's not what you are thinking."

"What are you, a mind reader suddenly?"

"Was it all that talk of dirty words in books? Did that do it for you? Charlie's place is not free, but there's a café down on the Western Road, near the border with Brighton. They have a place nobody notices, and even when they try the door they go away."

"What sort of place?"

"A sit down. Quite big too. You can stretch your legs."

"I'm not sure," Nick said, but his need was getting more urgent and the proximity of Greg was too strong to say no. He knew precisely what sort of room it would be.

Ten minutes later, after a rapid run, they were there. The café was dirty and filled with down and out men drinking tea out of grubby mugs. The toilet was at the back in a sort of courtyard. Once inside, they found it cleaner than the café. Greg was the first to hang his jacket behind the door, and he stuffed his handkerchief into the too large keyhole.

"Can't be too careful," he said.

They stood facing each other and Nick longed to kiss him, but he knew he had to accept less and just watched as Greg lowered his trousers.

"C'mon, you drop yours as well. Don't want to splash in your pants, do you?"

Nick lowered his trousers and he was startled to see how ready his penis was. It glistened with pre-cum.

"Give you a race," Greg murmured. "But remember, don't cry out when you shoot. It's pretty safe in here, but not *that* safe."

"Okay."

They both came within minutes. Greg splashed all over his black shoes, whereas Nick turned at the last moment and aimed into the toilet, but unlike urine, sperm doesn't always flow in quite the same way and it hung off his hand like white webbing.

"Feel better?" Greg asked, winking at him. "Now we've got to get out of this toilet and back into the café looking like innocent little lambs."

Out in the street, Greg seemed eager, in a casual sort of way, to meet up with Nick in the gardens the following day.

In his dreams, blurred grey-tinged dreams one after the other, Nick could see neither of their faces clearly. He had no exact idea of the definitions of his own face, and certainly not of Greg's face. He wanted it to be like that. Then suddenly in the grey he saw blue eyes, which then swam into being green. He had glimpses of vivid patches of colour like this in his mind: floppy hair, at first dark, near to black, then deep brown. He saw a sharp jaw, but no mouth, and then the mouth itself would slip into view. It was open in a gasp, in that moment of gasp when Greg came: a moment nearer to silence than cry. He heard rather than saw his own contorted lips, but then again in another moment, Greg's smile was fused into the contortion and they were blended together, totally one. He wanted it to be fluid, never fixed, always in motion, as their bodies were in motion when running. He watched the long legs run, and the dark hair on the legs, merge into the darker hair of the groin. He saw Greg's penis, but never his own. But then, in his dream, Greg's penis was his penis: the same length, the same head, glistening with liquid. He wanted it all to be oblique and seamless. Image chasing image. As impossible as it was to directly stare at the sun, so it was impossible to stare at all that Greg had physically. He never, ever wanted to see him in cold, solid perspective. Quite simply, he did not want the dream of themselves to break into two.

For a few weeks the dream of Greg, the ideal of Greg, continued. They spent most of their time together after school, sometimes returning to the café, sometimes just running around the town for the pure pleasure of it. They had fun on the Palace Pier ghost train where much to Nick's surprise Greg became a little claustrophobic and perhaps afraid. For the first time, he clutched Nick and held him to him, startled by a flapping thing that came out at them from the darkness. When they emerged into daylight his face was white.

"Shit, that was a ride," he said.

Nick observed how unsteady Greg was as he got out of his seat.

"I've got some extra money today. Wait here while I get us some candy floss," Nick said. When he returned with the gooey mess of pink, Greg took it and laughed.

"I really had you there," he said, taking the stick of floss from Nick.

"What do you mean?"

"Pretending like that. I thought if I was afraid, you'd be afraid."

The words sounded hollow and forced. Nick could still feel the tightness of Greg's hand where he had held on to his arm.

It was an embrace that Nick desired, but not in this way. He wanted Greg to remain true to his image of strength and daring. But this brief incident was soon forgotten, and the late afternoons continued in a round of stealing comics and playing pranks whenever and wherever they could. Later on, Nick realised it was in fact the end of their childhood and, certainly for Nick, the end of their innocence together.

The first shadow fell in May when the remake of *Dracula* opened at the Regent cinema. Usually they avoided the Regent with all its grandeur, generally because there was nothing on that they wanted to see. But Greg did look sixteen, especially in Nick's eyes, and he felt quite confident waiting for him in the foyer while he bought tickets for two. He glanced at the poster of Christopher Lee as Dracula and hoped it would live up to its bloodsucking publicity. Certainly the cinema was full, and as they hurried in, almost crushed by other eager viewers, Greg whispered in his ear that it was supposed to be even better than *The Curse of Frankenstein*.

"It's going to be gory this one. Just look at the stills."

Once inside and sitting next to Greg, Nick relished the palatial surroundings. There was only one snag. They had arrived late in the afternoon, just in time to see an X certificated French film called *There's Always a Price Tag*. It was a thriller, but to them it was dull. There was violence, it's true, but they were impatient for it to end and for the main feature to begin. *Dracula* was billed to start at five minutes past six and Nick was worried about getting home late.

"I thought you said *Dracula* was on first," he whispered.

"I got it wrong. So what? It's an X isn't it?

"I'm not really interested."

"I know, not much sex is there, and that blonde is too old."

Greg was like a merciless critic.

"Want to do something?" Greg asked.

"What?"

"You know what."

"I don't think I want to," Nick replied.

"Course you do. You're ready for it, anytime, just like me. The toilets are good here, and they're all into the film, so we won't be disturbed."

"I'm not sure."

Greg got up, tugging Nick out of his seat, and they pushed past tutting viewers to get to the aisle.

"Can't believe they're watching this crap," Greg said and led Nick to the toilets. Once locked inside a cubicle, Nick failed to rise to the occasion. Greg looked angrily at him and asked him what was wrong, but Nick couldn't reply as he didn't know what was wrong. He just felt he didn't want to.

"Well, I'm not gonna waste any more time."

He watched as Greg turned his back on him and began to masturbate and suddenly he felt sad. Was it always going to be like this? Greg came, buttoned up his trousers, and then with a stony face, pushed past Nick and out of the toilet. A puzzled man, urinating at the stand-ups, gave Nick a sinister look as he followed Greg out.

"He saw us," Nick said as they made their way back to their seats.

"So? Maybe it gave him a thrill. He probably waits for boys like us to go in there and do it with him. I caught his eye. He looked at me as if he was one of them. I can tell."

They reached their seats after a further bout of tutting, and they stared silently up at the screen, watching the downbeat end of the film.

"Didn't miss much," Greg said as the lights went up. "Got any money for an ice cream? I need one after that wank."

Nick gave him some coins and waited as Greg went down the aisle to the pretty usherette who had a full tray of ice cream tubs and chocolates. When he returned to his seat, he said to Nick, "I should have gone to that cubicle with her. I bet I could have had a real fuck with her instead of what we bloody do."

"Have you done it? Fucked a girl?" Nick asked, taking his raspberry ripple from Greg.

"Would I tell you?" Greg replied ambiguously.

The lights went down and the main feature began. It turned out to be as horrifying as they had hoped. The colour and large screen made moments of it truly terrifying for both of them. The first appearance of Dracula, fangs exposed and ready for action, made them jump in their seats.

"Bloody hell!" Greg exclaimed.

Then there was the staking, which while not as explicit as it could have been, was strong enough.

"We didn't see it all. The censor's been at it again," Greg whispered in a very knowing way.

Nick looked at him and asked if he had really wanted to see more.

"You bet," came Greg's excited reply.

By the end of the film, after Dracula had met his end by crumbling to dust in a particularly nasty way, Greg looked a bit shaken. He didn't look as bad as when he had come out of the ghost train, but he looked stunned all the same. Nick wasn't quite so affected by the film, but still thought he might get nightmares. Out in the street, Nick asked Greg what he had thought of it.

"I preferred *The Curse of Frankenstein*," Greg replied.

"Why? Wasn't this just as bloody?"

"I dunno. He was just a monster in the Frankenstein film."

"And what was this one then?" Nick asked, curious about the answer.

"He was an evil man, and the sex was abnormal. I don't think I like vampires."

They crossed the road to the Clock Tower, and Greg took out a packet of cigarettes. He lit one with a lighter Nick had never seen before and put it to his mouth.

"You smoke?" Nick asked.

"I nicked the cigarettes and the lighter. There's an easy shop in Portslade. You're too young to smoke still, but I'm not."

"Liar. You're too young as well. And anyway, I'd smoke if

I wanted to," Nick said defiantly.

"You'd never get away with it, you're too short."

Nick was angry at this, but hid it. He was also confused about the abnormal sexuality Greg had mentioned.

"What did you mean by the sexual stuff being abnormal? I thought you would have liked all those big breasts."

"Got nothing to do with that. Vampires have bad sex. Monsters don't have sex at all. It wouldn't be right. But this Dracula was just a plain pervert, sucking blood and doing those other things when the camera faded out. He even went after that man at the beginning of the film. Undead or not, he was a pervert. He had queer desires. Made me uncomfortable."

Nick was shocked at this sudden puritan attitude, and wondered how Greg could forget what they had done together. Wasn't that a perversion too in most people's eyes?

"I don't get it," Nick said, looking away from Greg. This was a different side to him that he hadn't seen before. His words seemed to come out with hatred.

"Like that man in the toilet. I'm sure he was queer. If he'd been normal, he would have told on us, and they would have come and fetched us. But he was old, and he fancied me, and he felt guilty about it."

"You don't know that, Greg."

"Like hell, I don't. Do you think I was born yesterday?"

"But what we do? Isn't that abnormal? I mean to you?"

"It's just a bit of fun. It doesn't mean we're like that. You saw that boy in the park I was talking to. He's going to end up like that man in the toilet. That's why I won't speak to him again."

The conversation was beginning to confuse Nick. He returned to the subject of Dracula.

"He was just a monster, Greg. There was sex—"

"—and there shouldn't have been! That Dracula would go with anyone, women, men—and look how he trained that young woman to go after children. If that isn't proof of what

I'm saying, I don't know what is."

"She was under his spell."

"She had that horrid, sick look on her face. She wanted to go after children, dead or not. The whole film was bloody sick."

Nick had to laugh, the conversation seemed so completely ridiculous to him. The film had struck a nerve with Greg that he could not understand and he wanted to get away from him. He recalled how in the toilet of the café, Greg had stared at Nick's penis and concentrated on it until he came. Was that bloody sick too?

"You're seeing things that weren't there."

"Fucking not. I saw what I saw."

Greg flicked his cigarette end at the base of the Clock Tower and began to walk away. Nick watched him go, not wanting to run after him. Greg turned once as if expecting him to do just that, but shrugged his shoulders when he saw Nick was going to stay put. He kept on walking in the direction of Cranbourne Street and disappeared. Nick crossed back to the main façade of the Regent cinema and looked again at the stills from the film. Then as he walked up towards the station, taking a longer route home than usual, he felt something break inside him and was almost overcome by a terrible sense of loss. His mind kept re-running the look on Greg's excited face as he had watched him, anticipating his orgasm. There had been real desire there. He was sure of it, but then again, he was suddenly not sure of anything.

"It doesn't make any sense at all," he said aloud to himself. Then his mind closed down on the subject.

In the long weeks that followed, Nick spent most of his free time after school walking the streets of Brighton. He began to notice other boys his own age or slightly older, identifying some as being desirable. There was also an incident with a man who was much older, who seemed to be following him as he walked through the Lanes. Nick darted down an alleyway to get away from him. He had noticed the man look at him, and knew that it signified interest in him. Of one thing Nick was sure; he desired boys around his own age, not older men.

It was on one of these walks that he discovered a run-down bookshop in a side street off the London Road. Some of the books in the window had cellophane wrappers around them, as if they enclosed a secret that should not be read by all. The covers under the wrappers were mainly lurid, with badly drawn women in various stages of undress. Tight and sometimes torn dresses, barely concealed their figures, and in most there was a man in the background looking at them. Clearly this was a bookshop for adults, and feeling curious, he went in, expecting to be told to get out. On the wall was a sign that said, 'All Books Second-hand'.

"Can I help you?"

From behind the counter at the front of the shop, an elderly woman with too much rouge and lipstick smiled at him. She was knitting. She clearly didn't think he was too young, and when he answered in his deepest voice, which could become very deep when he tried, that he just wanted to browse, she simply nodded her head and smiled again. He wandered further in and she asked, "Fiction or non-fiction?" Her tone was pleasant and casual.

"Both," he replied, continuing his way further down the long room which made up the bookshop.

"The only books you can't buy are the ones in wrappers," she added. "It's not my decision—the boss, you know. I hope you understand. You have to be eighteen or over for them."

For a moment he felt ridiculously young, but she gave him an extra friendly smile and said, "As far as I'm concerned, I don't care. Most of them are pretty harmless once you get beyond the covers, but the boss is terribly fussy. He thinks it's the law—as if they care what goes on in here."

She started to knit furiously, as if showing her anger at the very thought of the law and its stupid rules. He walked to the rear of the shop and her voice followed him. She was obviously in the mood for a chat.

"I'm only too pleased that a good-looking boy like you is interested in books and not flick knives. It makes a refreshing change. The number who come in here asking for the book of *Blackboard Jungle*! I always tell them we haven't got it, but they still look around for other violent stuff. Personally I hate violence, but you don't seem the kind of boy who's looking for that—not like those Whitehawk boys. I suppose there must be some decent kids who come out of Whitehawk though. Where do you come from dear?"

"Montpelier Road," Nick replied.

"Very nice. Nice houses. None of that rubbish they've been building lately. I live in Hove, in a nice area. The flat's in an Edwardian house. Do you know much about architecture, dear?"

"I know a little," he said cautiously. In fact at Clifton College they hadn't gone into the subject in any depth. "I can tell the difference between Doric, Ionic and Corinthian columns. They gave us a lot, the Greeks."

She clicked away with her needles and gave a loud laugh.

"You know more than me then! Good looks and intelligence don't often go together. You seem to have both."

He too laughed, and blushed at the same time. He was especially pleased she had commented on his looks. If only Greg would do the same he thought and then tried to brush the persistent image of Greg out of his mind. He hadn't even been to St Ann's Well Gardens recently to see if Greg was there. She said something else, but he was listening to his inner thoughts. He realised that the other boys he had seen and desired, didn't measure up to Greg at all.

The shop was well laid out with books, classified in categories. He passed military and historical. He noticed that all the books were in alphabetical order according to the author's name. He stopped and looked at the section with the books in cellophane wrappers, but didn't dare reach out and touch them. He noticed various Mickey Spillane titles and there were two copies of the expurgated edition of *Lady Chatterley's Lover*. Following on from them was a row of Emile Zola novels including *The Human Beast* and *Nana*. He couldn't see the covers, only the spines and titles, and wondered about the images they had given for those books.

After this section which was smaller than the window display suggested he found the regular fiction section. These books had unsensational titles, and were mostly by authors he had never heard of or seen in the more upmarket second hand bookshops he was used to. He was intrigued by *The Foxes of Harrow* and wondered if a book on animals had gone in by mistake. He took the book off the shelf and saw a romantic looking couple in the foreground and some black people in the background. The blurb inside was all about a plantation somewhere in America and he put the book back on the shelf. Then as his eyes travelled from top to bottom down the shelves he noticed a few books tucked away in the furthest corner. He saw the title *Against the Law* and knew, having seen it once before, that it was about homosexuals and their lives in prison. This was followed by *The Picture of Dorian Gray* and the name Oscar Wilde jumped out at him. He recalled the afternoon at Charlie's place and sensed that this section was perhaps more forbidden and secret than the others. It was not long before he realised this section was solely concerned with homosexuality. There were three other titles and they were all novels. He had never seen a homosexual novel before and his hand trembled as he picked them out, one by one. The first was a battered copy of *The Charioteer* and, on reading the blurb inside, he saw that it was set during the Second World War. The explicit nature of the relationships between three men, battling with their feelings for each other, was made clear. Next to it was an even more intriguing title—*The City and the Pillar*—faded dark red, with no dust wrapper. He read a few pages at random and found he was excited both mentally and sexually by the words. The last book in this small section was called *Finistère*. The cover was faded and showed a yellow sky with the title emblazoned across it and beneath the sky, a purplish blue sea. At the bottom of the cover were the words, 'A new novel by Fritz Peters, author of *The World Next Door*.' He liked the cover and on opening the book, again read a few of the pages at random. At first glance the prose appeared dense, but then so had *The Charioteer*, but it was not so dense that he didn't quickly catch on that it was about a boy, more or less his own age who was in love with a young, handsome teacher.

"I want these books," he said aloud, so thrilled at finding them that he couldn't keep quiet.

The woman who had sharp ears heard him and called out, "Have you found something you like, dear?"

"Yes," he said. His voice now lighter in pitch, due to his excitement. Then he added, "But I'm not sure I have enough money."

"If it's more than one, we can do a discount for you. Would that help?"

He looked at the prices written in pencil in the top corner of the first page. The total added up to less than a pound, but it was nearly twice the amount he had. He took out the money he had brought with him, glad that he had saved most of it from the previous week, and added up the total. He had the large sum (for him) of nine and six.

"Busy counting, dear? How much have you got? How many are there and let me have a look at them."

He gathered the books nervously together, hoping that she didn't know the bookshop's contents off by heart, and that she wouldn't know they came from a section that didn't even dare to name its subject. The titles were all innocuous enough and not one betrayed the nature of what was inside. Yet he was still nervous as he made his way back to the counter.

"Oh, they do look in a sad state," she said as she glanced at them. "Not very exciting titles. Are they for your mother?"

He shook his head and looked down. He would have to hide them from his mother.

"Well, they look serious anyway. Very suitable for a boy with your education. Finistère, that's somewhere in France isn't it, dear?"

"I think it's in Brittany," he said, hoping she wouldn't open the book to find out.

"Seems you're good at geography too. You must go to a good school. But let me just look at the prices."

"I've only got nine and six," he muttered, dreading that she would refuse this.

"My boss must have lost his mind pricing them as high as this. Even the books in wrappers aren't that much. He must have had one of his off days. Novels with titles like these don't usually go for more than a shilling. Two shillings at most."

She paused, and he watched as she put her knitting aside. He felt confident enough now to ask her what she was making. He wondered if she could hear how hard his heart was beating.

"How nice of you to ask. It's for my granddaughter. Baby socks. Wouldn't believe I was a grandmother, would you?"

She glanced at him and he was perceptive enough to realise that she in her turn was expecting a compliment.

"You look younger than my mother," he said.

"What a flatterer," she replied, and hard though it was to tell, he was sure she was blushing underneath all that rouge.

"The girls will have to watch out with you," she said.

He looked down at the floor, relieved that she could not read his mind.

"That will be four and a half shillings, young man."

He counted out the money, placing the exact amount in front of her. She took it and put it away without even bothering to check if it was right.

"Intelligent books don't sell here," she said. "The few women who come in here are the only ones who buy books with decent titles. But even then, it's mostly Ethel M. Dell and people like Doris Leslie. You know—a woman's read."

He said politely that he hadn't heard of either author, which was true.

"Of course you haven't. There would be something peculiar about you if you had."

She smiled at him and asked, "Would you like a bag?"

"Yes, please."

She put the books into a large brown paper bag and the deal was done.

"It will be a pleasure to serve you again."

He wondered what else her boss would put in that section in the future, and promised her quite sincerely that he would return. Then he walked out of the shop as happy as if he had found treasure.

He was so exhilarated when he got home that he forgot to hide the books in his bedroom and went straight into the living room with the brown bag underneath his arm. His mother was hunched over the chair she usually sat on, clutching at her stomach. She was in too much pain to notice he had anything.

"What's wrong?" he asked, swiftly putting the bag down out of her view.

"My hernia," she said and then asked him for a glass of water. He went into the kitchen and returned with it, feeling a cold, sorrow at her sickness.

"Here you are."

She took it and drank it down in one gulp. Pityingly, he stared down at her, all exhilaration gone. This was the core of reality in his life, not his wanderings through Brighton and Hove. He wondered when she would die, and hated the thought.

"You're back late," she murmured.

"I went for a walk around town with a few boys from school," he lied.

"Have you made some new friends?"

There was a slight note of sarcasm in her voice, which he didn't understand.

"A few."

"You never told me."

"You've never asked," he replied.

"I hope you've chosen the right ones."

"Mother, it's a small private school. Most of them speak as you would like them to speak."

"No bad language?"

She got up from the chair, still holding her stomach. He knew she was trying to talk herself out of the pain.

"You should see a doctor," he said.

She shook her head in silence, brushed past him and went to the toilet. He heard her cry out in there. It was not the first time. Emptying her bowels often caused her extreme pain. He covered his ears, hating the sound, then picked up his brown bag and took it into his room. He closed the door and sat at the window, staring out at his view of the tennis court. It was deserted. In fact he hardly ever saw people playing there.

It only took a few moments for him to relax and to start to daydream. It was a familiar dream. He was rescuing a boy who was caught on a cliff face. He scrambled down and somehow with immense bravery reached out with his hand to haul the boy up to safety. The boy had no fixed face. Sometimes it was Greg, sometimes a boy who existed solely in his imagination. At moments of stress this fantasy gave him relief and comfort.

"Your meal is ready."

His mother's voice and her knocking on the door broke the fantasy, and reluctantly he got up and went into the kitchen where the food was waiting. They were silent during the meal and his mind thought of the books he had bought and which one he would choose to read first after he had gone to bed.

He went to bed early and left his mother sitting in her chair reading *Woman's Own*. For a long time, he looked at his books without opening them, as if they were the entrance to some hidden place. He longed to enter, hoped to read what he wanted to know (which was simply a sense of hope expressed in the written word), and at last opened the door and entered in. It was around three or four when he eventually turned off the light. The next day at school he was exhausted, and nearly fell asleep during the Bible readings that started the day. He may have escaped from the Catholic rituals when he left St Mary Magdelen's, but he had not escaped from the Bible. Mrs Stanley, who took the class, made sure of that. When it came to Lot and the city of Sodom, he smiled to himself thinking of *The City and the Pillar*. He felt very grown up knowing he was reading a text that would have made Mrs Stanley throw her hands up in horror. He couldn't wait for the late hours of the night to come when he could resume his reading.

He was most struck that in all three books there was a longing to find the 'ideal' partner. There was Jim in *The City and the Pillar*, searching for a boy called Bob. They'd had sex together in a riverside cabin, and he, Jim, had known it was right for him. They were very young at the time. He also hoped that the sexual relationship would continue once he met Bob again who had gone off to be a sailor. Jim, in pursuit of him had taken boat after boat in search of his lost lover. Nick was almost a third of his way through the book when he had put it down that first night, and was over excited about discovering the outcome. Again, he thought of Greg. His penis was hard, but although he tried to masturbate, he fell asleep half way through. In the morning, his pyjamas, which his mother insisted he wore, were wet with semen. He washed them hurriedly in the bathroom and then hung them up to dry in his bedroom, hoping his mother would be feeling too ill to bother to go into his room. The books, he hid under the bed, beneath an untidy pile of shoes.

The Charioteer came next a few nights later. He was puzzled by this book. There was a lot of talk in it about abstract things (he had never read Plato), but he did follow the basic plot. Laurie, who had been wounded at Dunkirk, met a conscientious objector called Andrew in the hospital where he was being treated. Andrew was repressing his homosexuality but all the same felt very close to Laurie. What Nick didn't quite understand was why when Laurie met a man called Ralph he should suddenly turn his attentions to him and start going to homosexual parties. Clearly Ralph was in love with Laurie, but the plot became complicated. The gist of it was that he gave up on Andrew, who had appeared to Nick to be right for him, and turned to Ralph instead. Ralph had a war wound in one of his hands, and Laurie equally had a disability in one leg. To Nick's way of looking at it, this seemed to be the thing they had most in common, but then he admitted to himself that he was probably a poor judge of the real meaning of the book and it had failed to excite him sexually. He was sure that if he had been Laurie, he would have persisted with Andrew, despite the obstacles of religion and repression. The ending, when he eventually reached it, was oblique—black and white horses mingling their manes together. He sensed that Laurie had had sex with Ralph, but the images of the horses, being all about the soul and Plato again, were very confusing. He regretted not having gone to a school like Brighton College where he imagined the boys learnt all about this sort of thing.

Finally after a couple of weeks, he had finished all three books. All of them, except *The Charioteer*, which had a sort of positive ending, ended in what his mother called melodrama. *The City and the Pillar* ended with Jim murdering Bob, the second, *The Charioteer*, with the horses and their obscure meaning, and the third with a boy, not much older than himself, throwing himself off a cliff—or did he walk into the sea? By the time he reached the end of *Finistère* he was too cross to pay much attention to what had happened exactly. He had quite simply killed himself and the wretched teacher, an older man, seemed to be responsible for it.

He felt these books had taken him on a rollercoaster. First

up on top, excited by the prospect of sexual happiness, then plunging down into obscurity and death. And yet, and it was a big yet, he had learned some important details about how homosexuals led their lives, even if it was according to their authors. The rollercoaster ride, despite ending in disaster, had had its moments of hope and joy. The hidden place had revealed some treasures. And he, Nick, was impatient to find other books on the subject and even one day, if he became a writer, write one of his own. He decided he would certainly give his story a happy ending that was a) clearer to follow and b) gave his characters their ideal partner.

"I want to be happy, even if it takes years," he said to himself on the night that he finished *Finistère*. He was rewarded with a night of very pleasurable dreams, all culminating in emotional and sexual fulfilment. Awakening sleepily, he had the best and most intense orgasm he had ever experienced.

"You look tired," his mother said when he went into the kitchen that morning.

"I didn't sleep well," he lied.

"The rings under your eyes are very dark. I had better take your temperature, and you should not go to school."

Intuition told him his mother was exaggerating the way he looked so she could keep him at home with her. No doubt, she felt more depressed than usual and needed his company. He resigned himself to a claustrophobic day.

"The College isn't pleased with me staying away so often," he murmured as a last defence.

"Don't be silly. They've said nothing to me."

"They have to me."

"Then they are making a mountain out of a molehill. Perhaps they got you mixed up with another pupil. As far as I know you have only missed five or six days this term."

He gave up. She took his temperature and it was normal.

"Well, you don't look at all well," she commented. "Perhaps you are in the first stages of going down with a virus. They said on the radio last night there was one going the rounds—bad for both children and old people."

He reminded his mother that in a couple of months he would be fifteen.

"And aren't you still a child when you are fifteen?"

He said nothing to this and ate his breakfast. She sat at the table and watched him as he ate, taking nothing for herself. Then she began to talk. A long monologue began about when she had been his age and how little she had learned at school.

"It's life that is the teacher," she said. "It's life that is the adventure."

He looked at her, struck by this. She was being nice to him and this was a rare pleasure. But even so, there was a sad smile on her face as she said the words.

"Why don't we go out this afternoon, mother?" he asked impulsively. "Let's get out of this flat and go to the cinema. If we go to the Embassy for the first showing, we can get in for a shilling. I can even pay for the seats out of my pocket money."

His enthusiasm provoked a definite uplift in the atmosphere. She patted her hair and replied that she needed to wash it first.

"But nobody will see us in the cinema," he replied.

"All the same, I must look my best. Who knows, we may meet someone who knows us, and if I take up your offer of paying for the seats, we can have tea afterwards in a nice café nearby. People will look at us there and I want us to be a handsome couple."

"What café are you thinking about, mother?"

"The one near Brunswick Square that I used to go to with Dora sometimes. There's a lovely room upstairs with a good view of the street. It's fun to watch the people passing by below."

She had forgotten by now all about his tiredness or the possibility of a virus. He could see that she was ready for a small adventure, and he remembered how when he was seven or eight, she had collected him from St Mary Magdalen's and they had gone out for a special tea. There was a look of rejuvenation in her face and he saw how beautiful she could still look when she was like this.

"I love the Embassy cinema," she said. "It's almost like walking into a hotel." Then she went to prepare herself to look ready for the world. As she left the room, she added, "They show my kind of picture. I just hope they don't bore you as you are now so grown up." There was a teasing note in her voice that implied she was playing.

"I enjoy any film," he said.

"Even those silly romantic comedies I like so much?"

"Even those."

"Well, anyway, we'll see what's on."

She took her time getting ready, putting on a deep purple dress that suited the tone of her dark skin. He thought of her as an ageing film star, and that he would be her companion in pleasure for the day. He picked out his best flannel trousers from the wardrobe and his smartest grey jacket. They had been bought the previous year, but already felt tight on him and the trousers didn't quite fall to his shoes.

"I'm growing," he said to himself as he looked in the mirror. Then he worried about getting new clothes, because she would have to ask for extra money from his father.

In the hall, waiting to go out, she looked at him admiringly. He saw the admiration in her eyes, but there were no words said.

When they got to the Embassy cinema he noticed that it was a bland double-bill with actors he knew nothing about. Who was Loretta Young? Both films had A certificates, but the man taking the money, smiled at them both as if they were a couple, not just mother and son.

"Did you see?" he asked his mother.

"What?"

"I'm grown up. I'm really grown up. The man thought we were a couple."

She patted his face with her hand and they descended the red plush slope that led into the cinema.

This was the last of the good days with her. Her health took a turn for the worst, and he stayed away longer from school to be with her. He rang his father once to complain that his education was suffering, but there was nothing his father could or would do.

"It's inevitable," his father said.

"What is?" Nick asked.

"That she should have this decline. It's mainly mental, but that takes a toll on the body. She won't do anything about her hernia and no doubt her blood pressure is high."

"Can't you come down and force her to go to the doctor," Nick replied, his voice sounding impatient.

"I can't take any days off. What would happen if my money was to dry up? I'm afraid my hands are tied."

"Goodbye father," he said and put down the phone.

He said nothing about the call to his mother and was surprised when two weeks later his father turned up for the weekend. He looked old and fed up, and nothing much was said for the two days he was there. Nick realised his mother was now either too exhausted or too ill to row with him.

"I want to get a job when I am fifteen," Nick said to his father the last night he was there. His mother had gone to bed earlier than usual and they were alone together in the sitting room.

"I suppose that could be for the best," his father replied. "But you wouldn't be able to take days off from a job like you do from school."

"I know."

"She'll make life hell for you. I hope you understand that."

"I'll just have to put up with it. And I guess so will she."

"What sort of job do you hope to get? It's not that easy out there, and they'll pay next to nothing for a kid of your age."

"I'll find something," Nick said hopefully. In fact, now that

106

he had said that he was going to leave school, he did feel hopeful. He desperately needed life to broaden out.

"I wouldn't tell her your plans," his father said. "I'll sort things out with the school." Then his father added. "I hope she dies soon."

"Father!"

He had thought it often himself, but somehow it sounded too horribly real coming out of the mouth of his father. Nick looked at him in amazement, and with weary eyes, his father looked into his. There was a look of despair that Nick had never seen before in anybody. It was the look of somebody who had lost out on everything.

"I do love you, you know that," his father said and his lips trembled as he added, "but I don't love her."

"Have you never loved her?" Nick asked, no longer feeling too young to ask this sort of question.

"I can't remember."

There was silence in the room for a while: the sort of silence that Nick imagined was heard after a funeral or news of a terminal illness. The air itself was stifling around them, and although it was a hot August day, the windows were shut. His mother, even in the heat, complained that she was cold.

"I guess you had better start thinking about the future seriously now that you have made up your mind," his father said.

"Yes, I had."

"What do you really want from life? You're so young, and all this is so old around you. It isn't healthy. You're beginning to sound old yourself."

"I think I want to be a writer."

"Do you have any real reason to believe that you could?"

"I get ten out of ten in composition. I'm always praised for my essays. One day last term at school I even had *excellent* at the bottom of a short story I had written."

"But writing for money is harder than that. I don't read much—except for Nevil Shute and a few westerns—but even

I know it takes a lot of imagination and hard work—all those plots and characters."

"Maybe I'll get a job eventually as a journalist. That would be a good way to begin."

"I suppose they can pay well for that, but for God's sake, don't get fancy and write poetry. That's death as far as money is concerned."

His father stood up then and drawing back the curtains, opened the windows. He stood there for a long while staring out at Montpelier Road and Nick joined him there.

"We need this fresh air," his father said, turning to face Nick. "How can you put up with being closed in every day?"

"I go out sometimes. My favourite place is St Ann's Well Gardens. It's only around the corner. I used to get tadpoles from the pond when I was small. Do you remember?"

His father laughed.

"On weekends, yes. I always told you to put them back, but I guess it was fun catching them in the first place. What else do you do besides going to the gardens?"

"I had a special friend. A boy from Portslade. I went out with him often, but now—"

"Now what?"

"We had a row."

"Children make up better than adults," came the reply. "I suggest you make up and become friends with him again. Childhood friendships can last a whole lifetime if they are cultivated well. You remember that."

At that moment Nick wanted to say they were more than just friends. He wanted to be honest with his father and tell him that he was homosexual. He was sure some boys of his age who knew girls, talked about their feelings, but then he realised with an inner pain that it was normal for them to do it. Admitting that he felt more than friendship with Greg would sound like an admission of criminality.

"I will remember," he replied neutrally, and they turned away from the window back into the room.

"School starts soon," his father said practically. "But it would be absurd to go back just for the few weeks before your birthday, and then again, I'd have to pay a whole term's fee."

Nick agreed, and after discussing a few more details about leaving the school for good, they said goodnight and went their separate ways to bed.

The first thing Nick did the following week was to go back to the bookshop where he had bought his three books. The same woman was there behind the counter, but reading instead of knitting. She smiled and put the book down, recognising him at once.

"I hope you enjoyed the books," she said, and asked if he had come to look for some more. "My boss told me which section they came from," she added knowingly and winked at him. "He always puts up his prices in that section. I don't think it's fair, but he says people who are interested in those kinds of books usually have more money. A bit like Jews."

His first instinct was to run out of the shop. This was the first time someone had hinted at what he really was. The feeling of criminality returned. Sensing this, no doubt by the look of surprise and perhaps panic on his face, she reached out with a plump and restraining hand.

"Don't run away just because I guessed," she said. "It's perfectly normal to me dear. I'm just surprised that a boy like you should know so much already. Life can be dangerous you know."

He didn't know what to say, so decided to say nothing at all. Then, after what seemed like an eternity, he said, "I'm not sure about it yet."

"Yes, I know, a phase. My own brother went through it. He said it was like a dark tunnel, and that when he got out of it he felt relieved. He was sure then, you see, that he was."

"Was what?" Nick asked stupidly.

"Queer dear. I don't like to use that medical word."

"Homosexual?" he queried, his voice a little more high-pitched than it should have been.

"Well, we others don't call ourselves whatever it is that's the opposite, do we?"

"Heterosexual?"

"Well, whatever sexual. My philosophy is, as long as no one gets hurt, then it's alright. Anyway," she continued, changing the subject, "what can I do for you today? He hasn't got any new books in that section, I'm afraid."

"I didn't come looking for that," he said.

"Oh, is there another section you're interested in?"

He smiled, laughing to himself that she probably thought he had a one-track mind.

"No, I'm looking for a job."

She was so startled that she stood up and coming round from behind the counter, placed the *Closed* signed on the door. She even locked it.

"Let's go to my cubby hole at the back and have a proper talk. How old are you exactly?"

"Fifteen."

He had lied, but at that precise moment he felt more than three times that age. Not only was he now firmly in the adult world, but the door had been locked behind him.

"I would have expected you to want to go on to higher education or whatever it's called," she said. "Anyway, we'll chat over a cup of tea."

He followed her to the back of the shop, where there was a small door he hadn't noticed before. She opened it with another key, and they entered a room no larger than two cupboards put together. In it was a tiny round table, an electric kettle that was new enough to have come out of Greg's father's shop, and a few cups and saucers. He saw no sign of a sink, and anyway there was no room for it.

"Let's sit down," she said.

They sat on stools that looked as if they had been made for children.

"Don't you have a sink in here?" he asked inquisitively.

"We should have. There's just room for one. I wash up outside at the back. There's a tap there."

He looked for a door but saw none, and wondered how they got out there. Somehow the situation was becoming surreal—a bit like Alice, he felt as if he were following her down a hole to another sort of life.

"Now dear, explain it all to me. And you must call me Tanya. It's a posh name, I know. My brother couldn't pronounce Antonia, which is an equally posh name, so I've ended up with this. I'm afraid I rather like it."

She said this rather guiltily as she made the tea. After the first cup, he gave her in as short a version as possible, the story of his situation at home, and the necessity for him to leave school and find work.

"But an intelligent boy like you. I call it a shame."

She then got up and from yet one more mysterious place produced a packet of biscuits.

"I like my Digestives," she said, opening a tin and offering him one. He took it politely and ate it quickly. He found that he was hungry, and she offered him another.

"Well, as it happens, I was planning to go to Eastbourne to work with my sister Claudia and, on my recommendation, the boss would be only too happy to take on a replacement. He might be a bit wary about your age, considering some of the books we sell here, but he's broad minded like me and he's not afraid of the law. Anyway, you could pass for eighteen, with a new haircut and some more stylish clothes."

He nodded his head excitedly, willing to take on the blatant lie that he looked eighteen.

"Some people say I have an old face," he said.

"Exactly, dear. That's what I meant. And you do act old for your age."

She paused and looked down at the empty tea cup in front of her, as if expecting the tea leaves at the bottom to tell her what to say next.

"When could you start?" she asked.

"Not before October."

"Well, that would suit me fine. It would give me time to sort out my things here in Brighton. Eastbourne is such a nice place—very me, dear, with the winter gardens and all that. My sister has a café there. Posh teas. You know."

He did know, all too well.

"And she's crying out for help and company. Both of us have lost our husbands, you see. But don't let's talk about that. I will talk to Alfred, the man who owns the shop, and don't worry, I won't say anything about your private life. Not that he would care, but I know it's private to you and personal and I respect that.

Nick said that he lived a quiet life and that really there were no secrets to hide.

"No, I'm sure there aren't, dear, but you are good-looking and something is bound to happen soon."

He thought of Greg again, only wishing it would, and quite suddenly he felt like seeing him and telling him about this turn, possibly for the better, in his life. His train of thought was interrupted by her voice. It was louder than usual and he realised she must have noticed he had drifted off into a daydream.

"Dear, I want to explain about the money. It won't be much more than just a couple of pounds a week, but it's a start. We open at nine and close at five-thirty. You'll have to take in the books people want to sell and Fred will look at them once a week. He'll tell you what he wants and what he wants to give back. It's not hard. Just get to know the books and the regulars, be nice and smile at them in a friendly way, which I'm sure you can, and keep the place clean and tidy. But I warn you, he does like all the books to be strictly in order and perfectly aligned on the shelves."

Nick said he quite understood and that he had been impressed with the neatness and order the first time he had come into the shop.

"And no doubt you'll be on the lookout for your special section, won't you? There's no quick turnover there, but we have regulars for that as well—even some nice looking young men."

He blushed visibly at this, and noticing this, she laughed.

"Well, let's have another cuppa, and I must say, young as you are, I'm glad you put yourself forward."

After more tea and more biscuits and more general talk, Tanya had one thing to add, "I expect Fred will need a letter from your Dad saying it's alright for you to work here. Just to be on the safe side—kind of like a character reference and all that."

This sounded a bit unconventional to Nick, but he said he would ring his father and ask him to send a letter.

"Not much point in opening the shop again now. Gives me a good excuse to go home early. Just come back in a few days' time and I'll let you know what Alfred says. But don't worry, he's fond of me and I'm sure I'll get my way with him. But remember, you're eighteen."

"Will I need any official papers?" he asked.

"Money in your hand, dear. Every week, regular as clockwork. So much simpler."

They parted outside the shop, and suddenly she bent over and kissed him on the cheek.

"Do you know," she said with a laugh, "I don't even know your name."

"Nicholas," he said, "but everyone calls me Nick."

"There's a smack of sulphur there," she said with a wink, "but it suits you—makes you more cheeky than you look. I bet there's a little bit of the devil in you wanting to get out, isn't there?"

For the second time he felt exhilarated as he walked away from the shop. If the owner agreed, he knew he would like it there. It came with its own X certificate, and as an adult, he would walk through its doors.

FIVE

Nick did not return to Clifton College and after a few rows and pleadings, his mother more or less accepted that he was entering a new phase of his life. His birthday came and went, and he immediately started work at the bookshop. His meetings with Alfred Jennings, the owner, had been brief and easy, and he found him not difficult to get on with. He was given a regular half day off on Wednesdays.

"I hope you will come and see me in Eastbourne," Tanya had said on the last day that he saw her. He promised he would, but never did, but occasionally she would send him a saucy postcard.

It was a couple of weeks after he had begun working that he decided to go and see Charlie. He still thought of Greg constantly, but didn't dare go to Portslade to try to see him. He thought that Charlie was the next best option to learn some news of him.

Charlie was in. He was watching a programme called *Mainly for Women*. He turned the volume down, but not off, and looked embarrassed that Nick had come to see him after so long. Nick wasn't a friend, only an acquaintance, and he asked him what he had come about.

"May I sit down?" Nick asked.

Charlie removed some cast-off clothes from a chair, and Nick sat down on it. Charlie sat on the sofa in front of a very bright and modern looking coffee table. On it were various magazines, and a bowl of nuts with a nutcracker. He asked Nick if he wanted one.

"No thanks."

There was a silence, and Nick realised he had not answered Charlie's initial question.

"It's about Greg," he said.

Charlie cracked a nut and put it in his mouth, watching the near-silent television set and Nick almost simultaneously.

"I haven't seen him in a long while. Not since May," Nick continued.

"Well, I haven't seen him for about a month either. He only comes here to use the flat. He don't care nothing for me. I'm just the sucker who lets him carry on here just as he likes. But not any more. I've made my mind up about that. Why don't you go looking for him yourself? You know where he is."

There was anger in Charlie's voice. Hesitantly, Nick asked what had gone wrong between them.

"Shouldn't I ask you the same question?" Charlie responded defensively. "After all, he's damn easy to find in Portslade. The shop is just off Station Road. He works there after all, and he's not likely to be going anywhere else anytime soon."

He crushed another nut, making as loud a sound as he could while he did it. Then he belched and said, "Scuse me," with a smirk on his face. Nick was almost ready to get up and leave. It was clear he was unwanted and Charlie's tone of voice made him feel angry. Why should he take it out on me, he thought. And yet he knew that if he was patient enough, he might hear something so far unspoken, so he remained in his chair.

"This programme is bloody boring," Charlie said. "Alan Melville and that lot. All sodding snobs. I don't know why I watch it."

"So why do you, Charlie?" Nick asked, his voice as quiet and pleasant as possible.

"Cos it's on, that's why. What else?"

It was a simple reply that even Nick could translate as another way of saying that Charlie was lonely. He asked Charlie why he wasn't at school.

"Breathing problems. My doctor says I need to rest for a while. I thought I might have a problem, but now I know. Got medication and everything. Had it for years, the doctor said."

"Sorry, Charlie," Nick said.

"Oh, I can live with it. I go out sometimes, but I get out of breath."

Nick noticed that since the last time he had seen him, Charlie had put on even more weight.

"Do you miss Greg?" he asked.

At first Charlie scoffed at the question. Then he turned the question again onto Nick.

"Do you?"

"Yes, I do, but I'm not sure we get on anymore. It's too much of a risk going over there to Portslade, and now that I'm working myself, it's practically impossible."

"What do you do?" Charlie asked.

"I work in a jeweller's," he lied. "Boring job, but I got tired of school. I'm fifteen now, you know?"

Charlie looked at him briefly, then turned back to the television.

"Charlie, why did you call him an Oscar Wilde, the last time I was here? I want to know."

He had not expected the question to sound so completely frank, nor had he expected to ask it, but he felt relieved that he had.

"Cos he is," Charlie said, still staring at the television. "He brings boys back here, or used to until I put a stop to it the last time I saw him. I told him he couldn't ever do it again. I still like him and all that, but it's not right what he was doing."

"Then why did you allow it?"

Charlie literally stumbled off the sofa and going over to the TV set, turned it off. He answered Nick with his back to him.

"Sometimes he gave me his week's pocket money for using my bedroom. He always pretends he's poor and hasn't got much, but he's more loaded than either you or me. His father pays him well."

Nick was determined to ram the point home.

"Is that why you call him an Oscar Wilde? Because of the boys he takes into your bedroom?"

Charlie turned around then and almost spat out the words, "Even if he's only playing at it now, he will be one day if he

116

carries on the way he's doing. I could call him worse words if you want to hear them."

Nick felt the pain of jealousy. There were others. He dreaded the question he had to ask, but he managed to say the words, "Did he bring many boys here?"

"I don't know where he finds them, but yes. Including you. Are you like that as well?"

The words were blunt and to the point and Nick avoided them. He was afraid Charlie would get into a rage. His face was red and his eyes glared at Nick.

"There's only been one person for me," Nick said, "and that has been Greg."

"Experimenting, were you?"

"Charlie, I don't want us to get angry about him. Call it that if you want to. But I like Greg too and I'm worried about him."

"And then there's his favourite," Charlie continued, as if he hadn't heard a word of what Nick had said. "One from his school. A ginger nut. He likes them ginger. You must have been an exception."

Nick saw the face of the boy in St Ann's Well Gardens and felt a pain inside. He remembered that he had been a redhead. He wanted to cry or be sick and didn't know which.

"May I use your toilet?" he asked.

"Yes," Charlie said. His voice was quieter. He looked tired after his little rant and, with fumbling steps like an old man, he made his way back to the sofa. Nick watched him with pity as he left the room. How much did Charlie really like Greg, and how much was he denying it to himself? Once inside the toilet, Nick burst into tears. He thought he would never stop crying. Images of himself with Greg on the bed in Charlie's flat flashed through his mind, followed by those times in the café toilet along the Western Road. He could just about bear all that, but what he could not bear to remember was the incident in the Astoria cinema when he had turned to kiss Greg, and the way he had been rejected. He had been so much younger then, or so it seemed to him. A stupid film and a stupid action, but he had wanted that action, and still did. He longed in his mind to be able to kiss Greg on the mouth, and even if it was just once it would be enough. To feel Greg reciprocate, to feel a warmth there, unlike the closed, cold lips he had touched with his eager mouth in the cinema. It should have ended then, he told himself, but in his too youthful folly, he had continued. He had accepted and desired their mutual masturbation, and now naively he had learnt that he was not the only boy Greg had known in the same way. The redhead in the park flashed again across his brain, and Charlie's words, "He likes them ginger," stung him deeply and painfully. So he may have been the exception, but what if Greg did other things with redheaded boys that he would not do with him? His mind raced on, and his tears continued. He just managed to prevent himself from sobbing out loud. In no way could he show this pain to Charlie. He clung to the bathroom sink and tried to control himself. As long as he doesn't kiss the others, he thought, as long as he doesn't do that. He washed his face with water and then dried his skin carefully with a towel. He looked again in the mirror and saw that his eyes were red. He saw too that his face was very pale and that his skin was tight against the bone. He smiled wryly to himself, thinking how old he had become since he had met Greg that first time in the park.

"I was a child then," he said softly to himself. "I could still run and play like a child. It was still all new and fresh."

He wondered how long it had been since he had run around Brighton and Hove with Greg. So short a time and yet so long ago. They had both been children then, but now it had all changed. He was well into his teenage years now, and the following year he would be sixteen. What will I know then, he thought with a bitterness he had never felt before.

He returned into the living room, having no idea how long he had been in the toilet.

"You took a long time," Charlie said. The television set

had been turned on again, but the screen was empty. For a while it appeared the programmes had stopped their relentless advance, but all the same, Charlie was staring at the screen, as if he was determined to wait out the break until the evening schedule began. "I was going to come and knock on the door in case you had passed out or something stupid." He turned his head and glanced at Nick. "You look pale," he said.

"I had an upset stomach. Something I ate for lunch—a fish paste sandwich that didn't agree with me."

"Nasty," Charlie replied, and then added, "I hope you didn't stink out the toilet. My parents will be back in an hour or so and they always insist on a clean toilet."

"No, it wasn't that bad," Nick said. "I used the spray as well."

"Doesn't do a bloody thing that. It's just smell on smell. They shouldn't waste money on that rubbish."

Nick returned to his chair, or rather the chair that had been chosen for him. He was much calmer now and had to know more. In his mind his thoughts said the contrary, telling him to get up and go. Yet despite the advice, he wanted to hear more about Greg and what he had done in the flat. To his surprise, Charlie wanted to continue talking as well. The anger had gone and his words came out flat and factual.

"My parents say Oscar Wilde was the most dangerous man in all history—that he did the unspeakable," he said.

Nick paused to think about this, not quite sure how to continue. Then he murmured, "I wish you would stop using that man's name."

"Why?"

"He was fat and ugly and old," Nick added. "Greg's not like that."

"I'm fat," Charlie replied.

"Sorry, I shouldn't have used that word."

"Why not? Everyone else does. One day I'll be ugly and old as well. You might be fat and ugly as well when you reach fifty."

Fifty, to Nick's mind, seemed an impossible number. To climb up to that appeared to him as improbable as climbing a mountain taller than Everest.

"But we're getting off the subject."

"Which is?" Charlie asked.

"Greg, of course."

"Yes, dear fucking Greg. The boy who can't keep his prick in his trousers."

Nick looked down at the carpet in silence. It shouldn't have, but the last sentence excited him sexually. He felt his penis stir. Then he pushed the thought, with as much brutal energy as he could muster, out of his mind.

"You were telling me about the red-headed boy before I went to the toilet."

"It was because of him that I told Greg he could not continue using the bedroom," he said.

"But you told me there had been others also."

"That's different. It was a game with them. Listen, Greg's got a high sexuality and he needs to wank every day. I understand that. I'm a boy too. I don't have the same needs, but I can understand others."

"Then why the Oscar Wilde bit?"

"Because to need to do it with other boys, when your cock is out and hard, isn't right. That was Oscar Wilde's problem."

Nick had read up about Wilde in the bookshop and had read that he had gone much further than that, especially with someone called Lord Alfred Douglas. Then his mind raced on again, painfully, wondering if this redhead wasn't a Lord Alfred Douglas for Greg. Maybe Charlie had something in his comparison after all.

"Oscar Wilde was a criminal," Nick said.

"I know."

"So you think Greg is a criminal as well?"

"Didn't say that. But he definitely will be if he carries on doing what I saw him do the last time he was here with that boy Brian."

"What did they do?"

Here it comes, Nick thought. I don't know if I can bear it.

"What happened?" he continued. "What happened exactly?" His voice trembled slightly as he asked.

"It was shameful."

Charlie paused on the words, stumbled up again out of the sofa and going over to a cabinet near the television, brought out a bottle of beer. He ripped the top off with a sort of savagery, drank some down, and then offered the rest to Nick.

"I don't drink," Nick replied.

"I shouldn't. I'll get a right telling off when they return, but I don't do it often," he added as if apologising to Nick.

"What was shameful, Charlie?"

Charlie drank down another mouthful and, still standing, looked towards the bedroom door.

"I went in there. They were taking so long. I promised I never would, but it was getting close to the time when Mum and Dad get back from work." He paused, drinking some more. "I didn't knock. I just barged right in and there they were, starkers on the bed. Greg was lying back. I couldn't see the rest of him because Brian was bending over in front of his body. I heard Greg say, 'Go on. Faster! Then I'll fuck you.' They were both groaning. Then, as I moved into the room, I *saw* what was happening. Greg noticed me and cried out. Brian still had Greg's cock in his mouth, and didn't realise I was there until I shouted at them. His mouth was dribbling and he looked bloody disgusting I can tell you."

Charlie finished off the bottle and slumped onto the sofa. There was complete silence in the room. Nick looked at him and then down at the floor. He suddenly felt very dizzy.

"I've got to get out of here," he said.

"You never did that to him, did you? Suck him? And he didn't fuck you?"

The words came out slowly, a small sound. Nick shook his head in silence, trying to control the terrible sensation he was feeling.

"I knew you hadn't, but I had to ask."

"Yes," Nick murmured.

"You really are sick today, aren't you?"

"Yes."

"Have your first drink. It'll perk you up. There has to be a first time for a drink."

"No."

Another long silence followed. Eventually the sensation Nick felt eased off and he raised his head and looked at Charlie.

"I can't believe he did that with that boy."

Charlie sighed and leant back. He was staring at the ceiling as he said the words, "I guess that's what makes him queer—you know—one of them. But I hope he isn't. I hope it's just that Brian who persuaded him and that it's just another experiment."

"I don't know."

Nick had heard the worst he could hear. Jealousy turned to rage as he suddenly shouted out, "I hate him for it."

"Cos he may be queer?"

"No. It's not that, Charlie."

He couldn't tell Charlie that in some of his sexual fantasies he had thought of doing precisely the same thing to Greg. He couldn't tell Charlie that he had also fantasised about Greg doing it to him.

"He says he likes girls," Charlie added. "Maybe he likes both. What do I know about the subject? All I know is, it made me so disgusted, I told them both to go to hell. The look on that Brian's face, his mouth open, and all that wet slime coming out of it."

"Please don't say anymore," Nick murmured. He dreaded the tears coming again and had to leave the flat. Unsteadily he stood up.

"I really do have to go now, Charlie."

"Maybe I shouldn't have told you."

"I think I had to know," Nick replied.

"If Greg comes back and says he's sorry and tells me he likes girls best, then I'll see him again. But somehow I don't think he will."

"Who knows, Charlie?"

Nick crossed to the door leading to the hall and said, "Thanks for being honest with me, Charlie."

"You can come back, you know. I don't have many friends. You're an okay kid, Nick."

"You don't know me."

Charlie smiled at him and didn't reply. Nick went out into the hall, opened the door and in a few moments had managed to get down to the street. As he was going down the steps his dizziness returned. He didn't dare look up at the tall houses in St Michael's Place. It took him a long while to get round the corner into Victoria Road. In the distance, he saw the red house he lived in and shuddered at the thought of having to face his mother.

He felt bad for weeks. He worked mechanically, not being as friendly with his customers as he should have been. A few of the regulars asked him if he was fighting off a virus, and he replied that he hoped not. They looked at him warily, hoping they wouldn't catch anything. Then slowly the feeling that he had somehow been betrayed by Greg wore off.

"You haven't been yourself," Alfred said a week after Nick began to be his smiling self again in the shop.

"I was a bit run down," he replied.

"Not good, young man. Iron deficiency. That's probably it. How well do you eat?"

"I eat well enough I guess."

"But your energy levels are low. Can't have that. Your young face has brought more customers into the shop than before. Especially the ladies. All that women's stuff is flying off the shelves. Never read a woman writer myself."

Nick thought of *The Charioteer*, which had been written by a woman. Was it because she was a woman that the sexual detail in the book was so vague? Not that the other two books he had read had been particularly rich in it, but they at least made it clear that sex happened, and *Finistère* was good in its descriptions of places you could go to for sex in Paris. Then he felt ashamed of asking himself the question. He had read Jane Austen, not that he cared too much for her, and the Brontës, whom he liked. He had tried George Eliot and the brother and sister in *The Mill on the Floss* appealed to him, despite the heavy prose. In the short period since seeing Charlie, he had read a lot of women writers, despite his depression and giddiness and tiredness He thought that possibly women had a better perspective on men than men did. He had also read *The Charioteer* again and decided he liked it more and more.

"I think some of them thought I was a virus risk," Nick joked. "I hope they are not slow in returning."

Alfred waved his hand vaguely in the air.

"Regulars. They always come back. We're even getting new regulars. I'm sure of that. The sales don't lie. Tanya was chatty, but I think her constant knitting put quite a few off. Some days we hardly had a sale, and that never happens now. Don't put yourself down."

"Thank you, sir."

"Don't call me sir. I hate it. You're not at school now."

He gave Nick a wink, then went on with pricing the new books that had come in.

It was during the latter days of November that a good looking young man came into the shop and bought a book called *Giovanni's Room*. It had only come in a few days earlier and Nick had seen Alfred put it in the section where he had found his first three books. He had meant to borrow it and take it home, but forgot. Now he would not be able to and he felt slightly annoyed.

"Would you like the book in a bag?" he asked.

The young man laughed.

"Why? Do you think I should hide the title?"

The young man who was blond and had blue eyes as intense as Greg's stared hard at Nick. He then grinned. A big, wide grin that appealed to Nick.

"No, I didn't mean that," Nick said, flustered.

"You are blushing."

The grin grew bigger and Nick felt his penis stir for the first time in weeks. He knew at that moment that he was attracted to the young man.

"It's a very appealing blush," the light voice insisted. "What's your name?"

"Nick."

"I'm pleased to meet you Nick."

He held out a strong hand and Nick, responding, took it and felt its warmth.

"And your name?" he asked.

He felt more assured with the young man. He sensed flirtation and not really ever having experienced it before rather liked it.

"Martin."

There was a moment's silence while Martin stared even more openly at Nick than before. His grin had lessened, but the look spoke volumes. Nick wondered if this was just his imagination, but Martin confirmed it wasn't a few seconds later by asking him if he wanted to go out for a drink once the shop was closed.

Caution, despite a desire to say yes at once, remained. He felt his face redden and knew that he was blushing again.

"I promised my mother I'd go home this evening. There's a play at the Theatre Royal she wants to see."

"What's on?" Martin asked.

"I can't remember—an important play."

He was floundering and knew it.

"Look, if you don't want to go out with me for a drink you can just say so. I just thought you might. I also know that the Theatre Royal is dark this week."

Nick looked at Martin and stumbled over his words, "Yes,

I'm sorry. It was stupid of me to lie."

"Then you will have a drink with me?"

Nick looked back at Martin, embarrassed by the fact that his erection was getting harder. The counter concealed this from view, but his trousers were tight and he was sure that it would have shown.

"I'll wait for you outside the shop," Martin said.

"No, please stay. There's only half an hour to go, and I could close a bit early."

Suddenly he felt ridiculously young again. Martin seemed really interested in him, and he was certainly interested in Martin. He looked closely at the man's figure as he walked back down the shop, heading for the section that Nick thought of as the homosexual section. He looked at his figure. He was taller than Nick and slimmer. He looked like he had what was called a swimmer's body, tight, firm buttocks and long legs. The back of his neck appealed especially to Nick. His blond hair was cut short and clung crisply to his head. Nick wanted to touch him there.

"I like to read," the light voice called back to him. "Do you?"

"Yes."

"Have you got a speciality? Something you are really interested in?"

Nick paused, about to tell Martin that he liked the classics, then he came out with the words that he really wanted to say.

"I've enjoyed some of the books from the section where you found *Giovanni's Room*," he said.

"We'll have a lot in common then," came the confident reply.

There was quiet then as Martin hid himself from view by bending down to look closer at the books. Nick could only see the very top of his blond hair. I usually like dark boys, he thought. I don't often look at fair ones. Why him? He shook his head happily like a young puppy impatient for a treat. Precisely fifteen minutes later, he had closed the shop and they were out in the street.

"Do you like pubs? Actually, are you even old enough for pubs?"

Nick now felt trapped. He wasn't sure of Martin's age, but it was certainly around nineteen or twenty. He didn't want to confess that he was officially too young to go into a pub.

"I'd prefer a coffee at this time of the evening," he replied.

Martin placed his hands on Nick's shoulders and turned him around to look at him under a street lamp.

"How young are you Nick?" he persisted.

"Almost eighteen."

"I'd say you look younger. Are you sure you're telling the truth?"

"Yes, of course," he replied, relieved to see what looked like belief in Martin's eyes.

"Well, you are delightfully young for your age."

Nick stared up at Martin who was grinning again. He was pretty sure that Martin was nineteen or twenty. But then again, he could have been more.

"Do you know what I'd like to do?" Martin asked, still grinning. The words sounded flirtatious again and Nick's sense of sexual excitement returned.

"No," he replied, hoping that he would like the reply.

"I'd like to kiss you. Right here on the street."

Nick began to shake a little and turned his face away. The words were said with a smile but he knew Martin was telling the truth and he wasn't sure he was ready to take such a risk. Martin still had his hands on his shoulders, and Nick was sure he must have felt the sudden trembling of his body.

"This is your first time, isn't it? I can feel it in your body."

"Yes," Nick murmured, and at that moment Martin took away his hands.

"I'm going too fast, aren't I?"

"Yes. I mean, no," Nick stammered. He could have kicked himself for behaving like such a kid.

"Well, I'll take it easy then. Anyway, I know a pub where

they won't mind you looking young. They do coffee there too. I know the people who run it. They'll make it especially for me and we can sit together in a bay by the window."

They walked in silence towards the Old Steine, and then up towards East Street. At the end of the street, just a few steps away from the side entrance of the Savoy cinema was *The Greyhound*. They went into a side entrance and up the stairs to the first floor.

The first impression was a surprise to Nick. The bar was full of men, mostly older than either Martin or himself and there was a loud whisper of murmuring voices as they entered. Nick felt as self-conscious as if he were walking onto a stage.

"Hi, Martin."

An elderly man spoke the words as they passed by and Martin replied with a smiling "Hello." Nick felt a slight thrill that this handsome young man was known. As they approached the bar he whispered, "Is this a place for—?"

Martin interrupted him before he said perhaps the wrong word.

"Yes. It's a bit of an elephant's graveyard, but the guys here are nice and friendly. I never feel I'm being pressurised."

Martin's voice sounded loud to Nick and he hoped no one close had heard him.

"They all seem very impressed by you," Martin added, this time whispering into Nick's ear.

They both had coffee and sat in a window seat. The window was fogged up and there was no view, but Nick began to relax, realizing that his close-up view of Martin was much better than the world outside.

"Not much Rock 'n' Roll going on, is there?" Martin said laughing, openly taking Nick's hand in his.

"I don't like Rock 'n' Roll much," Nick replied honestly, remembering when he saw *Rock Around the Clock* as a child. "What sort of music do you like?"

He felt Martin's fingers open his and then entwine. It was a wonderful feeling and no one around them seemed to care.

"They call it classical, but I call it modern. Prokoviev and Bartok—composers like that."

Nick was ignorant of the names and was honest enough to say so.

"I'll play you Prokoviev's third piano concerto sometime."

This was the first real sign that they had a possible future and it was the best thing that Nick could possibly hear. He forgot about his mother and the troubles at home; he even forgot about Greg, but only just—the ghost of his presence was still very much there inside him. He told himself that Martin was much better looking, which at that moment for Nick was true, and that his sex life with Greg was over.

The voices grew louder around them as early evening advanced into mid-evening and someone in the crowd (because the bar was now almost full) began to sing *I Cain't Say No* from *Oklahoma*. Martin looked at Nick's face which showed all the surprise of a new experience and laughed.

"Why are you laughing?" Nick asked.

"Because I feel happy. I'm in the company of innocence. You have no idea how good that feels."

Their hands which had released themselves returned to each other, and the grip between them became tighter and stronger.

"I don't believe I am innocent," Nick replied.

"That's the joy of it. I'm sure you don't."

Nick was puzzled, and with his free hand, raised a glass of orange juice, which had replaced the coffee, to his lips. Then as he put it down he turned and looked around him. The assortment of men there had become more varied. There were younger men in the crowd now, around the same age as Martin, but he saw no one as young as himself. This worried him a little. He felt like a fourteen year old again, with an older companion, trying to get in to see an X-film. He knew he was not the age he should have been to be there.

"What are you thinking?" Martin asked. "You seem far

away."

"I'm just looking. I didn't know that there were so many, and so open with each other. I'm glad that you brought me."

"Are you?" Martin asked.

"Yes."

"And what do you think about what you see?"

"It's so diverse—so many different kinds of people. You see, the only images I have had of people like this until now have come out of a few books and often the images were quite negative. I've tried to imagine, but the people here seem happy with themselves. I know quite a few have drunk quite a bit, but all the same they look as if they are having a good time.

"That's true," Martin said.

I wonder what they are saying to each other, Nick thought. I can't hear them clearly. Maybe their words are like those in *The City and the Pillar* or *The Charioteer*.

"I suppose it's the feeling of belonging together that is important. It seems so strong." Nick continued.

"There are quite a few lonely people here as well, you know."

"But aren't there lonely people everywhere?"

Martin laughed again and looked around the room himself.

"There's an old man over there, right in the corner, at the end of the bar. He has a gold chain around his neck. Do you see him Nick?"

"Yes."

"He is in his late seventies. Every time I have been here, he is there. But until two months ago he had someone with him. It was his lover of fifty years."

"And where is he now?"

"Dead. A heart attack. He is probably the saddest man here tonight, but he hides it by laughing, and I will laugh with him. He sits up at the bar there and takes every opportunity to talk to his favourite barman. He will cry at home perhaps, but he won't cry here."

Nick looked in silence at the elderly man for a long time. He wondered if the man felt any real consolation by being with others. Turning to Martin, he asked him that.

"I am sure he does. It's because in our different ways, we all understand the same situation. Even for those of us who have never had a lover, there is understanding, and an understanding for what he has lost. Maybe I am just being over sentimental, but we all have one thing in common here, and that thing binds us together."

Nick grasped Martin's hand tightly and looked at him. He liked everything that he saw, and he liked everything that Martin had said.

"Tell me about yourself," he asked.

The gentle clichés exchanged between potential lovers since time began came spontaneously to their lips.

"Well, I was born in Brighton twenty-two years ago. I spent my childhood here, when I wasn't in Lancing. I went to Lancing College you see. Then there was a brief space before my National Service which thank God is behind me." He laughed again and looked intently at Nick. "Lucky sod. You don't have to do it. Just missed out. You don't know how lucky you are. They tried very hard to make their version of a man out of me."

Nick hadn't thought about his National Service much, but had once seen a play, the title of which he could no longer remember, about day to day life doing it. The play had been a comedy, but to him it had seemed just the opposite. He had even asked his mother in the interval if he would have to go 'there' but she had just looked at him, not sensing his fear, and said, "I really don't know, dear, but it's very amusing isn't it?" It was one of the worst evenings he had ever spent with her at the Theatre Royal.

"Did they succeed in making their version of a man out of you?" Nick asked.

"No," Martin replied emphatically. "Not even having to watch those men do their bathroom business together changed me. God, they were a revolting lot."

Nick laughed loudly at this. It was the first slightly vulgar observation Martin had made so far. He thought how graphically Greg would have described it, then realised that Greg, like himself, would never have to know it.

"I can't imagine it," he replied.

"I don't want you to."

At this point, a man came over to speak to Martin. He was in his mid-forties and to Nick's ears had a rather effeminate voice.

"Martin, darling," he began, "have you heard the gossip?"

Martin stared at him, a look of irritation appearing on his face.

"Peter," he said, "first let me introduce you to Nick."

"May I pull up this chair and sit down with you for a while? My legs are so tired. I've been standing at the bar for over an hour and my feet are killing me. Unlike you, Martin dear, I'm on my feet all day in a shop and I don't come here to stand like I do there. All the same, I never manage to come early enough to grab a decent seat."

Nick noticed reluctance in Martin's voice when he said that of course Peter could sit down.

"I promise I won't stay long. How could I when you both look so, so happy together? Makes my tired middle-aged body quite jealous." He then turned to a wide-eyed Nick and complimented him on his looks. "Except for Martin, you are the best looking here. Not that I mean that as flirtation, so don't get me wrong. I'm not into young people like that. That's why Martin and I are such good friends. I made it clear he wasn't my type when we first met. My ideal is Tyrone Power, but then you are probably too young to know who he is."

"I've seen him in a few swashbucklers," Nick replied. "I can't remember him in a serious film though."

"Old head on young shoulders, my, my! That's an advantage in life. Take it from me. When I was your age—oh well, don't let's go into that." Then he turned to Martin and said, his voice lowering to a loud whisper. "Guess who's here tonight?"

"I haven't been looking around much," Martin replied blandly.

"The main actor—if you can call him that—from last year's pantomime. Oh, what was it called? I can never remember titles."

"I didn't see it."

"Well, anyway, we didn't know he was *so*, but now we do. He's over there by the entrance with that actor who lives in Kemp Town. I can never remember his name either. A friend of Terry Rattigan."

Martin turned away from Peter's boring dialogue and was so unforthcoming that after a few awkward minutes Peter got up and moved away.

"I'm sorry about that," Martin said.

"I thought he was a good friend," Nick replied.

"He's more of an acquaintance through other people. He likes to gossip."

Nick smiled and said he rather gathered that, then added that he reminded him of some characters he had read about in *The Charioteer*.

"Did you really read that?" Martin asked.

"Yes."

"I'm impressed. It's overwritten, but at least it has an adult intelligence. She doesn't talk down to her readers."

"Did you understand all the Plato bit?" Nick asked.

"I think so."

"I suppose they taught you all about that at Lancing?"

There was a moment's silence between them.

"And you, Nick? Where did you go to school? Didn't you want to further your education?"

"I wanted to learn about life," Nick replied, not wanting to mention Clifton College. Being a Brightonian, he was sure Martin would know where it was.

"I won't ask any more. I can sense it's a sore issue with you, and to be honest, I didn't like Lancing much."

Nick felt Martin was trying to be kind and that he had just been told a white lie. He remembered how when he went to confession he was never sure whether he should mention his white lies. Even his mother had told him they weren't important in the eyes of God.

"Shall we go?" Martin asked suddenly. "I can't hear myself talk, I don't know about you."

Nick looked at Martin and the expression on his face appeared distant. He was not looking at Nick, but staring around the room. He didn't seem to be looking at anyone in particular, and seemed bored.

"Are you alright?" Nick asked, sensitive to change.

"I'll be okay once I get out of here."

"Then I'm ready."

Nick stood up, ready to go, and at that moment, Peter rushed up to them, his face flushed, probably with drink.

"Martin," he said, his voice a bit slurred, "why are you going so soon? It's only nine-thirty, and there is someone who so wants to meet your friend Nick."

"Why?" Martin asked, standing up and staring at Peter coldly.

"Because he knows him from the shop where he works. He says he always buys his gay books there. Says it's the only place in Brighton he can get them."

Nick was not used to the word *gay*. He didn't like the sound of it. His mother liked gay musicals, and he recalled as a young child being taken by his mother to a cinema for the first time to see a musical. After two minutes of being bombarded with sound and images, and people seemingly rushing at him from the screen, he made such a fuss crying that his mother had to take him out. She slapped him across the face for making her waste money. He complained that she had wasted the money herself because she had chosen the film, and she slapped his face again. Despite his love of the cinema, this had been a bad experience to begin it with.

"Nick, are you with us?"

He had not realised that he had gone off into his own thoughts and apologised for not speaking.

"Peter is asking if you want to meet this customer of yours."

"Er, no," Nick replied, hesitantly and then focused his attention on Peter who looked even more flushed, and disappointed.

"Well, if you don't want to I suppose he'll understand," Peter replied petulantly. "He says he bought a lovely book called *Quatrefoil*, whatever that means—an import from America."

"I can't remember," Nick said.

"He says he doesn't want to meet the man," Martin said angrily.

"Alright darling, you don't have to adopt that tone of voice with me. He just wanted a chat, that's all. He's not interested in your friend's body. I'd hate you to feel jealous."

"Go away, Peter."

Peter lifted his head haughtily in the air, and Nick thought he was sniffing at it. This made him laugh, and Peter looked at him sharply.

"Maybe you don't want to meet older men," he said, turning on Nick. "At your age, you don't have to. But you wait around long enough and you too will be his age."

"I said go away, Peter."

Nick didn't like the menace in Martin's voice as he said this and, mumbling to Peter that he was sorry, he moved away from both of them towards the door. He heard the word *bitch* muttered behind him, but wasn't sure if it came from Peter's mouth or Martin's. All pleasure in the pub had disappeared, and Nick felt suddenly that he wanted to get away from all of them.

"What's wrong?"

Martin joined him at the bottom of the stairs by the street

entrance.

"It wasn't as nice in there as I first thought," Nick said. Then he saw Martin smiling again, and felt foolish—a childish fool. "I guess it's all new to me—conflicted feelings and all that," he added, sounding confused.

"Come on, we'll go down to the seafront and look at the waves. A bit of fresh air will do us good."

As they walked in the direction of the West Pier, Nick turned to Martin and asked him if he knew any other places like *The Greyhound*.

"I wouldn't tell you if I did."

"Why not?"

"Just because."

"But there must be somewhere you prefer. I mean, other than *The Greyhound*."

They stopped walking, and leaning at the railings, looked out over the dark waters.

"There's a bar in Middle Street where I go sometimes—a better class of clientele. They've got a good piano player there. He's a nice guy who would like to get into an orchestra, but he hasn't got the connections."

Nick stared out into the darkness.

"Is it what Peter called *gay*?

"Mixed," Martin replied. "A bit like *The Cricketers*."

"But what of other more exclusive places?"

Martin put his arm around Nick's shoulder and drew him close. The feeling was good and it made Nick excited. He wondered, and felt slightly ashamed as he wondered, what Martin's penis looked like.

"I'm not going to give you the addresses of the more dangerous places," Martin murmured, his voice near to Nick's ear. For a moment Nick felt the touch of his lips on his skin.

"Dangerous? Why dangerous?"

"For a boy with your looks? I'm not taking the risk. I'm not crazy. You wouldn't get out alive."

Nick laughed and felt at ease again. His penis was also

very hard. He desperately needed to be touched there. He drew closer to Martin, and before he could say anything more, Martin had taken him in his arms. They pressed their bodies against each other and, in the semi-darkness of the deserted seafront, Nick could see an equally urgent look of desire on Martin's face. Nick wanted to kiss him, but just as urgently as Martin had drawn him to him, he broke the embrace.

"Isn't it what you want?" Nick asked.

"Yes, but not here. I'm not a bloody idiot."

"The seafront is empty," Nick replied.

"You never know with the Police. One minute they're nowhere, the next you've got one beside you."

Martin moved away from the railing and began to walk on. Perplexed and more than a little sexually frustrated, Nick rapidly caught up with him.

"Are you that afraid?"

"Aren't you?"

Nick thought of what he had done with Greg in the toilets. They could have been caught there, but they weren't.

"No," he said.

"Then lesson number one. Learn to be. It's illegal even if you're an adult, never mind being a minor."

The words stung Nick. He felt shoved back into childhood and into the usual submission.

"I liked what you did," Nick said simply.

They were walking quite rapidly now. He wanted Martin to slow down. The pace was destroying the intimacy.

"So did I," Martin replied. "Too bloody much. And I felt how excited you were. The whole thing seemed too explosive."

"I wanted you."

He was shocked at his own words. An instinct in him, wanted to take control. He wanted to be the man he was so desperately near to being.

"Let's go back to my place," Martin replied, slowing his pace at last. "I live in Regency Square. Only a few minutes away now."

For a moment Nick worried about how late it was, but it was only for a moment. He felt so pleased at what Martin had said that he moved closer to him and very gently allowed his moving hand to brush against Martin's. It lasted only a few seconds, but it sustained Nick's desire and the intensity of his feelings.

Then Martin said, "I like boys who have a certain darkness, hooded boys—boys who hide with longing behind their secret closed desires. That is what I like, and you have it. You are so fucking sexy."

Nick listened in silence. It made him sound mysterious and he did not see himself in that description at all. Then before he was really aware of it they had arrived at Martin's house and had climbed the stairs to the top floor flat.

"I wasn't expecting company," Martin said laughingly as he opened the door and turned on the light.

"Maybe I should go down and ring the bell," Nick replied, laughing as well, the poor joke bringing much needed relief to the intensity.

"Welcome to my small flat—a living room, a bedroom and a separate kitchen and bathroom."

Martin looked at him. He seemed to be observing him as if making a study of his features. Was he looking at Nick's brown eyes? Was he looking at his even darker brown hair and regular, if not entirely handsome, face? Was he also taking in his slim and clearly very youthful figure or was he just looking to assess if he was really worthwhile? Then Martin turned away and moved around the room, turning on side lamps, and turning off the central one. As Martin did this, Nick glanced around him. It was the first room of its kind that he had been in. The walls were white, the modern slimline furniture all slender black, and the colour, where he found it, dazzled him—bright cushions in blocks of red and yellow were scattered along a long sofa, and on the walls themselves were paintings that made no figurative sense to him, but were so vivid in their colour that his eyes blinked.

"It's all so new," he said.

"We live in a brown decade," Martin said. "But not here. Not where I live."

"And the paintings, they're not of anything," Nick added.

"Why should they be? The term for it is Geometric Abstraction. A man named Malevich is my god. He was painting in Russia during that brief period of communism before Socialist bloody Realism kicked in. He managed to paint a few real masterpieces. One is called *Black Square*. It is literally that. A square of solid black, bordered by while. I would give anything to have it."

Nick was ignorant of all this, but was eager to learn. He was also turned on by the passion in Martin's voice.

"It's certainly not Constable," Nick replied. He was looking at a square of vivid red, with horizontal lines of yellow crossing it. Martin caught his look and said that a friend had found it for him in London. He added that he hated Constable, and that nature was best left to the cows. Nick laughed, and the next moment they were in each other's arms. Then came the kiss—Nick's first passionate kiss. He felt with a rush of emotion that he had come home at last. The mouth, like his, was firm and warm, but best of all was the mingling of their saliva. He had read about kisses, but all the descriptions had lied.

"This is unbearable," Martin moaned.

Martin pulled away slightly, but Nick was overwhelmed by the wetness of his lips. Again he wanted to take control and grabbed Martin tightly to him, once more exploring the inside of his mouth with his tongue. Then, finally, they broke away from each other, both a little out of breath.

"I've never—" Nick began.

"I know," Martin said. "I can feel it. You don't have to tell me."

He moved quickly away from Nick and turned off all the lights. Only the glow from a street lamp, way below the living room window enabled Nick to see Martin. And then the distance between them was closed again and they were in each other's arms. The sex when it came was simple. Martin made no demands and Nick took the lead. Instinct again told him precisely what to do. He was the one who took off Martin's clothes. He was the one who gently pushed Martin down onto the floor, and then standing, took off his own clothes. Naked at last, they explored each other. Nick kissed and couldn't stop kissing Martin's body. He was like an explorer who had at last discovered his territory, and he was impatient to get to know it.

"Have you never done anything like this before?" Martin asked, his voice a little bewildered, as if he couldn't quite believe what was happening.

"Never like this," Nick said and burrowed his face into Martin's neck, licking the flesh there with his tongue.

"I can't take much more," Martin replied.

Nick knew exactly what he meant and with his hand, he urgently brought Martin to orgasm. The cry, at that moment, from Martin's mouth was very loud. Nick stifled it with his own mouth, bringing himself to climax with his own hand as he did so.

"That was beautiful," Martin whispered as they lay back on the floor, but Nick could not reply. He was silently crying. He did not know why he was crying and did his best to hide it from Martin. When Martin did notice, he simply and gently licked the tears from Nick's face.

"I am sorry," Nick said.

"Why?"

"For reacting like that."

"Don't try to explain," Martin replied, and reaching out, held Nick close to him again. "I want what we do to remain as simple as this, Nick. Nothing dirty. Nothing other men do."

"Yes," Nick said, not really understanding.

At half past four in the morning, Nick crept silently into

140

his own house and quietly closed the door of his room. He would face his mother tomorrow. Hopefully she would not create too much of a drama. He knew too that he would be exhausted at the shop, but his mind was composed. He had parted from Martin with reluctance, but had promised to go back to his place in two days' time. Both of them in their own ways had to recover from the intensity of their meeting. He fell asleep as soon as his head touched the pillow and for the remainder of what was left of the night had a strange dream. He dreamt of an old man walking up Montpelier Road: a tired old man who paused and stopped many times, and then in the grey of the dream, he heard the man speak aloud. The words were clear and he, watching in his dream, listened.

"Little boy, how I would like you to be by my side; I would walk with you, talk with you, and comfort you in the unease that you feel. I would even take your hand, and you would be astonished at how I could stand the constant patter of your speech. No mother there to scold or control, but a stranger man, so familiar, yet unknown as rain on a plain of sorrow. And we would walk, you and I, up the hill, the childhood hill, and the night when it fell would encourage you to dream of future men: men who in their tenderness would equally understand. I dream of him now, old as I am, you, myself, that boy in a bewildering land."

Fragments of the words remained as he was woken abruptly by his mother. He called out that he was alright and that he would be out soon. He heard her talking from behind the closed door, but did not listen to the words. Sometimes a child who is not quite a man has to put on invisible armour to protect himself, and that morning as he dressed, he did so, and opening the door, faced what the day would bring.

SIX

The waking dream of his life continued with Martin. Nick would go and spend evenings with him, usually three times a week, and would return to Montpelier Road as late as on that first night. Occasionally Martin went up to London to make plans for his future. He was hoping to become an actor and explained that he had contacts there that would eventually get him a good place at a drama school. Nick wondered who these people were of course, but was discreet enough not to ask any direct questions. This was Martin's life outside of his rooms in Regency Square, and Nick knew that he was not a part of it. On his side too, Martin rarely asked questions about Nick´s life or what he wanted to do with it, much to Nick's disappointment. He would have liked Martin to have been a friendly guide in his life as well as a lover, but again he did not openly question it. Once though, as Christmas approached, he asked Martin how he was going to spend it.

"I will go to London as I have done for the past couple of years. I can't explain, but it's sort of family. You'll be with your mother and her friends I suppose?"

"Yes," Nick replied, dreading the prospect of a solitary Christmas alone with his mother.

Aunt Agnes wrote to say that she was not strong enough to make the long journey down to Brighton, and sent a big Christmas cake as a present through the post. His father sent extra money, and a brand new watch, but made no mention of coming down himself.

"He should be here, even if it is just for your sake," challenged his mother.

"But you don't want him, mother, not really, and anyway, you would both end up rowing."

"You're still his son and he should love you more than he does. A new watch is easy to send. After all, he only has to come a short distance, unlike poor Agnes who lives way up there in the North."

"He didn't come last year or the year before."

"That's because Agnes was here. He never got on with her—and there wasn't room for him in the flat with her staying. There's no real excuse now."

Nick sat as usual, watching her. He thought of Martin, who had gone up early to London for Christmas and he knew that he would not see him until a few days before New Year. They had promised each other that they would see the New Year in together, although Nick dreaded leaving his mother to face it alone. He had lied and told her that he wanted to spend it with an old school friend and she had looked at him sceptically.

"I thought you didn't have anyone special at school, at least, not so special as to see the year in with. Have you got a girl I don't know about? You are secretive enough to have one without me knowing."

"No, mother."

"Well, you'd lie to me anyway."

"I'm not lying."

"Then what's so special about this boy, if I have to believe that he is one?"

"It will just be fun."

His eyes looked at her angrily as he said this, angry enough to make her silent. She just shrugged and turned on the radio.

Christmas Eve came and then Christmas Day. His mother said she would like a short walk in St Ann's Well Gardens and, after she eventually got herself ready, they slowly walked there together. She had become slower in walking, and had to stop several times along Temple Gardens and at the corner of Furze Hill. They didn't talk much and, on arrival at the park, they sat for a while facing the pond. Nick went up to it and watched the large fish emerge from the bottom—big brown ones that moved quickly and strangely in the water—before sinking from view beneath a cover of weed. His mind wandered to thoughts of Greg, and he tried to imagine what he was doing in Portslade. He wondered too if Greg had forgotten him, and for a moment or two he felt intense loss. He couldn't deny it. He missed him. He missed him a lot, but he overlaid this depressing realisation with thoughts of how it would be with Martin on New Year's Eve.

"I'm getting cold," his mother said grumpily, and he turned to help her out of the seat. She looked at the pond once or twice in an indifferent sort of way. Then they made their way back through the park and up Furze Hill.

Christmas night was spent in silence. There was enough on the radio to give his mother pleasure, and he spent a short time in his room, quickly masturbating. At the last moment, just before climax, he visualised Greg instead of Martin. In his fantasy, he saw himself in the same position the redheaded boy, Brian, had been in on Charlie's bed. Then he came, and the image went. He lay back exhausted after the orgasm and wondered why the thought of doing it to Martin or Martin doing it to him seemed wrong. He realised that Martin seldom appeared in his fantasies when he masturbated.

"You look tired," his mother said as he went back into the living room.

"I had a short nap."

"Don't know why. You've done nothing much all day. You didn't even help with the washing up after the meal."

She reached over and picked out a date from a box bought for the festivities and chewed on it noisily. Eventually the radio stations closed down and she said she was ready for bed. She turned to him at the door and asked him if he had liked her present. It surprised him that she asked. She had bought him a new jacket—a very grey and boring one—and a dark sweater to go with it.

"It's fine, mother," he said.

"I'm just asking. You didn't mention it this morning."

"But I thought it," he added. "Sorry if I was silent about it."

"Goodnight," she answered and closed the living room

door behind her.

New Year's Eve arrived. He wore a new sweater of his own choosing, which he had purchased the day before with some of the money his father had sent him. He also took a bottle of French wine that he had bought the same day but hidden from his mother in the bedroom.

He rang the bell for Martin's flat and was surprised that Martin took a long time coming to the door. He was dressed very smartly in a blue suit that matched the colour of his eyes and Nick felt briefly ashamed of his own new clothes. He smiled and said, "Hello," feeling strangely shy and then handed the bottle of wine to Martin.

"I don't know much about wines," he said apologetically.

Martin looked at the label and replied it was just fine. It was only when they reached the first floor landing that Martin said suddenly, "I'm afraid we're not alone. We have a guest for a couple of hours—a friend of a friend from London. He's staying at the Metropole and wanted to meet you. I think you will like him."

Nick followed Martin into the living room and there, standing in the middle of the room, was one of the best looking men he had ever seen. He was dark haired, with dark skin and eyes that were so brown they were almost black. He looked like he had just come out of a play in the role of Heathcliff, and as it turned out, that is precisely what he had done.

"It was awful," he said an hour later, after they had talked for a long time about the theatre. "I went into acting to play roles like Jimmy Porter and what do I end up with—the lead role in an appalling badly written adaptation of *Wuthering Heights*. Everyone seems to be adapting that novel at the moment and, sure enough, I had to be cast in a touring company with it."

He smiled constantly at Nick as he talked, and Nick, totally in awe of the man's charisma, stared back at him. His stage name was Jason Croft, which if Nick had found him less attractive would have seemed pretentious, but as he did like the look of him, he found it suited him very well. He was reminded of an illustration in a book of children's stories he had had many years previously of Jason—also dark and handsome—standing there, holding up the Golden Fleece. He had often looked at that image and fantasised about it.

"You are just as good looking as Martin said you were," Jason said after a couple of glasses of wine. Nick looked away, blushing again, and again it was remarked upon.

"Do you really blush so easily?" Jason asked.

Nick turned and looked at Martin who was preparing a side table with more bottles of alcohol, and accompanying snacks. Martin avoided his look and remained silent.

"Have you been an actor for long?" Nick asked hesitantly, realizing at the same time that they had already been talking about Jason's career for long enough. Jason laughed and asked Martin for a glass of gin and tonic. Martin poured him a drink and handed it to him.

"What do you think we have been talking about?" Martin said softly to Nick. "Do we need to know anything more about Jason's career?"

Nick replied, flustered, "I meant when did Jason start, and how easy was it to get into drama school."

"Hasn't Martin told you all that?" Jason asked. "I got in easily because I had a recommendation. Martin is having a harder time."

Martin was seated facing Jason who was on the sofa, while Nick, a small distance away, was seated on another chair. Nick noted that the room looked cluttered, and he thought how much Martin must hate its geometrical precision being disturbed by the shifting of chairs.

"Don't exaggerate, Jason," Martin said.

"Well, Martin, you have had a difficult time of it. Why shouldn't Nick know? It's not easy for a lot of people out there, and it has nothing to do with talent. I have known some young actors with buckets of talent who have got nowhere. You always have to be a friend of a friend of someone, or to be lucky enough to get into a well-known touring company like I did."

"I know that," Martin said.

"Tell me how good Martin is, Jason. He never says."

"He's very good, and I'm sure if he could blush like you, he would. Let me tell you something about him."

"No," Martin said rather harshly.

"Why not?"

"Because I hate any kind of flattery about my acting, and you are bound to do that in front of Nick. Only a few weeks ago you criticised my reading of a part and that was only for an amateur company. Good, but still amateur."

"It was the first time," Jason insisted, again waving his empty glass in the air. This time he got up, and going over to the side table, poured himself a very large glass of gin. "And anyway," he added, "you have made a fine friend in London. Denise. She has influence with the school you want to get into. There will be no refusal."

"How can you be so sure," Martin retorted.

"I know Denise. She has an eye for talent, and she told me herself that you have it. She heard you read that dreary bit from *Man and Superman* and said you were the first person she had ever heard who had managed to bring it to life. If you can do old Bernard Shaw with vigour, you can do anything! I couldn't do it."

Martin laughed and Nick could see that he was pleased, despite his supposed dislike of flattery.

"But I thought you said Martin was finding it difficult," Nick said looking at Jason. "If he has met someone who will help him then surely it's getting easier."

"Nothing is sure," Martin interrupted. "Denise does have some influence, but all the same, I'm not through the door yet."

"As I said, Martin has had difficulties," Jason replied, his voice now slightly slurred with drink. "But you had better believe me, Nick, one day Martin here will have his name up in lights somewhere in the West End, or better still at the Royal Court. That's where all the really talented people want to be, or at the Theatre Workshop in Stratford. But I'm not sure Joan Littlewood's stuff is quite for him. Too common."

"Oh, shut up Jason, you're rambling," Martin said with a smile on his face. Then he went over to the table where Jason had spilled some gin and wiped the liquid away.

"When is it midnight?" Jason asked, suddenly changing the subject which had so far dominated the entire evening.

Nick despite being attracted to Jason's looks was now longing for him to go so that he could be alone with Martin.

"Half an hour away," Martin said, glancing at his watch.

"I was going to go somewhere else," Jason murmured to no-one in particular, then turned to look at Nick. "But I'd much rather give that dreary party a miss and see the New Year in with you." Still looking at Nick he added, "Is that okay with you Martin?"

Martin said nothing, but looked helplessly at Nick. There was a brief silence and Jason returned to refill his glass. Nick thought he would soon be really drunk if he continued like that.

"Haven't you had enough?" Martin asked, breaking the silence.

"Rubbish. I never get drunk," Jason replied, "I just look as if I am. When have I ever behaved like a drunk at anyone's place?"

"I haven't seen you at anyone's place."

"Funny Martin. You've known me long enough to know it's true."

Jason turned then, drink in hand, and said to Nick, "Do you know we've known each other since school? We went to Lancing, but I was a couple of years above him. We still had time for a wank together though, didn't we Martin?"

Nick didn't want to hear about this and decided that his

first impression of Jason was changing. He was becoming not only a bore, but he was saying things that should have been private between him and Martin.

"I am sure Nick doesn't want to hear about all that," Martin said firmly. Then he nervously went to the window and opened it despite the fact that he was letting in cold air. Nick joined him at once and briefly touched his hand. He was desperate to touch him. Martin glanced at him and smiled.

"Come on you two, come back into the room, and entertain me. I didn't come here to be lonely."

Martin remained where he was, leaning out for a while, looking in the direction of the West Pier. Nick went back to his seat.

"You look so uncomfortable on that so fashionable chair, Nick. Why don't you join me here on the sofa? I prefer Victorian furniture myself. I think it's much more fun than this austerity, but then I suppose I don't have good taste. I like a good old pile up of stuff in a room."

Nick ignored the invitation and Martin, closing the window, returned to join them.

"I'll go into the kitchen and prepare something a bit more substantial than these snacks. It will absorb the drink."

He looked at Nick pointedly and left the room. Nick felt uneasy being alone with Jason.

"So tell me about what you do," Jason said, turning to Nick.

"I work in a bookshop. Nothing as exciting as you two."

"The bookshop was exciting enough for you to have met Martin, wasn't it?"

Nick felt slightly cross that Jason already knew this and looked down at the floor as he usually did when he wanted to be away from a situation.

"What did he buy from you, or shouldn't I ask?"

Nick continued to stare at the floor obstinately, knowing that he was perhaps being rude, but no longer caring.

"Oh well, it must have been something good," Jason said

airily, then persisted with another question. "Have you always lived in Brighton?"

Martin returned at that moment and prevented Nick from having to answer by asking if they would both like some cold meat and potato salad.

"I don't feel hungry," Nick said, looking at him. "Really I don't. I ate a big lunch today."

"Was this food for you two once I had gone?" Jason asked.

"Yes," Martin replied and gave Jason a cross look. Nick could see that he too was fed up with the man's presence.

"I'll have some after the clock strikes twelve. In the meantime, couldn't you show some of your talent to Nick by doing a scene with me out of say, *Variation on a Theme*? You could play Ron, the ballet dancer."

"No," Martin replied now openly hostile. "I hated the bloody awful play, and I'm not a performing bear."

"What's *Variation on a Theme*?" Nick asked, interested in something that he had heard was on in London.

"It's not a bloody awful play at all," Jason said. "It's got great parts for actors, male and female and it stars Margaret Leighton as a sort of Lady of the Camellias and lovely Jeremy Brett plays Ron—so much younger than her."

Martin replied, "It was Rattigan at his worst. I wasn't impressed by any of it."

"It's got a strange title," Nick added. "Intriguing."

At that moment there came the sound of excited shouting from the square and a firework shot up in the air in a blaze of blue and red. Nick pointed excitedly to it as it passed out of view and all three of them looked out of the window expecting more, but only one more burst of colour came as another cheer went up from outside.

"Well, it's time we all gave each other a kiss," Jason said, standing up. He held his glass up unsteadily and slopped some of the gin onto the carpet.

"Happy New Year, Nick," Martin said first, coming over to Nick and kissing him on the mouth. Nick responded warmly to this and for a moment forgot that Jason was still there. Then Martin turned away and wished Jason a Happy New Year as well.

"No kiss?" Jason asked.

"Oh, alright."

Martin gave him a peck on the cheek.

"And a happy one for you too," Jason added, then looked over at Nick, winked at him and asked, "Aren't you going to come over and share a kiss with me?"

Reluctantly, Nick went over to Jason. He still thought the man was stunningly attractive, but there was something about him that he wasn't sure of. He couldn't call it dislike, but he felt uneasy with him. He looked into Jason's face and was about to speak when he felt Jason grab him and start to kiss him fully on the mouth. Nick's lips were open, and despite himself, he found that he was responding. He felt the tip of Jason's tongue in his mouth, and although he should have pulled away, he didn't. He didn't even mind the taste of gin that was there.

"Steady on," Martin said loudly. "Break it up you two."

Nick broke away and looked at Martin helplessly. He couldn't admit that he had enjoyed the kiss. Martin glared back at him, then turned to Jason and said, "What else should I have expected from you? I know you of old as they say."

"Yes, and I was a good kisser then too. Or have you forgotten?"

"You were precocious and, if I remember correctly, I didn't particularly want to kiss you."

"Ah, but in the passion of the climax, you had to."

Nick turned away from both of them and looked at one of the abstract paintings on the wall. He focused on a big red patch in the middle of one of them and tried to clear his mind of all thoughts, but he didn't succeed. He wondered where Greg was and what he was doing. The erection that Jason had begun to give him now grew bigger.

"Why are you bothering to look at a sodding painting

which says absolutely nothing?" Jason barked at him from across the room.

"He likes my paintings," Martin said.

"More fool him. Come on over and tell us what New Year resolutions you have in mind."

Slowly Nick's erection went down, and even more slowly, he turned to face them. Greg too had gone from his mind. He stared fixedly at Martin, longing to be alone with him. He desperately needed sexual relief and he wanted Martin to know that he needed it.

"So what are your resolutions?" Jason insisted.

"I never make any," Nick replied truthfully. "Anyway, they never last, do they, for anyone?"

"Tut-tut, cynicism at your deliciously tender age. That won't do at all."

Martin interrupted with the words, "Now it's time for some champagne. Even you must have some, Nick."

"Don't you drink, Nick?" Jason asked, and laughed.

Nick said nothing in reply and offered to help Martin wash up some glasses.

"No, I have special ones ready."

"Ah, the lovely fluted ones," Jason added. "I remember them."

"I've had them a long while," Martin replied, "and I haven't broken one yet."

"We could throw them in the fireplace, like Russians do in badly made American films." Then he looked around the room mockingly. "But this room is so modern it doesn't have a good old fashioned fireplace. Let's throw them at the pictures on the wall instead. What's another splash on splash?"

Nick couldn't help but laugh at this, but checked himself half way through and looked at Martin apologetically.

"It's not my fault, Jason, if you don't understand the visual arts," Martin replied crisply.

"Oh, I wouldn't say that, Martin. I look at Nick and I

believe I understand the visual arts quite, quite, well."

Nick coughed an artificial cough and Martin went to the kitchen to fetch the fluted glasses.

"Hope you don't mind me comparing you to a painting," Jason said, turning to Nick. "I think maybe a Caravaggio. You're not as black-haired as most of his models, but you have the face. Martin, strangely enough doesn't like Caravaggios. I think that is very hypocritical of him. He likes it well enough in the flesh."

Nick could not deal with this banter. He didn't understand Martin's relationship with Jason sufficiently to know when enough was enough. He was also beginning to feel tired.

"What do you really hope for in 1959?" Jason asked.

Nick shrugged his shoulders. He knew he wanted his next birthday to come soon, but realised that was a childish wish. It would come soon enough. He had no answer to hand and no time to think one up. Martin was soon back with the champagne glasses on a tray with an unopened bottle of champagne.

"Who's going to open it?" Martin asked.

"Can I?" Nick wanted to take control again. He smiled and said he had opened one the year before at a party with his mother. This was a lie of course, but he had seen lots of films with his mother with an awful lot of champagne corks popping and figured that he knew precisely what to do.

"Very smoothly done!" Jason cried as Nick not only opened the champagne with a sufficiently loud pop, but also poured the fizzy liquid into the glasses without spilling a drop. Nick felt quite proud of himself.

"Quite the man around the house," Jason quipped.

They raised their glasses, wished each other a Happy New Year again, and listened for a while to the sound of neighbours below them, shouting merrily to each other.

"The whole square is awake," Martin said.

"We're in the heart of Brighton," Jason replied, "of course it is. I bet there's even more life in this house than there is in the whole of the Metropole hotel."

They all laughed and then there was a refill. Nick declined, saying he really would be drunk if he did.

"Coward," murmured Jason, and drained his own glass in one go.

Martin sipped at his, then discreetly set it aside. Nick noticed the gesture and thought, I'm not going to get home before it's light, and I don't care. Then Jason collapsed on the sofa, and to Nick's surprise Martin sat down beside him.

"The last year of the decade," Martin said. "The fifties will soon be bloody over."

"Good riddance," Jason replied. "A decade of rationing, dirt and grime, and the poor picking themselves up out of the shit the war left behind. Plus all the arrests of people like us, and don't let's pretend it has got any better, Wolfenden Report or not. We are a long, long way from enlightenment. In fact, I don't think it will come in our lifetimes. And that includes you too," he said turning to Nick. "I'm twenty-six would you believe and Martin here is twenty-two. The mathematics don't make so great a difference between us all."

Nick didn't really want a potted history lesson. He knew about most of it, but it was distant to him now. He supposed of course that it was closer for the two men he was with, and once again he thought of Greg and imagined him saying, fuck rationing, and fuck Wolfenden—whoever he is. He laughed to himself.

"Why are you laughing?" Martin asked.

"He's laughing because it's New Year and he wants some fun. Am I right, Nick?" Jason asked, winking at Nick again. Nick, not understanding, looked away.

"It's the end of a lousy decade chums. So why don't we three have some fun together now?"

Martin looked at him sharply and stood up. Nick looked on, wondering what would be said next. He saw Jason get up, go over to Martin and put a hand on his shoulder.

"Oh, come on, Martin. Nick's got enough for two. I can

see that through his trousers. He won't mind once he's asked properly. I could tell that from the way he and I kissed." He turned to face Nick as he added, "You won't mind will you, Nick, a little spark between the three of us?"

Martin said coldly and quickly, "You'd better go, Jason."

Jason laughed. He was still looking at an astonished Nick as he said, "He always says that in the beginning. The colder he sounds now, the hotter he'll sound later."

Martin turned on him and shouted, "Shut up, Jason. It's not, not funny."

Jason looked at both of them in turn, then sighed, and sat down again.

"Nick," he said, "don't look so innocent. It's very sexy, but don't look like that. It's giving me a hard-on, and I'm sure as hell it's giving Martin a hard-on. I'm only talking about a threesome. Surely you've heard of that."

"In books," Nick murmured, his mouth dry with desire despite himself.

"Well, they must be good books!" Then Jason turned again to Martin. "And as for this handsome blond here, he knows what it's all about. He only has a few books, but my, you should see those books."

Nick wasn't quite so stupid that he didn't notice the sarcasm in the last sentence.

"You should indeed take a look at those books," Jason continued. "In fact, I underestimated the number. I remember now there are stacks of them hidden in his bedroom cupboards. He has all the respectable queer books of course, Peter Wildeblood's *Against the Law*, and *The Charioteer* by that maiden aunt of a writer—not a book to wank your cock to. Then I understand he has that depressing *Giovanni's Room*, and even a copy of *Peyton Place*. Now that is lowbrow, but it does have a hot scene in it if I remember— you could almost beat off to that. Oh, and yes, he's got *Sixteen: Told by a Boy*."

"Shut up," growled Martin.

"Plus all the modern greats. Kafka, Gide—*The Immoralist* particularly."

Jason paused for a moment in the now silent room, then regaining his breath said, "And in the second cupboard, he has piles and piles of books on the visual arts—his speciality as you know, and lots of theatre books and theatre mags. *Theatre World* is a favourite. And then, underneath the *Theatre World*'s if you really look, you will find a stuffed envelope full of photographs of naked and very active young boys. Oh, and I'm not forgetting all the *Physique* magazines. All those bulging cocks, trapped behind such tight jock straps."

"Shut up, shut up, shut up," Martin screamed, trembling with anger.

"Okay boys, I've got the message. No games tonight."

Jason stood up, brushed his trousers down as if he had crumbs on them, and then looking up, smiled at both of them.

"Martin, Nick, I wish you a Happy New Year for the third and last time. I still don't regret not going to that dreadful party. This has been fun. But it could have been extra special if your inhibitions, and your trousers, had dropped. Good night and don't end the night looking as gloomy and disapproving as you do now."

"Is that the end of your monologues?" Martin asked.

"I told you I wanted to play Jimmy Porter. My dialogue's not as good as John Osborne's, but I tried. At least give me an A-minus for trying so hard to prove I am a good actor."

He bowed mockingly to them both, and then went out of the door, closing it quietly behind him. Nick stared at Martin who looked washed out, then going up to him, took him in his arms.

"He talked a lot of rubbish, didn't he?"

"Yes," Martin replied, holding Nick close.

"Then let's forget he was ever here. Anyway, the old year has gone and he has gone with it. We have the New Year. Are you ready for us to go to bed now, even if it's only to take pity on me and relieve me of a lot of tension?"

Martin couldn't help but laugh and led him off to the bedroom.

"Before we do anything," Martin said, and Nick sighed hoping he was not about to hear more talk, "before we begin I suggest we undress, lie down on the bed and enjoy a glass of champagne together. Let's toast the New Year in, just you and me."

"I'll get drunk," Nick warned, then took off his clothes. Martin did the same and they lay down.

"Don't be silly," Martin said. "It's only fizz. It'll be just fine."

Naked, Martin got off the bed and Nick told him to stand still so he could just look at him. Both of them had erections.

"Now I feel silly," Martin said, looking down at himself.

"I like the thick blond hair you've got down there," Nick murmured, then reached down and touched himself. He began to move his penis up and down, gazing all the while at Martin.

"You want us to do it like this? Apart from each other?" Martin asked.

"I can. Can you? I just want to see you come. With the light on. I want you to caress your balls, and above all I want to watch the expression on your face. When we're up close, I can never quite do that."

"Pervert," Martin laughed.

"Please," Nick said. "I want it more than I want the champagne." They both smiled at each other and almost lost their erections. For the first time, Nick observed that Martin looked shy, but after a while, he began to pull on himself like Nick. Soon his eyes were closed and Nick, holding off his too ready and too soon orgasm, looked closely at the twisting of Martin's mouth, and the slight distortion of his face. Then as Martin accelerated the rhythm of his hand and cupped his balls with the other, Nick exploded. He wanted to scream out, but instead, bit on his tongue. His eyes became blurred with excitement as the climax subsided, and clear vision returning, he was just in time to see Martin spurt his cum all over the carpet. They both laughed and Nick said he hoped the stains would come out.

"It's a red carpet," Martin moaned.

"Now, I want champagne," Nick said.

"First I go to the bathroom and wash up."

"No, you don't," Nick ordered, surprised at how deep his voice was. "I want you to come and lie here beside me and I want to rub the cum that is on your cock into your balls."

"You are a pervert," Martin exclaimed.

"I can't help it, you are so fucking beautiful."

"I'm not sure I've ever heard you talk like that before. It's horny."

Nick blushed again. For a second he had heard Greg's voice and he realised that in his own way he was imitating him.

"Where did you pick that up?" Martin asked mockingly. "Surely not in Miss Renault or any other book on the subject."

"I just felt like it," Nick replied, then smiled at Martin and asked him to get the champagne. "My throat's dry."

"Don't gulp it down now. Sip it slowly."

When he returned, they toasted each other again and then lay back in silence. Nick lay on the bed and looked around him. He noticed the cupboards and felt curious.

"Was Jason right? Do you have photos hidden in there?"

"No," said Martin, but Nick wasn't convinced by the moment's hesitation there had been before he said it.

"It's just—well—I've never seen photographs like that before. Where did you buy them?"

Martin laughed, more at ease now.

"You don't buy them, stupid. It's illegal. Really illegal."

Nick always fascinated by what was prohibited to him, begged Martin to describe one to him.

"No, I won't. I'm too tired to get a hard-on again."

"But you don't mind if I do?"

"That champagne has really got to you."

"Maybe it has. Please describe one to me. I'm sure you've seen one even if you haven't got any here like Jason said."

"You didn't believe me when I said no, did you?"

"You might be embarrassed—a sort of white lie."

"White or black, you don't believe me."

Nick leant up and looked down into Martin's face.

"I'd be really happy if you did have some. I mean, I've read books, but they never give descriptions. I always have to make up the descriptions in my head, when I wank alone at home or when I used to wank in the school toilet."

"Okay, okay," Martin sighed, and got out of bed. Naked he went to one of the cupboards and Nick got turned on because he could see Martin was turned on. After a while rummaging, Martin brought out a long white envelope and came back with it to the bed.

"Have you got magazines as well?"

"Yes, but this is more what you want."

"Can I open it?" Nick asked, sounding like a child at Christmas.

"No you can't. It's for me to select."

"And censor," Nick giggled.

Martin opened the envelope, and then after handing a photograph to Nick, went to get himself another glass of champagne. He came back with it.

"It's the last of the bottle," he said, "so you can only have a little."

Nick was too surprised and excited by what he saw in the photograph to answer. It was his first objective sight of others 'doing it' and he couldn't take it all in in one look. Eventually the image fell into place. Two young men were standing facing each other and their erections were much bigger than either his or Martin's. They were caught in the moment of reaching for each other's cocks. He looked at the photograph more closely, wanting the hands to reach their destinations.

He wanted the image to move, like in a film. Then his look travelled to the expressions on the young men's faces. They both looked as young as or perhaps younger than him. They had their mouths wide open as if in wonder at what they saw. He wondered if it was perhaps inappropriate that at this moment he found the image quite simply beautiful.

"It is beautiful," he said aloud.

"What is?" Martin looked over, then down at the photograph. "God knows when that was taken or by whom. There's never a date on this kind of thing. I'd say forties. The haircuts give it away. The hair is too cropped."

Nick thought they looked ageless, and said so.

"What is it that you find so beautiful?" Martin asked. "Is it their arousal or the size of their cocks?"

"It's not really their cocks, though I guess they are impressive. No, it's the look on their faces—as if they've just discovered something they always wanted to see."

"Romantic!" Martin exclaimed, and took the photo out of Nick's hand and put it away. "I think that's enough for one night."

Nick lay back on the bed and closed his eyes. He reached down and touched himself again.

"Make me cum," he whispered.

Martin kissed him on the mouth and in the dark that is never quite dark when the eyes are closed, Nick felt Martin touch his penis. He came very quickly and then quite suddenly fell asleep.

He returned to the flat the following morning to find his mother sitting at the kitchen table with a jam sandwich and a cup of tea in front of her. She was dressed immaculately, as if she had herself just come back from a party, or was waiting for a taxi to take her away on holiday—bright dress, fresh make up, too much lipstick—and a look of fury in her eyes.

"I have been up since six," she said, staring up at him. "It's eight-thirty. Where have you been?"

160

"I told you where I was going."

"To see an old school friend, yes, I know you said that. But where have you really been?"

Wearily (and he really was) he sat down at the table and faced her.

"I drank a little champagne," he said. "I fell asleep on a sofa."

She remained silent for a moment, as if assimilating this possible truth.

"I think you are hiding something," she said.

"Well, I'm not."

"Like a girl."

He laughed and she raised her voice and told him not to laugh in her face.

"But mother, really—"

"Nothing," she interrupted, "nothing you are saying is true. I can tell by the tone of your voice."

"Then I can't convince you," he said, reaching out for a cup and then for the pot of lukewarm tea. He was halfway through pouring it when she screamed out, "Don't act as if this is a normal day, because it isn't."

"I know, mother. It's New Year's Day. Happy New Year." He hadn't meant to sound sarcastic, but it came out like that. Normally he would have kissed her, but he decided against that move.

"I can't say I return your wishes, if this is how the New Year is to begin. I am not running an hotel here, and you are still only fifteen. If you do have a secret girl, you had better be careful. I presume you know the facts of life."

"I learned those in the playground at St Mary Magdalen's," he replied sharply, then tried to be calm, and sipped his tepid cup of tea.

"Then you know the possible consequences."

This so-called conversation was becoming ludicrous, but he kept quiet. After a long silence he couldn't help but burst out, "Yes, I could make her pregnant."

His mother looked at him as if he had uttered a four-letter word.

"I am glad you can be so crude about it."

Nick looked at her then, wondering if she had finally become mad.

"Crude? Pregnant? Crude?"

"You make it sound so knowingly casual," she replied.

"I don't know what you mean. I am using ordinary language. But it's a stupid discussion because the last thing I would have done last night was to go anywhere near a girl."

He desperately wanted to tell her that he'd had a mutual wank with a handsome young man and that he had also looked at what she would have called a dirty picture, but somehow he managed to keep his mouth shut.

"It's obvious," she said, "that I'm not going to get to the truth about last night. But, if you stay out all night again at your age, I will contact your father."

He stood up and walked away from her to the kitchen sink where he ran himself a glass of water.

"I hope he laughs at you," he said, suddenly really angry.

"What did you say?"

"You heard."

She then came up behind him, turned him around to face her and slapped him hard. A ring on her finger caught the skin beneath his right eye, and he raised his hand to feel if she had drawn blood. The place felt sore to touch, but when he looked at his fingers, he didn't see any blood.

"Don't you ever do that again," he growled at her.

Too shocked to answer, she stepped back from him, and when he eventually was able to look at her, he saw that she was shaking. He saw, for the first time, that she was afraid of him.

"This is my flat," she said, as if that signified something.

"No mother, it is a rented flat paid for by my father. And please, don't try to hit me again for saying that. It's the truth. I am sure father would quite understand that a boy of my age occasionally stays out all night."

She laughed at this.

"Yes, perhaps he would understand," she replied. "He was a wastrel himself. Secret girls. He knew all about that. The things he wanted to do to me. Things you certainly wouldn't have heard about in the playground. Things too shameful to mention."

"But you are mentioning them by hinting," he said. "I know all about sexual positions, and I have an imagination."

"Disgusting," she murmured, and looked away.

"That I know of the various ways of having sex?" he replied mockingly.

She shook her head at him and slumped down again at the kitchen table.

"Go to your room," she said. "I don't want this filthy talk to go any further."

"Despite the fact that you have made allegations about my father's sexual life and hinted that it was disgusting? How do you think I feel about that?"

"It *was* shameful," she repeated.

"What, mother, what? Sex is only shameful if it is made shameful. I am old enough to understand that."

She raised her head and stared at him for a long time in silence, clearly doing her best to make him feel uncomfortable.

"You *do* know all about it, don't you? I can tell by the way you say the words—as if you have experienced it. God, to think of it."

"Then don't," he said. "I have experienced nothing more than a boy of my age should have. Now I'm hinting, and hinting because you don't like honest words. If I have experienced anything, it has done me no harm at all."

"Then there has been someone. There is someone."

"I didn't say that."

"Then you mean by yourself? That filthy thing you do to yourself?"

"I didn't say that either. I think it's best if I keep the details of the few things that I have done, to myself. I feel it is my right to do so."

Suddenly he felt he was in court, or worse, in an Embassy cinema melodrama.

"You'll have rights when you come of age," she said.

"I am a grown boy, mother, as you must have noticed—fully developed."

She put her hands to her ears, and suddenly did look like one of those movie queens from the Embassy.

"Disgusting," she repeated. "Men disgust me."

There, it was said. He looked at her in silence, realizing she had said something acutely real at last. He felt a sudden rush of pity towards her. Slowly he went up to her and placed his hands on her shoulders. She tried to shrug him off, but he kept hold of her.

"I am sorry I have caused you this distress, mother, I really am. But there is no need for it. I have done nothing I am ashamed of. I would know if I had. I am able to tell right from wrong."

"Can you?" she murmured between her hands.

"Yes."

He squeezed her shoulder lightly, trying to impress on her the only sign of affection he could muster. He sensed her sorrow and her loss, and the possible fact that she had never known sexual happiness.

"I am also sorry that perhaps life has not been good to you," he added.

"What would you know about it at your age?"

"I have read a lot," he replied.

"Books lie," she said, and her hands fell from her face. She placed them on the table. The brown spots on them were very brown, and he saw that she was old. Despite the still remaining remnants of youth in her, she was old.

"Not all books lie."

"They do," she said. "I read when I was your age. Even

then, I knew it was all lies. The words meant nothing to me. Now when I read, I read simple women's stories that have no filth in them, just pleasant fantasy. It is all I can bear and the lies in them are all white ones."

He kissed the top of her head, wished her again a Happy New Year and in a state of exhaustion went to his room.

The beginning of 1959 was a happy one for Nick. His mother was polite to him, but distant, and the relationship between them was bearable. He worked hard in the bookshop and soon Alfred gave him the extra responsibility of buying in the books himself. He was also given a little more money each week and he felt valued. As for Martin, the feeling of happiness continued, and the sex slowly changed from being urgent to a more quiet state. Nick told himself that he was fulfilled by it.

It was late in the month of February that he and Martin decided to go out again into Brighton's homosexual nightlife. Nick liked Buddy Holly's music and was saddened by the news of his death. He especially liked the song *Oh, Boy!* and read into it a double meaning and a longing that Buddy Holly probably hadn't intended. He knew the expression 'oh boy' was a common one, but in the song he sensed a hidden layer, a hidden message. He sensed the longing of boy for boy and told Martin about it.

"I've heard the song," Martin replied, "not that I like that kind of music much myself."

"I know," Nick said, smiling. "You've introduced me to Prokoviev, Bartok and Stravinsky. I know your tastes now, and I like your music as well. I'm not sure I quite understand it, but I like the sounds. Maybe that is the essence of appreciation, liking the sound."

"My, you are getting big with words," Martin said, opening his eyes in faked wonder.

"It's true. I especially like Stravinsky. I like the rhythms."

"God!"

"You're laughing at me?"

"No, I mean it. You like the modern paintings I've shown you and now you like my music. It makes me happy that I'm educating you."

"Now you really are laughing at me."

"Honestly," Martin laughed. "But I can't honestly say that I feel much for popular music. I heard something dreadful the other day. Something about lollipops. It sounded thoroughly obscene."

"I know it. The Chordettes," Nick said. "It's from last year."

"Sorry for being out of date!"

Then Nick asked if there was a bar for men that had a decent juke box. Martin replied that there was a place on the sea front called the 42 Club.

"Can we go there?"

"If we really must."

"I'll play you some of my favourite hits," Nick said. "I'm young. You're young. I can educate *you* for a bit."

They fixed on a Saturday night, when Martin thought it would be at its most crowded.

On the way there, Martin asked, "This pop music you like. Isn't it all for teenage girls? And when did you have time to listen to it?"

"Lunchtime. When I close the shop, I go to a local London Road café and the radio is always on. There's a station that plays all the tracks and they're always tuned into it. Every day."

"You never stop surprising me," Martin said with an edge of sarcasm in his voice.

They arrived at the 42 Club early. The sea facing the club was churning away, pounding heavily on the pebbled shore. There was nobody around as they approached the place.

"Kind of quiet, isn't it?" Nick observed.

"I guess we're too early. And remember, only mineral water for you. Once it's busy I'll buy you something stronger, but no more than a couple of glasses of that either."

Nick felt he was being treated like a child again and resented it. At the same time he knew full well that officially he was too young to go into the place. They went up a flight of stairs (why was it always upstairs to these places in Brighton?) and entered a long room, with lusty murals of stereotypical hunks dressed as Spartans or something out of ancient Greece on the walls.

"They're not very sexy, are they?" Nick said.

The barman was just out of earshot and didn't hear them. Martin replied quietly, "Not to you or I, Nick, but they are to someone."

"They must be desperate."

"No. They just like to think that's how the Greeks or Spartans or whatever they are dressed. It's a form of camp."

"What's camp?"

Martin laughed, and the barman turned round, happy that someone was breaking the monotony of the evening.

"It means laughing at something that is serious," Martin said, "and *knowing* that you are laughing at something serious. It's a defence mechanism against society and so-called normality, like *Gentlemen Prefer Blondes*? Did your mother take you to see that one?"

Nick shook his head.

"It wasn't suitable for children, and anyway, my mother wasn't interested. Did I miss something?"

"Pity," Martin replied. "It was a musical, and you would have learned about camp all in one go—and early in life too."

Nick made a face. He was surprised his mother hadn't been interested, she liked musicals, but maybe it was on at an expensive cinema.

Then the door opened and a young man, only a year or two older than Nick came in. Nick and Martin both looked at him and he looked at them. It was around eight-thirty already and still they were the only people in the place.

"Hello, Paul."

The barman knew him. Paul smiled at the barman and asked for his usual. It turned out to be a glass of sherry.

"He's almost as young as me," Nick whispered.

"No, he's not," Martin whispered back. "I've seen him in The Greyhound. He's older than he looks, or at least I think so."

Paul had realised they were talking about him, and with a flashy smile he came over and introduced himself.

"I nearly got blown away," he said and patted his hair.

Nick thought it was a rather effeminate gesture.

"Yes," Martin said, "and the 42 is quiet."

"It'll busy up later I expect."

"I wonder what's on the juke box." Nick said.

Martin groaned. Leaving Paul with Martin, Nick went over and found two tracks he wanted to hear. The first was by The Teddy Bears, *To Know Him is to Love Him*, and the second was inevitably *Oh, Boy!* He took his time going back to the others. By the window, he tried to make out the white crests of the waves in the darkness. He hummed to both tunes, and when they were over he put them on again.

"Oh, no!"

Nick heard Martin's loud exclamation and turned to look at him on the other side of the room.

"Not again," Martin added.

Nick returned to join them.

"It's rather sweet," Paul said, looking at Nick with the sort of look that Nick understood only too well. He looked back at Paul with a look that silently said, no, I'm not interested.

"I'm glad you think so, Paul," Martin added. "Sweet that music is not."

"Personally I prefer *Sweet Sixteen*," Paul replied. "Have they still got that one? There's an awful lot from last year."

"We are only just into this year," Martin pointed out.

"But things go fast, darling," Paul said in a high squeaky voice. Then he finished his drink and asked Martin and Nick if he could buy them a drink. They declined, saying their

168

glasses were still full, which they were.

"Oh, don't be silly. I can afford it," Paul said. "I know I look young enough for people to believe I have only pocket money, but my daddy is very generous with me."

"I wish my father was," Nick replied.

Paul let out a scream of loud laughter.

"Not my real father, silly. You know, my daddy!"

"Do you understand?" Martin asked, turning to Nick.

Nick shook his head. Paul by now had his back to them, ordering more sherry and talking to the barman.

"He means he is being kept," Martin whispered, out of Paul's hearing. "He has a sugar daddy. In plain words, he is a paid whore, but he wouldn't exactly put it like that."

Nick again looked wide-eyed in Babylon and took another sip of his drink.

"That surprises me," he said at last, and blushed again. He wondered how Paul could possibly do it with an older man, whom he probably didn't like, just for the money.

"Maybe he loves him," Martin said. "It's pretty common in The Greyhound—older man with younger man, or boy. You just didn't see it the night we met.

"Can we go?" Nick asked, suddenly deciding he wanted some fresh air.

"Not on your life. I want you to play me some more of your songs. That's my excuse anyway. Let's go over to the juke box and I'll choose some at random."

Once there, Martin went at it blind, and chose an awful Pat Boone song and something called *Tequila*. Nick had heard neither of them before and disliked them. Martin moved away, and looked so disappointed and embarrassed by what he'd done that Nick couldn't resist pulling him back and kissing him on the mouth. Martin pulled away at once.

"We mustn't kiss in public," Martin said. "We could be thrown out for that. Even a bar like this has to be discreet."

Nick mumbled that he was sorry, but felt quietly furious that he could not show affection for his lover in public—as if a closed off bar like this with only a handful of people in it could really be called public. It was no larger than a long living room after all. Grumbling inwardly, and no doubt looking outwardly moody, he returned to the bar with Martin. Paul was still in full flow with the barman and at that point Martin agreed that it was a dead evening and that perhaps they should go after all, but just as they had made up their minds to do so, the door opened and a whole group of about ten or twelve burst into the room. Among them was a young man Martin knew and he excitedly whispered to Nick that he was a successful actor, much more successful than Jason, and that he had even appeared in a play on television.

"Hello there, Martin!"

The young man, sandy-haired, not quite a redhead, came over to them. His name was Bruce and they all shook hands.

"Please don't talk about the weather," Martin said, "or about how quiet it is in here. We have heard it all already, plus a few songs from the juke box."

"That bad?" Bruce said.

"That bad."

"Well, I'm resting at the moment, so I thought a night out with the crowd I know might be fun. Of course it was the youngest among us who chose this place."

Bruce turned to Nick and smiled at him in an abstract sort of way. Nick was relieved that he did not see any sort of desire in his look and for the first time that evening he was completely relaxed.

"Is this your new friend?" Bruce asked.

Martin said yes, and looked surprisingly a bit embarrassed. Intuition rang loud and clear in Nick and he figured Martin was just a little ashamed of owning up to this man that he was with someone quite so young. But Bruce's eyes had already moved away from him and he was once more talking to Martin. Nick heard snatches of the conversation—inevitable talk about the theatre, who was who and who was doing what. Bored with the theatre, Nick moved over to the juke box again. A few minutes later, after he had put on *Oh, Boy!* yet again, a young man joined him and stood by his side.

"I'm Andy," he said. "This is a good song."

"Are you with the others?" Nick asked, turning to look at him. He was slight of build, pretty, but not at all feminine-looking and he had black hair and blue eyes. He looked to Nick like Greg's brother and he asked himself whether Greg did in fact have a brother, and his mind drifted away.

"Hey, am I boring you?"

The music stopped and Nick chose The Teddy Bears once more, then turned to face Andy.

"I was lost for a moment in my thoughts," he said. "I hope I didn't appear rude."

"Not at all. You asked me if I was with the group. We met up earlier in The Cricketers, which is where I normally go. It was their idea to come here. Bruce probably told you it was mine, but it's not true. They are just people I know from that pub."

"Do you know Martin?"

"Our paths have crossed," Andy replied, his voice rather deeply and delightfully gruff.

Nick smiled, thinking of The Teddy Bears and what a strange name it was for a group. Then he looked at Andy once more and had the laughable childish thought that Andy looked rather like a sexy teddy bear himself.

"*To Know Him is to Love Him*," Andy said. "It's nice. I haven't heard it before. Is it a B-side?"

Nick looked down at the juke box.

"No, I don't think so."

"B-sides can sometimes be better," Andy added as if to keep the conversation going. He looked down at the juke box, and then turned his look on Nick again. Andy's smile came and went. It was not as bright as Martin's, but darker and somehow more mysterious. If a smile has a sexual attraction all of its own, which it surely has, then Andy definitely had it. Nick liked it a lot. Just as he was thinking that, Martin came over and joined them.

"I'm glad you two have met," he said, "Andy's a nice boy, and intelligent with it—rare these days. You should appreciate that Nick."

"I'm not a boy," Andy replied. "I am nineteen. I left boyhood a long, long time ago."

"Sorry Andy, no offence," Martin said, then went on to say that Bruce had a fascinating script for him to read that the Arts Theatre in London was considering putting on.

"The Lord Chamberlain will ban it, but the Arts is all set up for that. Anyway, I'm going to disappear for half an hour. I hope you don't mind, Nick. Bruce's car is parked a few streets down and he has to go through a pile of scripts to find it. I said I'd go with him."

"That's okay with me," Nick replied.

"Anyway, perhaps Andy will see you are not approached by any unsuitable men with unsuitable thoughts while I'm gone."

"If any do," Andy quipped, "they'll be with the group from The Cricketers. I know them all."

"Well, I'll be going."

As Martin left, Andy asked Nick, "How long have you been with him?"

"A few months now."

"And are you satisfied?"

Nick was shocked by this direct question, and was not quite sure what it meant exactly or how to answer it. He chose, 'yes' hoping that the obscure subject would rest there, but it didn't.

"Well, there's quite a bit of talk about him which I think you should be aware of," Andy said. "I heard him being discussed among Bruce's friends. They are all theatrical types and know about Martin's attempts to get into the theatre, and about his private life as well it seems."

Nick remained quiet. He looked closely at Andy and for once didn't believe he was just out to spread gossip.

"He has a bit of a reputation, especially in London, and it isn't for his talent as an actor."

This sounded unfair and Nick said so. He told Andy how he had heard Martin was potentially a very good actor.

"I'm not into the theatre myself, so I can't comment on

that. I'm studying to be an accountant, which may sound boring, but at least I'm not playing at being bohemian with my life. You work in a bookshop I hear. Books, I like. Serious ones as well."

Nick smiled at this and leant up with his back to the juke box. There was no use putting on any more music. There was enough noise in the room already.

"Well, what do you want to tell me?" he asked, facing Andy. His look must have seemed to the point and direct as Andy appeared a bit taken by surprise and stared down at the floor.

"He's apparently a lot on the London scene," Andy continued. "He has a rather limited scope concerning his sexual partners, and that doesn't appear to be going down too well. The law being what it is, he could get into even more serious trouble than the rest of us."

Nick thought of young men like Paul, and of male prostitution, which seemed bad to him at first, but having met Paul, he realised it was just another point on the spectrum they were all on. He had never thought of the issue until that evening. He said nothing and waited for more information from Andy who was now looking at him equally directly with a sombre expression on his face.

"Making us legal, which is being fought for in some quarters, would not cover what Martin is supposedly up to, I'm afraid."

"Perhaps I know," he said. "Threesomes maybe, or is it that he pays sometimes? Or that they are really young? Is that it?"

"Perhaps it is just rubbish they are spreading," Andy replied, now appearing to backtrack a little, "and if you do know, then you won't need my warning—except of course, not to get too deeply involved. Can I ask if you are in love with him?"

Nick sighed. He had read too much about love and its gains and losses in books to know its full meaning, but he did know about the intensity of sexual attraction, which he had been sharing with Martin, even if it had been a little bit less intense recently.

"Love is a fire that can burn itself out a bit too quickly," Nick stated, surprised at his own words. "I mean the sort of love we homosexuals experience." Then his mind turned to Greg. Greg was still burning there, somewhere at the back of his mind. He knew deep down that fire had not gone out. It is love that I feel for him, he thought.

"A bit too profound for me what you have just said," Andy replied, then stared at Nick and murmured, "A boy like you will be told all sorts of things. You must be cautious. Easy words said in passion can turn sour. I'm nineteen, and I already know that." He paused for a moment then rushed out the words, "Oh, hell, even I like the look of you. You've got it. It's not beauty exactly, but it's very desirable. And before you tell me to fuck off, I must add that I would like to get to know you better. I'm not just a disinterested troublemaker. I already care enough not to want to see you hurt.

"Thanks," Nick mumbled, and the more he looked at Andy, the redder Andy became in the face. It contrasted strongly with his black hair and Nick resisted the urge, sexual in nature, to touch him. As if sensing this, Andy hesitantly touched him instead, putting his hand on Nick's hand which was resting on the juke box. Nick did not move his hand. He liked the feeling.

"Do you mind me touching you?" Andy asked.

"No."

The noise in the room grew louder: a whole chorus behind them. No one seemed to be looking their way, or caring. Then Andy reached forward with his head and whispered in Nick's ear, "No one will see," and the next moment, Nick felt Andy's lips on his. They were a little rough and insistent, not at all like Martin's softer lips, and he responded at once. It was new and exciting, and all thoughts of what they had said before went out of his mind. He allowed himself the pleasure of relaxing and enjoying. The more Andy kissed him, the more he wanted. He liked his rough probing tongue which suggested a much stronger need for sexual discovery than Martin's kisses had. As the kiss prolonged itself, he felt Andy

174

reach out and touch the bulge in his trousers, pressing hard. His reaction was to do the same, and he touched Andy's groin. Andy's penis felt long and big, and the thought of seeing it made him want to ejaculate there and then. He drew back from Andy's mouth and they stared at each other, knowing precisely what they wanted. Andy continued to rub him and Nick felt his orgasm approach.

"Please stop," he whispered. "I'm almost there."

"So am I," Andy whispered back, "but don't let's get it over with quite so quickly. We can't hold back now. Come with me." He grabbed Nick by the hand and led him towards the toilets. "No one will notice," he said on the way.

Nick followed, too far gone to care if anyone did, and soon they were inside the tiny cubicle. He watched as Andy pulled down his trousers, somehow simultaneously also pulling down his own. He watched as both of their penises jerked upwards, eager for freedom. Then, in the next quick move, Andy was on his knees and taking him into his mouth. This had never happened to Nick before. The newness of the sensation startled him and filled him with joy at the same time. He came in a rush into Andy's mouth, and gasping with pleasure, looked down, intent on both the fierceness of his release and the look on Andy's face as he took it all inside him. He cried out, "This is fantastic," and Andy, rising, urgently pushed Nick's face down to take him. Nick had just the briefest of moments to see the glistening red tip of Andy's penis, before opening his own mouth. He gagged at first, but soon knew exactly what to do, and cupping Andy's balls with his hand, urged him on to his climax. He liked the taste, especially when the full force of Andy's sperm hit his tongue and throat. He swallowed, and thought obscurely of salted peanuts which made him laugh to himself. After the last paroxysm has passed, he leant back against the bulk of the toilet and stared at Andy's erection. He caressed the black hair, wet with sweat and cum, and admired the beauty of what he saw. He thought how superbly proud Andy's genitals were—solid, big, and still looking as if they demanded further pleasure.

"Do it again," Andy said, and Nick immediately returned to please him. This time it took longer and Nick wanked himself at the same time. Then, just as he came, he felt Andy's cock stiffen in his mouth, and he let it happen for a second time, swallowing him. His mouth felt full and satisfied, and he enjoyed hearing the cry that came from Andy's lips.

"Fuck," Andy whispered as they faced each other. "Fuck, you are so hot."

They kissed again briefly, tasting each other, and then there was a knock on the door. Shamefaced, but happy, they quickly did up their trousers, smiled at each other and left the cubicle. A middle-aged man looked at them and winked as they passed saying, "Don't worry, I won't tell mother," before closing the cubicle door behind him. They laughed at the words as they went back into the bar.

They sat down near the window and suddenly Nick felt guilty about what they had done, and that he had betrayed Martin. And yet he felt happy. It was a contradiction that he could not quite reconcile.

"I knew a boy a short while ago, a bit older than me," he said to Andy, opening up about his relationship with Greg for the first time. "I was much younger last year than I am now, but he always said I looked older anyway." He stared out at the darkness: lit only by the seafront lights and the tips of the furious waves. "I wanted him so much," he continued, "but he was not like us. I think he had a part of him that was, but maybe that's just my fantasy. I guess I just wanted him to be, and he was fond of me, and we did have a kind of sex together."

"What was the sex like?"

Nick explained about the time at Charlie's place, and the masturbation that took place in the café toilets.

"I see," Andy said.

"I supposed it was just experimentation for him," Nick said. "But sometimes I thought I saw desire. I don't know. I'm confused. Then I found out he had been sucked off by another boy and wanted to fuck him. That was confusing. And on top of that, I've had too much sex in public toilets. I mustn't let it become a habit. It isn't normal."

He looked ruefully at Andy who suddenly looked serious.

"Don't imagine I wouldn't have wanted a better place for both of us," Andy said, "but the urge was too great. We both felt it."

"And it was great," Nick said. "It was the most fulfilling I've had yet. I felt I was beginning to have the sex I have fantasised about, wanked about. I wanted more too."

Andy smiled at this. "I think I know what you mean."

Nick turned his face away. He thought about being inside Andy. He tried to imagine putting his penis inside him, and his body responded immediately to the thought.

"You haven't done it yet, have you?" Andy asked hesitantly.

"No," Nick said. "Martin doesn't want anything more than masturbation." Then he felt ashamed that he was revealing too much.

"Does he treat you like a child?" Andy asked.

"It kind of feels like that. It's childish sex. But it wasn't with you. I felt it wasn't."

"No, it wasn't. I really wanted all of you. I can sense what you need, but I'm not going to put it into words. The words are too harsh for something as fulfilling."

"Thanks," Nick said and looked into Andy's eyes. "You're really beautiful," he said.

"Nonsense," Andy replied and fumbled in his pockets to get out a packet of cigarettes. "I really need this," he added. "Do you smoke?"

"No."

"Don't. It's a waste of money. It started after my mother walked into my bedroom and I was well, you know, masturbating. It was terrible, but do you know what she said? Nothing. She laughed, and then she just left the room. Never mentioned it afterwards. First thing I did though was to rush out and buy my first packet of cigarettes, and now I'm addicted."

Nick thought of his own mother and looked at Andy in surprise.

"She really said nothing at all?"

"Nothing at all."

"You must have a bloody nice mother."

Andy lit his cigarette, and after a while brought out a piece of paper and a pencil from the same trouser pocket. He laughed as he did it.

"I'm still a kid who keeps too much in his trouser pockets. I'm really untidy. Anyway, I'm going to give you my number. No demands. I just want you to take it. I live in a simple room in Kemp Town. I hate all the snobs who live around me, but hey ho, the room's nice and it's got a good large bed."

He winked at Nick as he wrote down his full name, address and telephone number. His pretty, but masculine face made Nick long to hold him to him again.

"The phone is right outside my door. Could be my own really. No one else seems to use it. Now take this, put it away and don't lose it. Tomorrow, next week or next year, you will be surprised to know just how welcome you are.

Nick took it in silence, folded it and put it away. He was glad that Andy had given it to him, but he felt his life was too crowded already and that in all probability he would never use it. There was Martin, whom he still desired and felt close to and there was his mother and his job. There was too much clutter, but he didn't like to think of it as such.

Martin came back, looking as excited as a puppy and would probably have been carrying the playscript in his mouth if he could have. He had theatre written all over him.

"Have you read it?" Nick remarked, looking up at his smiling face.

"We sneaked into a pub and I had a quick look. The dialogue is marvellous. It's in my jacket over there." He pointed towards an invisible place in the crowded club, and Nick and Andy both looked vaguely in that direction. "I hope Andy has been saying nice things about me," he said flippantly. Andy looked down and coughed. Nick smiled and said of course he had, and all good. Martin laughed at this and then bounded off to join Bruce and the others.

"He looks happy!" Andy said.

"He's in his element over there with them," Nick observed.

"Well, I expect they flatter him to his face," Andy replied dryly. "They are all very theatrical."

"Like Kemp Town?" Nick quipped.

"Exactly."

"I've had months listening to who's who up there. But I can't remember names."

"Good. Keep it that way. But I must go now. Just looking at you makes me want to drag you away and be alone with you."

Nick smiled at him and murmured that he felt the same, and then patted the pocket where his telephone number was.

"I'll keep the number safe," he said.

"Yes. Please do."

These last words were said with such a tone of sincerity that Nick dared to hope Andy really was as nice as he sounded. Those three simple words seemed like a very tempting way out of the maelstrom that was swirling around him. But Andy hadn't finished. Just as he was about to leave, he turned again to face Nick and said, "It meant something, what we did. I know you felt it too." Then he was gone, and Nick felt sad that he had gone. Why didn't he just get up and run after him? He asked this question to himself as if he was speaking about another person.

"I'm not ready," he whispered as he looked down at the table.

Half an hour later, he left the club with Martin.

"He took a shine to you, didn't he? It was written all over his pretty little face. Even I thought you looked good together."

Nick was silent.

"You both looked so young and innocent."

The words came out of Martin's mouth with a hollow sounding laugh.

"He was nice to me," Nick said simply.

"Did he talk to you about me?"

Nick, with surprising animosity, was tempted to say they'd had better things to say and do, but he realised it wasn't quite the truth. They had talked about Martin. He decided on the flippant approach.

"Only about how famous you'll be one day, and how good-looking you are."

"I'll bet."

"It's true."

"Did he mention how they gossip about me as well?"

Nick was silent again.

"I can see you're being tactful. I have a reputation for liking younger boys too much, and them seeing you with me will only feed into the gossip machine."

"Will it?" Nick asked.

"Most of them want older protectors, or hunks out of *Physique Pictorial* magazines. They lack another kind of appreciation."

Is that what it's called, Nick thought.

"Maybe they just prefer older partners, or men of their own age."

"Romantic," Martin replied. "They are all promiscuous, even Bruce, and I really do like him. He's into guardsmen. No one talks about that, because it's what they all want. The big uniformed man to take control of their lives."

The words came out with such ferocious bitterness that Nick found it hard to recall the happy young man who had come up to him and Andy only a short while ago.

"I don't listen to gossip," Nick said.

"Well, as long as you don't listen to their fairy stories, it's okay. Of course, they commented on your looks as well, and on the way Andy and you had stayed in each other's company. One of them said, 'youth must have youth' and 'good luck to that rubbish.' But as I said, I like Bruce. He preoccupied me and distracted me from their comments."

"Did he talk about this new play?"

"Yes."

"Is there a good role in it for you?"

"I wish," Martin said with a sigh. "Strictly professionals only. I don't qualify just yet, but who knows, with Denise's help, I might stand a chance."

Nick thought, here we go about the bloody theatre again, not acknowledging that he had started it.

Martin wanted to cross over and look at the sea and Nick followed him. They walked down to the lower level and onto the pebbles. The sea itself was not that loud, but there was a strong wind which made it difficult for them to talk or be heard. They crossed the pebbles to the edge of the water, and a wave suddenly splashed water over their feet. They laughed at the cold feel of the water as it went through their shoes and socks.

"We will have to walk home with wet feet now," Martin said.

"What?"

"My feet are soaking. Aren't yours?"

As he said this, Martin grabbed Nick to him and held him close. It was completely dark where they stood and there was no sight or sound of anyone near.

"Let's do it here," Martin whispered.

"But we never—"

"It's safe. The police don't like getting their feet wet either."

He then guided Nick's hand to his trousers and whispering in Nick's ear, asked him to open them.

"Take yours out as well," Martin whispered.

Nick did what he was told and as if obeying orders his penis cooperated. Despite the time it had just had with Andy, it was still ready for more.

They clung together, leaning back against a sea wall. Martin murmured how sexy he was and how attracted he was to him, and with surprising quickness Nick's semen spurted all over Martin's hand. Martin held the wet hand away from him while his other hand guided Nick to increase the speed of his fingers as he jerked his penis.

"Christ!" he cried loudly as he came, and Nick was afraid the word would carry on the wind and alert someone to their presence.

"I needed that. I really needed that," Martin said, gasping after the pleasure had subsided.

"So did I," Nick said, not entirely telling the truth.

Then they kissed and Nick could just about see Martin's face up close. The expression of desire on it still turned him on and for a while he forgot about Andy in the sudden urgency of their kisses and passionate embraces.

"Shall we wash our hands in the sea?" Martin suggested. Nick laughed and they ran to the water's edge. Once more, Nick got wet, this time right up to his chest. His shirt was soaked.

"The waves have got it in for me tonight," he said.

"What? I can't hear because of the wind."

"Bloody sea water."

"It's the first time I've done this," Martin said, loudly so that Nick would hear. "It's the first time, and it seems so natural out here. Thank God the waves aren't fucking people."

Nick looked at the water and understood what Martin meant. The sea was a living mass and each wave was so different and yet the same, like people, but without morals or judgement. They walked slowly back up the pebbles, onto the concrete.

"I'll walk you to your door," Nick said.

"Hadn't you better come in and dry out a bit first?"

"No, I don't have far to go from Regency Square."

They were quiet as they walked the remainder of the distance and Nick was deep in thought. He felt the act they had just committed no longer meant as much as before. He asked himself why. In the end, he had got lost in Martin's kisses, but an inner voice had reminded him that he needed the intensity of fresh experience that he'd had with Andy and he remembered too that he had wanted to go further with Andy than they had been able to. He had not seen Andy's buttocks, but he had felt them briefly. Equally briefly, he had run his hand down the cleft that that separated one from the other, and touched with his finger at the hairy protection that surrounded Andy's anus. There was more, so much more to trace with eye and hand and mouth, to go into, to be at one with. He wasn't satisfied to return to the safe, restricted land of masturbation. He wanted, young explorer that he was, to move on.

"A penny for them?"

Martin came out with the trite expression as they approached his house in Regency Square.

"Your thoughts, Nick," he added.

"I'm just dreaming. Nothing of importance. Tired, I guess."

"All that sea air," Martin replied, laughing.

On the doorstep, Martin held Nick's hand briefly, then without making any further arrangements, took out his key, said goodnight to Nick, opened the door and was gone.

Nick walked home slowly, and as he approached Preston Street, which with its elegant shops and cafés was his mother's favourite street, a rush of disturbing images flooded his mind. He felt intense pressure in his head as if somebody or something was pressing down on his brain. He thought of Jason and of New Year's Eve. He wondered what Martin would have said and done if he had shown a real active interest in having a threesome. After all, Jason was attractive and Nick had found him attractive. He wondered how it would have been, and whether Jason wouldn't have forced Martin, with the sheer force of lust, to be more adventurous sexually. He almost regretted it hadn't happened. He would have been able to discover more of Martin's body, to sniff and lick and probe—all the things Martin refused to do. But then he wondered, did he do those things with others in London or with Jason? Was he less inhibited with other people than with him? What was wrong with him that Martin didn't want to discover more? And the more he questioned, the more complex and impossible it became for his young mind to unravel. He had no idea, except that he knew there was a barrier in their sexuality. Then there was the photograph of the two youths. They were younger than him. Did their youth turn Martin on? Martin must have used the photograph himself as stimulation. What did he see in his fantasies? It was dark and Nick felt dark inside himself as he reached the top of the street and crossed over Western Road. He made his way up into the Montpelier area, going a roundabout way, through the shadowy beauty of Montpelier Villas, then turning left he saw his house: the great lumbering red house that was so unlike the others, stark against the night sky, almost threatening. He thought of his mother and what he endured with her, and then exhausted, he walked up the flight of steps to the side door and let himself in, walking in darkness until he was safe enough in his own room to turn the light on.

He was shivering now, and felt hot as well.

SEVEN

For the next few weeks Nick was ill. At first his mother dismissed it as a simple cold and insisted he should go into work as usual. She now seemed happy that he was not at home with her. He managed to stay on his feet for a couple of days, sorting out books, pricing them, smiling his usual smile to the customers. But the regulars who liked him told him that he looked ill and that he should go home. It was late on the third day that he felt a sudden rush of giddiness and Alfred, who was in the shop with him, called for a taxi and sent him home, telling him he was foolish to play around with his health.

"You've got flu. Do you want to give it to everyone who comes in here? Anyway, it's a good thing you're young. I don't know what kind of flu it is this year, but it seems to be bad. It was in the papers, but then you don't read the papers."

"I can't afford a taxi," Nick said. "I can walk back to Montpelier Road."

"In this state? You'll collapse in the street after a few steps. Look at you, you've gone grey. You need your bed. And as for the fare, I'll take care of it."

"But Alfred—"

"The taxi will be here in a moment. Here's a couple of quid."

"I don't need all that."

"Take it just the same. I'll feel better knowing you've got sufficient money in your pocket."

Nick took the money and for a moment he felt better. He had drunk two glasses of water which Alfred had given him, and had taken a couple of aspirin.

"I'd give you tea," Alfred said, "but there's no time."

When the taxi arrived, and Nick walked out onto the pavement outside the shop, the giddiness hit again. The taxi man and Alfred helped him into the back seat.

"Is he very sick?" the man asked.

"I don't know," Alfred replied, almost gruffly. "Just take him to Montpelier Road as soon as you can and if you could help him up the steps at the other end that would be good."

"Of course," the man said, and Alfred called out to Nick through the glass, "Get well soon, and take your time. I can sort everything out here. Don't you dare worry about it."

The taxi drove away and Nick sat back into the seat. Despite feeling so ill, he liked the luxury of being in the taxi. Even when he was out with his mother, and she was overtired, she always insisted it was an expense she could not afford. The driver was silent during the trip and Nick looked out of the window. Familiar places he knew so well, looked unreal as if they were floating just above the ground. He saw St Nicholas's Church in a daze, and the houses in the Montpelier area seemed to wobble, like white jellies.

Once at the house, the driver helped him out of the car and with fumbling fingers Nick pulled out his money and paid. He took his change and the man insisted on helping him up the steps to the door.

"Which bell is it?" he asked.

Nick told him, too exhausted to reach for it himself.

"You really need your bed you know," the taxi man said. Then the door opened and his mother was standing there. He looked at her, said simply that he felt ill, and then everything went black. He passed out.

When he came round, he was in bed. His mother was standing over him and explained that the kind taxi man had helped him into bed. Nick thanked her, almost as if she were a stranger. She then made him sit up, and slowly he drank sips of warm sweet tea.

"Now, lie back," she said, "and get some good sleep."

He slept for a long time, and in his sleep he saw the faces of Martin and Andy. They were both pursuing him, and he was crying out, "I'm too tired. I'm too tired." Then the image melted and Greg was there, calling him a fucking idiot for getting his feet wet in the sea. He liked Greg being there in his dream. He had cool hands, and he passed his hands across Nick's forehead. Then the dream shifted and for some reason he was standing naked in front of the Royal Pavilion, looking up at the architecture: the crazy, wonderful architecture of the building, oblivious to the crowd of people around him all laughing at the sight of his body. Then a splash of bright red sliced across the image and he heard the sound of the waves in his ears: long, drawn out waves, drawing him in to their wet silence, then plunging him back onto the shore. "I can't swim," he cried out. But the waves were not human. They did not care, and continued to throw him onto the pebbles and then suck him back into their fluid, icy grasp.

"I can't swim," he cried out and woke up suddenly, feeling a dreadful panic. His mother rushed into the room and pushed his raised head back onto the pillow.

"Don't do it to me any more," he shouted, and she told him to be quiet, that he was delirious.

"What's delirious?" he heard himself ask.

"It's bad," his mother said. "It's very bad." Then he felt smothered again as he was drawn backwards into sleep.

Eventually the fever broke and he was well enough to sit up, but not yet to get out of bed. He needed to urinate, but knew he had to control himself. He called out for his mother to come to him, and told her that he needed the toilet.

"I've got this," she said, a note of disgust in her voice. She drew back the blanket and sheet that covered him and presented him with the nozzle of an object into which to put his penis. She held it as the urine flowed out of him. Then she hurried away, leaving him to cover himself again with the sheet and blanket. When she returned, still with a look of distaste on her face, she asked him coldly if he wanted anything more to drink.

"I'd like something to eat," he mumbled weakly.

"A bit of toast?"

"Yes. Thank you, mother."

As he lay in the bed, the smell of hot toast came into the bedroom. He found the smell unpleasant, but all the same, he knew he had to eat something.

"Here you are," she said, handing the toast to him.

He took the plate and held the toast up to his lips. The butter tasted bad in his mouth, but he forced the food down.

"Do you want some more?"

"No, thank you. I feel better already."

He tried to smile, but his jaw ached. His mother then put a thermometer in his mouth and when it was ready she looked at the result.

"Still high," she said. "You're not well yet. A few more days in bed."

He leant back onto the pillow and asked if he could have a book. He had a sudden desire to have his favourite childhood book *The Wind in the Willows* by his side. He told her what he wanted and where it was.

Once he was on his own he reached for it. He had been given it on his tenth birthday, or was it the year before? Anyway, it was the year there had been snow on the tennis court; snow for the first time in his life; a long stretch of white, dazzling him. He had never seen anything quite so magical. He read and re-read the adventures of Ratty, Mole, and all the other characters, especially the chapter called *The Wild Wood*. He got confused when he reached *The Piper at the Gates of Dawn*, and was slightly irritated with Toad. But he never tired of reading the opening chapters and knew them almost by heart.

Now, years later he needed it once more. Tired, but happy with the book in his hands, he read through the opening chapters, then laid it aside and fell asleep.

This childlike ritual got him through, and for the next few days in bed, the book was his companion. He spoke the dialogue out loud, enjoying hearing it echo back at him from the high ceiling. It even made his mother laugh.

"You big kid," she said, ruffling his hair. It was the only

moment of tenderness throughout his illness. The rest of the time, she grumbled quietly about how all the extra running around was taking it out of her and how it was affecting her hernia.

"I am sorry you have to do so much for me," he would say. "I am trying to get better as soon as I can. I don't want to go on feeling like this."

He felt sorry for her though; sorry for the pain she endured constantly from her hernia. He knew he would get better, but realised she would only decline. He was aware of this, but he was also exhausted, bearing this knowledge alone.

In a couple of days he was able to get up, put on his clothes and sit by the window of his room. The tennis court looked bleak in the late winter weather. The grass was still there, dirty green, almost dark brown in places. Occasionally he saw a few people cross it, but he had no idea where they had come from or where they were going. If anything, their presence made it look even more deserted.

"I've seen him again," his mother said one day, bursting in on his silence.

He was startled. She sounded panic stricken and, frighteningly, she looked as if she had emerged from one of his nightmares.

"Who?" he asked.

"A boy. I've seen him three days running now. He stands at the bottom of the steps, looking up at the door. I can't imagine he's a friend of yours, and if he is, why doesn't he come to the door instead of just lingering outside like that?"

"What does he look like?"

His heart was beating fast as he asked, already knowing.

"He looks wild, unkempt, older than you, darker, but still a boy."

"About sixteen?"

"I don't know. All I do know is, he makes me feel uncomfortable. He looks as if he wants to come in and cause trouble."

"I think I know who it is," Nick replied. "His name is Greg. I knew him at school."

"Then why doesn't he come to the door? And why is he here so often, just standing about? Soon the neighbours will be talking."

"He's probably afraid to ring the bell."

"Why?"

She sat on his bed and looked at him wearily.

"Because he knows you do not like any of my friends to come here. He knew that when I was at school."

She shook her head, still not understanding.

"I'll go and see if he's still there," she said, getting up heavily off the bed.

Nick's heart was beating rapidly and he felt both dread and desire at seeing Greg again, if it was him.

"He's gone," his mother murmured as she returned into the room. "Next time he comes, I hope you are well enough to look for yourself." Nick nodded his head. "Because he scares me!" she continued. "There's something wrong with him. I can feel it."

"Perhaps he's had some bad news and wants to tell me," he answered.

"Why should he come to you with it? Hasn't he got a family of his own? I suppose you haven't seen him for a while, have you?"

Bombarded by these unanswerable questions, Nick longed for her to leave the room so he could ponder them alone. There was a remote chance that it was some other boy than Greg. Or maybe someone waiting for someone else in the house, although this hypothesis seemed unlikely as there were only older people living above him, including one woman who would have liked to have been more intimate with his mother, but his mother refused it, referring to her as common.

"Greg," he said aloud, once his mother had left the room, and he felt a surge of energy for the first time since his illness had begun. And for the first time, he felt his penis grow hard, but he couldn't allow himself the consolation of sexual relief as his mother could burst in on him at any time. And anyway, he told himself, I am not ready for that yet. It could bring the fever back.

That night he had troubled dreams. Greg was a vague shadow in them, but he was not entirely defined and Nick couldn't see his features. In the dream Nick was standing on a dark plain and he knew he was being threatened: threatened and confronted. A harsh wind blew around him, a cold wind that made him shiver. He cried out, afraid, and woke up at dawn, his body wet with sweat. Unsteadily, he went to the bathroom and washed his body down with a flannel at the sink. Then he returned to his room, sitting by the window, until the weakest of suns rose in the sky, its pale rays bathing the court with their feeble light. His mind felt empty.

"Nick, Nick."

His mother came in.

"He's there. Come in to the living room and look, but don't let him see you. You don't know if he's the boy you think he is."

He hurried after her as best as he could and looked cautiously out of the window. At first he saw only the top of a head. Then the body beneath it moved into view.

"It is Greg!" he said.

"Are you strong enough to go and talk to him?"

He replied that yes, he had a little energy, and that as long as he had his warmest sweater and his coat, he would be fit enough to go down.

"And you won't stay long with him?"

"No," he replied.

He wrapped himself up quickly, and went out of the house almost running down the steps. He felt both exhausted and exhilarated at the same time. Greg stood there and looked at him in silence. He neither smiled nor spoke, but just looked at him. It gave time for Nick to assess what he saw as well. Greg's body looked strangely thin, sharper than before. His blue eyes, once so familiar were familiar still, but they seemed bigger, rounder in his lean face. His dark hair was more floppy than ever, and his clothes were scruffy. But one thing Nick noticed more than anything else was that he looked much older than he had the last time he had seen him.

"I had to fucking come to you," Greg said at last. "I couldn't wait any longer."

"Wait for what?" Nick replied, his voice sounding more mechanical than he had expected.

"To see you again you fucking idiot. I thought you would come to me in Portslade. I'm working in the shop now—not that I'm any good at it."

Nick continued to stare at him. He began to feel unsteady in his legs and had to hold on to the side of the red wall.

"You ill or something?"

"I've had flu," Nick replied. "I still feel a bit weak. It's my first time outside."

"Can you manage a short walk to the bottom of the road? I'll steady you, if you like. We can walk slowly."

Then, as the sun started to shine brighter in the sky, a smile broke up the harsh, older lines on Greg's face. His cheeky look returned and there was a warmth in his voice. Time, and all that had happened in it, appeared to slip away when Nick saw that smile and felt the subtle tenderness of Greg's words reach him.

"Okay," he replied, "but my mother will be bloody furious. She's seen you hanging around outside for days and thinks you're up to no good. I'd better go in and tell her I'm going off with you for a while."

"No," Greg cried out, "don't do that. She might not let you come out again. I'll take care of you if you feel bad. Trust me."

Nick looked up at the window and saw his mother pressed up close to the glass. She made questioning gestures with her hands. He waved to her, smiled and pointed down the street. She understood and shook her head vigorously.

"Come on," Greg urged. "Don't take any notice."

Nick looked at him and for the first time in what seemed a long time laughed his own young laugh. He felt a flush of happiness being close to Greg again and felt too weak in the head to question any further.

"There's a café, just off Western Road. Waterloo Street. You can walk that far, can't you?"

"I can try."

He walked slowly. He felt unreal, but somehow he had just enough energy to put one step in front of the other.

"Look," Greg whispered. "We're on Western Road already."

Nick looked around him. The rush of traffic disorientated him at first; that and the scurrying of people on their way to do their early morning business.

"What's it like this café?" he asked.

"Not like the one we used to go to," Greg said with a laugh. "More to your taste than mine, but the cakes look good and I'm hungry."

"But surely you'll be expected at work this morning. And what about those other times you've been round to the house?"

"Oh, my Dad's quite easy going. I've had a rough period too, but enough about me."

Reaching the top of Waterloo Street, Nick felt unsteady again. The steepness of the road leading down to the seafront suddenly seemed too much for him. He could see the water in the distance and the light of the morning sun glinting off the top of small incoming waves.

"Is it far?" he asked.

"No, it's just there, on the corner of Cross Street."

When they reached the café it looked more like a tea shop with porcelain ornaments in the window and antique pots hanging on the walls.

"My mother would feel at home here," he murmured.

"Good. What will you have? Breakfast?"

"Just tea."

"No scrambled eggs?"

"No, I don't feel like eating yet."

"Real bad was it? Your flu?"

A waitress came up, curious at seeing two such young men in the place so early in the morning. As if anticipating trouble she made it clear almost at once that she was the owner and not just a waitress. Her hair was tied tight in a bun at the back of her neck. Nick thought it made her look rather old and ugly.

"He wants tea," Greg said, taking over. "I'll have a Coca-Cola and a piece of that chocolate cake." He pointed to a pile of them on the counter.

"Chocolate cake? For breakfast?" she queried.

"For breakfast," Greg replied.

"And you don't want anything to eat?" she said rather coldly, turning to Nick.

He replied in his politest voice that a) he had been unwell, and b) he wasn't hungry.

"So it's just your friend then for food?"

"Yes," Greg said firmly and she went away. "The old battle-axe," he said when she was out of hearing. Then there was an awkward silence between them until the cake and pot of tea was put on the table. Greg had to wait before she brought him his Coca-Cola.

"I thought she'd keep me waiting," Greg observed sourly. "Thinks I'm too common to be in her café."

"You're not common," Nick replied.

"Compared to you with your accent? You must be deaf. Just remind me to watch my language. I don't expect she's heard the word fuck much in her life."

Nick watched as Greg ate his cake hurriedly, stuffing it into his mouth almost all in one go.

"You look like you haven't eaten in ages," he said.

"Oh, food and me," Greg shrugged. "All I want to do right now is eat cake. It was a bit stale though." Then he said seriously, "I have missed you, honest I have."

Nick put down the cup he was holding and stared hard at Greg.

"Tell me about yourself," he said.

"The truth?"

"Of course."

"It's been bad. I had to leave school. Me and learning. Forget it. I can do one thing, and *that* badly. I know what to do in the shop, but somehow I don't seem to do it right. As for my personal life, well, I tried it out with a girl—Diane." He grinned. "Posh name isn't it?"

"I don't know," Nick replied neutrally.

"Well, she was sort of posh. Lives in Shoreham. Rides a horse and all that. Seventeen. And for a time I was okay with her, until I thought of you. I even fucked her. Oops, here I go with the bad words again." He looked around him with a grin. "No one's listening though." He turned back to Nick. Then he was silent again.

"You said you thought of me?"

"Yes," Greg whispered, as if he was suddenly ashamed of admitting it again. "What we did in the toilets and at Charlie's place. I couldn't get it out of my mind. It kept my prick hard, and I wasn't really *with* her if you know what I mean."

"Didn't you think of the other boys?" Nick asked suddenly, recalling his conversation with Charlie.

A much longer silence followed. Greg fiddled with the chocolate crumbs on his plate, then called the woman over and asked for another piece. Only after she had brought the cake to him did he reply.

"Charlie told you then?" he said with a rather shaky voice.

Nick nodded his head. He hated having this conversation, but it had to be talked about. He looked sideways at Greg and felt a surge of emotion. What was that song in the juke box at the 42 Club? *To Know Him is to Love Him.* He remembered the tune and the words.

"Was he lying?" Nick asked.

"No."

This single word was said sullenly. Then Greg bit into his cake and munched on it loudly. He ate with anger.

"I knew two redheads. Charlie probably turned it into many more. It wasn't like that."

"Wasn't it?"

Nick realised he sounded pitiless.

"Coincidence they were redheads," Greg said between mouthfuls. At last he had finished eating and looked down at the empty plate.

"Charlie also told you he found me and that boy on the bed, didn't he? Don't bother to answer. I know he did. I bet the fat little bastard didn't spare you any details."

"What about the boy on the bed?" Nick asked, swallowing the last of the tea. He felt desperately thirsty and slightly feverish.

"He went and killed himself, that's what! A great bloody shock it was. He went to some shithole of a shed in his back garden and hanged himself with his shoelaces."

Nick felt himself tremble involuntarily and had to ask the woman if she could bring him a glass of water. When he had drunk it he felt slightly better, but weak. He needed to go home. He knew instinctively why Brian (he suddenly remembered his name) had done this. He was probably in love with Greg and couldn't bear it any longer. It was a flash of intuition, like lightning, but it seemed clear enough to him.

"Do you know why he did it?" he managed to ask eventually.

"Things got out of control between us. It's partly my fault, but it wasn't like between you and me. He took it hard when I wouldn't be serious with him, and he was jealous of you. I used to talk a lot about you to him. He thought he had a rival and being sort of intense and feminine-like in his feelings, I guess it got too much. He had family problems as well. He was afraid they'd find out how he was and put him away."

"I see," Nick said quietly.

"I hated myself. It was a few months after I last saw you. I was seeing Diane then as well, and I got really angry with Brian one day and told him I wasn't a queer like him."

"Oh," Nick replied.

"And I'm not a queer," Greg added. "I like sex with guys my own age, yes. I like sex with boys, but I'm not queer. I liked it with you more than anybody. I even had feelings about doing more with you. Strong feelings. Even now, right this moment, I'd go somewhere with you. My cock's so bloody hard."

Nick felt suddenly strong then and, in a rush of words, he told Greg about the books he had read and how he knew definitely what he was. He also told Greg about Martin and Andy.

Greg shook his head.

"I don't want to believe it," he said. Then he got up, went to the counter and paid. Nick remained seated. Greg returned to the table and looked hopelessly down at him. That's more of a fucking shock than anything, and the worst of it is, I feel jealous. But I'd fucking lay into those guys you've been with if I met them." Then he sat down and said slowly, "Have you ever fucked any of them? Or have any of them fucked you?"

"No," Nick replied.

"You're not lying now?"

"Would it make any difference if I had?"

"I'd bloody murder them if I knew you had. I know fucking someone or being fucked by them can be really special. You have to do it to know it."

"Was it special with Diane? You did it with her, and what about Brian?"

Greg looked distant and didn't reply.

"You said you were thinking of me when you were with her," Nick said, then added, "Were you thinking of Brian as well?"

"I don't want to talk about it."

"You mean you can't."

Then Greg hissed at him, "Yes, yes. But don't you understand what that makes me? It makes me a fucking poof—a nancy-boy. And I'm not. I'm not." He looked at Nick and there was a look of terrible desperation on his face. "I can't face a life like that," he said loudly.

The woman who owned the café coughed loudly and came to clean the table. She looked at them suspiciously again and clearly did not like what she saw, or what she had probably heard.

"We'd better get out of here," Greg said.

"No, you go. I want to stay. I need to be alone. I have some money in my pocket. I'll have some more tea. It will give me enough strength to get home."

Greg stared at him helplessly, then getting up, hurried to the door and closed it loudly behind him.

"What a rude young man," the woman said as she returned to the table. "Is he a good friend of yours?"

"No," Nick said.

"I'm glad to hear it. I wouldn't want any son of mine to associate with a boy of that type."

"Could I have some more tea please?"

"Of course. You look as if you need a strong pot. Then you'd best forget all about him. That's my advice, for what it's worth."

When she brought the tea back to him, she lingered a while at the table as if wanting to talk to him some more, but noticing how distressed he looked, she walked away slowly, back to her position behind the counter. Eventually, after drinking some of the tea, Nick got up unsteadily. He felt in his pocket for the extra pound note Alfred had given him and went to the counter to pay. He thanked the woman for her advice, picked up his change and left.

Looking to the top of Waterloo Street, he saw that Greg was standing there with his back to him and a sudden fear hit him: a totally irrational yet intuitive fear that Greg would do him harm if he went to him. He sensed a desperation of violence in Greg. His back looked lean and hard and his strong legs were wide apart as if ready to take on an opponent. They were no longer the legs of a boy kicking a ball, but of a youth waiting to tackle someone, to fight. As fast as he could, Nick turned into Cross Street behind him and made his way back home from there.

"Where have you been?" his mother shouted at him as soon as he opened the door.

"I had to walk with him," he said simply.

"I watched you closely with him. There's something going on between you two. The more I looked at him the more I thought he looked like a thug. He looked as if he were up to things that are no good."

"I went to a tea shop with him. Not far from here. He's got serious problems, that's all. He just needed to talk. He's not a criminal or even a potential criminal."

"So far."

Nick shook his head, tired of her.

"He's young like me, mother. Sometimes young people need to talk to each other about matters that concern them."

"Has he got someone into trouble?" she asked, walking into the kitchen.

"What do you mean?"

"A girl. Is there a girl involved, and if there is, what do you have to do with it?"

"He spoke about a girlfriend, yes. But he's a year older than me. He's worried about the future."

"Marriage, I suppose," his mother said, putting away some dishes.

"He's confused. Can't we just leave it at that?"

She wheeled on him then, and dropped a plate to the floor. It smashed.

"Look what you've made me do I'm so anxious," she said.

He bent down, and picked up the pieces. It was from a set of Willow pattern plates that she liked but that he hated. He threw the broken pieces into the bin.

"I'm sorry," he said, "but now I really need to rest."

"Stay here. I haven't finished talking to you yet. I can't leave it at that, as you put it."

"What more do you want me to say?" he asked, exasperated.

"I want you to promise me not to see that boy again. I don't want you to be drawn into anything."

He laughed and, just by looking at her reaction, saw that she wanted to hit him again, and that she was only just restraining herself.

"You are growing up too fast," she said. "You'll regret the end of childhood when it comes."

"Will I?" he murmured and then added, "Maybe, mother, it is already behind me."

She looked at him with suspicion as he walked out of the kitchen to his room. Quietly, he closed the door behind him.

EIGHT

When he was well again, Nick returned to the shop. The weeks passed quickly, and when he was not tidying up and sorting out, he read behind the counter. He had already found another book called *The Heart in Exile*. It didn't touch him as much as the others, but he found the dustjacket beautiful. It was a charcoal drawing of a sad-eyed boy. He had wide eyes, gentle in their attentive look, with the sadness focused there. There was the hint of a smile on his face and he seemed to be looking sideways at someone out of the picture. His thick, forward thrusting hair appealed to Nick and he wanted to reach into the drawing to touch it. He also had a very broad nose and a strong neck. He looked neither like Greg, nor like Andy, but in some obscure way appeared to be a blend of them both. As Nick turned the pages of the book, he often paused to lay it down and look at him. It was definitely one to be added to his collection and he kept it under the counter, so that no one else could pick it up to buy it.

To his surprise, he rarely thought of Martin. The intensity he had felt in those months before had dissipated, as if drained away during his illness. He wondered if Martin would come to the shop, hoping that he wouldn't, and as the weeks turned into months, he felt more at ease. He had, quite simply, no desire to see him again, but still he needed time to get over that loss, if it was one. Of course, he could recall Martin's good looks and his attraction to him, but realised that it was burnt out and gone.

"I will soon be ready to move on from there," he repeated to himself aloud so as to make it more real, more of a promise. He had also kept Andy's address and number, and had it continually on him. But that too had to wait.

As the year lengthened and then shortened, he began to think of his approaching birthday. He would be sixteen. The age of admission at last to go and see any film he wanted without pretence. He smiled to himself as he thought he would soon be part of the 'Adults Only' crowd. But as for specific plans for his birthday, he had none, and he knew his mother never gave it a thought.

"You should go out more often," Alfred said to him one day, catching him reading a book. "Just because you sell the books, doesn't mean you have to be stuck with them. It's a job."

"But I like books, Alfred," he said.

"They corrupt the mind, you know—and I don't mean the ones behind the wrappers. More often than not, the ones in the wrappers are tamer than the rest. Talk about a come-on. But they sell, don't they?"

Nick laughed.

"Especially that expurgated *Fanny Hill*," he said.

"Have you read that too?" Alfred asked.

"I dipped into it. It's well written. Cleland knew how to write."

"Well, I wouldn't know about that. Haven't read it myself. I like *The Naked and the Dead*. Good war book. Refused to put that one in a wrapper."

They talked a bit more, then Alfred asked him a really personal question for the first time.

"Have you got a girl yet?"

"No," Nick answered truthfully.

"Well, I'm not like that, so don't get me wrong, but even I can see you're bloody good-looking."

Nick looked down at the counter, turning red.

"Save your blushes for the girls," Alfred said, laughing. "Do that with them and they will be queuing up! Nothing like a shy boy to make them curious. As for me, I was never shy. Never got the pick of the crop either." Then Alfred busied himself around the shop, pretending to do things until it was time to leave. "Remember what I said. Go out. Do a bit of partying. Art students are supposed to be fun. You could take up painting. They won't mind if it's bad. Most of the stuff they produce looks like Van Gogh on a bad day."

"I'll remember," Nick said, and once again he was left alone in the shop. Nick had no idea what Alfred did with the rest of his time. With Nick back in good form he only turned up once a week to check things over and pay him.

October 1st arrived at last. Nick's birthday. He woke that morning after a vivid dream. It was of a Brighton he no longer knew. He was standing, for some reason, in the middle of a road leading towards St Peter's Church. Crowds of people flanked him on either side, and although it was a bright day, the brightness of the lights of the Astoria cinema further down on the left, glared out as if in defiance at the ferocious gaze of the sun. A few yards ahead of him, a bizarre figure was dragging itself slowly towards the church. It appeared hardly human, dressed in a garish pink costume, feathered from top to bottom, a train of dirty pink material slithering along the road behind it. He stared at this monster (or so it seemed to him) as it advanced painfully forwards like a flamingo Christ without a cross. The crowd on either side were silent or had open mouths like clowns, mimicking laughter. They were enjoying this solitary, grotesque parade, for it was, unlike them, so tall and alien, and like an alien, forbidding. He knew they dared not accost it, nor attempt to hurt it for fear it would either contaminate or hurt them. Then as Nick looked closer, he saw that the one of it was actually two. It had a companion, identically dressed, but so small was the space between them that it looked like one. The 'couple' of it suddenly appeared to him as a travesty of a bridal pair, with the church as destination. This monster that could have crawled out of a horror film playing at the Astoria was seeking either blessing or curse, and was not afraid of the equally alien crowd. And he, Nick, was alone: the only person bold enough to follow their train, there in the middle of the road, like them, the twinned creatures, and he screamed out against this solitude, for unlike them, he had no twinned partner. The scream awoke him. His mother, hearing him, knocked loudly on the bedroom door.

"Nick, what is it?"

He raised himself up and slowly got out of the bed. As he did so he called out, "It's alright, mother. I had a nightmare." He heard her say something, but he was still halfway in his dream, trying hard in his sudden wakefulness to shake it off. But remnants of the images still clung to him like pieces of alien cloth.

"You look awful," she said as he appeared in the hallway, making his way to the bathroom. He did not reply but ran himself a bath and he lay for a long while in the soothing warmth of the water. Again she knocked on the door.

"I cooked you a special breakfast. It's getting cold."

Like the twinned creature, for he still felt it was with him, he dragged himself out of the bath, dried himself, patted his face with cold water, put on his clothes and combed his hair. When he got to the kitchen, semi-cold fried eggs and bacon greeted him. His mother was not there. He sat and dutifully ate the greasy food down, trying to drown the taste of it with several cups of tea.

"Happy birthday," she said from behind him. He had not heard her come into the kitchen. She sat at the table, facing him, looking unwell, and he realised it was one of her particularly painful days.

"Thank you, mother," he said and smiled at her.

"I was going to buy you a present, but now you are sixteen, and you already think of yourself as a man, I had no idea what to get you, so I decided to give you money instead."

Nick thought to himself that a small gift of anything but money, as long as it had been given with open affection, would have been better. He watched as she silently passed a white envelope across the table to him.

"Here," she said.

He took it, and opened it. It was a very bright card with a bold scarlet '16' surrounded by multi-coloured festoons hanging off or falling away from the central numbers. Inside was the usual meaningless rhyming jingle, and a couple of folded notes. He saw that they amounted to ten pounds.

"Thank you," he said and smiled at her again. Then he got up and kissed her on the cheek. Her face smelled of too much powder.

"Has the nurse been for your injection yet?" he asked.

"She came at seven."

He returned to his seat and nibbled on a piece of toast. He wanted to ask if there were any other cards for him, but his mother got up and left the room.

He had arranged with Alfred to have the day off work and he hoped he would be able to go out as soon as possible and that his mother had not planned anything special for him like a birthday tea. Reluctantly, he followed her into the living room.

"Look behind you on the side table," she said. "There are more cards."

He turned and saw two cards. One was from his father with yet more money in it, and the second was from Aunt Agnes. Both were signed 'with love' and both contained more of the relentless jingles. He wondered how much these off the peg poets got paid for their rubbish.

"What do you plan to do with your day?" his mother asked, looking up at him from her usual chair.

"I haven't thought about it," he replied, relieved that she was clearly not going to propose anything.

"Well, it's your day," she replied. "I remember as a girl that my sixteenth birthday felt different from the others. But what happened on that day I can't remember. It's a long time ago." She sighed, then picked up a copy of the *Radio Times*. "My eyesight is getting poorer," she said. "Can you read out what's on the radio this afternoon?" He took the magazine from her and looked at the afternoon programmes. He told her what was on and she nodded her head and replied, "Nothing out of the usual. I needn't have bothered to look."

"I think I'll go to the cinema."

She looked up at him, as if startled by this banal information.

"I'd have thought you'd have had enough of the cinema by now. Heaven only knows I'm responsible for taking you to see so many films." She paused, then added, "but not recently. We haven't gone recently, have we?"

He looked at her and shook his head.

"Anyway, they don't make films I like any more. It's all as common as a seaside postcard now. All vulgarity and dirty innuendo. I've read about them."

"I don't know," he replied. "I haven't been old enough to get in to see them." He was lying of course. Only a month or so ago he had seen a French film called *Nana*. It was based on one of the wrapped books he sold at the shop. He was curious to see what all the fuss around writers like Zola was about. The film told him nothing. It was simply a film, lavishly made in colour about the life of what the French called a courtesan. He had been bored to tears by it.

"I expect you are now," she said. "Isn't sixteen the age for it?"

"Yes."

"Well, I doubt you'll learn anything you don't already know."

She looked at him with a smirk on her face, then turned away and fiddled to get a copy of *Woman's Own* out of a pile of magazines at her feet. Taking advantage of her momentary lack of attention towards him, Nick left the room.

He spent a couple of hours in his bedroom, sitting by the window, reading a book by an author he had not heard of before. It was a battered paperback of *Moira* by Julien Green. He had opened it at random at the shop and had been immediately drawn to the red-headed protagonist of the book: a young man, tortured yet caught by religion, who had left his backwoods American town to go and study at a university. It was there that he met a good-looking youth called Bruce and an equally attractive girl called Moira. His reaction of desire and antagonism towards them fascinated Nick and he could, or so he thought, think of nothing better than to spend the whole of his birthday finishing the story.

Halfway through the book he felt stirrings of desire. It was induced by nothing he had read, but simply made itself known to him. The window was closed, the room was stuffy and he could smell his own masculine smell around him. Perhaps he was aroused by the smell. Images of the male naked body began to appear in his mind. He got up, made sure the door was firmly shut, then lay down on the bed. He pushed his trousers down to his knees and started to jerk himself off. Then came the inevitable knock on the door. He only just managed to pull his trousers up in time as his mother entered the room.

"Have you been sleeping again?" she asked suspiciously looking at him lying out on the bed. His erection had not gone down, and perversely, he hoped that it showed. "Aren't you going out?" she asked.

"What time is it?"

"It's almost one."

"Is there anything in for lunch?"

"I wasn't well enough to stock up yesterday. A sandwich will have to do. There's also a piece of cake from two days ago, which reminds me, I haven't got a special cake for you. I'm sorry about that."

The last sentence came out almost grudgingly. He got up from the bed, his penis quiet now, and felt ready to face her and the world.

"Don't worry, mother," he replied with a muted note of sarcasm in his voice, "I wasn't expecting a special cake." She looked at him sharply, wondering no doubt if this was a slight against her. He patted his trouser pocket where the ten pounds was and added, "I can always buy myself one if I want to."

After she had left the room, he changed his clothes, putting on a clean shirt and a pair of grey flannel trousers. He then picked out his best sweater and looked at himself in the thin tall mirror that was attached to a wall in a corner of the room. He asked himself if he looked any older. During the past year he had at least grown taller. He was now about five foot ten and his body was sturdier and fuller. This had only recently happened, and he was pleased. His hair was now floppy like Greg's and he thought he might treat himself to a haircut.

"I'd like it short," he said aloud, as if rehearsing the line he would use.

Then he looked closely at his face. His eyes, he thought, were more knowing, less wide-eyed, narrower if anything. And his face unlike his body had grown thinner, leaner. He supposed that he could pass for good-looking, but he was not a born Narcissus and certainly had no desire to trade on it like certain characters in books he had read. He turned away from the looking glass and went straight for the door.

"I'm going out now, mother," he said.

She waved to him silently, a vague smile on her face.

The day had begun with a bad dream. He hoped the rest of the waking hours would be different.

He had his hair cut in a hairdresser's for men at the Seven Dials. He hadn't given any specific directions except for it to be short, and he came out with a haircut that looked as if he was ready for the army. He was slightly shocked at the eventual outcome, but the man who had done it was quite old, and seemed a little deaf.

"Well, it's done now," he whispered to himself.

He wandered up the hill, towards his former school and the Dials Congregational Church, and carried on over Dyke Road, downwards to the Clock Tower. Once he had reached it he had an urgent need to urinate and went down into the public toilets. He had always found it difficult to pass water in public and stood for a long time at the urinal. A short distance from him, two men were standing together and he glanced briefly at them. One of them had an erection. It was sticking out and upwards and the sight of it appeared crude to Nick as he tried desperately to pee, wanting to get out of the place as soon as possible. He wondered how he had ever had the nerve to have sex with Greg in public toilets, even if it had been in closed cubicles. He had only just thought of that when he caught a glimpse out of the corner of his eye of a figure appearing from the shadows behind him. The figure went straight up to the man with the erection, placed a hand on his shoulder and whispered something in his ear. Then he heard a shocked cry from the man who had been accosted and Nick knew with sickening realisation that he was in the presence of an arrest. Out of fear, he peed at once and quickly putting himself away, he moved from the stall. As he passed the three men, he noticed that while the accosting man was in uniform, the other man was in on the arrest as well and was gripping the arrested man's arm tightly. He was in his mid-twenties, handsome, and Nick understood immediately that he had witnessed an entrapment. Shaking with sudden and very violent fright, he made his way up to the light of the entrance and quickly crossed over towards West Street. He almost ran down it, fearful that someone would be after him as well. He imagined a hand being placed on his shoulder.

"My God," he said to himself in a half-whisper, "that could have been me. I could have been that bloody stupid man."

He reached the promenade and leant up against the railing, looking down at the half-deserted beach. Thoughts raced through his mind. The man had been stupid certainly, but then so had he with Greg, and he hadn't cared enough himself back then. Desire had been too strong—a desire that had seemed uncontrollably natural. And what about the man who was working with the Police? Did he have an erection as well? He must have shown desire to encourage the man, and no man gets an erection without desire. How could this man have done it? How could he have pretended to be attracted when he wasn't? And was he working for the police, or was he a policemen himself, in plain clothes? No one works for the police, he told himself. He was a policeman. Just like the other. A policemen who could call up a hard-on at will.

"How dare he?" he said aloud, stirred by a rush of anger, the bitter sound, carried away by the wind from off the sea. Then he had a violent desire to vomit. He rushed down the steps to the lower promenade and made it just in time to get onto the beach. In full sight of anyone who wanted to see, he brought up the thick bile of greasy food he had swallowed that morning. Even the hungry seagulls circling above him appeared to wheel away in disgust. The image of the entrapment returned, of the two policemen standing on either side of the man, grasping him by the arms, and of the man's futile struggle. To protect himself from it, Nick had more or less blocked the image from his mind as he left the toilet, but now it returned with force, with all its implicit violence, and he bent over again, vomiting the rest of what was left in his guts onto the harsh pebbles.

"You alright, mate?"

A youngish man held his arm and Nick flinched from the touch. The last thing he wanted was that.

"I'm fine," he said, straightening himself up.

"You look bloody pale. Too much drink is it?"

Looking at himself in the mirror earlier that day, Nick had had his first recognition that he now looked old enough to drink. If he had felt better he would have smiled.

"Really, I'm okay."

The man looked at him dubiously, shrugged his shoulders and walked on along the beach. Nick waited for a while to see if he really did feel a bit better, then slowly moved on, up the beach to the lower promenade. He made his way up the steps to the top, stared up at West Street and, still feeling shaky, realised that he was safe. He had not been followed. He began to walk towards the Palace Pier and on his way he glanced over the road to the 42 Club. It made him think of Andy, and he reminded himself that this was his sixteenth birthday, and that he was alone.

"I don't know him," he murmured to himself. "It's been a long time. I can't ring him up just like that, and anyway, he is probably working."

He was more or less alone on the promenade and felt comforted by the sound of his own words. He needed to hear a voice that was familiar to him and at that moment he only had his own.

He stopped and looked down at his clothes and his shoes, hoping that none of his vomit had marked them. None had and he moved on again, feeling a little more confident. But as he approached the Palace Pier fear struck at him. He began to shiver, not with the cold, but because, despite his need for them, he had a sudden aversion towards his fellow men. Do I really want to see anybody, he thought. Do I really want to take that risk? Inside him he still heard the cry of the man in the toilet as he had been seized. Arms were dangerous. They could hurt as well as embrace. And what had that man felt when he was being so brutally held by the man next to him: a potential lover who had become, in an instant, an enemy?

"I can't face anybody," he whispered. "I'd better return home." But home was where his mother was and the thought of seeing her, unwell and unloving, forced a certain amount of courage onto him. He had to remain outside. He paid he entrance fee and began to walk along the pier.

He stopped off once to look at the booth where he had bought and collected *Classics Illustrated* as a child. The rack of comics was still there and new titles. As he glanced at them he felt nostalgia for an innocence that seemed already completely gone. Two titles that he remembered from the past now took on sinister connotations: *Crime and Punishment* with its drawing of a haunted man and a woman holding up the scales of justice in the background, and close to this, *Dr Jekyll and Mr Hyde*. The incident in the toilet returned to his mind again and superimposed over the faces Jekyll and Hyde he saw images of Greg's divided self. He hurried away from the booth, up towards the Ghost Train with its own memories and crossed over to the theatre entrance. He looked at the billboard, wondering if there was anything he could come and see by himself, but the title of the show became blurred as he looked at it. He found he was crying and that he could barely see. He brushed away his tears, realising that he had perhaps been crying since he left the magazine booth and he wondered how many people had seen him like that. Self-consciously he looked around him, turning his back on the theatre, but the hurrying crowd, eager for pleasure, swept past him, oblivious to anything that did not concern them. I will go crazy if I remain here he thought and reluctantly, becoming one with the crowd, he headed back towards the pier entrance.

Once on the street he crossed over and went into Forte's restaurant on the corner. He sat at the window and having ordered a plate of fish and chips, which he didn't really want, but felt that he needed to fill his empty stomach, wondered what to do next. Loneliness hit, more savagely than the call of hunger, and he wondered if they had a phone. After eating a little of his food, he felt disgusted by it, and pushed it aside. He got up, drank his tea while standing and not bothering to look for a telephone there, placed his money on the table and walked once more out into the street. It was now five to five. He would wait another hour and would then try to ring Andy. To kill time, he sat by the fountain in the Old Steine, and watched as the seagulls perched on top of it, drinking from the small jet of water. He tried to make his mind a blank, not wanting to think about what he would say to Andy if he did manage to get through. He had no words prepared, and would let whatever was said on either side just happen. At least it would break, if only for a few moments, the terrible isolation he was feeling.

He looked at his watch again. Time had gone quickly. It was nearly six. He got up from his seat and made his way to St James's Street. He found a telephone booth and went into it. He rang Andy's number, fished out by nervous fingers from his trouser pocket: the same trousers he'd had on when he had met him. The number on the piece of paper had remained there and, as the phone rang, he was glad they were rarely worn, and that not once during the long months since their meeting had they been cleaned. Then he heard Andy's voice.

"Hello?"

"Andy?"

"Yes."

"It's Nick."

His mouth felt dry. He heard a sharp intake of breath.

"Nick. It's been so long."

"Yes," he said. "I know. I'm sorry. I meant to."

"Okay, slow down. You sound a bit panicky. Anyway, I told you to ring anytime, and at last you have."

"Yes."

"I'm glad you have."

"Are you sure?"

Nick recognised the sound of light laughter coming from Andy's mouth at the other end.

"Look, it's obvious you can't talk to me on the phone. You sound as if you are being pursued by wolves. Why don't you come round?"

"You mean now?"

"Stop playing hard to get. Where are you?"

"St James's Street."

"I live just around the corner. You know that, don't you? I gave you the address as well as the number. George Street."

Nick glanced down at the paper. There was the address, written as large as the telephone number but, the day being what it was, he had only taken in the numbers written there.

"I see it," he said.

"Come round at once. You sound weird, as if you're in trouble or something. Are you?"

"No." Nick tried to force a laugh, but it didn't sound convincing.

"There are only two bells," Andy said. "Mine's the first one. I'll be waiting."

"See you in a minute."

He left the phone booth and there were beads of sweat on his forehead. He wiped his brow with the back of his hand and the shaking began again. He moved slowly and it was more than a few minutes before he had walked the short distance up St James's Street to Andy's place.

"At last."

Andy opened the door. There was a short flight of stairs behind him. He was standing in shadow and Nick couldn't see his face clearly. "Wait. I'll put some lights on."

Once the lights were on, they stood looking at each other in silence. Nick took in the strong yet pretty features of Andy's face, his blue eyes and black hair. Then he felt himself being pulled in; hauled in almost, as if he was being rescued.

"You sexy little sod," Andy murmured and took him in his arms. They stood there for what seemed to Nick a long time, but he no longer cared about time. He was being held at last.

"Andy," he whispered.

"Come on upstairs."

They separated. Andy held out his hand and they both went up, stopping at the first floor.

"There's not much to these small houses," Andy said and opened a door. "You go in first."

Nick walked into a room that appeared more crowded with things than any other room he had been in before. It was untidy and cluttered with piles of clothes and books (mostly on mathematics Nick was to find out later) and on the wall, a poster of Bobby Darin next to what looked like an original Victorian oil painting of a country scene: a small brown cottage, set off by lots of tall trees and pinkish clouds. Nick fascinated by the painting, went up to it.

"I like it," he said, glad that he had found something so easy to say.

"I picked it up in a junk shop, cleaned it up, and hey presto, I've got myself a work of art. Trust you to pick out the most cultured thing in the room."

214

Nick turned to face him and again looked closely at Andy who was doing exactly the same to him.

"You don't look well," Andy began, then looked down awkwardly as if he had made the wrong observation.

Nick blushed, much to his annoyance, but was consoled by the warm, concerned sound in Andy's voice.

"But you look, well, you look just right," he said.

He was surprised at his sudden confidence and daring. It was as if Andy had given him an injection of life. And Andy did look just right to him. He had on a pair of tight jeans, deep blue in colour, like his eyes, and a brightly coloured shirt that was open at the top. Nick noticed the darkness of his skin. A moment later, they were in each other's arms. Nick buried his head into the hard softness of Andy's shoulder, then he raised his head and their lips met.

"I want you," Andy whispered, and they tumbled onto the bed. For a while they fumbled awkwardly with each other's clothes, laughing as they did so. Then, naked at last, they looked at each other's bodies for a long while. Admiration mixed with lust—lust with genuine longing for each other. As the room darkened around them, they explored each other with their hands. The caresses and the findings, tentative at first, then became fiercely eager. Nick took control. Andy lay back on the bed and Nick covered his body with his own.

"I've wanted you to ring me so much," Andy whispered as Nick, straddling his body, looked down at him.

"You'll never guess what day it is," Nick replied softly. "It's my birthday."

This both broke and added to the sexual tension between them. The words seemed funny and they started laughing again. Then Andy drew Nick closer to him and Nick, silent once more, slid down his body, taking the tip of Andy's moist sex into his mouth.

"Not too fast," Andy said. "I don't want to let go for a while yet."

But Nick could not stop. He was too eager, too hungry. He

let the shock of the day pass from him by immersing himself in Andy's body, blinding himself to all memory of it by exploring parts of the body he had never explored before. He was not using Andy, but losing himself in him, trying to find the home that he so urgently needed in Andy's flesh, wanting above all not to be alone and to feel secure. He raised Andy's legs up, instinct alone making him do it. The newness of this did not surprise him and he sensed Andy wanted it. He licked first at Andy's balls, then his tongue travelled down to that most secret place, the place that Nick had often experienced in dreams and fantasies, but had not as yet felt. He licked there tentatively, then his tongue grew bolder and he buried his face into the divide of the body as he had previously buried his face into Andy's neck. He heard groans coming from Andy's mouth, and this drove him on. Andy relaxed and Nick's tongue went further, tasting and relishing the muskiness of his taste, and the hidden smell of him. Nothing was wrong about it, nothing put him off. After a while, he drew back, then he leant forward and their lips met again. Nick sucked on Andy's tongue, drawing it in.

"I want you," he said at last. "But, I have never, I have never done it. Will you help me?"

He said the words roughly, but there was tenderness in them. Andy didn't reply, but with his hands, guided him, into himself. They cried out simultaneously as the experience began.

"It's beautiful," Nick cried out.

Andy reached up and closed his mouth with his fingers. For a while they paused, then as Nick plunged further in, the rhythm and the intensity grew. Both of their bodies, wet with sweat, responded to each other, and after what seemed too short a time, both of them climaxed and, sighing with pleasure, they lay back on the bed. The room was in darkness, and lying side by side, they murmured all the usual words, the familiar old words, that took on again the ever renewed imprint of youth.

216

Much later, after they had joined their bodies together for a second, longer time, Nick confessed that he was hungry.

"I'll make you something to eat," Andy said. "There's a shared kitchen down the hall. The people above us are out and won't be back until late if I know them. I'll make us a fry up."

Remembering the food he had had earlier, Nick discreetly asked if there wasn't something easier, simpler.

"There's some ham and a tin of beans, I think. Will that do?"

"Fine," Nick replied contentedly, but he was reluctant to get out of bed and even more reluctant to let Andy get up.

"It won't come to us," Andy said at last, stepping over Nick and reaching for his clothes. Then he stood there, and with a smile on his face, ordered Nick to get up and join him.

In the kitchen, which was surprisingly tidy and clean, Andy put plates on the table and started to prepare the food. Nick sat at the table and watched him, taking in his every move. He liked watching him move. He was swift and graceful and his delicately good-looking face had a determined look on it.

"Stop looking at me as if you could eat me," Andy said with a laugh. "Cut up the bread, will you? And when the kettle boils, will you turn it off?"

Nick did as he was told and when everything was ready they stared at each other and quite suddenly, both of them looked shy.

"The light is bright in here," Nick said.

"I know. What time is it?"

Nick looked at his watch.

"It's half ten."

"An hour and a half before the end of your birthday. Let's celebrate."

Nick smiled and said that he had already celebrated it with Andy, but Andy did not reply to this, and started rummaging in the kitchen drawers.

"Found them," he said, and brought out a box of candles.

"I'm not going to ask how old you are, because I can't remember. So let's say ten candles, because that's all there is."

He found a big red plate and dripping hot wax from the first lighted candle, fixed them all into a circle. He then turned off the light and asked Nick to make a wish and blow.

"But don't say it out loud," he warned.

They were playing like kids now, and Nick found it fun. He bent forward, made his wish, which he wasn't going to tell yet, and then blew out the candles.

"Happy Birthday," Andy said in the semi-darkness, the only light coming from a dim bulb in the hallway. Then he came over to Nick, bent down and kissed him on the mouth.

"I'm sixteen," Nick said suddenly, and for a moment he thought, oh hell, why did I have to say that? I can't remember if I lied to him back in the 42 Club, or even if we talked about my age. I know he is nineteen. He may not want me now. Please let him want me.

Andy was standing by his chair and Nick, getting up, drew him tightly into his arms. He felt relieved when Andy responded to him in exactly the same way as before.

"I wish I had a present for you," Andy said at last.

"I've got all I want," Nick murmured.

They ate the simple meal that Andy had prepared and afterwards Andy took Nick by the hand and they returned to his room. He turned on a small lamp in the corner. Nick looked around the room again, and it appeared so comfortable and warm, with the shadow of the lamp casting a soft light around them. They sat on the floor together, pushing a pile of books and clothes to one side.

"Let's get undressed again," Nick whispered.

"I want to wait a while," Andy replied. "I think I know what present I want to give you."

He stood up briefly and went to a writing desk standing against the wall underneath Bobby Darin and the Victorian painting. He opened the lid and brought out something so small that Nick could not see what it was. Returning to his place on the floor, he asked Nick to close his eyes.

"Is this a game?" Nick asked.

"No," Andy said. "Now close them tight. No peeping."

Nick did as he was told and felt a piece of material with something hard in it being pressed into his hand. The material was so thick he couldn't make out what the object was.

"I give you three guesses," Andy said, "but I still want you to keep your eyes closed."

"Now you are making it a game," Nick replied.

"Okay, so I've changed my mind. A birthday should be fun."

"Is it a stone?"

"No," Andy laughed.

"Alright, second guess. I feel that it's small, but I can't make out the shape. The material is really hiding its form."

"That's not a second answer."

"Is it something I can wear? Like round my neck? A pendant?"

"No again."

"I give up."

"One more try."

Nick tried again to feel what it was, then blurted out, "I've got it. It's a very small frame with a picture in it. Maybe a passport photo of you that you like and have kept."

"That's a wild guess," Andy said. "You'd better open your eyes and look. It was a very romantic last guess though and I like the thought that no frame is as small as this."

Nick opened his eyes. He looked down at the blue material, silky to the touch but as thick as velvet.

"It's part of an old curtain," he exclaimed.

"Go on, open it. It comes from the heart, this."

Nick unwrapped the folds and at last saw what it was—a simple key, attached to a key ring with the number of the house written on it.

"For me?" he asked, and looked at the key in some sort of wonder. He felt light inside, all darkness gone. The hard experience of the first half of the day seemed to evaporate.

"It's like I'm holding the key to Aladdin's cave," he said.

"You really are a big romantic, aren't you? But it makes me happy you are. And if you are wondering why there is only one key, it's because I never lock the door to my room. The people upstairs are like us, and very friendly. I know them well. One is older than the other. He is a writer and the younger one wants to become an architect. They have dreams, and I love them for it, and above all, I totally trust them. I wouldn't dream of locking the door."

"But what of the landlord?" Nick queried, afraid that he was getting a bit too realistic, and slightly tarnishing the dream of what was happening.

"The older man is my landlord. This is his house. His name is Oliver and his friend's name is Frank."

"I don't know what to say," Nick said. "I want to cry and laugh at the same time. It feels wonderful to be so wanted by you."

"I'd like you to stay the night," Andy said.

Nick thought of his mother and the cross examination she would give him if he returned home in the morning to change for work. It didn't matter what he wore to work in the bookshop, but if he didn't turn up until the following evening his mother would think he had gone missing and would probably do something stupid like ringing up the police.

"I can't tonight," he said, hating saying it. He felt like a dependent child again, and was ashamed that that same idea might enter Andy's head.

"Then come back tomorrow evening," Andy added. "I'll make you a real meal then."

"Shall I ring the bell or use the key?" Nick asked cheekily, feeling happy again.

"The key of course. Just give me a moment's warning, by knocking on the door of my room."

Then they played around a little, and Nick thought of two squirrels he had seen in St Ann's Well Gardens chasing each other about. It made him laugh even more, and Andy, tickling him on the bed, only made him laugh even louder. The play was followed by yet more undressing, but this time Andy insisted their love making consisted only of kissing and exploring each other with their fingers, and finally masturbation. At around one in the morning, Nick said that he really must go.

"I have to get up for work as well," Andy said, "I'm an accountant remember? I wear a suit every day which I hate, and usually get thoroughly bored around mid-afternoon. I'm a grouch when I get back here, so I put on either *Splish Splash* or *Dream Lover* and lie on the bed dreaming." He sighed. "But if you were here, I wouldn't have to dream, would I? You'd still get the music though. Can you bear it?"

Nick grinned, and said he was already longing to bear it.

They kissed on the doorstep and Nick walked away from George Street, knowing that a definite turning had taken place in his life. His sixteenth birthday wish, for him and Andy to be happy together, had been granted when Andy gave him the key and an unspoken promise of its endurance. As he crossed the Old Steine the town was totally quiet around him and for the rest of the way back to his house he hardly saw anyone. This gave him time to think more clearly. He decided with surprising boldness to tell his mother that he had found himself a flat, or a room that was cheap, and that he wished to leave home. He wasn't sure if Andy had meant this, but he hoped he had and he clutched the key in his hand in his trouser pocket, making another wish for that to be the case. Then the thought struck him that they hadn't mentioned Martin once all evening.

"Well I guess it doesn't matter any more," he said to himself as he reached the red house, but a fleeting image of Greg passed through his mind as he closed the front door behind him. He tried to dismiss this intrusion and told it not to return, then went into his room and went straight to bed.

NINE

Nick's mother gave him the silent treatment the following morning. She was dressed and made up, looking as if she was ready to go out herself, and passed him without a word as he met her in the hallway on his way to the bathroom.

"Good morning, mother," he said, but she closed the living room door behind her: a sign he knew all too well meant she did not want to be disturbed. He shrugged his shoulders, pretending he didn't care, but all day at the shop he felt a dread of returning home that evening and telling her that he was going out again.

"You are the silent one," a familiar customer said to him as she handed over a pile of romantic novels.

He smiled and replied that he had a bit of a toothache and she clucked over him, "You go to the dentist before it gets any worse, but don't let them give you any of that awful gas."

"Surely that's just for extractions," he replied, putting the books into a large bag.

"Well, some dentists can't be trusted. I go to Mr Malcolm. He's in the book and very good. I had a filling and it didn't hurt a bit. Try him if you are unhappy with your own."

To prove that her dentist had done a good job, she leant over the counter and opening her mouth wide, showed him a long row of very uneven top teeth. She pointed at one that looked whiter than the others.

"He brushed it up nice," she added. "Spent a great deal of time and attention on me, and that's rare."

He smiled his approval and handed over her change for the pound she had given. The books had been no more than sixpence each and had titles like, *Last Year's Passion* by Victoria Holding, whoever she was.

"I hope you enjoy them," he said, hating himself for his hypocrisy. He also hated the thought that he was becoming a snob. Then he noticed in the pile, a book called *Intimacy* by

Jean-Paul Sartre and knew yet again that quality had slipped through Alfred's hands. He supposed that just knowing a Jean-Paul Sartre book was worth more made him a snob. Then he recalled a book called *Iron in the Soul* by Sartre which he had read in the shop a few weeks back. It had a homosexual relationship in it, and he had thought the book was well written.

"Is your mind wandering, dear?"

He looked at her, surprised that she was still in the shop.

"Oh, I'm sorry Mrs Langdon. I guess I was miles away."

"Somewhere nice, I hope," she said, patting his hand, then adding, "Cheerio," before leaving the shop.

He looked at his watch. Time was dragging. He had four more hours to go. He attempted to read and then, giving up on that, dusted the same books he had dusted two days before. He even spent time carefully aligning all the books on the shelves. Finally, a little exhausted with the work he had done but grateful for the exercise, he made himself a cup of tea. Then there was just one more hour to go. Soon he would be with Andy, after another bout of silent treatment from his mother.

He closed the shop promptly at five-thirty and caught a bus home. His mother, unlike that morning, was fully vocal when he opened the door.

"I've got news for you," she said crisply, before he had time to say anything. It was his turn to be silent now, and he waited. He was about to go into his room when she caught him by the arm. "I rang your father today," she exclaimed, her voice rising to anger pitch.

"Why?" he asked.

"You'll see when he arrives tomorrow. He'll be waiting outside your shop when it closes. He wants to talk to you."

"You mean you want him to talk to me?"

She glared at him and released his arm.

"Wait 'til tomorrow," she replied ominously, then went into the living room where he followed her.

"Mother, I don't want another row with you," he said. "I just want you to be honest with me. Why did you ring my father?"

"He won't be coming here," she said, evading the question. "I made sure it's strictly between you and him. He knows more about the subject than I do. And anyway, I don't want to see him."

"What subject?"

"I asked Mrs Granger upstairs about it," she replied. "We went out for a bit of lunch."

"But I thought you didn't like her?"

"That's not the point. She's proving to be both considerate and kind, and she listens to me. She's also very intelligent, which I hadn't realised before."

Nick was now beginning to feel really angry.

"What bloody subject are you talking about?" he shouted.

"Need I tell you?" she snapped back. "And don't you dare use bad language to me now after all the disgusting words I had to read in that filth I found under your bed." He realised at once and his face became red. She noticed this and remarked, "You might as well turn red—red with shame no doubt. To think they publish such dirt."

"I have very few books under my bed," he said quietly, trying to restrain his anger and to gather his forces for a defence.

"Few they may be, but you have them and you hid them. *The City and the Pillar* indeed! Dirty books hiding behind respectable covers. There is nothing more despicable."

They were standing facing each other in the centre of the room and Nick asked her if she wouldn't be better sitting down.

"I will sit down when I want to," she replied, sounding like Gladys Cooper in a play he had seen with her at the Theatre Royal.

"Okay," he said, "we will talk standing."

"I suppose that bookshop you work for provided you with

them?" she said.

"No, mother," he replied, lying. "I bought them from a bookshop in the Lanes. You would call it a very respectable shop, and there are no dirty words in *The City and the Pillar*."

"You don't need four letter words to make words dirty," she said, and passed a hand across her face, as if wiping away a tear, which she did not have.

"So now you know," he said flatly.

"That you read books about pansies? Yes, I know that. I glanced at the others too. The disgusting dialogue. To my horror I even saw that a woman was responsible for one of them."

"Mary Renault," he replied.

"Whoever," she said, then resumed her attack. "The rest of course were men—*The Heart in Exile* with that pretty boy on the cover. In the theatre in my day, horrible old men used to like pretty boys. I could tell you something about what I saw then."

"Why are you contradicting yourself?" he asked. "Why do you need my father to talk about a subject you seem so familiar with? I only wish we could sit down sensibly and talk seriously about this. And when you were in the theatre, was a long time ago."

"I wouldn't soil my mouth talking about those days," she replied, "or those perverted men."

He wanted to reply that she had already soiled her mouth, but he erred on the side of diplomacy.

"Look, mother, why can't we talk about this decently, without anger or outrage?"

"You are sixteen years old and you are reading criminal books. That is why your father is needed. He may even be familiar with them himself."

"That is uncalled for," Nick replied, and turned his back on her.

"Turn around at once," she ordered, "and look at me when I am talking to you."

He obeyed her reluctantly, but stared down at the carpet. He counted the number of whirls in the design as he did so.

"Well?" she said.

"Well, what?"

"Are you or aren't you? Is this simply adolescent curiosity with filth or is it real?"

He paused before answering, counting again the whirls that now appeared to take on dragon form, then slowly he raised his eyes and looked at her.

"What do you want to hear?" he asked.

"The truth. Are you a nancy-boy or aren't you? It's a simple enough question."

He laughed at this, and she shouted at him to not laugh in her face.

"I'm laughing at the words you use," he replied, and suddenly he felt very strong and stared hard at her. He noticed her lips were trembling.

"If you want to know if I am homosexual, then yes is the answer. I have known for years."

"How could you?" she cried out. "You were a child, an innocent child."

"Oh, please, mother, I reached puberty by the age of eleven. But you're right about one thing. I was as you say innocent, until—" and here he stopped.

"Until what?" she demanded.

"Until I was ready for it. Until I saw with my own eyes, someone that I desired."

"Filth. More filth."

She gave in and sat down heavily in her chair. "I would like a glass of water," she said, and he noticed this was said with just an edge of drama in it. He went into the kitchen, poured out a glassful of water for the tragedy queen she had become and took it back to her. He felt he needed one himself, but did not want to be distracted from what they were saying. He hoped that at last it might be sensible, but first he had to cut through the fake melodrama.

"It may be dirty in your mind," he said, "but it is not in mine and I have had a long time to think about it."

"Influenced by those books." She glared at him after drinking the water.

"No, mother, you are wrong. I only read the books after I already knew I desired boys. I wanted to understand more about what I was."

"This is more than one can bear," she whispered. "You are even making a case for this perversity."

"It is society that makes it a crime and a perversity," he replied.

"Nonsense. The Bible is wrong too I suppose, even if we forget, and I certainly can't, the laws of the land."

He remained silent at this. She suddenly looked again as if she was on the Theatre Royal stage.

"Ah," she said with a cold smile, "I can tell by your silence that you may at last agree with me. Try to be loquacious about that!"

He disregarded the pretentious word of the last sentence and replied simply, "I desire other boys of my own age, and some a little older. I am like any other boy of my age, except that they look at girls. There is nothing more to it than that."

"Isn't there?" she said with a sneer. "And I suppose you can settle down and marry one of these boys and have children with them? You can be normal like everyone else and not have the police sniffing around you, watching your every step? Do you think it makes me happy to imagine you could end up in prison?"

"Love is love," he replied simply. He was now tired and wanted the discussion to be over.

"Love! What does a boy of sixteen know of love? I barely believe in it myself. If love is the degradation and the disgust I have witnessed in my life, then it had better change its name."

"That sounds hard, mother. I am sorry."

"Sorry?"

She looked at him as if he had lost his mind.

"You are sorry for me? Shouldn't it be the other way around? Haven't you twisted things slightly to say the least?"

He faced her barrage and found there was little hope of him trying to explain or defend. She had hatred on her side and he could not fight that.

"I have nothing more to say, mother," he replied.

"Then neither do I. Let your father have his say."

He made a move towards the door and she told him to stop. He turned and faced her.

"What?"

"Those books. I want those books out of the house. I won't have them here."

"I will take them with me tonight," he replied.

"Oh, and where are you going?"

"To see a friend," he said.

"A queer like you?" she asked.

"Yes, mother, a queer like me. Now if you don't mind, I will get myself ready. I am already late."

"Put on some of my perfume while you're at it," she jeered. "The nancy-boys did it back then. I'm sure you still carry on the custom."

"Times have changed," he said as he opened the door.

"Quite the man, aren't we?"

He stared at her from the open doorway, her full hatred glaring at him in silent rage. He then closed the door and it was then that he allowed himself to cry.

Inside Andy's room, he took out the books and put them on the table. He had a small suitcase with him with a few extra clothes in it. He told Andy what had happened with his mother.

"This means you must stay here," Andy said.

"Are you sure, Andy? I mean, I know I brought the suitcase, but I didn't dare to presume—"

"Of course I am sure."

"She's in a pretty angry state, but she hasn't shown it fully yet. And then there's my father. He's meeting me after work tomorrow."

"Calm down. Face that tomorrow."

Nick didn't dare ask what would happen if his mother went to the police, but he knew her, she wouldn't. She may have looked at him with hatred, but she would not go to the police. And yet, the doubt lingered in his mind, and he didn't want to put Andy at risk. He was sixteen, and soon Andy would be twenty. Suddenly he felt more afraid for Andy than he did for himself.

"It's a risk for you," he said at last. "I'm not sure I can allow that. I had better go back."

"I want you to stay," Andy replied firmly. "It's right that you should. Not many mothers would betray their own children. But anyway, I've made up my mind. You have to get away from that atmosphere."

There was a knock on the door and Nick looked startled.

"It's only Oliver from upstairs," Andy said. "I'm proud of what you've done. Just believe that and behave normally. Nothing nasty is going to happen."

Nick would have taken Andy in his arms if the knock hadn't been repeated.

"Come in," Andy called out. Then he looked at Nick and smiled. "You'll like Oliver," he said.

Oliver was tall and in his early forties. His hair was slightly grey, but he had a youthful face and his brown eyes had an immediate look of warmth. He looked as if he liked people and instinctively Nick liked him. He was dressed casually in brown corduroy trousers and was wearing a light brown jacket. Nick thought he looked 'artistic' whatever that dreaded word meant, and his overall look seemed to come from about two decades before.

"Hello," said Oliver and reached out with a big broad hand to shake Nick's. "I'm Oliver, but you know that already, and I already know you must be Nick."

Andy laughed, winked at Nick, and told Oliver that he mustn't make Nick blush. He then added that he liked to see Nick blush as it turned him on, and Nick on hearing him say that, promptly blushed. Oliver sat down at the table and asked if there was a cup of tea to be had.

"I'll go to the kitchen and make a pot for the three of us," Andy said.

Alone with Oliver, Nick felt momentarily awkward, but Oliver looked at him so kindly that the feeling did not last.

"I'm glad you two have met," Oliver said. "Andy's one of the nicest guys in Brighton and, if I may say so, you seem to be a nice guy yourself, and I'm not talking about the way you look. It's a feeling I have. It's called intuition. Most people don't seem to know what the hell it means."

"I do," said Nick.

"You look as if you do. And by the look of the small suitcase over there, it appears you have come to join us."

"I hope you don't mind?" Nick queried.

"God, no. I hope you're happy here. Andy tells me you work in a bookshop?"

"Yes, but it's a bit of a jumble. There are some good books in the shop though."

"Do you read a lot?"

"I do now. I'm also trying to write. I make notes, sometimes in the shop. Poetry attracts me, but I haven't told anybody about it. I have a volume of 1940s poems behind the counter. I like David Gascoyne's *The Vagrant* best."

Nick was suddenly surprised at what he had said. He had not as yet formulated this quite so clearly either to himself or anyone else.

"I know it," Oliver said, and then quoted a couple of lines.

The city's lack and mine are much the same. What, oh what can
A vagrant hope to find to take the place of what once was
Our expectation of the Human City, in which each man might
Morning and evening, every day, lead his own life, and Man's?

"Beautiful," he added, "and what a hope."

"Yes," Nick murmured, and looked away.

"You seem a bit troubled. Is it your parents?"

"Yes, did Andy tell you?"

"No, I can feel it. I can see the sadness in your eyes. At your young age it usually means family. Do they know?"

"I told my mother earlier on this evening."

Oliver smiled at him and asked, "Do you want to talk about it?"

"I think it's a relief I told her, but I'm afraid. I don't want to risk anything that might hurt Andy."

"Andy can take the risk," Oliver replied. "He's made like that, and I sense you are as well. We need more people like you two in the world."

"I'm glad you said that," Nick said, now looking openly at Oliver's kind eyes. "I believe truth is best. I couldn't lie about it. I used to tell what are called white lies—but I was a kid then."

"Catholic?" Oliver asked.

"Yes, does that show as well?"

"I must admit I don't like organised religion, but the Catholics for all their prejudices seem to really hold to their beliefs. The trouble is they don't like us homosexuals."

"I know," Nick said.

"Well, Catholic or not, I am sure you are strong enough to stand up to them."

Andy came into the room, precariously holding a tray balanced on one hand with a pot of tea, some cups and a packet of biscuits. Nick jumped up and immediately took the tray from him and placed it on the table.

"What are you planning to be?" Oliver laughed, staring at Andy. "A waiter?"

"Don't laugh. I nearly tripped in the hallway with it, and it's your best cups."

Nick looked at the cups. They were on saucers, and they were beautifully decorated in bright colours and jazzy designs.

"Real thirties," Oliver said. "Like everything else in the house, bought in a junkshop. I hope you don't mind Nick that we are all more or less poor here?"

Nick smiled and Andy poured out the tea. There was silence for a while as they drank and ate some of the biscuits.

"I hope this is not your only meal for tonight," Oliver said.

"No, got something special for Nick and I," Andy replied. "It's a delayed birthday meal."

"May I ask how old you are Nick?" Oliver asked.

"Sixteen."

"You look older. And that's a compliment. To think I am old enough to be your father!" Oliver then turned to Andy, adding, "I'm old enough to be yours as well."

"I know, daddy," Andy replied laughing. Then the conversation changed and once again, Nick felt relief that there was such a simple acceptance of his age. They, Oliver and Andy, talked about the 'scene' and what they liked and disliked about it. Nick listened, but his mind wasn't taking much of it in. He was thinking about his father the next day and what his actual daddy was going to say to him. He dreaded emotional blackmail.

"You seem far away," Andy observed.

"Sorry," Nick said, and hurriedly took another biscuit.

"Can I propose something?" Oliver asked. He looked at both of them in turn and continued, "There's a drinks party the night after tomorrow. I'm not exactly in their club, but they've invited me along plus a couple of friends. I think you are an ideal couple of friends, so why not come with me? They'll be mainly rich folk and they'll talk like the rich do of course, but there may be one or two interesting people there. My lover, Frank, won't come. He knows some of them—a few who are on the council—and he hates the plans they have for developing this town and doesn't want to spend the evening arguing."

"Doesn't sound your sort of thing either," Andy said.

"I know, but they've heard I've got a book coming out." Oliver turned to Nick and explained, "It's a book of short stories—about this town. They're probably hoping for some gossip or secret revelations, but I'm afraid they'll be bitterly disappointed if they get to read it. They won't of course. Theirs isn't a crowd that reads. But I now have the slightest touch of celebrity, and they want to be in on it.

"Patronising bastards," Andy murmured.

"Come, come Andy. Don't be so young and harsh. Let's just go along and have a few free drinks, and maybe, if we're lucky, some caviar. Who knows? After all, they don't know as yet that I haven't written the Brighton equivalent of *Goodbye to Berlin*."

"What's that?" Nick asked, genuinely curious.

"An author to read, Nick. Christopher Isherwood. Stories about Berlin just before and after Hitler came to power in the early thirties."

"I'll hunt it down," Nick replied.

"No need. Got it upstairs. Read it any time you like. Now I really must get back. Frank is working on a drawing for some building he would like to see made. He'd have come down, but I told him it would be a bombardment for Nick here."

"I'd like to meet him," Nick said.

Oliver laughed and said he would soon, but that Frank was reclusive and had a habit of staying away even from people he liked. Then he got up and going to the door, turned and said, "Can I count on you two for the drinks party?"

"We'll be there," Andy said, then looked at Nick who nodded his head.

"Goodnight, you two," and Oliver was gone.

"I like him," Nick said.

"I'm glad. He's my best friend. I knew you'd have a lot in common. He even tolerates my love for playing *Splish Splash* and Duane Eddy really loud."

A few moments later they were on the bed and Andy gently ordered Nick to lie back so that he could take off his clothes.

"With the lights full on?"

"The brighter the better. I want to see every detail, every part of you. The whole landscape of you under the artificial sun hanging from the ceiling."

Nick lay back, and his body ached with the pleasure of being so lovingly wanted.

The following afternoon his father met him outside the bookshop. It was only when they were inside a tea shop in Imperial Arcade that Nick asked him what he thought of his place of work.

"I'm sure there are better bookshops, but it's a good job for you and you seem to like it there. It's not quite the Sodom and Gomorrah that your mother thinks it is." He looked at Nick and his smile was weary. "But that's not why I'm down here, is it?"

A waitress interrupted them, prim in her black and white uniform, and his father placed their order.

"Tea for two and a nice plate of cakes please." He smiled up at the young woman, but she just noted the order down and didn't smile back. "Not very friendly here, are they Nick? I've been here a few times with your mother. A bit snooty."

Nick tried to laugh, but his throat felt tight. He had no idea how to open up the conversation with his father.

"You look shy, Nick, as if you are ashamed of something. Has your mother already told you why she asked me to see you?"

Nick nodded his head in silence.

"Well, are those books as dirty as they are supposed to be?" he asked. The words came out thinly, as if not wanting to really be heard. Nick felt a surge of courage and replied to his question.

"What do you think, father? Do I look as if I have filth under my bed?"

"No, you don't."

234

"They are just books on a certain subject. That's all. Mother was even surprised that a woman wrote one of them."

His father tried to smile, but failed. Then the waitress was back and busy laying out the things on the table. The creamy meringues and fluffy pastries made Nick feel a little sick as he looked down at them. His father poured the tea.

"You look pale," he said as he did it. "Drink this first before we go on talking."

Nick drank down a cup of tea quickly and his father poured him another.

"I suppose you don't feel like one of those cakes?"

"No, father, I don't."

"Neither do I. They look as false as the rest of this ghastly town—all frills and no real substance. No plain Bath buns here."

Nick had to smile at this and suddenly the tension was gone.

"I don't think I could even face a slice of Battenberg," he said.

"Well, Nick, I'm not exactly a firing squad you know. This isn't supposed to be a last meal."

"Anyway, as I was saying father, she was shocked that a woman could lower herself to write on the subject."

"Your mother would find something shocking in Jane Austen if she was bothered enough to read her." He paused. "I guess we're not talking about an imported edition of *Lady Chatterley's Lover*? Why don't you tell me what these books are all about?"

Nick watched as his father raised his cup of tea to his mouth. He saw that his hand was shaking slightly.

"They are about love," he said simply.

His father lowered his cup.

"You mean a certain kind of love that your mother doesn't understand, don't you?" he responded.

Nick nodded his head again.

"I don't want to use the word for it, father. I don't know

235

why. It's not shame, but there is no word that fully encompasses it; that doesn't make it sound either medical or sordid."

"If it helps, Nick, I read a book a few decades ago. It too was imported from France. I can't quite remember who leant it to me. A woman friend I think, but that's not the point. It was called *The Well of Loneliness*. I opened it with, well, the distaste that I had been taught to feel and closed it, finally with a feeling of sadness. It was a sad book and I felt not disgust, but pity for the main character. She was very unhappy at the end of the book. I don't want you to feel that unhappy."

Nick felt relief that his father had made it easy on him. He had not read this book, but he had heard of it. One day an elderly woman had come into the shop and asked for it. She said she had lost her copy and had missed it. The book came in a few weeks later and he read some of the pages, but put the book down and did not return to it. It was not that the subject of lesbianism didn't interest him, but the heavy style of the writing. Snobbery about the writing had made him turn away from a book that had moved even his father.

"I haven't really read it," he said. "I only glanced at a few pages. Eventually it was bought by a woman who had lost her copy. She was very happy to find it again."

"And the books under the bed? Are they more explicit than *The Well of Loneliness*?"

Nick paused and a particularly harsh meringue with a cherry on top of it seemed to stare up at him, daring him to answer.

"Yes, in a way they are. They were published later than *The Well of Loneliness*, but all of them in this country, and without any sort of prosecution."

"I know the issue is being discussed now," his father said. "The Wolfenden Report and all that. I don't want these people to be treated like criminals either."

For a moment, Nick was stung by the words *these people*. It must have shown on his face because his father said hurriedly, "I didn't mean to offend you in any way." His voice was gentle and Nick smiled back at him.

"You know I am one of those people, don't you father? One of *them*, as the crude press puts it."

His father placed his hands on the table. He looked down at them with a sort of wondering look. Nick had no idea what he was thinking.

"You've chosen, or it has chosen for you, a dangerous life. I wish it wasn't so, but I know that it is true. It will demand a lot of courage from you."

"Then you don't condemn me?"

Father and son looked at each other. A silent understanding seemed to pass between them. Nick realised that there was no hatred there and that he had nothing to fear from him.

"Of course I don't," but his father's hands trembled as he said the words. He was feeling pain, and Nick could see that.

"But you are disappointed, aren't you?" he asked.

"That you may not have children? Yes. That you may not grow out of this? Yes. Somehow, I don't think you will. I sense it has been inside you since you were born. I don't know why. And I'm not going to be a crackpot and give out any theories about it. Only fools go down that road."

"Thank you," Nick said.

"But the essential thing is, do you believe you will find happiness in it? I know happiness is in short supply in this world, but I can't expect you to live a life of misery because the world is not yet ready to accept you."

"I hope the times will change," Nick replied and then drank some more tea. Then he got up and said, "Excuse me, father, I must go to the toilet."

"Yes, of course. You know where it is. Must be the nerves. I get it too."

Inside the toilet, Nick held his head in his hands. His head was now pounding with pressure. He felt sadness for his father and the quandary he was now in. How was the situation with his mother to be resolved? And what if it could not be resolved? He washed his face with cold water, then realised that he did indeed have an urgent desire to pee. He took his usual long time, and wondered about the small part of his body that he held in his hand, and how much it inspired desire as well as needing that desire. It suddenly seemed an urgent mystery all of its own that needed answering, but he had no answers. He put the fragile thing back into his trousers and went back to face his father.

"What am I going to do about mother?" he asked as he sat down at the table. "She has been very ugly about all this."

His father sighed and looked down at the cakes.

"Have you any ideas?" he asked, looking up at his son.

"I'd like to move out if I have your permission."

"Do you have a suitable place to go?"

"I have a friend. His name is Andy. He's not much older than me and he cares for me, father, he really does."

For the first time, his father looked embarrassed, as if he could accept the fact of Nick's nature, but not quite yet the practice of it.

"Is it, I mean, is *he* important to you?"

"Yes."

"I see."

Suddenly his father reached for one of the dullest cakes on the plate and, with a fork, tore a piece out of it. He then dangled it on the edge of his fork, brought it to his mouth, then put it down again.

"When do you want to move in with him?"

His looked at his son and the expression on his face was so tired that Nick wanted to reach out and touch his hand. Only an instinct of reticence prevented him. Touching another man's hand, even his own father's, appeared to be a new and dangerous thing to do.

"I took a suitcase there last night. I had to. Mother was so abusive. I couldn't stand it any longer."

"That bad was it?" His father's voice sounded bitter. "I know what she sounds like when she's like that. I left her too."

"There's room in Andy's house for me. The house is very pleasant. Simple and no frills."

"You must pay your way though," his father replied, his voice practical. "I will find the necessary. Give me the address and I will see you get what you need each week."

"And mother?"

"I'll deal with her. She won't add to your troubles. I have some control over her, even now."

Nick sensed a rather sinister tone and looked at his father questioningly.

"I pay her rent. She'll want to stay on in this town. As for her illness, we'll see about that when the time comes if she gets really bad. She can't hold that as a gun to your head, but she'll try."

"I don't want her hurt, father," Nick said.

"Don't be too generous, son. You've other things to think about. As for this friend of yours, I hope he is good for you and kind. You need that. Can I ask what he does for a living?"

"He is an accountant with a firm here in Brighton."

"Good. Something sensible. He's obviously got his head on his shoulders."

They smiled at each other, and at last his father put the dull piece of cake in his mouth. They parted with a handshake after Nick had given him the address, and they had agreed an amount for the rent that Andy might need.

"Ring me if there are any problems," his father said. "I'll walk to the station by myself. It's not far and I want to think. But above all, you, you must take care of yourself and remember the dangers with the pleasures. It's hard to think about, but you must."

Nick nodded his head in silence, and with a warm sounding goodbye, his father left the tea shop and the arcade.

Mrs Granger was with his mother when he got home that evening.

"Did you meet your father?"

She stood there, with Mrs Granger behind her. Both were dressed up and made up, their faces, it seemed, competing for rouge and powder. Mrs Granger had a black sort of lipstick which revolted Nick and his mother's mouth was its usual slash of red. He stared at both of them in silence. They seemed like a wall of opposition against him.

"Well?" his mother asked.

"I saw him," he replied, as politely as he could.

Mrs Granger was staring at him as fiercely as his mother. He sensed she knew the whole story.

"And?"

"And I'm leaving here tonight, mother. He has given me his permission. He was quite calm and reasonable about the whole thing."

"Do you want me to go?" Mrs Granger asked. Her voice was high-pitched and seemed to squawk.

"No," his mother replied, hurrying to her new friend, and then asking her to sit down and to listen in to this 'nonsense'.

"Mother, I don't want to row with you, especially not in front of a stranger."

"Your mother and I have met before," Mrs Granger said as she sat herself down on the sofa. She then lit a cigarette and looked quite at home there. His mother meanwhile was slowly pacing the room; slowly as if she was yet again on a stage. Nick thought how young she looked suddenly and how pleased. He wondered if she felt that once more she had a captive audience.

"You may have met my mother, but I can't remember meeting you," Nick replied. "When did *we* exactly meet, Mrs Granger? I really can't remember."

"Don't be rude," his mother said.

Nick made a move to go to the door. He was only just inside the living room, but wanted to pack his other suitcase, his big suitcase, so that he could take almost all his things.

"Where are you going?"

"To my room, mother. I have things to do."

"I want to hear in detail what your father said."

"Then ring him, mother. He'll tell you himself. I am tired of explaining."

"You shouldn't talk to your mother like that," Mrs Granger piped up. "She loves you and is frightened of what you're getting into. Any decent mother would feel the same, and you are only just sixteen."

"Thank you," his mother said, turning to her with a smile.

Nick stood there looking at them and remained silent. He wanted to tell Mrs Granger to mind her own business, but he no longer cared if she thought it was her business. He just wanted to be free of the situation.

"I suppose you think you are very adult, insulting me in front of Mrs Granger," his mother said facing him, her face a mask, trying to hide her anger.

"No, I'm not proud of anything, mother. I just want to pack my big suitcase and move to where I am really wanted."

"The same *queer* friend?" his mother asked.

"Yes, and my father knows all about it."

"And he understands?"

"He loves me, mother. He will support me and, I hope, stand by me whatever happens."

Mrs Granger let out a small laugh. Nick looked at her and sought her eye and she looked away.

"Yes, it is laughable, Anne," his mother said, clearly now on very intimate terms with her neighbour from upstairs. "He thinks his father has the last word, but I am equal to him. I know the man I married. No doubt he was as shameful as Nick is being now when he was young. Maybe they have something in common that I know nothing about."

"How can you say that?" Nick cried out. "What do you really know about him, or about his inner self? He is suffering because of me, but he doesn't want me to suffer because of that. He is good, mother. Have you never known that side of him?"

Mrs Granger shifted uneasily on the sofa and his mother went and sat beside her. As she did so, Mrs Granger reached out and patted her hand in a visible show of sympathy.

"Let him go," she said.

Nick looked at his mother and she looked at him.

"I don't want you to be one of them, Nick, don't you understand?" she said. "I cannot believe your father would be so calm about the dreadful life you are contemplating. It is not only a sin, it is unhealthy and repulsive and goes against everything that is natural. How can I accept that? I gave birth to you."

Nick thought he was listening to a speech from a play. It was delivered with smart clarity and quiet force and almost demanded applause. She was playing to the house.

"You know nothing about sex or love between men, mother."

She got up then and the stage act was gone. She came over to him and slapped him across the face. It was a strong slap and his face stung.

"I know nothing about the dirt of life, no. I know nothing about the dirty acts of disgust that take place between people of your kind. I never want to know the details, ever. I forbid you to use those words again in this house. Sex between men!"

"I wasn't exactly giving descriptions, mother. We do more or less the same things that you do." He looked at her coldly, up close to her. "Would you prefer me to use the words of the gutter? I know them, mother. Shit-pusher. Shirt-lifter. Pansy. Bugger. Don't you think the simple word homosexual is better than that?"

"Shut up, Nick."

"Please stop this," Mrs Granger said in the background, also standing.

"I have used all the filthiest words I can think of, mother. Personally I would still prefer to call it the physical loving of men for other men."

242

She tried to slap him again but this time he caught her wrist and gripped it hard.

"Don't try to show your power over me, mother. I might just hit you back."

She wrenched her arm free and he saw tears in her eyes.

"Go away," she said. "But remember this, because I may choose to never see you again. I am the only mother you will ever have. I suffered when you were born and I looked after you all those years—years of difficulty while your father took no notice of how hard it was for me. Hard for me to do it alone and in bad health." She paused and the tears flowed. "I am the only mother you will ever have. One day when you are old you will remember this day with shame. You will suffer for it then. Suffer, when you are at last alone."

He could no longer bear any more of it and left the room. In a state of shock he quickly packed his suitcase, then without looking in on them, left the house. Once outside, he looked up at the red building and fought back the memories of all the years he had lived there: of the years when he had been a child.

He was exhausted when he reached George Street. Andy looked at him, seeing at once how upset he was. He put him to bed and lay down in the darkness with him for a long time. Then Nick fell asleep and there were no dreams.

He woke, surprisingly refreshed. Andy was asleep by his side with his back to him. He lay there for an hour, looking around the room, taking the measure of his new home. He felt that he wanted it always to be home to him, but as he thought that, an inner voice reminded him that this was but the first step of his new life, and that it would probably not last forever. He would eventually have to move on. Andy turned in his sleep and Nick reached out and tentatively touched him with his hand. He felt no sexual excitement, just a need to hold Andy close to him. This may not last forever, he thought, but I want to care for him for as long as I can. Then a feeling of sadness came over him: a light shadow covering the pleasure he felt lying there, temporarily, if nothing else, in a new place that appeared secure.

"You are awake," Andy said sleepily. "How do you feel?"

"Fine," Nick said.

Andy snuggled against him, and reaching up, caressed his face.

"This is our first morning together," he said, his voice still sleepy. Then his hand moved down the rest of Nick's body, and Nick, aroused, let him continue caressing him there. He wanted Andy, but he knew that it was already getting late and he had to open the shop.

"The shop," he murmured. "I've got to get ready for work. Don't you?"

"I'll be late for once," Andy replied.

"I have to go in," Nick said. "The shop will stay closed if I don't."

"But you were tired out last night. Ring the boss. Tell him you are unwell."

"I can't. I left his number at the house. I really do have to go in.'

Andy removed his hand from Nick's all too willing sex and sighed.

"I want you," he said.

"So do I, Andy."

"Then, please open the shop an hour later. Please?"

Nick laughed, and turning to Andy, moved on top of his body. They rubbed their bodies together until the feeling became too unbearably pleasurable, and Nick, moving slightly away, put his hand between Andy's legs and gently put a finger inside him. Andy moaned with such intensity that Nick pushed him over onto his stomach and this time, guided himself into Andy's open flesh. The climax for both of them was not long in arriving, and they both cried out so loudly that they looked at each other in embarrassment.

"Do you think Oliver and Frank heard?" Nick asked.

"I expect they are doing exactly the same thing," Andy replied, "but yes they probably did and they're probably having a good old chuckle about it."

"I mean, it was loud!"

"Operatic!" Andy replied, his face grinning with delight. "It will enhance their love-life no end. They won't be so quiet themselves from now on. Now I'm no longer alone, they don't have to be discreet for my sake. I imagine they hated being so tactful."

"Surely you weren't always alone?" Nick queried.

"Okay, well, there were occasions, but I wasn't ready for love then."

Nick got out of bed and stood by the side of it. Still erect, he looked down at Andy. He no longer felt embarrassed, but as Andy gazed up at him with obvious pleasure, he was happy that he was so wanted by his lover.

Andy said wistfully, "Why can't time stop?"

Nick moved away from the bed and the moment was broken. He hurriedly put on his clothes and said that he was going to the bathroom.

"Was I being too sentimental?" Andy asked, sitting up in bed. "About time stopping? Like some lyric from a corny pop song? Maybe just a bit of a cliché?"

"Clichés are true," Nick replied, opening the door. "The familiar words are the best. I like those songs as well. Especially *Dream Lover*," he added in a voice that almost broke into song.

"Go and wash," Andy said laughing and flung a pillow at him.

On his way to the bathroom, Nick met Oliver going to the kitchen.

"Did you have a good night's sleep?" Oliver asked.

"Yes, and now I must get ready for work."

"Are you sure? Andy came up to me briefly after you fell asleep. He said you looked worn out after what you had been through. I'm sure it would do you good to take it easy today."

Nick was grateful for everybody's concern, but was beginning to be slightly irritated by it. He felt in control of himself, clear in his mind about the previous evening, and ready to resume his daily ritual.

"Going into work will help me forget about last night," he replied, opening the bathroom door. Oliver smiled at him and went into the kitchen. Although Nick had not met Frank yet, he could hear his voice calling out that the toast and coffee were ready. Nick, realising that time was moving fast, closed the bathroom door and began to wash. As he was about to step into the bath, there was a brief, hard tap on the door.

"Yes?" he called out, half expecting Andy to join him.

"Just to remind you not to forget about the drinks tonight."

Nick smiled, recognising Oliver's voice.

"I won't forget," he called back before stepping into the hot water.

Nick was slightly nervous and subdued when they arrived at the front door of the house in Brunswick Square. Despite the fact that the square was in a state of disrepair, there were houses that retained their full grandeur. He had never previously entered one of them, nor did he know anyone who lived in one. As he passed through the spacious hallway, Nick glimpsed one of the biggest rooms he had ever seen. He blinked with astonishment at the many side lamps and the large glittering central chandelier.

"It looks like a fairy tale," he whispered to Andy without any sense of irony.

Oliver overhearing him said, "It *is* a fairy tale, Nick. The goblins from Whitehawk come down and clean at dawn."

They were then ushered into a small room, piled high with coats and hats, and someone (a servant?) murmured to them that they could put their 'extras' there.

"Is it safe to leave our things here?" asked Nick.

Andy laughed. "The wealthy don't bother to steal from each other."

"Oh, I wouldn't say that," replied Oliver, placing his rather threadbare duffel coat on top of a coat with a Savile Row label. "Those with light fingers are always on the lookout for an opportunity. And anyway, the rich *do* steal from each other. I knew a woman who—"

Andy interrupted. "Oliver, I've already heard that story and it takes a lot of telling. Let's go into that hideous chandelier room and face the music."

"But they're not playing any music," Nick commented, still somewhat bemused.

"It's an expression," Oliver explained.

The room was not particularly crowded and Nick and Andy were relieved to see there was enough of a social mix for them not to feel out of place.

"It looks like a gentleman's club with guests," Oliver said. "But I guarantee that after a while it will not be quite so gentlemanly. A few more drinks and the masks will start to fall."

As he finished saying this, a rather overbearing figure came up to them, tall and rather fat, and immediately shook Oliver's hand.

"Congratulations on the book," he said. "I haven't seen a copy yet, but it's on my reading list."

"Thank you Adrian," Oliver replied. Then silence fell on the group and the man drifted away.

"You've got one reader," Andy said.

Oliver laughed at this, and there was a note of bitterness in the sound. Then someone else came up to him and said more or less the same thing before he too passed gracefully on, gliding over the floor as if being pulled along on invisible wheels.

"Who was that one?" Nick asked.

"I think his name is Alan. We met at a reading in a London bookshop a while back. He made a pass at me and I declined, but not before he had told me in exhausting detail about a book he was writing—something about the aristocracy at the time of the French Revolution of all subjects! I think he was particularly sorry about Madame du Barry. Needless to say, he had absolutely no interest in my work."

"It all seems so brittle here," Nick said. "Hard."

"You've hit the nail on the head."

Oliver looked at him and smiled, and Nick found that he liked the smile a lot. Andy was standing to one side with a humorous look on his face. Clearly he was drawing his own conclusions about the scene in front of him. Nick, noting this, went up to him and touched him gently on the arm.

"What are you thinking about, staring at them all?" he asked.

"I'm not sure," Andy said, "I'm not sure they know who they are or why they're here. I don't think any of them are particularly happy."

Oliver overheard him and said, "Money often cushions you against self-knowledge. Maybe if the masks do fall, they will only reveal further masks."

"Would you like a drink?"

A man dressed like an Edwardian butler came up to them with a tray of drinks.

"I'm afraid I only have sherry," he added, "but there are other drinks near to the window. I can personally recommend the wines." Oliver took a glass of sherry and thanked him. Andy and Nick politely refused. Before moving on, the butler looked at Nick in particular and said in a very quiet voice, "There are soft drinks as well if the young gentleman would prefer."

Nick, startled, nodded his head, and Andy, noticing the look of surprise on his face, whispered, "You should be proud you're the youngest here. After all, you are the future!"

"Don't speak too soon about who is the youngest," Oliver added. "I can see someone who looks about twelve sitting next to the man against the wall on your right."

Nick turned and looked and saw Martin. He was seated on a plush sofa with a youth beside him. Above their heads was

248

an old portrait of a rather nasty looking man with a thin face and a beaky nose. He was dressed in Victorian clothes and had a cane in his left hand. It was raised as if he was on the point of striking someone. Both Oliver and Andy noticed as well.

"Is he going to come down and chastise us?" Andy asked.

"He may be one of the original owners of the house," Oliver added.

"I don't like him," Andy replied.

"His type is probably one of the reasons why Edward Carpenter wanted to leave Brunswick Square and move up North. This may even be the house where he lived out his early years."

"Who's Edward Carpenter?" Andy asked.

"A great man," Oliver replied. "I'll tell you about him another time. All you need to know is that he desired men like we do, but probably wouldn't have liked the look of this lot." Then Oliver turned to Nick who was still staring more at Martin than at the portrait and said to him, "I really didn't expect this lot to be quite so stereotyped. Carpenter knew we were not all like this. He would seem uncouth to them now if he was here. They would sense an enemy in their camp immediately—no pun intended."

Andy looked more closely to where Nick was staring and said softly, "It's Martin and he's not alone."

"I can see that," Nick replied.

As if by osmosis, Martin looked in their direction as Nick said that and, as the crowd was not particularly thick, he noticed Nick immediately. He got up from the sofa and came towards them.

"He's coming over," Andy said. "I'm sorry we came, Nick."

"Don't be. I'm not that surprised."

Nick held out his hand as Martin came up to him. Martin shook it briefly and gave a smirk which passed as a smile.

"I see you and Andy are an item," he said.

"Do we know you?" Oliver asked, turning to face Martin. He had been looking elsewhere and had no idea about the situation that was taking place.

"I know Nick very well," Martin said, "and young Andy here. I more or less introduced them, and now I see they are an affair."

"I'm not sure I understand," replied Oliver.

"You don't have to," Andy interjected. Then he turned to Martin and said coldly, "He's my lover if that's what you mean."

"Sorry, I thought the word 'affair' would be more appropriate." Martin looked at Nick and continued, "Wouldn't you consider the word affair more appropriate?"

Nick looked down at the floor and he too wished they had not come.

"I can see you are still shy," Martin persisted, "but you look older. That very young look with blushes no longer seems to suit you."

Nick glared up at him and clenched his hands at his sides in anger. Andy saw this and put a tentative hand on his arm. Oliver then took over.

"I don't know anything about what is happening, but I think I can guess. Martin, excuse me by calling you by your name as we have not been introduced, but I have the tiniest feeling you are trying to be rude or jealous or both."

Martin stared at Oliver with a look of disgust.

"And you are the chaperone, I presume?"

Oliver laughed loudly at this. So loudly, that a discreet group nearby turned round to stare.

"Jane Austen is alive and well!" Oliver said. Then he gently added to Martin, "Go back to your underage friend and leave us alone."

"Yes, please go," Nick said.

Martin mockingly bowed to them, looked at Nick and said, "You really must listen to the Adagio from Mahler's Ninth Symphony. I heard it recently and would have introduced you to it if you had still been with me. Very resigned music it is."

"What is he talking about?" Andy asked.

"Mahler," Martin replied. "I believe, Andy, if memory serves me right, that you don't respond to good music much, or am I remembering wrongly? Mahler is not for you, but he will be for Nick one day—one very sad day in the future, of that I am sure." Then he walked away, joining his young friend who immediately started plying him with questions.

"It looks as if the portrait did come down off the wall," Oliver said quietly.

"Do you want to go?" Andy asked Nick.

"No, it's alright. I'd like a drink though. A real one. Something strong."

"I'll see what they've got," Oliver said, moving away.

"Are you really alright?" Andy asked gently turning Nick round to face him. He could see that Nick looked upset by what had just happened and that he was trying his hardest not to collapse in his arms.

"I'll be fine. I'll show you how much in bed later when we are free of all this."

"Martin's not a good man," Andy said. "Really he isn't."

"I can't judge that," Nick replied. "I think he's very confused and sad about his life. Life, I believe, is being unkind to him."

"In what way?" Andy asked.

"From being grown up. He wants to be grown up, but it may be a little too difficult for him to achieve that."

"Well, you're grown-up. Far more than I am."

Nick looked to one side, and to Andy, he appeared deep in thought.

"I haven't heard any Mahler yet," Nick said as if he were talking to himself. "But one day I might, and I might recall what Martin said and understand why he said it."

This time, Andy could no longer resist and drew Nick into his arms. His kissed him passionately on the mouth, and Nick responded. An elderly couple passed by and tutted. Then, laughing quietly, Nick and Andy separated.

"We must be careful," Nick said ironically. "They may have some plain clothes policemen here. Some of the younger ones look as if they might be."

Another couple passed.

"Do you like animals, dear?" The voice was high-pitched and meant to be heard.

"No, darling," his partner replied, "but if I know any turkeys who want some more neck, I will tell them to come to you."

"You bitch!"

The couple floated away and Andy said, "At last the masks are falling."

"Here's your drink. A scotch and soda."

Oliver was by their side and handed a glass to Nick. "God, it was crowded by the drinks table. All the young ones have left their daddies to get drunk. It was quite a crush."

Nick drank his scotch and the three of them began to wander around the room. The noise had grown louder and the comments made were no longer said politely or discreetly. The place was beginning to resemble a bar.

"Well, well, I never thought I'd hear that," Oliver remarked about something he overheard. "The things these people get up to."

"Sorry," Nick said, "I need the toilet."

Andy noticed he looked a bit pale and pointed in the direction of the hallway. "I don't know the layout of the house," he said, "but I bet there is one down there somewhere."

Nick moved away from them, feeling giddy. He had drunk too fast and his nerves were also on edge. The meeting with Martin had destabilised him more than he had initially thought. He went into the discreetly lit corridor. There were quite a few doors. He opened one towards the end, hoping he had opened the right one, but he was wrong. There on a single bed in a narrow room, underneath an unexpectedly bright light two young men were fucking. Fascinated and repelled he stood in the entrance. The fucking continued. The two on the bed were half-dressed, with only their lower halves naked. The younger of the two was being penetrated from the side, and they both faced outwards. At first they were oblivious to Nick's presence. Then one of them looked up and attempted a smile on his contorted face.

"Look, we have company," he cried, and for a moment, they stopped what they were doing.

"Come on handsome," the other who was doing the fucking called out, "Timmy likes to be sucked off while he's getting fucked. Couldn't ask for a better threesome than with a cute kid like you."

"I'm sorry," Nick said, still standing at the open door.

"Close it," said the young man who was being fucked. "We don't need a crowd."

"I've got the wrong room."

Nick's head began to feel strange and he realised that he might be really drunk, but how that was possible on just one drink he didn't know. Then he shut the door and he was inside the room. He had needed to urinate, but now no longer did. Slowly he moved towards them, hating himself for feeling so attracted to what he saw. So this is how I look with Andy, he thought. This is how it is! Then the young man in front, who was now being penetrated with some force, reached out a hand and pulled Nick to him.

"Kiss me," he said.

"No, suck him. He's my boyfriend. He doesn't get kissed."

Nick knelt down by the bed. The fucked young man's penis was fiercely erect and throbbing with its need to be touched. Nick reached out with his hand and felt the wetness of it.

"Suck me. For fuck's sake, suck me."

Nick took the head in his mouth and closed his eyes. He felt as if he was about to pass out, but the force of desire was too strong. He took out his own penis and began to jerk it off.

"Suck me faster," the young man said, his voice almost pleading. "I want to come. I want to come before Alec does. Then I can really feel his cum inside me."

The words alone seemed to excite him and the youth promptly came. Nick took the semen down, swallowing it all, then felt sick and, jumping up, noticed a sink in the room. The room was spinning around him, but he made it there and tried to spit out what was left in his mouth. He heard a loud cry behind him as the active partner came, but Nick didn't turn round, feeling shame and sorrow at what he had done. He held on to the rim of the sink, realising that his trousers were open. He briefly looked down at his now flaccid penis and his sickness returned.

"Let's get out of here," he heard, and there was a rustling of clothes and then a quick slamming of the door. Nick was alone in the room. His immediate thought was how he could possibly go back and face the others. Then someone, whose room it possibly was, came in and said quietly, "Excuse me, I didn't know anyone was in here."

Nick turned and faced a youngish man.

"Did you feel unwell and want to lie down?" the stranger asked. Then he looked at Nick's open trousers and his eyes looked surprised. "Were you peeing in the sink?" he said.

Nick adjusted himself, brushed past him and hurried back down the corridor. He did not look for Andy and Oliver, but went over to where the strong drinks were. He saw the two young men who had been in the room standing there drinking.

"I think I owe you a drink for services rendered. You weren't bad," said the younger of the two with a wink.

Nick smiled weakly at him, said nothing and poured himself a drink from a bottle that was nearest to him.

"It's pink gin," the same young man murmured. "Do you want our telephone number? A kid like you could come in handy when we give parties at our place. We don't have to be so discreet there about liking threesomes."

"Sometimes more than three," his partner added.

Nick moved away and drank the gin in one go. It burned as it went down. Then Oliver was by his side.

"What happened?" he asked, his voice sounding alarmed. "If I may say so, you look awful. Were you sick?"

"Yes, I was sick," Nick repeated, suddenly sober and quite clear in the head. "And I'm sick of this bloody party."

"I suggest we go home where we belong," Oliver said.

"I agree," Andy added, having found and joined them. Then he looked at Nick and said, "That sodding Martin. Trust him to make you feel awful. It was him who made you sick, wasn't it?"

Nick stared at him as if he was suddenly a stranger.

"No," he replied, "it was me. I made myself sick."

Oliver and Andy looked at each other questioningly. They must have seemed like Nick's bodyguards as they led him out of the room and then on to the front door.

Outside, the night was cold.

What Nick saw that night in that room in Brunswick Square marked the end of his childhood. It was to him like having watched the ultimate 'Adults Only' film, and not only having watched it, but having participated in it also. Before he had gone into this cinema for one, he had dreams of finding the ideal partner and of sexual desire being in its ideal state an act of beauty. Instead of an act of beauty, he had seen two young men playing out a scenario of crude lust, only too willing to have not only witnesses, but people like Nick to add to their sport.

I wanted it too, he thought to himself over and over again, and I can't defend that wanting with the excuse of drink or of having had that encounter with Martin. I was drawn in by a parody of what I do with Andy, like looking in a distorted mirror on the pier, and I felt the same lust as those two men.

His work at the bookshop was affected and so was his relationship with Andy. He became moody and depressed, and his physical need for his lover became more desperate and frantic. He continued to take the active role, but in his mind he saw the two men and his erection would fail him. Andy at first pretended that nothing had changed, bringing himself to climax more quickly than usual, but Nick knew he was doing this to avoid making him feel guilty in any way. He never questioned Nick, but later they began to avoid penetration completely and started doing other things to satisfy themselves. Nick would lie back while Andy sucked his penis and Nick would use words to cover up the void that was opening up between them, and to maintain his erection. He used the words he had heard the young men use, and now he had brought these obscenities to their own bed.

TEN

Christmas came and both Andy and Frank went home to their respective families. Oliver and Nick were left alone in the house and it gave them time to get to know each other.

"Frank's family know," Oliver said, "but they would still rather not meet me. It used to hurt. Christmas can be a dreadful time to be alone, especially for people like us. It's all geared for families and silly gifts which no one ever really wants. I saw a film a few years ago, *The Holly and the Ivy*, it said it all."

Oliver and Nick were sitting in the kitchen and Oliver was looking gloomily at the stove.

"I don't cook very well," Oliver said.

Nick laughed and replied, "I can try. After all, what can go wrong with a chicken? I can do stuffing too. I used to do it for my mother when I was small. It was my main Christmas task, that and making paper chains."

Oliver got up from the table and prepared another pot of tea. He was laughing at Nick's description.

"I would have liked to have seen you do that."

"My mother used to hit me if I got it wrong."

"Did she?" Oliver said with a note of sadness in his voice. "Are you going to visit her this year?"

"I rang my father recently and asked him if I should. He said not to. A woman from upstairs in the house, Mrs Granger, is looking after her and more or less staying in the flat with her the whole time. Also my mother wrote to my father and said she didn't want to see me again."

"That will pass," Oliver said, returning with the tea.

"I'm not sure I want it to, Oliver. She already seems so distant to me."

"I have a feeling most people seem distant to you at the moment. Is it because of what you experienced at that party? If so, it has gone on for too long."

"Has Andy talked to you about our relationship?" Nick asked.

Oliver sat and faced him across the table. He looked tired himself.

"I love Andy very much," Oliver replied slowly, "and I think he is sad at the moment. That is all I know."

Nick remained silent and began to play with the teaspoon in his cup. For a minute or two neither of them seemed able to advance the conversation.

"Shall we go upstairs to the flat?" Oliver said. "It's more comfortable there, and I think I have some music you'll like. A small collection, but good. I think you are tense and music can ease tension."

Nick said he would like to do that, and carrying their cups, both of them went up the short flight of stairs to the small flat that Oliver and Frank occupied.

"The place is a total mess," Oliver said when they entered the living room. "What with my notes for my next book—if it ever happens—and Frank's designs for the perfect building, there is very little space to move."

In fact the room looked tidy to Nick. It was comfortable and lived-in. There were bookshelves full of books and some paintings on the walls. He thought of Martin's flat, but this was not in any way similar. The pictures were mainly landscapes, no doubt from antique shops, and next to these were framed designs of buildings. He went over and looked at the designs.

"*De Stijl*," Oliver said, "founded in 1917 in Leiden in Holland. That's the Rietveld Schröder House, and next to it is that impossible chair no one would dare to sit on today. I like the colours, and I can see the ideas were necessary to blow away the stuffy cobwebs, but I dread seeing lesser men and women trying to create similar buildings or objects. How long before we see some of that damage inflicted on Brighton?

"Too sterile?" Nick queried.

"Don't say that to Frank, but yes I fear it is. But then I like clutter, so what do I know about it? All those verticals and horizontals. Despite protests from people who defend it, I can't see it having anything to do with nature's idiosyncrasies. Now shut me up. I will sound like a bore."

"You're not boring to me," Nick said, and turned to smile at him. Oliver looked away at once and began sorting out some things that were scattered around on the floor.

"Well, anyway," he said, pointing to a large sofa that almost occupied the whole length of the room, "make yourself comfortable on that."

Nick sat down on the sofa and hoped Oliver would join him there. He liked the feeling of being near him and he felt lonely, but Oliver sat on a chair by an open window, and lit a cigarette. He looked out of the window and for a few minutes they did not speak. It was Nick who broke the silence, which was in fact quite peaceful between them and not at all uncomfortable.

"Why do we, Andy and I, see so little of Frank? He always seems to be in the kitchen when we are not, and only occasionally in the hallway. Is he really okay about me being here? Andy mentions him quite often and he gives the impression they have at least talked."

"Haven't you met him at all yet? Not in all these months?"

"Once, by the kitchen door. He was very nice and shook my hand and smiled, but I can't remember him saying anything."

Oliver stubbed out his unfinished cigarette on the window-sill, and came up to the sofa. He stood there looking down at Nick.

"It's nothing to do with you. Frank said to me he liked the look of you and how polite you were. I guess it's my fault I haven't introduced you properly or brought you up here when he's here. It's really my fault."

"But Andy has been up here, hasn't he?"

Nick didn't know why he was asking all these questions, and suddenly they seemed important to him. Part of him was curious about Oliver's relationship with Frank and what it was really like, but he didn't dare ask. He saw Oliver being older and attractive, and Frank being much younger, and he wondered how it had happened: the miracle that they were happy together. There was also another reason, but it was nowhere near the surface of his mind.

"Yes, he has been here, but that was long before you moved in. Frank was more outgoing then. He had a nervous breakdown, you see, and people—all people—for a while intensely scared him. He is only slowly getting better."

"Andy never mentioned that."

"No. He is discreet. He knew if I wanted to tell you that I would. Frank too said he didn't mind you knowing about it, but I still felt it was too private."

"Then why are you telling me now?"

Oliver sat beside him and looked him in the face.

"Because I've got to know you. I respect you and I like you. I am also interested in your writing: in your response to poetry. It is rare in someone so young."

Nick turned his head away.

"You dislike being considered young, don't you?" Oliver said.

"I don't know," Nick mumbled.

"I know how old you are, but I also know that there is wisdom in you, even a certain oldness about you, as if you've been on this fucked up planet much longer than your years."

Nick smiled and blushed again for the first time in months and turned to face Oliver once more. He was happy Oliver had said that.

"Thank you," he replied.

"For what?"

"For not expecting me to conform to an image. Most people do with me. They see only the surface."

"And you trust that I see more than that?"

"I feel a warmth from you that I haven't felt before from anyone. It doesn't demand anything, and it makes me feel I am wanted for myself. You accept my moods, even more than Andy does. You have patience."

Oliver sighed and looked down at his hands.

"Don't put me too highly up there on a pedestal. I'm not that—well, let's forget about what I'm not." He paused, and then added, "I'm sorry about you not talking with Frank. He's such an intelligent guy. More of an intellectual than me, and sharper in his artistic perception than I am, but strangely enough, he doesn't respond to poetry."

"And you do?"

"Yes," said Oliver looking again at Nick. "Poetry can be ugly and beautiful, disgraceful and even transcendent. It is a way of seeing that can incorporate all of life within it and still retain ambiguity. You are never quite sure what the best poetry is about, and yet it can contain images that both uplift and disturb."

For a moment there was a feeling of intense intimacy between them and in that moment Nick longed for Oliver to kiss him. He blushed again at the thought and the moment passed. Then he remembered Brunswick Square again: the corridor and the room. That had been the very opposite of poetry: a travesty of it, and a visual degradation that filled him with disgust. And he had been touched, literally touched by it. He could taste the sperm in his mouth and recall his attempt to retch it out over the sink. The worst of it was that during the heat of his lust for the young man, he had taken that semen into himself. He felt with total self-hatred that it would always be there, clinging to the insides of him.

"What's wrong?" Oliver asked.

"Nothing," Nick said, and he wanted to cry.

"No, it's not nothing. And my intuition tells me it has something to do with that night at the party. Something really went wrong for you there, didn't it? Something that wasn't meant to happen to you."

"Please, don't let's talk about it," Nick said, and his tears began to flow. He was crying silently and he was not ashamed of Oliver seeing it.

"Nick, dear," Oliver murmured, "whatever anyone did to you that night, wipe it out. Wipe it clean. If you believe it has changed you, let me assure you it has not. You are a poet. It is your essence. Nothing bad can reach that. As for Martin—"

"It wasn't Martin," Nick said.

"Whoever it was, let it go. If it tries to spoil what you are, what your essential self is, then fight it out with all your force from your system. I don't believe in a conventional God, but I do believe that we are more than we know. Cherish that mystery. What you are is hidden to you; the poet keeps it hidden so that ultimately you cannot be spoilt by others."

"I don't understand all you're saying, but please don't let's talk about me any more."

Oliver covered Nick's hand with his own and pressed it briefly.

"Come on now, wipe those handsome eyes."

Nick wiped his eyes with the back of his hand, and getting up, wandered around the room, pausing here and there at the bookshelves, looking at titles.

"You like Italian poetry," Nick remarked.

Oliver joined him and took down a book from the shelf.

"There is a poem by Montale that I like especially. It's in manuscript form inside the book. A friend of a friend gave it to me recently as a birthday present."

"When was your birthday?"

"Never mind that now. The poem is very fine. I'd like you to take it away and read it. It's about suffering and the apparent indifference of the universe. I think it might inspire you. Take it with the rest of the poems in the book. They are all in translation with the original Italian facing the translated page."

"I'll see if I can make out the text in Italian as well," Nick said, his face brightening. "I'll read it before I go to sleep."

Oliver changed the subject then, returning to Frank.

"Frank likes you," he said. "He likes you despite the fact

that you haven't talked. But try to remember, he is still afraid of people, even of someone like you. He is only really comfortable with me. He will eventually get better and his former adventurous self will emerge again. I expect he is struggling with that right now with his family and the relatives he barely knows and is so distant from. It's a big challenge. He wasn't capable of doing it last year."

"I'm not surprised he is comfortable with you," Nick said, then excused himself to go downstairs to the bathroom. Suddenly the closeness of Oliver was too much for him and he had to absorb what had been said.

He went into the kitchen and placed the volume of poetry on the table. He read a few of the poems very quickly, not really taking them in. Eugenio Montale was difficult to understand, but he didn't mind. The words appealed to him and their hidden meanings. He read one called *I clear your brow*, and all he could think of was Oliver's hand on his. And the opening words of the poem, *I clear your brow of the icicles*, made him recall the warmth of that hand, and how he had opened his door to that warmth, and to a touch that was generous and meant well.

"Shall we plan the Christmas meal?"

Oliver was in the kitchen and beside him. Nick picked up the book and said, "This might get soiled in here. I'll take it into Andy's room."

Inside the room he paused as he put the book safely in a place by the side of the bed, and wondered why he hadn't said, *our* room. Then he let the thought drop and returned to the kitchen. Oliver smiled at him and they sat together at the table and drew up a list of things to buy.

Later that night he read through Montale's poems again, and as he read, certain meanings and symbols became clearer. He left the poem in manuscript form to last, and when he eventually unfolded the page and read it, he found that he understood the words almost at once. The first line, *Often I have been acquainted with the worst of living:* drew him in and line by line he read about images of decay. Then the second stanza with its reference to *divine Indifference* struck him like a confirmation of his own lack of belief in a God that could be known, and images of St Mary Magdalen's church returned as vividly as when he had been a young child. But then came the statue and its *near sleep of noon*, and he thought of warmth again, heat even, and in the last line there were clouds in the sky and a *falcon soaring.* He saw that falcon, that most supreme of birds rising up, way up above human life below. For a moment he felt he could be that falcon as well, rising above, soaring above the ills of living and the portents of divine indifference. How high could he go like that falcon, he wondered. How high would the sky permit him to go? He lay back on the bed and he longed to be free of the *gasping rivulet* and the *dried out leaf curling tight.* All those images in Montale's poem spoke of the Earth's inevitable dying. The falcon would be free of that, and he too if chance, or luck, would permit. Then he saw Oliver's face in his mind and the statue at noon, hot and alive perhaps with the noon day heat. And most strangely of all, the statue became Greg, caught in stone, unable to move beyond himself, and he, Nick, as the falcon, longed to return to Earth to make the statue come alive. How I love him, he thought, then his mind went blank and he fell into a deep sleep. In the early morning hours he dreamt, and he recalled his dreams when he awoke. Both Oliver and Greg were intertwined around his body, not in a sexual way, but in the dream sense that they were part of him, not to be divided. Even their faces were split in two: one half Oliver, one half Greg and they were part of his face as well.

He sat for a long while, waiting for the winter light on the edge of his bed and felt that, if he had allowed it, the dream would have drawn him in completely and he would have become a part of it and would never have come out of it. Is that death, he wondered, and as the first grey appeared at the window, he got up and opened it. The window looked out on George Street: a long line of houses, small but full of people like himself. He breathed in the cold morning air and leant his head out. He could just make out St James's Street. This brought him back to reality again. He was young and alive and completely his conscious day self again, waiting for the noise and the bustle of things and people to begin.

The next thing he knew was Oliver tapping on the door, telling him to get ready for breakfast, and that there were a lot of things they had to do that day.

Andy rang Nick on Christmas Eve. Oliver answered the phone and after a brief conversation he knocked on Nick's door to see if he was there. He opened the door after he heard "come in" and found Nick lying out on the bed writing.

"It's Andy," Oliver said.

Nick looked up at him, pretending surprise. He had heard the phone ring and Oliver had spoken loudly enough for Nick to know who he was talking to.

"Ask him to wait a minute," Nick said. "I'm just finishing this poem."

Oliver, looking impatient, told him Andy was calling long distance and to put his pen down.

"Where are they?" he asked Oliver.

"Scotland, I think. Come on, Nick."

"Alright."

He put down his pen, got off the bed and walked slowly to the door. He didn't particularly want to talk to Andy. He was not sure why, but he had hoped he wouldn't ring. He took the phone out of Oliver's hand and Oliver made his way towards the kitchen.

"I forgot to send him my love," Oliver said without turning around.

"Will do."

Nick held the phone in his hand for a few moments, his mind blank at what to say. He felt that he was about to talk to a stranger. Then he put the phone to his ear and spoke into the mouth piece.

"Hi, Andy, it's me."

"What took you so long?"

"I was sleeping," he lied.

"On Christmas Eve?"

"I did the shopping this morning. I was tired. And anyway, I've got you a surprise for when you get back."

Nick heard Andy's laugh and felt saddened that he had so little enthusiasm for this young man who seemed so far away in his mind as well as in space. He wondered exactly how many miles it was to where Andy was calling from. He had never been to Scotland and had no desire to go there. He tried to imagine lochs and castles and picturesque places like Edinburgh.

"Is it nice where you are?" he asked blandly.

"I'm in the middle of nowhere with my parents. Relatives as well. I'm bored and I miss you."

"Do you?" Nick replied.

"You sound as if you are away in one of your daydreams. You don't sound as if you are there."

Nick paused before answering, "I lied to you before. I wasn't asleep. I was writing. I've got this poem I want to finish. I have a few more lines to go."

Andy laughed again, this time with an edge of sarcasm, "Has Oliver been corrupting you?" he asked. "Poetry is one of his things. I know you want to be a writer, and I'm glad you do, but couldn't you give it a rest on Christmas Eve? I mean, can't the inspiration wait? I wish I had something to occupy me here."

"You've got family," Nick said. "There must be lots to talk about. They love you, don't they?"

There was silence at the other end of the phone, and finally Andy asked in a subdued voice, "Have you seen your mother yet?"

"No. I'd rather not talk about it. You know how it is."

"But Christmas?"

"I left home, Andy, because of her. Don't you remember?"

There was a note of anger and frustration in his voice. He suddenly saw Andy as being a wall. Had he no memory of why he had come to him? Then the word *love* crossed his mind. He had also gone to Andy because he had both a desire for him and strong feelings towards him.

"I'm sorry," he said. "I'm feeling depressed today. Again. I know. It's bad at the moment. I will explain when you get back. I can't really talk fluently on the phone, and anyway, it's expensive?"

"Don't worry about the money," Andy said. "Have you seen a lot of Oliver? I mean, you have plenty of things in common and Frank is away as well—"

"I know," Nick replied, interrupting. "I expect Oliver misses him as much as I miss you, but I guess we'll both manage. I bought a chicken today and the veg—holly too. It was cheap. It's always cheaper to shop on Christmas Eve. They don't want things to remain over."

"Well, at least you said it," Andy said.

"What?"

"That you miss me. That's what I rang to hear, not a rundown of your Christmas buys."

"Don't you want to know what kind of present I've bought you?"

Quite abruptly Nick's mind had changed. He had talked himself into a sort of Christmas spirit. He remembered years past, and his very first years in the red house. He wanted to play like a child again, the game of guessing, the game of guessing about presents.

"Guess?" he continued. "Three guesses. Please. It will be your Christmas present to me."

Andy said he thought Nick sounded like a child, then chuckled down the phone at the thought of it and began to play the game.

"Is it animal, vegetable or mineral?"

"What do you mean?"

"I'm referring to the television programme."

"I don't know anything about television," Nick replied defensively. "Oliver and I aren't concerned about that, and anyway, we have no TV."

"Well, I may have a surprise for you on that score."

The guessing game had stopped before it had really begun. Nick said, "You don't mean we're going to have a TV set?"

A disappointed voice asked him why not. Nick looked at the phone in his hand as if he had received bad news.

"I know that Oliver and Frank are above TV, but I'm not. I want to see Bobby Darin and the other pop stars like anyone else. Don't you want that as well? I mean there's—"

"Aren't the records enough?" Nick interrupted again. "Or does Bobby Darin have to play live in our room?"

There was an awkward silence.

Andy broke it by saying, "That's unkind, Nick. There are other things on television as well. Culture programmes. I've looked through the *Radio Times* while I've been up here, and there's lots you'll like. It's not only what you would call superficial."

"Wouldn't you? *Even* the culture programmes?"

"Well, there's not much other action going on in our room at the moment, is there?"

The pain in this sudden attack from Andy was all too evident to Nick. He held the phone away from him, feeling suddenly cold. He desperately wanted Oliver to appear and to take away the phone from him. He wanted the conversation to end.

"Yes, at the moment, that's true. I feel—well—is withdrawn a good word? It won't last."

"Won't it?"

"No," Nick said, putting as much force in the one word as he could. "You know what a time I've been having. At work too. I'm not exactly popular there at the moment. Soon the customer's will be complaining. I don't even smile much at them any more."

"Couldn't you try?"

"It takes time, Andy, it takes time. For fuck's sake, you were sympathetic enough when we first met, when I first came to you. You knew I was not some feather brain from the 42 when you met me."

"I thought I would satisfy you," Andy said slowly. "I thought I could help you, and yes, love you. I feel so much for you. I want to share your interests with you too, but more and more you've become distant—even in bed!"

"Again, that!" Nick said.

"It's important, Nick. What do you expect me to do, have a wank by myself while I'm lying there beside you, trying not to shake the bed too much in case I wake you and you find I'm horny for you? Or would that turn you on?"

"Now you're being—"

"What, Nick? I'm telling the truth. Do you lie beside me with a hard-on waiting for me to notice? Even longing for me to notice? Tell me truthfully."

"It's depression, Andy. It's not an abstract thing, depression. I just don't have—well, I don't have much desire any more. I guess I should see a doctor."

Andy laughed, and the phone now felt hot in Nick's hand. He realised his hand was running with sweat. The cold feeling had gone away. He felt trapped: closed in with this dialogue between them.

"I thought I was a good enough doctor for you. Didn't I listen? Aren't I intelligent enough to listen, or do you think that deep down *I'm* just a feather brain you met and had sex with in the 42 Club? Has the size of my cock lost its appeal? Do you want—or have you discovered—that you want to take the passive role? Were you acting butch only to please me? If that's so, I can tell you now, I've thought of fucking you as well. I just thought you weren't into that. I thought you had a strict idea about what role you wanted to play."

Then the voice stopped and Nick felt shocked at what he

had heard.

"I don't know what to say," he said helplessly.

There was silence again for a few seconds, and then Andy, his voice now almost choking (was he crying?) asked, "Do you love me? Tell me, one way or the other. I have to know. I need to know. I have these awful thoughts that you've turned cold on me. People do. I know that. People change."

"I haven't changed," Nick replied with a sudden warmth in his voice.

"Something happened at that party. I'm no fool. Why don't you tell me?"

"I saw something," Nick said.

"What? What, Nick? Tell me?"

Nick tried to think of a suitable lie. He felt too much shame in his own complicity to be able to tell Andy that he had been unfaithful to him. Up until that moment of choice in that room, he hadn't even remotely thought of having anyone else except Andy. Then the words shot through his brain, but what of Greg? What of him? Haven't you seen him in your dreams? Felt him there? Seen his body there? Haven't you been unfaithful with him?

"Did Martin come after you? I wasn't following his movements. I didn't think of doing so. Only now, the thought has entered my mind that he may have followed you to the—"

"To the toilet?"

"Well, did he follow you?"

"Yes, he followed me," Nick said. He knew he had to lie and let Martin be the fall guy. Why not? Martin would deny it if Andy got around to asking him, but he sensed somehow that Andy wouldn't ask him.

"The bastard!"

"He just tried his luck, that's all. Out of malice. Boredom. To break us up, I don't know. But it made me sick, him standing there next to me with his cock sticking out. It's as simple as that. Needless to say, I didn't reciprocate."

"I understand now," Andy said softly. "He's caused you a

lot of damage, hasn't he? One way or another."

Nick felt relief at the believed lie, and if Andy could have appeared before him magically there and then, he would have responded to him sexually.

"I've got an erection," Nick said, and he had.

"Then go to your room. Think of me, and get some fucking relief. I'd talk dirty to you on the phone now, only my father is hovering in the background. Just think about the black hair around my cock and the wetness of its tip; of how you like to rim me, and how I suck you off. Anything to bring you alive again."

"Stop," Nick said, feeling very excited.

"Danger. The family Gestapo are approaching. I'll have to call off. I'll ring tomorrow after lunch. And come, please come! That's the only present I want from you—you coming, thinking of me—to know that you still love me in the completest way possible."

Then they said goodbye and Andy added before ending the call, "First thing when I get back, I want you so frustrated, so frustrated," then the line went dead and Nick hung the phone back up on the wall. Then he went into the bedroom, closed the door quietly and taking out his penis, jerked it until the sperm came into his hand. He looked at the white pool of it in his palm and the trickle that was running down his arm, and he screamed. He ran to the bathroom, and washed his hand over and over under the hot water tap that was so hot it almost scalded him. Oliver knocked loudly on the door and asked him if he was alright.

"Yes," he cried out, then, "no," and when he left the bathroom, Oliver took him in his arms.

"I don't love him any more," Nick sobbed. "I don't want him to touch me any more."

"Quiet. Be quiet. You don't mean it. You know you don't mean it. You are good together in every possible way. Don't you think my eyes are old enough to see that?"

Nick wondered why he could let go, let go so freely in the

true sense of the term, with Oliver. Slowly he released himself from Oliver's arms.

"It will all work out when Andy returns," Oliver tried to reassure. Then he smiled and added it was about time they started to feel some Christmas spirit.

They spent Christmas Eve upstairs. Oliver had tidied up the living room, hiding away as much as possible any signs of disorder. There were lighted candles dotted all around, and above the pictures was the holly that Nick had bought. It all looked festive and clean, and had a feeling and look of simplicity that Nick had rarely, if ever, felt before during Christmas. Above all it was calm and he did not have to dread the visit of his father and the inevitable rows that always ensued with his mother. He did not have to watch them tearing each other apart in their violence as he had had to do so often when he was a child. He told Oliver all about this and Oliver listened attentively, passing a comment here and there, reminding him gently that he was away from it now, and that he could call the place where he was, home.

Oliver opened a bottle of white wine and asked Nick if he would have a glass with him. Nick said yes and sipped the wine slowly. It tasted good and after a while he felt totally relaxed.

"What about you, Oliver?" he asked, and Oliver looked surprised.

"What about me?" he replied, pouring himself another glass of wine.

"We never talk about you," Nick said. "I know next to nothing about your life and yet you know so much about mine. I would like to hear you talk about yourself."

Oliver's look of surprise changed to a look of doubt and placing the glass on a small table in front of the sofa, he stared down at his large hands.

"Please, take me out of myself," Nick prompted. "I feel there is so much inside you that is good, and that would be good for me to hear."

"Then for you, I will," Oliver said at last and raising his head, he looked at Nick and smiled. Nick thought how young he looked suddenly, the candles flickering around him. He imagined that Oliver was the same age as himself and that they were on an adventure of discovery.

"What do you want to know?" Oliver asked.

"About when you were my age, or Andy's age. What was it like for you then?"

"Confusing," Oliver began. "I'm in my forties now. It was over twenty years ago. The war was impending, but most people were in denial that it would happen. My family were quite well-off. My mother was a writer. She taught me my love of literature and the finer things in life. She made me listen to good music, and like any child I found that hard work. But I liked Beethoven, I remember that. I used to ask her to play Beethoven symphonies constantly. The house in Hove was full of records and books."

"And your education?"

"It was good, and I was the only child. Then when war broke out, they were both killed in a street in London during an air raid. They'd gone up to visit an aunt of mine. Travel was not recommended, but they took a risk and the risk killed them. I was in the army myself by then. War had reached England and to be honest, none of us seemed prepared. You have no idea how much we tried to fool ourselves about Hitler before the war, but that's another story. No one wants to hear about that now. We were all heroes."

Nick listened attentively. He had been born during the war, but it was never discussed in his family, as if the subject was best forgotten, almost taboo, and yet all the time around him, he heard men and women talking about the war as if it was yesterday, which of course it was to them. And now Oliver was talking about it as if it was alive, terrifyingly alive.

"Brighton of course got bombed as well, but not as much as places further north. An aunt of mine who lived in Hull told me how it had been up there. Horrible. Relentless. And we in the South knew nothing about it. It was all hush-hush."

"Hush-hush," Nick whispered to himself. "What a strange expression that is."

"Everything had to be hidden, Nick. I suppose because of morale, and no doubt security reasons. But it was appalling what my Aunt saw and went through up there. The toll of death was so great, and never knowing for all those long years whether you would survive until morning. Whatever Brighton had it wasn't that bad, or anywhere near that bad."

Nick had never heard about any of this from his Aunt Agnes, but then again, she never mentioned the war at all. Oliver was breaking the silence about it and he was glad.

"Then after the war was over, and I came out of it with all my limbs and my hearing and my sight, I fell in love. I was, believe it or not, almost a total virgin then. I'd done a bit of playing around in the army, but you can imagine how furtive that was. I was just there to be used by some guys who had no access to women, and I enjoyed it, but I never thought of it as anything serious."

"Where did you fall in love?" Nick asked.

"Here. In Brighton. His name was Eric. Brown eyes. Soft skin. Slightly older than me. A handsome young man. He looked a bit like you."

Nick smiled, pleased that Oliver had said that. There was a short silence between them, and once more Nick looked closely at Oliver. How young he looked, sitting there on the sofa, his long legs stretched out in front of him. The leanness of his body appealed to Nick. He wished suddenly that they were both the same age, and that this Christmas Eve could lead to a closer reaching out. He felt his penis stir in his trousers. The feeling of sexual need was intense and spontaneous. His desire, seemingly lost after the party was at last beginning to awaken, as if arousing itself after the shock of a crippling nightmare. He hunched himself forward on the chair, just in case anything showed and tried to dismiss the thought of sex between him and Oliver.

"His name was Eric," Oliver repeated. "He'd had a rough time in the war, and unlike you, he had a disability. A physical disability. The lower part of his body had been blown away on the battlefield and he'd had surgery on his penis. When we made love, he never took off his underwear. I was naked, he was not. He came, but I never saw him come. He would crush himself against me, and would scream as if he was in the most dreadful pain, and then he would get up and go to the bathroom. He would be in there for a long time and often I would have to satisfy myself. Then when he returned, we would try to behave normally. We would kiss and fondle each other, but I was never allowed to touch him below the waist. This lasted for a few years, into the early years of this decade."

Oliver's voice sounded strained as he related this. He poured himself another glass of wine and Nick asked if he could have another as well.

"Are you sure?" Oliver asked. Then he added, "God, I'm a fool. Of course you're bloody sure, and why shouldn't you get drunk over Christmas? I think I can handle that. I might even get drunk myself, but it would have to be something stronger than this wine. It's potent, but not that potent." He laughed, but the laughter sounded artificial. Then he leant back on the sofa. "I really loved him," he said slowly. "We had a lot in common. He used to paint. His work wasn't very good. He knew that and I knew that. But it didn't matter. He loved the smell of paint, and the feel of it on his fingers. The smell of turpentine was often on him when we went to bed and he would talk about the work he had done that day. His paintings were a riot of colour. Almost abstract, with only the slightest suggestion of a human form. An eye or a suggestion of an eye in the suggestion of a face. A limb not quite there, but a vague sense of it there on the canvas. A shape of a leg that was not quite a leg. Oh, hell, you can't describe painting! And how can I say his work was not very good? Was it because I was young then and stupid enough to listen to the opinion of others? He knew Duncan Grant. I even went once to Charleston with him one glorious summer's day. Grant was brutally honest with him, but then maybe he just didn't like his vision. Who can tell? His paintings disappeared when he disappeared. One day he just left. I tried to trace him, but every attempt failed. He could be somewhere now, but I'll never know."

"Why?" Nick asked.

Oliver shook his head in the shadows.

"I don't know, Nick. I don't know. I investigated as much as I could. I don't believe he killed himself. I think he just wanted to leave us all behind him. He said to me once that he wanted to enter the monastic life, not as a believer but as a way of life. He'd read the Gospels and loved Christ as a truly great model of how a man should be, but he did not believe in His divinity. He believed simply that Christ meant for us to love each other. He believed only in that. So maybe he has another name now, and he is leading his monastic life. I like to think that."

There was a long pause. Nick was shy about making any comment about this relationship. He felt it would be patronising to say anything at all. Words would have all sounded so easy.

"Now I've done with talking about myself," Oliver said and stood up. "It must be almost midnight. Shall we have a few mince pies? I'm famished."

"I'd like that," Nick replied.

When midnight struck, Oliver took Nick briefly in his arms and with tenderness kissed him lightly on the lips.

"Happy Christmas, my friend," he said.

Nick wanted more, but made no gesture to suggest it. Later, lying in bed, waiting for sleep, he thought more about the love story he had heard. No novel he had read had moved him so deeply.

Christmas lunch went well. There was even a box of crackers and they enjoyed laughing at the corny jokes and putting on the paper hats. After the last cracker was pulled, Nick said it was the bangs he had enjoyed most, which sent them into fits of what Oliver referred to as wonderful juvenile laughter, and then they exchanged presents. Nick gave Oliver a pair of gloves and a poem he had written for him: the poem he had been finishing when Andy had phoned. Oliver read it in silence, then pressed Nick's hand saying it had images of great power in it. Nick knew that it was not very good, but he wanted to show Oliver that he could produce something in recognition of Oliver's encouragement and belief that he could write. Oliver's gift to him was a portable typewriter in a case with Nick's name embossed on it.

"It's beautiful," Nick said. "It's the most wonderful present I have ever had."

"I'm happy you like it. I hope it will help you write many, many more poems."

Then the phone rang and it was Andy. The conversation this time was brief. He said he would be home for the New Year and that he missed Nick. The words seemed to slide off Nick as Andy said them. Oliver took the phone and wished him a happy Christmas and the conversation ended there. There were too many people in the background and it sounded loud, very loud.

"He's having a good time," Nick said, but he was conscious that his voice sounded flat.

At around four in the afternoon, Oliver left the house to visit an old friend. Left on his own, Nick felt very much alone, and after cleaning up the debris of the Christmas meal, he put on his coat and went out himself. It was dark and cold, and he decided on the spur of the moment to go and visit his mother. On his way to Montpelier Road he realised he had no present for her, and that he had never even once thought of getting one, but there was a small shop open in a side street off the Western Road. He had been there previously on Sundays with his mother. The couple who ran it were elderly, and his mother had told him, for he had questioned why they were open on Sundays, that they were refugees from 'the war situation' and that they had settled in Brighton. He wanted to say Happy Christmas to them, but the woman looked unhappy, as if she had just received bad news, and her husband looked the same.

"Can I help you?" the woman said, in her strong Eastern European accent.

He asked for a large box of chocolates from the window: the largest in the shop, and the man took it out and handed it to him with a pale smile. He paid them and left the shop, making his way upwards into the Montpelier area. He passed St Mary Magdalen's, pausing briefly to look at it. The school house next to it looked cramped and the small annex which had been the headmaster's study seemed dark and as reduced in size as the rest. How big it had all been in his early years. He recalled the day he had done something wrong in class and had been sent to be strapped. He had held out his hand and the whacks had come down very hard on his burning palm. He had tried to smile through it and the headmaster had given him a brief lecture which he could no longer remember and he had returned to the classroom.

He hurried on.

By the light of a street lamp he saw the red house with its three pointed roofs, which were so different from the rest of the architecture of the street. He paused before going up the steps, not sure if he really wanted to ring the bell. His hands felt clammy holding the box of chocolates, and he almost dropped them as he climbed the steps. Then, hesitantly, he rang the bell. No one came, but then he saw, by a light that was on in his former bedroom, the silhouette of a figure behind the curtains. The curtain moved slightly and a face looked out and he saw his mother. The porch of the house was lit and she would have been able to see who it was quite clearly. Then the curtains fell back into place and she disappeared.

He was about to go, sensing her refusal to see him, when the door opened and he turned to see Mrs Granger standing there, half in shadow as the light in the hall was falling behind her. She stepped forward, to stand half inside the house, half on the porch. She was dressed in a long, green dress which didn't suit her features. She also had a Christmas paper hat on her head in the shape of a crown.

"I came to see my mother," he said, staring at her. "I'd like to give her these chocolates if I may."

"Have you changed your behaviour?" she asked.

"I don't think that is any of your business," he replied.

"Since I look after her now it is my business. There is no one else but me."

"But my father?"

"He no longer comes now that you are no longer here. I care for her welfare completely."

"That is kind of you, but I would like to see her."

"I don't want her to be disturbed by you," she said, once more withdrawing into the house. She stood on the threshold like a guardian, upright and rigid in posture. He thought of an aggressive dog. "I cannot ignore your illegal practices," she continued, the words ringing out loud and clear in the stillness of the evening. "As I assume they are continuing, you have no right to remind her of them."

"I haven't changed," he replied defiantly. "If you hope for a conversion to your rules, then you will both be disappointed. I have a right to lead my own life."

"I don't think she would want to hear that."

"Then I'm definitely not allowed in?"

"You have another home now, so go back to it. You are not wanted here."

"My friend is away with his parents and I thought she would like to know how I am, even if I am as unwanted as you say I am."

Out of the corner of his eye, he saw the bedroom curtain twitch again. His mother had been watching.

"She's behind my bedroom window," he said. "I saw the curtains move."

"It's my bedroom now, Nick."

Suddenly angry he cried out to Mrs Granger, "You have no right to do this. At least go and ask her if she is really so determined not to see me."

"She is," Mrs Granger said. Her head bobbed forward and the paper crown fell off onto the porch. Nick bent down and tried to hand it to her, but she made a dismissive gesture with her hand.

"Did you make her Christmas lunch?" he asked, trying to regain some normality between them, some element of reality to break the grotesque nature of their encounter.

"She made it for us," she replied, her voice still cold. "Your mother can walk and do the usual things, but her state of health is too fragile to be shocked. Your presence and the reminder of what you are would make her ill—much more ill than she already is. She believes that what you are now is bad, and until that changes—"

"What should I bring then?" he interjected. "A signed paper from someone, someone of the church, or the law, to say that I am 'normal' again? Normal like you? Would that piece of paper let me in? If someone was ludicrous enough to give it to me?"

"You are a criminal," she hissed. "Remember that. A criminal of sixteen. Your father may accept that fact, but she does not. If the police do get you I hope she never knows about it. Turn to your father for help, and anyway, why didn't you go and stay with him?"

"I didn't ask him," Nick replied, tired of standing there protesting, and also trying to be rational to this woman who had taken over, taken control. Then his mind closed down. He knew that it was hopeless.

"Will you at least give these chocolates to her?" he asked.

"I would have to tell her who brought them. I don't want to do that."

"But she has already seen me from the side window."

"Her sight is very poor now. You could be anybody—a tramp, a vagrant who wants money—anybody. She keeps everyone away thanks to me." She paused, as if to catch her breath, then said, "I don't want to talk to you any more. I'm going to close the door."

"But she is my mother," he exclaimed. He realised he was almost screaming out the words, and as he reached the word 'she' he felt as if he was going to fall apart. He threw the box of chocolates onto the porch. "I'll leave them there," he said.

"It's up to you, if you want to remind yourself of the obvious—that you are still a child, with a child's reactions. Go home to your friends."

She slammed the door on him and he stared at the solid wood. He wanted to ring the doorbell again. He wanted to see his mother. Then he shouted at the door, "One day you'll be gone, Mrs Granger. You will leave her like everyone else has, even me. You will leave her and once I know from my father that you are no longer there I will return."

The solid door seemed to throw his words back at him. Then the light on the porch went out, followed by the bedroom light. In semi-darkness he made his way down the steps to the street, and the urge to return to the warmth of Oliver's affection and understanding made him begin to run. Very soon he was once more in the bright lights of the Western Road. As he ran by *Wades* he looked up at the department store and stared at the Christmas decorations. He felt like a child running finally, once and for all, away from home.

ELEVEN

Andy returned to celebrate the beginning of the new decade and so did Frank. The house became, to all appearances, the same as it was before. Nick returned to his job as normal and his relationship with Andy resumed itself once more. They had sex regularly and, despite a feeling of distance between them, Nick succeeded in making his lover sexually happy. Oliver and Frank kept mainly to themselves.

At the bookshop however, while he was arranging books on a shelf, Alfred spoke frankly about the changes he had noticed in Nick.

"You have lost your glow," he said. "You had a light inside you when you first came here—an enthusiasm for life. I'd almost go so far as to say an infatuation for life. I feel it has gone. The light has become dimmer. Soon I fear it will go out." He approached Nick at the counter. "What *is* wrong? I like you. I don't want to see you like this."

Nick was silent, and did not look Alfred in the face.

"I feel it myself," he said at last. "I don't know what I need."

"May I speak freely?"

"Of course."

"I think you are in love with a girl. I've not seen her. I think you lost her a while back. Maybe you didn't even know then that you loved her. Did you go to school together?"

"You're presuming a lot, Alfred."

"Am I wrong?"

Nick paused before he replied. "There is a person at the back of my mind, yes, but I feel lost. I have friends, but I feel lost. Cold too."

"The customers have noticed."

"I'm sorry. If you want to get someone better, tell me. I don't want people to avoid the bookshop because of me."

Alfred coughed into his hand and for a moment he looked

awkward. Nick observed the man and recognised his kindness. He could have tried to tell him the truth about himself, or maybe Alfred already knew and was being tactful about calling the person a girl. Or did he simply prefer to think it was a girl?

"Alfred, maybe I should go."

"Is it what you want?"

"No, really it's not, but—"

"Look, son, you are going through a rough patch. Don't you think when I was young I went through rough patches? People stood behind you more then, helped you more than now. Society was less selfish. I got through thanks to them. I remember I had a job like you and I thought I was a disappointment." He smiled at Nick and asked him if he would like a cup of tea.

"I would, thank you."

"It's a second home here for you Nick, this place. I'm sure you're the best man for the job and, who knows, one day you may be able to run it yourself. I'm not going to last forever. My doctor said as much only last week."

"Anything serious, Alfred?"

Alfred laughed: a dismissive laugh.

"I went through a bloody fucking war—excuse my language—and I am still here. I'm just saying, one day I won't be. I have no one in my life and I would like the shop to continue in good hands. Oh, damn it all, I am tired of all this talk. You just get yourself that living spark again. Talk to the girl!" Then he went to the room at the back of the shop and spent a long time making the tea.

The months passed and Nick forcibly tried to make himself outwardly happier and friendly. He saw so many others wearing masks that he knew he wasn't incapable of wearing one himself. He supposed that if you were lucky, like a right hat, the right mask would fit. He tried many and one day he looked in the mirror and even he believed the light, as Alfred had called it, had returned and that he was as fresh and youthful as before. He even fooled Andy and the romantic words he had once used with him now flowed again all too easily from his mouth. But there was someone in the background who did not look as if he was convinced. It was, of course, Oliver.

"You've stopped writing," Oliver said to him one late April day in the kitchen. "I miss the poems."

"Maybe it was a phase," Nick replied.

"Don't try to fool me like the rest of them," Oliver said softly. "Write me a poem and prove to me that the flame is still there."

"Oh, you too!" Nick said.

"What do you mean?"

"At the bookshop, Alfred said the light in me was dimming. My enthusiasm for life was dimming. He scared me."

"He's an older man, isn't he?"

"Yes. Does that matter?"

"Perhaps we see more," Oliver said, smiling at Nick. He then returned to the meal he was preparing.

Nick went away and promptly wrote a lyrical poem about a figure in a park who was half Pan, half boy. This boy-god played upon a magic pipe and all the animals responded to him. Afterwards Nick read it through and even though he was alone he blushed. He tore it up as if it were pornography and at that moment he thought the light really had died, and his invisible mask tightened itself even more firmly to his face.

Then it happened. He saw Greg. It was a warm day in early May. Greg was sitting in the window of a brand new coffee bar that had just opened in St James's Street. It had brightly coloured seats and a juke box in a corner at the back. Nick saw him through the window as he approached. He was sitting on a bar stool, looking down at the coffee cup in front of him. He appeared lost in thought and as far as Nick could tell had not noticed him. He was wearing a black leather jacket and his hair was slicked back and neatly cut. Then he got up and moved from the window towards the juke box at the back. Nick stood in the doorway of the café, and a girl who was standing with a group of boys, smiled when she saw him and beckoned him in.

"Why don't you come on in?" she cried out. "The place is jumping. Have some fun."

She was dressed from top to bottom in yellow and looked like a canary while the boys were all wearing tight trousers and bright sweaters as if to match the décor. Nick smiled back at her. He was wearing his duffel coat and looked distinctly dull. I am being teased, he thought.

"Dressed like this?" he replied. He was not looking at her, but staring at Greg's back over by the juke box which had just finished playing Fats Domino's *Ain't That a Shame*.

Another boy call out, "Can't you put on something a bit more lively?" Greg turned slightly in the boy's direction, but didn't answer back. *What Do You Want to Make Those Eyes at Me For?* began to play.

The girl who was still looking in Nick's direction called out to him, "You're cute. Doesn't matter what you're wearing."

Nick thought she looked like a tomboy, despite the canary colours, and walked into the coffee bar.

"Hi," the girl said. "I'm Stella."

"I'm Nick," he replied, feeling more confident about himself.

Stella started to talk to Nick about the way he looked and whether he was an art or drama student because he looked the part. Nick turned away from her towards Greg who was still at the juke box. The choice of song had no doubt been his. Nick hadn't heard it before and liked its raucous sound.

"Well, are you?" Stella questioned.

"Am I what?" Nick answered, realising he had not been paying attention to her machine-gun patter.

"Oh, never mind," she replied and, laughing, turned to one of the boys beside her. Nick now felt free to move, and made his way towards Greg. His jacket looked new and was almost as out of place in this café as the clothes Nick was wearing.

"Hello," he said, and Greg turned to face him. He looked white in the face at seeing Nick. The music had stopped and Nick felt in his pocket for some money to choose a record for himself.

"What are you going to put on?" Greg asked.

"A song I like," Nick replied, his voice slightly trembling as he said the words. He put his money in and selected *It's Only Make Believe*.

"I thought we'd never see each other again," Greg murmured. The music began to play and Nick felt the urge to take Greg in his arms and dance with him there in the bar. He suddenly wanted them all to see that he was close to Greg and proud of being close to him.

"It's a small town," Nick replied. "It had to happen some day." Then he added, "You look great like that."

Greg tried to smile, but couldn't. His face was still pale and Nick had no idea what he was thinking behind his blank expression.

"I wouldn't have thought this was your kind of place," Nick said.

"Nor yours. Look at you. Duffel coat. Hell, the real intellectual." Greg's face now began to take on some colour and there was a wild look in his eyes as he said the words. His blue eyes stood out in stark contrast to the slicked back darkness of his hair and the black of his leather jacket. Nick badly wanted to touch him.

"Anyway, I like it here," Greg added. "I found it a few weeks ago. I know a girl here."

"Stella?" Nick asked.

"Course not. Her name is Hope. Like Hope Lange in *Wild in the Country*—the Elvis film."

Nick said he hadn't seen it.

"Did it play in Portslade?" he asked.

"Don't be fucking condescending. I suppose you look down on Portslade now you're all dressed up like a fucking bohemian in that coat and happy probably with your own sort. Anyway, I go to the flicks in Brighton remember?"

"I didn't mean to—" Nick stopped talking.

Greg hurriedly put on a Cliff Richard song. A small group around them cheered at this and looked over in their direction.

"I hate the fucking sound of this boy," Greg said.

"Then why did you put him on?"

"I thought you might like it—pretty boy and all that. Or would you say no to him?"

"Look, Greg, do you want me to go away? You seem to be pushing me out of the door. You're trying to be insulting, but I'm older now and not quite so easily offended. And I wasn't knocking Portslade. I've no reason to."

Greg looked at him in surprise.

"Perhaps you'd prefer me to go?" he asked jokingly. "Stella over there seems to like you. I heard you both talking. I couldn't turn round. I was in too much shock."

"At hearing my voice again?" Nick asked gently. "I thought I was speaking fairly quietly."

"My hearing is *abnormal*," Greg replied, and they both burst out laughing.

"That's better," Nick said.

"Is it?"

Greg looked at him and his blue eyes had a look that seemed to be both aggressive and tender at the same time. The music stopped again and they stared at each other for quite a long time. Nick became conscious that maybe the others in the bar were looking at them, but then as before he wanted them to look. He was also glad that neither he nor Greg looked as if they fitted in with the gaudy brightness of the place. He was glad they both looked like outsiders.

"Put some more music on," someone called out.

Greg veered round and shouted out, "Put some fucking

music on yourself. Haven't you got any money, or are you all just tight fucking fisted?"

"Just cos your girl's not here," another said. "Hope! You haven't got a hope with her. She may like you as a friend, but she prefers boys like us. Smart looking."

"Quieten down now," the man behind the counter added. Then he came out from behind it and put some music on himself.

"Don't start a brawl," he said turning to Greg as he put in the money. "Any trouble here and we'll be shut down. This is England remember, even if Brighton tries not to be."

"Okay, okay," Greg muttered. Then he turned to Nick and said, "Let's get out of this shithole place."

Stella called out, "Goodbye boys," as they left.

"I still can't see why you go there," Nick remarked once they were out on St James's Street.

"I told you why."

"Is Hope your girl?"

"No. She's nice though. I like being with her. She understands me."

This sounded ambiguous, but Nick made no reply.

"Well, where are you living now?" Nick eventually asked.

"I'm still in Portslade."

"Working in the shop?"

"Yeah. It's alright."

"I see."

They walked together in silence to the Old Steine and made their way to the fountain. It was its usual playful self and the warm, frisky wind was spraying water capriciously over the people walking near to it.

"That's funny," Greg said, pointing as a couple got wet. His voice sounded as it had sounded when they had first met—fresh and open and only too willing to go and have fun and maybe make trouble.

"Shall we go stealing comics again?" Nick said, responding to the sudden playfulness.

"Why not?" Greg replied. "The place in Trafalgar Street is still open. I go there sometimes. The books are a bit racier now."

"I never went back there," Nick replied.

"Why should you, now that you're a man of the world?"

"Are you being sarcastic? I'm only sixteen, Greg."

"You look fucking forty in that duffel."

They laughed again and Greg reached into his pocket and took out a small bottle. He turned his back on Nick, but Nick was quick enough to see that the bottle had some kind of alcohol in it. Greg was rapidly swallowing as he turned round again.

"What are you drinking?" Nick asked.

"I need it at the moment. And if I want to drink I'll drink!"

"But in the street? You take out a bottle and you drink it in the street? Do you want to become an alcoholic?"

Greg shrugged.

"Bit of whisky to brighten me up when I'm down. I also drink before I go to bed. Helps me sleep. Insomnia."

"That's not right."

"Don't let's get heavy, Nick. I don't want to talk about it."

"So you don't sleep well?"

"I said don't let's get heavy. The whisky helps. That's all I care about. I've got a sleep problem. Lots of people have sleep problems."

"But this is the afternoon, Greg. It looks as if you can't live without it."

"Just felt like it. Now lay off."

"So you drink at all times of day? At work as well? What do your parents think?"

"I don't drink at work. And I said lay off!"

"Okay, it's none of my business."

"Shit right it isn't. Now let's have some fucking fun for Christ's sake."

Greg smiled at Nick and went over to where the water was spraying. He stood there for a long while getting wetter and wetter. His leather jacket and blue jeans were soon soaked. A small group were watching him and laughing. Then he ran back and joined Nick.

"Now I feel really cool," he said, laughing. "Come on, let's go down to Trafalgar Street."

On the way they talked, but Greg asked no questions about Nick's private life. Nick however did manage to get a few details from Greg about his life in Portslade.

"This drink thing isn't really serious," Greg said. "I mean, I do my job well enough. At least Dad thinks so. It's got stability and one day I could run the whole business. Thing is, do I want to?"

"Do you?"

"Well, shit, I don't want to tie myself down to anything. I dunno. I feel a bit messed-up inside at the moment, and I didn't come to Brighton to get a sodding interrogation from you. All the same, it's nice to know you care."

Standing in front of the shop in Trafalgar Street, Nick noticed there was sweat on Greg's forehead.

"You okay?" he asked.

"Just a bit jittery. Bit of dizziness. I'm used to it. Now for fuck's sake let's go in and plunder the place. The blind old geezer is still there."

The shopkeeper seemed warier than usual and they didn't stay long in the shop. All the same, Greg managed to sneak two comics into his open jacket.

"Let's get out of here," he whispered.

They were in Kemp Street when Greg took them out.

"Not here," Nick said. "It's dangerous. Someone could see?"

"What's the fun if there isn't any danger? Let's at least get a bit of a kick out of this. Let's see what I've got."

"Didn't you choose?"

"Fraid not. It was lucky-dip time."

Nick looked down at the two comics. They were for kids. He waited as Greg leafed through a few of the pages.

"Sod it," Greg said, and then he laughed. "Well some of the kids in the street might like them."

"Greg, you can't."

"Watch me."

At the end of Kemp Street, two little girls were skipping rope. Greg stopped them and handed them a comic each.

"Don't tell your parents," he said, and then he walked away followed by Nick.

"The police could have seen us," Nick said.

"Don't be such an old woman. When did you last see a policeman round here? They don't give a shit for this area. Really, Nick, you are getting quite old." He nudged Nick and then winked. "Only joking," he said. "And anyway, the comics were for boys. Bet they don't get to see those too often. *Gosh, Peter, I bet that blue Supreme was touching eighty.*" He mimicked a posh voice and a line read from one of the comics.

They turned back towards Trafalgar Street and climbed the rest of the hill to the station.

"Let's hang out for a while in a real dive," Greg said. "I'll take you on a ride. Got any money?"

Nick said he had and they hopped onto a passing bus.

"Never guess where I'm taking you," Greg added.

Nick felt young again and didn't care where Greg was taking him. He was out on a spree with the one person he knew deep down he really wanted to be with. Even the thought of sex between them didn't cross his mind. He was just happy.

"I'll close my eyes until we get there," he said and closed his eyes.

"You big kid," Greg said warmly.

The conductor came round and Nick held out the necessary change for their tickets, his eyes still playfully and firmly shut.

"I need sixpence more," the man said.

Nick felt as Greg reached out and put a hand into his duffel coat pocket and took some extra money.

"He's blind," Greg said.

"I'm sorry," came the reply and Nick began to giggle. He heard the conductor move away.

"Do blind people even have their eyes closed?" he asked Greg, without opening them.

"Search me, I don't know."

Then he felt Greg nudge him.

"Only a few stops more," he said. "The bus is quick today. Not much traffic."

When they arrived, Nick opened his eyes and found himself at Boundary Road. He was in Portslade.

"Shall we go and see what's on at the Rothbury?" he asked.

"Fuck, no. The woman behind the till in the afternoons knows me. I don't want her to see me. News will get around like wild fire that I was there with a boy in a duffel coat."

"Bugger it then, I'll take the bloody thing off," Nick said.

Nick took off the coat and carried it over his arm. Greg laughed at him.

"We'd still better not go there though. It's too near my dad's shop. Better go up towards the station. There's a café up there full of layabouts. They're too poor and fed up with life even to gossip."

Nick looked up towards Portslade station.

"I expect it's cleaner than you thought. Portslade, I mean?" Greg asked, a note of sarcasm in his voice.

"Don't start in on that again," Nick said.

"Well, this dive we're going to is filthy. I'll warn you about that. I look like I've come out of a poof's paradise compared to them."

"Cut it out."

"Okay, okay, no harm intended."

They reached the tiny café which sold hot snacks, coffee and tea. Nick wanted some tea and they sat at a small table at the back. The wall was covered with calendars dating back to the forties. The men (and they were mostly men) all looked as if they dated back even further.

"Poor old fuckers," Greg said sitting down facing Nick with an unappetising sandwich in front of him. He started to munch into it, sipping some of the foul looking coffee beside his plate. "This is muck," he said, after tasting it.

"Then why did you order it?"

"To make it taste better of course!"

Quick as a thief, Greg took the bottle out of his jacket pocket and poured the remainder of its contents into the coffee.

Again Nick looked shocked and Greg grinned.

"The tea's worse, but you haven't tasted it yet. And only the sandwiches are edible. The rest of the food will give you the shits."

"Is there a juke box here?" Nick asked.

Greg let out a whoop of laughter.

"There is," he answered.

"Where?"

"In the corner. You missed it when you walked in. No one ever plays it. It's got Rosemary Clooney, Doris Day and of course Frank Sinatra. There's only about two tracks worth playing—try Jerry Lee Lewis and *High School Confidential*."

Nick went over, brushing past a crowd of men who were not quite as run-down as Greg had described them. There were a few women also, all bangles and dangly earrings. Everyone was conversing loudly and Nick thought how much friendlier and more sociable people seemed to be than in either Brighton or Hove. He put on the Jerry Lee Lewis track.

"Bloody noise!" someone grumbled as he returned to the table.

"I hope you put it on twice," Greg said. "Just to annoy them."

"No," Nick replied.

"I'll do it then."

"Thought you didn't have any money?"

"Got enough for the juke box. Always got to have enough for the essentials of life. Fun first, eating last. That's how it is in Portslade."

Greg got up from the table and pushed his way through the crowd. He also selected *Oh Boy!* and *Rebel Rouser*.

"That'll last us a few minutes," he said, returning to the table. "That sandwich was lethal." he said before reaching into his pocket and taking out a hip flask.

"More? You didn't say you had two bottles on you."

"You didn't ask, and I've got big pockets."

Greg drank the last of his coffee and then poured the contents of the hip flask into his empty cup and swallowed it down in two goes. Then in silence he put the cup back on the table.

"No more lectures, Nick, okay?"

"You've had a lot!"

"The first bottle was tiny. This flask was my standby in case I needed more.

"And you need more now?"

"Oh, sod off with your interrogation, Nick. You sound like a blasted girl. I thought you was a boy. Boys don't care. That's why I like them—"

He stopped talking and stared down at his empty cup.

Nick looked at him and said nothing. The juke box was playing *Oh Boy!*

"I like Buddy Holly," Nick said.

"Yeah. So do I. Pity the others in here don't like it. Come on, let's get out of here. It was a mistake to have come to Portslade."

"But I'm glad you brought me here," Nick replied.

"We'll catch a bus at the station. Take us straight back to Brighton. You still got enough of the ready?"

"Yes," Nick answered, smiling. I was born to pay, he thought.

They got on the first bus that came along and Greg slumped back in his seat, visibly relieved. Nick turned and looked at him and felt Greg's leg brush against his. Then the leg pressed hard against Nick.

"I want to," Greg whispered.

Nick didn't reply, nor did he move his leg away. Greg's voice sounded as if it was sleepy.

"You sound tired," Nick said.

"No, just resting. That fuck awful place gave me a headache. Couldn't hear the songs over the din."

The bus reached Western Road and Greg suggested they should get off. He touched Nick's thigh as he said this and for a while let his hand remain there.

"Where do you want to go?" Nick asked.

"What time is it?"

"It's gone seven."

"Come on."

They got off and walked up Lansdowne Place. Nick knew where they were going. They turned right at the top and a short while later found themselves in St Ann's Well Gardens. The park was quiet, despite it being a warm evening and they wandered over to the pond and looked down at the big brown fish.

"Big," Greg said. "Real fucking big."

He turned to look at Nick and his eyes looked a bit glazed. He was also unsteady on his feet.

"Let's sit down," Greg said. They sat on a bench, and Greg murmured that he'd be feeling better in a minute or two. "A dizzy spell," he said. Then he reached out and put his hand on Nick's groin.

"Not here," Nick whispered.

"Okay, okay."

Greg moved his hand away and a sulky look moved across his face. His eyes were shut and he pretended to snore. Then a few moments later he jumped up and cried out, "Fooled you, didn't I?"

"Yes," Nick said.

"Let's walk through the park."

Greg walked over to the bench where he had first seen Nick. Clouds had covered what remained of the sun, and the park was now both quieter and darker. Nick looked at his watch again. To his surprise he saw it was now past eight o'clock. He suddenly thought of Andy, wondering whether he was at home in George Street and waiting for him.

"Go and sit on the bench," Greg said. His voice was harsh and it came out as an order.

"But Greg—" he began, wanting to tell him that he was expected elsewhere.

"Do as I say!"

The expression on Greg's face was wild and Nick thought again of the amount of alcohol he had consumed.

"I don't take orders, Greg. I'm too old for that now."

"No, you're not. You're still a kid. A kid in a coat. Only it's a duffel coat now. Sit down on the bench where I first met you—and open your legs."

Nick remained standing and Greg came over and steered him forcibly to the exact spot where he wanted him to sit. Nick refused to sit down, but despite the anger he felt towards Greg's aggressive tone, continued to look at him. In his stomach he felt sick with a longing for him. They faced each other in a stand-off as if ready for battle. Greg was no longer the boy that he had met in the park, but a rough looking young man: a man with stubble on his face and slicked back hair which made him look even older than he was. His clothes fitted him like a glove they were so tight. The bulky leather jacket was zipped up right to the top and the blue jeans made his long legs look extra muscular and strong. He seemed encased in a fierce and terrible armour.

"Sit down," Greg repeated, "or I'll push you down. I want to see you as you were."

Nick sat down, suddenly afraid. He could not beat that armour or the defiant body inside it. He felt strange, as if he too had taken too much to drink and reality seemed to be slipping away from him. The trees in the distance looked tall and ominous. The green of the grass was darkening. There was nothing of beauty or comfort in the place. He heard a rustle and saw a large sleek rat slip out from behind him and run out towards the open. It was the only creature he had seen so far in the gardens that night, apart from the fish, and its thick dark body ran across the grass at great speed. He shuddered and, although it was not cold, he felt cold. He didn't like rats, and this one, in his mind, in his suddenly exaggerated state of mind, appeared particularly malevolent.

"I don't want to stay here," he said. "I have to get home."

"To your boyfriend?" Greg sneered. "Let him fucking wait. You have got a boyfriend, haven't you?"

Nick realised that whatever he said would be a useless waste of language. Greg was close now, so close to him and yet somehow far away. Nick looked up at his face; his fixed and determined face. He saw a hard and brutal desire in it. The statue in Montale's poem came to mind: the indifference and yet the beauty of it, and he saw Greg as if also made of stone. He imagined that he would not be able to escape from the gardens, that he too would be turned to stone and that they would remain like this, unable to escape from a desire that was so impossible for them. His mind too was hardening with distress and the impending threat of a final heaviness in his head: a terminal stillness that would last forever, enclosing him in the living coffin of his body.

"I'm afraid," he murmured, his lips feeling thick and heavy.

Greg moved backwards then.

"Open your legs," he ordered. "I want to see you in the same position you were in. I want you to open your trousers and show me your cock."

"I won't," Nick replied.

"Do it," Greg cried out. His voice was loud, but in the darkening gardens, there was no one but themselves to hear.

Mechanically, Nick opened his legs wide, but he did not undo his trousers. He was relieved that his imagination had not taken on a physical truth. He was not stone. He had not been transformed as he had feared. In the thin light of the fading day he saw Greg's face, and it appeared red to him in the semi-darkness. He saw a deep red line slashing across it, a bright glistening red making a last gesture of burning brightness. Nick's mind was now spinning out of control and he knew it. It was as if he were in a parallel world and the gardens were an imitation of the gardens: a twisted reflection of themselves thrown back at him. The trees loomed larger, more than ever threatening, advancing towards him.

"I want to go," he cried out.

"Open your legs. Show it to me. Show me your cock. I want to see your cock. Make it hard for me."

"No," Nick said, but his penis *was* hardening. He was not excited, but it was hardening. It was separate from himself, a parody of real desire with its own determined will. It belongs to Greg, he thought. It no longer belongs to me. It belongs to Greg.

Greg moved forwards and slipped down onto his knees in front of Nick's open legs. He then shifted his head under the seat and his body twisted itself into a grotesque misshapen encased form: a twisted line of flesh in the semi-darkness, leather-held and quiveringly alive. Nick thought of the rat returning to its lair.

"I'm getting the ball I kicked towards you," Greg said.

Nick heard the muffled sound of the words, and then the body straightened and Greg's face sprang up at him.

"It's gone," he said. "Come on, let's find it together."

Greg stood up and to Nick he was transfigured. He saw again the boy he had met. The jeans were now dirty and the jacket soiled, but the face returned to its former self—still red with excitement, but the excitement of physical exertion and youth. He watched as Greg's hand reached out for him, pulling him off the seat.

"It's gone towards the pond," Greg said. "The ball has gone there!"

Then Nick was being pulled along the path towards another path that wound its way next to the pond itself. Tall trees to the right of him flashed by, and then there was a dense enclosure of green. He felt himself being thrust into that green darkness, and although cramped in the tightened space, he was still standing. He felt Greg move behind him.

"I want you. Don't you *know* how much I want you?"

Nick heard the garbled words. Then his trousers were being pulled down to his knees and his clothes were torn away from his body. He shivered at the feel of Greg's body pressed against him and knew in an instant what was going to happen.

"Don't," he said.

"I love you. I love you. I don't care anymore."

Then Nick's body was bent over and a searing pain went through him. His anus was tight and Greg was large and thick. He felt himself being ripped open; felt as the hard penis thrust to its limit. His anus struggled but opened wider to receive it, resisting, then partially relaxing, as the pumping force began. Greg's hands encircled him, drawing him inwards towards him. He heard the panting sound behind him and the words fuck and shit exploded in Nick's brain. He could no longer see, the agony of the entering of his body was so great. Automatically he reached down to his own sex and felt it pulse in his hands. He came himself and almost immediately afterwards he felt a wet warmth inside him.

"I've fucking come," Greg cried out.

They both cried out and Nick fell forwards, feeling the softness of the grass beneath him. Greg fell with him, covering his body with a sticky, firm hold. Nick could not move from under it. He smelt the leather of Greg's jacket and then he blacked out. As he did so he heard the words, "I love you. I will always love you," cleave to the last remnants of his mind.

He awoke and it was dawn. Greg was lying half naked

beside him, hidden by the green undergrowth. He was fast asleep and Nick gently pulled Greg's trousers up, lifting up his body slightly as he did so. He then collected and put on his own clothes and crawled out onto the path. His mind was still in shock at what had happened and he slowly made his way out of the gardens. No one was around.

The sky was bright and clear as he walked down Lansdowne Place. He continued down until he reached Hove Lawns where he entered a public toilet and locked himself in a cubicle. He squatted over the toilet bowl and expelled some liquid. He then brought up some of the water and washed his anus before looking down into the bowl to see what Greg had left within him. He saw it, Greg's sperm, like a paper flower that when put in water becomes a real flower, opening white on white, artificial no longer, but becoming a glowing reality. He looked at his hands and there was blood on them. Strangely he had not seen blood in the bowl. He needed a sink, but the sink was outside the cubicle. He did up his trousers and going out, went to the sink and washed his hands. A man came into the toilet and Nick hurried out of it quickly. He then walked westward along the lawns. A few people were already out walking their dogs. He thought about what had happened and quite suddenly felt a lightness grow from within him. He no longer cared about the physical pain he still felt. He had no feeling of disgust or of shame. Greg had said that he loved him, and that was the only thing that truly mattered. He admitted to himself that he had felt pleasure himself, but now it was over and he also experienced, with the light feeling, a burden being lifted. He could move on from this and perhaps one day he and Greg would meet again. Perhaps Brighton itself would always draw them to each other.

"I don't want to think about the future," he said aloud, looking up at the blue sky. There was no wind and the sea was completely calm. So calm that it looked like a lake. He wandered down past Courtenay Gate to King's Esplanade and stood by the railings, looking out to the horizon. There was a skiff in the middle distance, still in the still waters of the sea. Nick leaned over the railings and looked as closely as he could at it. He saw a figure move inside the skiff. A tall man, standing, and Nick with his clear eyes thought for a moment that he recognised Oliver. He waved and the man waved back at him. The day was so sharp with light that Nick realised he had been seen. He was happy, imagining Oliver's smile and he smiled back. Then slowly, the skiff moved in the water and appeared to be coming towards him. The stranger he thought of as Oliver was responding to him and drawing closer to the shore. Nick was ready for the response.

Thank you for reading *Nick & Greg*.
Please share your thoughts and reactions with others.

Don't miss the next book in the *Nick & Greg* series!

Time of Obsessions
Publication date November 2016
ISBN 978-1-899713-56-1

Sign up to receive information about this and other
forthcoming titles from Wilkinson House
http://bit.do/gayreads

CPSIA information can be obtained
at www.ICGtesting.com
Printed in the USA
FSOW02n0955041016
25721FS